To A and my boys whose love and smiles give me

constant joy and hope.

To Mum and Dad for being there.

To all those women who keep going.

In memory of Cal.

Music, when soft voices die,

Vibrates in the memory—

P B Shelley

The Discovery

Devon, December 2010

No, I don't have a daughter. All my friends have daughters: Clare, Holly, Rose, and Jane. Between them they have ten daughters. Perhaps I would have liked a daughter, a future friend, a bride for my husband to accompany down the aisle, but it hasn't happened. Or maybe it has? The miscarriage that happened between Ben and Reuben was quite possibly a daughter and the boys have given her a name: Hope. She lived for only eight weeks and we have planted a delicate pink Flamingo Salix sapling in the garden to remember her by. The boys lay pebbles and shells beneath it; a place we can talk about her. Sometimes I cry about this loss, quietly by the tree. You are not supposed to grieve for a miscarriage, are you? Especially when you already have one healthy child. 'Probably for the best,' 'Nature's way,' 'You can always try again.' The platitudes people fill the empty spaces with. You know some of them are thinking, 'Just a blob of cells.' All I know is that I grieved quietly, for at least a year. Despite the loss, I cannot imagine loving a daughter any more than my sons. I cannot imagine being more in love with my boys.

It isn't always bliss. Why do boys take so long to toilet train? How many thousands of nappies have I had to chuck into landfill before one, even just one of my boys manages to wee into a toilet? Three years each before they got the hang of it; that's six years of nappies decomposing at a rate of 250 years per nappy. By Reuben's third year of nappies I was brutal and would almost throw him on the changing mat with a scowl, my aching back, bending over him as I tugged away at his trousers, whilst he gazed nonchalantly up at the light bulb, a fountain of fresh wee landing in his new nappy.

Then there is the food issue. The daily battles. Ben hated potato in any shape or form – even chips! Tomato ketchup became one of his five a day, twice a day. Reuben hated slimy textures, and any form of vegetable, especially baked beans. I don't remember being this fussy. I blame their father, who managed to gag on a tomato at boarding school and has since developed every imaginable phobia about peas, pulses, strawberries and grapes... but these memories fade as they grow and every night, as I watch their sleeping faces, I fall in love with them all over again.

I heave the damp laundry from the washing machine into the plastic basket and hang it out to dry on the old wooden airer in the dining room. I shake out a tiny pirate T-shirt with a faded blue shark embroidered onto the front and enjoy the smallness of my younger son. I press the damp shirt to my face and smell the cleanness of it, smiling as I remember the loud, shouty Pirate Party he had on his fourth birthday, ten boys tumbling around the garden, brandishing wooden sabres and screaming 'Walk the Plank!' whilst Tom joined in as Captain Hook, leading the band around the garden in the hunt for golden chocolate coins. The fabulous pirate treasure cake my mother and I made for the day with sweets oozing out of a sponge treasure chest and dripping down the chocolate butter cream. But not even the excitement of that day quite matches Reuben's mounting frenzy at the arrival of December. Every time Christmas is mentioned, his whole body trembles and his eyes sparkle. Even this morning, he has scrutinised the advent calendar and counted down the days with his little four-and-a-half-year-old fingers.

'Only twenty days until Christmas, Mummy!'

Every day his dark brown mop of hair and toothy grin explodes out of the Reception classroom, as he talks non-stop about the latest enormous cardboard model the wonderful Mr Parks has been creating for them that week; a huge train with carriages has now given way to a giant igloo. He hugs me tightly around the waist as I try to dodge the crumpled, still-wet paintings he thrusts in front of me, and hand in hand we stroll around to the Junior playground and collect Ben. I envelop him in an enormous bear hug, lippy kisses all round, cold cheeks on warm freckled ones.

'Do you have a treat for us, Mummy? I'm starving!'

'What are we doing today? Is it cubs tonight?'

'I got nine out of ten in my spellings, Mummy!'

I finish hanging out the washing and glance at the detailed drawings on the table, the architect's plans for our new extension. We dream of a large family kitchen where we can have space to run and play and relax on big, soft sofas, with huge windows opening out the view towards the distant dunes and the eddying channels of the estuary.

Perfection.

The builders are due to start work straight after Christmas and say it will only take three weeks. I clear away the breakfast bowls, scraping out the sludge of syrupy porridge in the bottom to reveal tigers and monkeys grinning at me and head upstairs to run the bath, liberally pouring in the last of a bottle of blue bubble bath. The school run was the usual rush this morning of picnic bags, bottles of water, teeth cleaning and shoe searching – thank heaven for velcro, and as usual I look as if I have been pulled through a hedge backwards with hair scraped back into a ponytail and yesterday's clothes thrown on. Time to relax for twenty minutes before heading out again into the cold air and the jobs of the day.

Sinking into the hot, soapy bath, I gaze up at the mould gathering in the corners of the ceiling, and tick off the list of things to do this day - end of term Christmas plays are on the horizon next week and I still need to get the tickets, a shift at the parent café, a few more presents for the boys' stockings, cards to write, mince pies to make and freeze... I close my eyes and drift momentarily into a half-sleep. I am tired, more tired than I have been for a long time. This crazy autumn term is always so exhausting. Roll on the holidays.

I dry myself off, running my fingers along the crease below my breasts to check they are dry before I put on my bra. Wet. I pat it dry and feel again. Small bumps are perceptible. Hadn't noticed before. Bit like a string of tiny grapes. Bit odd. Probably my period playing tricks on my boobs again. They are always a bit sensitive at this time of the month. I will get Tom to have a look later. Lovely Doctor Tom who keeps me from having to darken the GP's surgery.

I brush my long, thick dark-blonde hair and look at myself in the large hall mirror on the landing. I am slimmer than I have been in years and brown leather boots seem to add to the effect. The horrible stomach virus a month ago was worth it after all when the pounds just seemed to drop off. I have kept an eye on my figure and have resolved to continue eating smaller portions. Losing weight after a second baby has been difficult but the resolve has been there this time. Without a doubt I am slimmer now as I approach my forty-seventh birthday than I was on my wedding day.

Joy.

I pat my flat stomach, stroking the pink, cashmere cardigan and smile to myself smugly. Time to finish that Christmas shopping.

I speed along the coastal road that wraps itself around the estuary and head into town, parking outside the library. I comb the shops for the last presents and bargains, shoulders sagging with the weight of plastic bags that pinch my fingers, and head for the market café, slumping into a chair in the corner. Tired shoppers and locals, here for the farmers' market have squeezed themselves into the tightly packed tables, almost back to back with one another. Warm, rich Devonshire burr, reminiscent of my grandmother, mingles with the incomer stall holders from the West Midlands, as greasy plates of bacon and egg sweep around me. The waitress is a thin, elderly woman with a lined face. I order a mug of milky coffee and a tea cake. It would have been nice to meet up with a friend in a smart high street café, but life has been so busy that I am glad of a moment to draw breath and sit quietly here in this comfortable space and just watch. I glance down at the presents for the boys that nestle at the tops of the bags: pick-and-mix sweets in retro bottles, a jumper, trousers, and shirt for Tom's new job and two snow shakers for the boys' bedside tables. I pick one up and shake it as tiny flakes of snow swirl around a beaming snowman. I smile as I catch the eye of a toddler gazing up at it from a neighbouring table and shake it again. She giggles.

December is the magical month, the month of all months for me - a month full of sparkle with the promise of sledging, snowy walks, and snowball fights. Magical childhood visits to the hills of Derbyshire in the snow mingle in my memories with the smell of gingerbread wafting through my mother's kitchen, the baking cupboard crammed full of spice packets, and the sight of our small hands and large wooden rolling pins finely coated in flour. Magical December, the month of my birthday when presents and cards poured in, and then Christmas Eve when my father would drive off to find the tallest tree for the living room and fill the air with pine. My mother decorating the tree with straw stars and lametta and real candles! My grandmother sitting by the tree, reading to us the sacred story, and praying reverently for us all with a multitude of 'Thees' and 'Thous', and then the sharing of those magical presents and carols sung around the piano. The table in the kitchen laden with a hot buffet of sausage rolls, warm bread, salads, puddings, and cake.

December.

How I long to fill the boys' memory banks full of these delicious moments, even if it seldom snows in Devon.

'What do you think these are, Tom?' I casually ask my husband later that evening as he climbs into bed beside me. Tom leans over to feel the area I am pointing to below my left breast. It is not hard to find. I am grateful that my husband is a doctor, even if his GP days are behind him.

'Looks like your boobs are growing boobs.' He laughs - 'Probably cysts. 95% of the time that is the case... wouldn't worry about it at all,' he says fairly dismissively.

I don't want to say this, but I push myself.

'Do you think I should get it checked out?'

Tom doesn't rush his response,

'I guess it wouldn't do any harm to see the GP at the surgery and let her have a look, but I really wouldn't worry about it.'

I lie back onto the pillow and feel the string of tiny grapes and convince my mind that they are cysts. Reassuring words are like balm. My breast tingles a little as it has done periodically over the last few weeks. I shut my eyes and sleep comes quickly.

A week later

I sit at the end of a long row of empty chairs, facing a huge television screen a week later in the Outpatients department of the hospital. The visit to see my GP, Doctor Homsi, happened last Monday, with both boys crammed into her small room. She pulled a curtain around the examination bed and felt the affected area with swift but careful professionalism.

'I suspect it is only cysts, but let's book you into an appointment at the hospital just to make sure.' She too has a confident breeziness in her voice.

I cram the pile of half-written Christmas cards into my handbag and gaze down at my crossed legs. I stand up and wander across the gleaming white floor of the spacious, open-plan waiting area and gaze through the large hospital windows. Small flakes of snow are swirling over the rolling Devon hills surrounding the hospital, and a flurry of excitement causes a child-like grin to spread over my face. This is special. Snow in Devon is incredibly special. This comes once every ten years. I am lost momentarily in a reverie of excitement about how the boys will feel, seeing these big fluffy flakes, as they sit in their classrooms. I run my fingers through my hair and sweep it back over an ear and sigh deeply.

'Krista Templeton? ' A short, middle-aged nurse appears in the waiting room and smiles. My heart jumps, and I quickly gather my handbag and jacket and follow the nurse into the ultrasound room, boots clicking on the white tiled floor. It is a small, rather claustrophobic space, made even

7

smaller by the presence of an enormous chair with screens hovering around it.

'Please remove your top and bra and sit on the chair. Here is a sheet to hold around yourself. The radiographer will be in shortly. I will come back before he arrives.' The nurse leaves me to get ready.

I remove my top behind a curtain and place the white sheet over my chest and sit down, a little uncomfortable at the thought of a man looking at my breasts. Hopefully, I can get this over with quickly and get on with my shopping. This is a similar room to the one I visited ten years ago when Ben was wriggling around inside on that hot August day. Tears filled my eyes as I saw his tiny form on the screen. Tom squeezed my hand - we chose not to know whether it was a boy or girl. The surprise would be half the fun.

A small, stocky radiographer wearing thick glasses pads into the room and nods at me, explaining the procedure briefly. He removes the sheet and smears thick gel over the lower part of the left breast, moving the monitor around slowly and steadily, thick lenses fixed inscrutably on the screen in front of him.

Time passes slowly.

I had asked Tom that morning what the 'cyst' would be like if it were bad news. I hang onto the one question I have rehearsed in my head from our conversation.

'Is it dense?'

I suddenly wish Tom were here. Of course, it was senseless for him to come on a very busy working day with an important board meeting in

Exeter to attend and it didn't even occur to me to ask him to come along just for a check-up. But there is something in the long silence that is disturbing me.

The radiographer doesn't meet my gaze... He just studiously analyses the screen as if I am not in the room, as if he is just engaging with the grey and white images on the screen. It is as if he doesn't want me to ask that question, as if by answering it he is being forced to say something that professionally he is uncomfortable with saying.

'Yes, very dense.'

The Consultant

I stare at the silent radiographer, who wordlessly leaves the room.

I grow numb.

Quietly I get dressed and am asked by the nurse to sit in the waiting room until I am called for by the consultant who had questioned me at the start of this process.

The waiting room is completely empty. I sit down and place my bags on the chair beside me and turn to the Christmas cards I have stuffed in my bag and start to write the next one.

'Wishing you all a very happy Christmas...'

And I stop.

Pack the cards away.

Start to shake gently and speak audibly but in a whisper.

'Oh shit.' My body starts to tremble almost imperceptibly. Tears come silently. I am aware I do not want to be noticed by any of the staff wandering through the area. Disbelief. I can't have cancer. There is no significant history of cancer in my family. Tom was so reassuring last night. What was it he said? 95% of cases are cysts? Shit!

All I can think of is whether Rose is in the hospital. She is stationed on the orthopaedic ward, but part-time, so she may not be there. I need to text her - 'I am in Outpatients. No time to explain, can you come down quickly?'

A few moments later I am ushered into a room filled with medical professionals, students, specialist nurses and the consultant who has questioned me at the beginning of this one-stop shop before the ultrasound. He is overweight, with puffy cheeks and dead eyes. He asks me to sit on the bed that is already surrounded by three other people in uniforms.

There is a heaviness in the air before he begins to speak. He waits until everyone is looking at him, and as he begins, all eyes fall on me.

'There is a high index of seriousness in your ultrasound scan, Mrs Templeton. There is a sizeable growth on the left side and what looks like spots of calcification on the right side, but we are less concerned about that.'

High index of seriousness? Calcification? What is that supposed to mean? Does he expect me to understand medical jargon because I am a doctor's wife? Or is this just for the benefit of the students?

Rose peers around the door in her blue uniform, grinning at me, unaware of what has just been disclosed. She sits next to me on the bed and looks at the consultant and me quizzically.

'This is my friend, she works here,' I say weakly.

The consultant ignores this information and continues.

'We need to take a biopsy straightaway. We use this cylindrical gun to slice out the tissue. It will enter at various angles four times into the breast. You will hear a sudden noise like a pop. It may sting a little but it's very quick.'

Gun? I hold Rose's hand tightly and stare at her. Is this really happening? There are presents to buy, things to do. It is Christmas. Snowflakes are falling outside. This is the magical month, the month of all months!

Rose realises immediately what is going on, not least because of the frantic look I give her.

'Can I help? I work on Orthopaedics,' she says confidently.

The consultant grunts as he prepares the instruments. Once again, I have to take off my top and remove my bra, watched by all the students. She holds my shoulders tightly and as the biopsy needle comes against my pale, smooth breast she prays quietly but audibly over me. The needle jolts each time as it efficiently withdraws the breast tissue. Once again, my body is exposed to other men. Of course, to them it is probably nothing more than a day's work, an organ that needs to be analysed, probed, and operated on, but to me it is embarrassment, invasion, exposure. I esteem my privacy highly, especially my physical privacy. I am not someone to flaunt my body on the beach or go topless in France. These are the parts of me that only Tom may see or occasionally my boys at bath time when I plunge in to join Reuben amongst the bubbles. Even then, I stroke the cloud of foam over my breasts out of modesty to conceal them again.

Rose is an angel that day. She never works on Mondays but has miraculously swapped a shift so that she can see her children's Christmas production later in the week. Rose understands shocks. Her husband died of a stroke two years before, leaving her to navigate the tsunami of grief that erupted over her and her children who are similar ages to mine. I held her shoulders on the day that she gazed down at her husband's dead body, lying in an open coffin at the undertakers.

'Thank you for being here,' I whisper, choking back tears.

This is not the place to fall apart. Too many students and junior doctors.

'I thought I was going to find you with Ben and a broken arm being plastered,' she whispers to me, smiling nervously.

The consultant continues, gesturing to a bespectacled older lady standing near him.

'Barbara here is a specialist breast care nurse and will answer any of your questions.'

He clearly has little time to discuss the matter. Another one to process, a wonderful case study to discuss with these junior colleagues later.

I have questions.

I turn to Barbara and they tumble out,

'What will happen? Will I lose my breast? Will I need chemotherapy? Will my hair fall out?'

The nurse is kindly looking. She is experienced and truthful and holds my hand.

'You will probably need an operation to remove the tumour, possibly a mastectomy, then probably chemotherapy or radiotherapy or both.'

There is a bizarre relief in this truthfulness, even at this shockingly early stage of what is clearly an unfolding drama in my life. I now begin to wrap my mind around the idea that is exploding in my mind in slow motion -

'I have cancer.'

This is ridiculous. No one in our family has had cancer. We do diabetes. My grandfather, uncle, cousin, nephew... they all contracted diabetes... we do diabetes... four generations of diabetes. We don't do cancer.

Rose has to get back to her ward and I have to tell Tom. I wipe my eyes and blow my nose as I walk through the main floor of the hospital into the biting winter's day. I think about the words the consultant has spoken. How many times has he thrown these grenades at unsuspecting women? I later discover that it is on average once a week. I send Tom a text, knowing that he is waiting for news, conscious that he might be in the middle of a meeting. Will he snatch a glance at the text just as he is about to lead a major item on the agenda? The message is brief.

It's serious, looks malignant.

A prayer is whispered under my breath as I press the Send button and head off to the car.

The Secret

I walk numbly to my car, turn on the ignition and head straight to my parents. They only live five minutes away and, trance-like, I drive on autopilot through the winding streets of their village, past the church where my grandmother is buried and into their cul-de-sac. My parents have been awaiting the result of the morning's investigations. I know they will be at home. I ring the familiar doorbell of my grandmother's old semi-detached house with its pebbledash white painted walls but walk in without waiting for it to be answered. Four years after her death it still 'smells' of Gran - a familiar, indefinable smell of carpet and furniture polish and her dresses. The barometer on the wall and the old rag rugs scattered on the parquet floor are a comforting reminder of that special little ninety-five-year old lady. My father meets me in the hall. I fall into his arms and begin to cry.

'It's not good. It looks serious.'

He just holds me. My mother appears from the kitchen and puts her arms around us both, squeezing my shoulders. We wander into the living room, the small, cosy room with its arched red brick fireplace and ticking mahogany clock on the wall, and memories of Gran flood into the small space. Here we would sit of an evening chatting while I held baby Ben, 'Sonny Jim' she would call him, and her thin, bony arms would cradle him whilst she cooed. How good that Gran was no longer alive to bear this news; it would have broken her heart. Her death on New Year's Eve when I was pregnant with Reuben was not lost on me. In a world that was becoming increasingly frightening, with the spawning of global terrorism, I wondered if my grandmother had pulled her crisp, linen white sheets under her chin that night, fingered her beloved black Bible, read her favourite Psalm and decided that it was time to leave this world behind at the end of a year and walk into the arms of her loving Saviour. The Psalm was engraved upon a bench where she used to sit and watch the Atlantic waves crash on the rocks. *Though I travel to the far side of the sea, even there Thy hand will guide me* - I could recite it all in my head, I had heard it so often.

Dad, tall, gaunt, and silver-bearded, swept back his grey hair and looked stunned. I sit down in one of my grandmother's old, patterned, wing back armchairs, the sort that so often inhabit old folks' homes, old, but wonderfully comfortable. My mother passes me a hot mug of tea and she and my father sit opposite me, concern etched on their faces.

'They think it's serious,' I explain.

'They did an ultrasound on my breast and the lump is very dense, which means it isn't a cyst; that would have been transparent. They took a biopsy and we are now waiting for the results, but I could tell from the doctors' faces that they know it is going to be bad news. The results will just confirm what they already know.'

'When will you find out for sure?' my mother says softly.

'In a week. That's when we will meet the surgeon.'

I explain all the events of the morning and that I have texted Tom. My parents are full of reassurances and comfort.

'We are here for you, we will help, we will get through this. We can get through anything,' she adds with a strength in her voice I have not heard for some time.

'Mum, we can't tell the boys, I don't want them to know. I don't want them to be frightened.'

She senses the urgency in my voice.

'Don't worry, love. We'll follow you home in your car and help you with the school run. One step at a time.'

I am enormously grateful that my parents are here, that they are at home and that they are coming home with me. It will help distract the boys while I get my head straight.

I drive home trembling, stifling tears but strangely strengthened by the need to protect my beautiful sons. As each boy tumbles out of their classes, I am smothered by kisses. All they can talk about is the snow. Even rehearsals for Christmas productions are forgotten. I beam at them and their innocence and realise, in a moment, that this is how I shall stay sane, by keeping this cup of life clean and pure and unsullied by worries and anxieties. I manage somehow to make small talk with friends. Now is not the time to tell anyone what has just unfolded at the hospital. Revelations will be selective and can wait. I need to consider who I can trust.

A few hours later Tom eventually arrives home from Exeter. It feels like an eternity of waiting. I meet him in our hallway. He stretches out his arms, tears in his eyes and holds me tight.

'I'm sorry,' he says, 'I'm sorry.'

I am startled by his tears - and moved, and together we weep silently for a brief moment before two flying boys crash into us out of the kitchen and living room, in spite of my parents' best efforts to hold them back for a few minutes. We wipe our eyes quickly and put on delighted faces,

'Daddy! Daddy! Have you seen the snow?! Can we build a snowman in the garden?'

'Hi Ben! Of course, we can. Let Daddy have a cup of tea with Mummy first.'

I head up to our room with Tom bringing the tea and we sit on the edge of the bed while the children watch their favourite video.

'What were you doing when you got the text?' I ask him.

'We were in the middle of a meeting and I glanced at it and then pretended to answer the 'phone and field an important call. I managed to excuse myself as I had told them I was on-call... I wanted to find a quiet room – all I could find was a disabled toilet - and think for a moment before trying to ring you. I just wanted to hear your voice. How could I have missed this?'

'Don't blame yourself, Tom,' I say, leaning into his shoulders. 'No one could have imagined this would happen. I still can't believe this is happening. Tom, I don't want us to tell the boys. They don't need to know. We don't even know for sure yet what exactly is going on. Please can we carry on as normal and not tell too many people. I don't want it slipping out at church or in the playground or at work. I've already told my parents. Do you agree?'

Tom hugs me and whispers in my ear, 'Not a word.'

Later that week, on the Friday before Christmas, I return with Tom to the hospital to hear the results of the biopsy.

We walk up the steps past the maternity unit where I gave birth to Ben. The irony of the moment is not lost on me. How many women are lying there in their post-natal beds, suckling their new-born babies, breasts like rocks as they start the first few feeds, the overwhelming orgasmic sensation of milk being drained away with almost immediate relief for the mother. What joy to see my 34A breasts bulging into a D cup and my cleavage oozing sensuality. I felt bigger, more beautiful... more feminine. There had been weeks when I had put a book into my mouth to bite through the pain barrier of that latching-on moment, clearly not doing it quite right, yet determined to press on through. It was worth the agony for the delicious luxury of just sitting and half-snoozing as a baby fed and slowly drowsed off, mouth dribbling milk onto my nipple. Often, I would just sit and gaze at this miracle of life we had made and be thankful.

Here I am walking up those same steps without a baby and with a breast that has been invaded by a 'serious' tumour. At least I have had my children, I say to myself - how terrible to be diagnosed before experiencing this wonderful time.

We are met at the top of the stairs by a different specialist breast care nurse called Carol. She is small and plump with a beaming, comforting smile. She beckons us to come into the waiting room and informs us that Dr Browne will be up shortly. Time passes awkwardly and I try and reassure the nurse that I am not expecting any good news. Carol chirps slightly nervously until she spots the surgeon, a diminutive man in his early fifties, ambling across a courtyard below in a short-sleeved, checked shirt. An age later he appears and introduces himself as one of the team of surgeons specialising in breast surgery. I like him. He is not a typical surgeon; none of the brash, slightly brutal air that some seem to enjoy emanating. He is clearly aware that this is a different type of surgery, a different type of malady.

'Well, er... the results have come through,' he begins in a soft Australian voice, leafing through the notes in front of him, 'and er, it's been identified as a moderate grade two cancer. The tumour is about four centimetres long and quite close to the chest wall. What we need to do is check whether it has gone into the lymph. We'll need to perform a mastectomy and check out the sentinel node at the same time.'

I sense that in the presence of two hospital consultants, the terminology is inevitably going to be medical. *What does grade two mean? What is a sentinel node? What does the lymph have to do with it? JUST tell me in simple language,* I think to myself whilst nodding intelligently at everything he says - I need to know what this all means.

Carol explains that there are two options. One will be to shrink the tumour first with chemotherapy and then later to operate with perhaps a less invasive operation, the other to operate as soon as possible. I sense Tom's agitation. He wants the operation to have happened yesterday.

'We'll take the earliest possible date,' he says, knowing full well that this is going to be a challenge with Christmas looming. It is the 17th of December and highly unlikely that an operation can take place until at least January. Every day the tumour will be growing larger - I need to get rid of it as soon as possible. Does Dr Browne take note of the fact he is sitting opposite a fellow consultant or is he simply full of compassion for his patient? I sense the latter, though am aware that Tom's presence can only help. He scrutinises his diary carefully, scratching his scruffy brown hair.

'I have a slot free on the 22nd of December. It would also be possible for you to have a reconstruction with a specialist in Plymouth, although the likelihood is that it will be sometime in January now, after the holidays.'

'I couldn't care less right now about reconstructive surgery,' I hear myself saying, knowing nothing really about it,' I just want this lump out as soon as possible.'

Tom nods in agreement and murmurs assent. The surgeon continues,

'The day before the operation, you will need to drive to Exeter to have an injection of nucleic fluid which will show me during the operation where the sentinel node in your arm is. This will have to be investigated to check if it has been affected by the cancer.'

'What does this node tell you?' I ask.

'It acts like a gateway to all the other lymph nodes that serve as the body's drainage system. If it has been invaded, then it is likely that others have as well and perhaps that the cancer has spread.'

I nod silently, absorbing this new thought. Tom rises from his seat.

'Thank you so much, we really appreciate you making time in your diary to do this.'

The surgeon smiles.

'We'll get you sorted,' he says reassuringly, patting my arm as we leave.

On the journey home to meet the boys on the last day of school, we are both compelled again to protect them.

'I don't want to scare them about this operation, Tom, at least not beforehand. I don't mind them knowing I am in hospital after it has happened, but they mustn't know what sort of operation it is. We can tell them I have an infection in my breast that needs treating. I'll sort out some play dates for them on the day.'

'I could take Ben for a long walk,' interjected Tom, 'he would enjoy a bit of Daddy time on his own.'

'Great idea!'

My mind is buzzing. Days of uncertainty lie ahead but I am determined to deal with one thing at a time and not to jump too far ahead.

It is Christmas, and nothing is going to spoil the magical month for my sons. They will have the best Christmas ever. Fresh snowflakes begin to float slowly down from the heavens and settle on the cold, frosty hills behind the hospital. The sky is a mass of grey, billowy clouds and as I look up from the school playground later that afternoon, they grow thicker and thicker, kissing my lips and melting. In the midst of this surreal week, my heart, though besieged by racing thoughts about an unknown future, is suddenly filled with peace and a joy at the sight of the snow. I need every bit of help I can get right now to distract the boys. This thick blanket of snow is rescuing me. The sickness bug that has ravaged half of the school has missed the boys and we are all free from it. Another blessing.

'Please God,' I whisper, 'Please let me stay *well* over this next week. I can't be ill right now, I can't get the 'flu or a bad cold or this sickness bug. I need to be well for this operation.'

The 21st of December.

The roads are icy. Blizzards have been forecast and we set off in some trepidation across the rolling hills of Exmoor en route to the motorway. The journey is madness, and against all traffic police advice, but we have no choice. Thankfully, the main road has been gritted the night before, but even so, the overnight blizzard has made driving a torturously slow affair. Two lanes become one and Tom strains through frantic windscreen wipers to see where the darker tracks are. The merciless hills and slopes of Exmoor are treacherous and the car slips and slides occasionally. At last we reach the motorway and driving conditions are easier, albeit still with only one lane open.

After an age we reach the hospital and book ourselves in.

A middle-aged nurse welcomes me into a side room and explains that she wants to go over the procedure again.

'In seven out of ten cases, the lymph is not affected, and no further surgery is needed,' she begins reassuringly.

'Can you explain exactly what is happening today,' I ask, 'my head is swimming with medical terms I don't understand.'

'Of course,' she smiles kindly, 'It is very straightforward: we will inject a small amount of albumen into the area around the nipple. This albumen has been tagged with some radioactivity. This fluid will follow the lymphatic drainage system in your body and will lodge in the nodes for about twenty-four hours. You will then be scanned in a couple of hours and the results will be sent through to your hospital so that your surgeon can detect where your sentinel node is by using a gamma probe and can remove it easily. The node will then be examined by the pathologist and he will inform your surgeon of the results.'

I ask the inevitable question. I am getting used to pushing for the truth.

'And if the node has been affected?'

'Then you will need further surgery to remove any other nodes that appear to have been affected.'

'Right, let's do it,' I say resolutely and lie down on the bed.

The Scalpel

I sit on the edge of my bed and look down at my naked body.

'Your last chance to look,' I say almost casually to my husband. He kneels down and holds me close. His soft blue eyes look into mine tenderly, his hands cup my face and his lips brush my lips with the softest of kisses. He looks at me with the same look of love I saw on our wedding evening, a mixture of gentleness and desire. I break the moment with an attempt at humour.

'Do you think we should take a photograph? Just for old time's sake?'

I know he won't. I feel the string of bumps underneath the left breast. Still there. Spreading. How long has this tumour been there? How quickly is it growing?

Tom doesn't know the answer to these questions; he just stays kneeling beside me and smiles at me.

'I am just grateful that they can remove it quickly,' he says quietly.

I smile too. At this moment I do not want any part of this breast. I want it gone quickly. It is like a gangrenous foot that needs to be amputated, an appendix that is about to rupture - just get it out. The breast has done its job, the boys were nourished by it, and now it's simply packed in and needs to go. That's all there is to it.

I climb into bed and switch off the light, massaging my mind with thoughts of how much better Christmas is going to be, knowing that this sinister malignant thing won't be spreading during the holidays. Exhaustion overtakes me, and sleep comes mercifully quickly.

I wake early and sit bolt upright in bed with the immediate wakefulness that comes on important exam days or when you have an assembly to deliver in front of a thousand pupils. Stomach tightens. I stare at the floor, stroke my breast again and hold it tenderly for a moment, cradling it.

Nil by mouth.

An iciness has gripped Devon. Grey clouds hang in the sky, more snow clouds ready to release their magical cargo. Another blessing. Oh, for more snow, as much snow as possible. Anything to conceal the black reality of this day.

And it comes.

The snow begins to fall softly, extraordinary in this normally damp and warm region of England, but yes, the snow is coming for Christmas and for me. A wave of excitement will break over my children and immerse them in other thoughts. They will have no suspicion that anything is amiss, that there is anything to worry about, that there is any change in our lives at all.

'Hurrah!' I whisper to Tom, 'It's snowing!'

He smiles back at me, transmitting hope and strength and support, just relieved, I sense, that I am not dissolving in a mess.

I have no time for messes right now. I'm not particularly tolerant of people who wimp out of difficult situations, who seem to fall apart and blub on their families at the first difficulty in life. This is not going to get the better of me, overwhelm me or destroy my family and their happiness. I shall be positive, and I shall re-define what it means to be a cancer patient. I shall inspire those around me that life can go on as normal, a bit more slowly perhaps, but still carry on as if nothing is happening. I shall do it all with great humour too. This is my new challenge. I shall manage it. I certainly won't expect Tom to drop his career and be at my beck and call.

'The boys will have a great time today – don't you worry about a thing – I've got their boots ready,' says Tom.

'I'll be down in a minute - you go and have some breakfast.'

I finish dressing and tiptoe along the landing, peering through the cracks in the bedroom doors at my sleeping sons, blissfully unaware of what their mother is about to undergo. I gaze for a moment at their beautiful faces, even more beautiful when asleep. They are breathing deeply, peacefully. I look at their pale, freckled skin, small noses, long eyelashes, tousled brown hair, smell the warm, human heat that fills their room. I breathe deeply, swallow my emotions and creep out of their rooms. They will sleep for at least another hour or two.

Padding downstairs, I see the front door crack open and Becca, my sister-in-law peering into the hallway. She knows not to ring the doorbell. She has come to babysit and look after the boys until one of my friends comes to collect Reuben for a playdate and Tom returns to take Ben on a walk.

She squeezes me in a warm embrace.

'The boys will have a fine five-star breakfast with me, don't worry about a thing,' she whispers, still holding me tightly.

'Thank you so much, Becca. Here we go.'

The drive to the hospital is shakier. I feel my stomach starting to churn. I have resisted the temptation to look at pictures of mastectomies on the internet and I do not know what I will look like after the operation. Ignorance is an easier path right now. At the hospital I undress and prepare myself for the arrival of the anaesthetist. Another woman next to me is to have a lumpectomy, another much younger is very tearful and being consoled by parents. There is no desire for small talk. We are all locked in our own worlds. I want to be with my thoughts.

'You go, love, I'm OK. There's no point you staying here any longer. I would rather you were at home with the boys, so they don't start worrying.'

'You'll be fine. You'll still be beautiful,' he replies reassuringly and squeezing my shoulder he strides off out of the ward. Tom always knows the right thing to say. I sit and imagine the day the boys are going to have: excited Reuben off to play in the snow with his friend Toby and Tom driving off to the beach with Ben. At the end of the day Tom will tell the boys Mummy has had an operation on her breast for an infection that had to be treated. Not a lie, not the full truth, but not a lie. The truth will be told if specific questions are asked, but in the absence of those questions, a lighter version of reality must be acceptable. I sense that these questions won't come for a long time; the boys are trusting and accepting of everything they are told and neither are they insatiably curious to know every detail - perhaps girls might have been different, perhaps older children would have had to be told... but not my little sons.

After the anaesthetist checks that I am 'well' and have no temperature, a nurse marks the area around my left breast with a felt-tip pen and escorts me down for surgery. It is a long, cold walk down into the bowels of the hospital. Freezing draughts of air shoot between my bare legs as I slipper my way to theatre. It is a surreal experience, alone with this nurse; half naked in a flimsy hospital gown, walking to my fate, plodding towards some form of execution.

I am greeted by friendly, chatty members of the surgical team, keen to put me at my ease. I confirm my identity and that I am here for a mastectomy of the left breast. I lie down on the bed. I am in buoyant mood, strangely buoyant. All I can think of is how wonderful it will be to get rid of this evil tumour, how grateful I feel that the operation didn't have to be postponed because of a bad cold. A cloudy liquid is injected through a cannula in my hand. The 'champagne' does its trick. My head feels wonderfully woozy and light and I begin giggling and drift off.

I wake up in recovery later that day, vaguely aware of nurses hovering around me. A nurse stands beside me.

'Are you awake, Krista, are you hearing me? You've been asleep a long time.'

I murmur, my head still swimming from the anaesthetic.

'How are you feeling? Would you like a drink?'

I nod. My throat is parched.

The kindly nurse fetches a cup of water and a straw to help me sip.

'We've given you some morphine to help with the pain. Just press on this pad if you need more.'

An instinct tells me I am about to gag and I ask for a bowl, thankfully just in time. I lie down again and close my eyes, aware of various trolleys being wheeled in and out of the theatre next door. The nurse takes my temperature and blood pressure and after another half hour I am wheeled onto one of the wards. I am aware of bandages around my chest with a thin tube coming out from under my armpit. A nurse explains that this is necessary in order to drain fluid away over the next few days.

So, it is over. The cancer has hopefully all been cut out with a skilful scalpel, and tissue around the site has been sent off to Pathology to check that they have caught it all.

Later that day I am aware that my surgeon is hovering by the bed.

'Good afternoon, Mrs Templeton. How are you feeling?'

'Uh, OK I guess. Bit spacey.'

'Are you in any pain?'

'No, the morphine helped when I came round but the other pain killers are keeping on top of it at the moment.'

'That's good,' he says sagely, nodding, 'Well, erm, the surgery went well. I think we got it all out.' He speaks slowly and deliberately. 'I've taken a biopsy of tissue around the site to check that it is not affected and we should know the results of that soon. How's the tube doing? Draining well?'

'Yes, I think so. Thank you so much for what you have done.'

He pats my hand and smiles and plods away, this diminutive 'giant' of a man who has just saved my life.

I lie back again on my pillow and doze. So, it is over, and the cancer has gone. I hold onto that thought. The worst is over. Thank you, God.

Friends visit with lovely beauty creams and bouquets of kindness. As they come, I often cry at the love they show and perhaps at the enormity of what has just happened. I feel cocooned by the love and concern of those around me and the care of the nurses.

I need to get home and be with my boys for Christmas. It is difficult to rest on the ward. At night I am kept awake by an elderly lady who shouts every half an hour,

'What's it all for?!' 'What's it all about?!'

Unlike her I am not in the mood to ask the ultimate questions of life. I just want to sleep.

Thankfully on Christmas Eve morning I am released home with a bag full of painkillers and a small heart-shaped cushion given me by Carol, my breast care nurse.

'These are sewn by a group of ladies who want to do something to make your life a bit more comfortable. Put the cushion under your arm – it will help while you heal.'

I choose a small pink one with a tiny flower print, and thank her.

'I will 'phone you soon, Krista, to let you know if the sentinel node has been affected.'

Holly, one of my besties, texts a few times that day, always perky, always encouraging – 'Well done old chum!' 'The worst is over!' 'Did they get the right one ?!' Her messages are always accompanied by emojis of hysterical faces - and I am grateful for a friend who knows me so well albeit long distance. She never texts very much, so it is all the more precious. Her favourite thing is to 'phone me on one of her days off work when she is upcycling a piece of tatty old furniture she has found in an old antiques emporium and transforming it into some beautiful, pale blue shabby chic piece. Conversations often strayed into her beloved Indian cuisine.

'So, Krista, I've found this amazing new curry recipe... it's all in the cumin... and please don't ever stir the rice while it's cooking. That absolutely drives me nuts when people do that!'

It's probably a good job she can't 'phone me in the hospital as I would be roaring with laughter over something she said and the shaking would be painful with all those stitches in my chest. Even the memories of past conversations can cause me to giggle uncontrollably. Conversations of the time when we shared a house tumble back to ease my mind.

'Krista?' she asked, lifting her head from her patchwork sewing project one evening, 'so who exactly is Sinn Fein? We're always hearing about him in the news but we never see him? Who the heck is he?'

Once I had dried my eyes and literally picked myself up from the floor I explained to her in the kindest tone I could think of that Sinn Fein was an organisation and that what she probably meant to say was, 'Who is Gerry Adams, its leader?' What was even funnier to experience was the guffawing of laughter that erupted from her at this realisation.

Tom arrives to take me home and help me dress. Gingerly I manage to put on a button-up blouse and a cardigan, careful not to disturb the tube. Snow continues to fall outside as Tom drives me out of the hospital car park. I sense his relief that I am coming home. His voice is full of life,

'The boys are very excited. They can't wait to see you.'

'Have they wanted to know why I have been away?' I probe, curious to know what kind of questions they have asked.

'No, not really – I told them you had had an operation and that you were fine and looking forward to coming home.'

'I guess hospitals don't scare them much.'

I think back to the endless weekend days when Tom has been on call in the hospital whilst training and I have taken the boys to visit him. How they loved racing down shimmering white corridors and turning their noses up at the strong smell of disinfectant. Hospitals were fun places to run into and visit Daddy in cafés, not scary, frightening places where people die.

We pull into the drive and, shielding my left side from the boys, I am enveloped in excited cuddles.

'Mummy, we have made you a poster – look! Welcome home Mummy!' Ben shouts excitedly, pointing to the large felt-tipped banner above the kitchen door.

'Look, Mummy, we bought a tree!'

Reuben tugs my cardigan and I follow into the living room filled with the fragrance of fresh pine.

'Wow! That looks amazing, boys, thank you so much – and you have both helped decorate the tree?'

'Yes!' they both chime together, fingering the sparkly, home-made snowmen and Christmas trees they have made out of salt dough in previous years at play groups.

Christmas can begin. I am grateful that all the presents were organised before the operation and that the food shopping has been ordered and delivered. Everything will be as normal. Even more cards than usual have flooded in along with flowers, and the house looks wonderful. Everything is perfect, quite perfect: the snow, the carols around the piano, the meal my parents help me prepare on Christmas Day... and the boys don't suspect a thing. The snow continues to fall over Christmas and Lego models are sprawled all over the living room floor on trays, both boys cordoning off a corner of the room for their pile of presents and model-making. Tom is lying between the two zones, rolling from one boy to the other in an attempt to quell any frustration that 'the model looks different from the one in the picture!' or 'I can't find that tiny red piece, Daddy, I've been looking for ages.'

We decide to take them out for a break and head for the hills with Becca and Tom's brother Richard, a muddle of mittens and woolly hats stuffed into a plastic bag alongside hot chocolate in vacuum flasks. The perfect slope is found and in spite of an operation only five days before, I find myself tucked behind my husband on a red plastic sledge, whizzing recklessly down a slope, shrieking in delight.

It is good to be alive.

A week later

The 'phone rings early, shortly before New Year's Eve. A week has passed since the operation and I am slowly recovering. It is the warm, chirpy voice of Carol, my breast care nurse.

'Hi Krista, it's Carol here. Just wanted to let you know that you need just a little bit more surgery to check out some more of the lymph nodes. OK? We will send you a date very soon.'

'Was the sentinel node affected?'

'Yes, it looks like it.'

I sit on the edge of the bed. Tom is stirring, aware that it is the hospital. Tears fall silently onto the duvet.

The Elderflower Tree

'Rough winds do shake the darling buds in May,
And summer's lease hath all too short a date.'
(Shakespeare)

Northern Germany June 1938

Georg Hoffmann gazed down at the document before him and exhaled wearily through his nose. He rolled his black, ebonite fountain pen between his fingers like a fat cigar and dated the document for his own records, before placing it neatly into the right-hand drawer of his oak desk and turning the small grey key in the lock. Leaning back in a creaking, well-worn leather chair, he gazed out through the surgery window at children playing soldiers in the road, practising their marching in step to the shouts of the alpha boy in the group. The sash window was open a little and the curtains stirred in the breeze. The scent of honeysuckle below the window wafted in and Georg closed his eyes for a moment, listening to the faint strains of piano music being played across the road. The melody was haunting, melancholic, and deeply stirring, but above all, quite quite beautiful. As he listened, a sadness seeped into his soul. There was something wistful about the piece being played, a longing within the cadences, something that transcended even the ideas of the composer and it perfectly matched Georg Hoffmann's mood that day. He was worried. He sat there a while, lost in thought, his mind wandering between the documents in his desk drawer and the house from which the music wafted so seductively. Hannelore could play the piano well, but those hands were blessed by a divine kiss.

Georg almost drifted off in his chair, nothing disturbing the stolen peace of that moment in his mostly contented life, which was as orderly as the rows of bottles of morphine, chlorinated lime solution, cotton wool, bandages and jars of sulfa that lined the large glass vitrines by the wall. Trays of syringes, forceps and scissors lay in perfect lines on shallow dishes, ready to be sterilised afresh after minor surgical procedures. A steam autoclave sat proudly in the corner of the room, a recent acquisition to improve the sterilising of all his instruments. And by his feet, his trusty, well-worn brown leather bag ready for patient visits to all the good people of Borkhausen and outlying farmlands. The all-pervasive smell of disinfectant from Irma's daily floor scrubbings was something he had grown used to, making the delicate sweetness of the honeysuckle most welcome. The music stopped and ten minutes later there was a knock at the door. He could hear muffled voices at the front door.

'Ah yes, Frau Rothstein, do come in, Eva is in the garden.'

Irma showed a small, petite lady into the hallway. She wore a blue silk dress that was sucked into her tiny waist. A shiny black belt reinforced the point. Georg rose from the creaking chair and strode over the threshold of his surgery, his heart pounding beneath the carefully arranged white shirt and bow tie, waistcoat, and linen jacket. Even on these warm early summer days he rarely took off his jacket in the week. Leah Rothstein's dark eyes met his blue gaze and she smiled.

'Good afternoon Doktor Hoffmann, and how is my young student progressing today?'

The scent of Vol de Nuit lingering in the air around her was quite intoxicating and Georg smiled broadly as he spoke.

'Ah, I think you will have to judge that for yourself, Frau Rothstein. Eva has been rather overexcited about her birthday last week and I am not too sure her head has been focused on the scales you set for her.'

 'Papa! Papa!'

A mass of brown curls brushed past the piano teacher and Georg's ten-year-old daughter Margarete stood gasping in front of her father.

'Komm, schnell! Eva ist vom Baum runtergefallen!'

Eva had fallen out of a tree.

'Will you excuse me, Frau Rothstein.' He strode heavily across the polished parquet floor of the hallway without waiting for a response and made his way quickly down the stone cellar steps with Margarete racing ahead into the garden.

The fragrant lemony smell of elderflower hung in the air. His wife, Hannelore, had that morning been gathering flower heads to infuse overnight in great enamel bowls of boiling water, lemon zest and tartaric acid. The ritual was deeply ingrained in the family life of the Hoffmanns. June signalled the start of the elderflower cordial season and all the children would help gather the best flower heads. The first beautiful, sun-drenched day had arrived.

'Remember,' instructed their mother, 'only heads which are half open and half in bud. They will give the best flavour.'

Eva, in all her seven-year-old eagerness, had picked the lower blooms but then out of boredom had scrambled as high as she could up into the gnarled branches of the ancient tree, oblivious to the relative height she had gained. She was more interested in climbing than gathering the blooms that rested on the outer canopy. She had edged towards the end of a large branch, hoping to pop her head out for all to see and to shriek with laughter at her sister below when, with an ominous scream, her feet slipped, wrenching her hands away from the thin branches they were holding. Tumbling down, arms flailing around her, larger branches breaking her fall, she landed with a great thud on the dry ground below. Hannelore waited for the scream, but it didn't come. The crumpled heap of blonde hair and lifeless limbs alarmed her. Eva's face was white.

'Margarete! Schnell! Fetch Papa!'

Panic.

Hannelore was not medical and in spite of giving birth four times would almost always call Georg if there was an accident involving her children. She whirled round as Georg ran up to his motionless daughter. He knelt down and felt Eva's pulse. Slow, but there.

'She fell before I saw what was happening! I didn't realise she had climbed so high!'

He leant over his crumpled daughter.

'Eva! Can you hear me?'

Eva murmured almost inaudibly and her eyes fluttered open, squinting in the sunlight. They looked quite green in this light, and her white cotton smock dress, dirtied by branch stains, made her seem quite angelic. Leaves and tiny twigs had caught themselves in her blonde, wavy hair.

The murmuring gave way to tears and sobs of pain as she reached out for her father and wrapped her small grazed arms around his neck.

'Papa! My foot! It hurts! My foot!'

Eva's ankle was swollen, and her foot turned in at an odd angle. Georg examined it gently and then laid it carefully down on the grass again.

'What were you doing so high in the tree?' blurted her father, a rare flush of anger rising in his temples - 'You know you are not allowed to climb so high. That was so stupid, Eva.'

Eva stared at him momentarily, her eyes frightened even more by his anger than the pain in her leg. It wasn't her fault she had fallen out of the tree. Why was he so angry?

The sobs continued, sobs of pain.

Georg raised himself to his full height, his eyes catching the consternation in Leah's face. He wanted to address her but thought better of it and turned to his wife and spoke in calmer, lowered tones. He regretted his outburst almost immediately. The anger came from somewhere beyond the incident, somewhere in the drawer of his desk. He lowered his voice.

'I am fairly certain her ankle is broken. We need to get her to hospital immediately. I'll telephone a message through to say we are on our way. With any luck, Hermann will be on duty today. Frau Rothstein, if you will forgive us...' Georg brushed past her and headed up to the surgery.

'Please do not worry yourself, Frau Rothstein,' Hannelore added, 'there is nothing to be done today. We shall send a note when Eva is quite recovered again. Sorry for your inconvenience.'

'Well, if you are quite sure I can do nothing to help, I shall get back to the house, but I shall enquire soon, Frau Hoffmann. Get well soon little Eva.'

And Leah Rothstein turned and scurried up the driveway to the cobbled road leaving the patient with her mother.

As Hannelore lifted her daughter into her lap, taking care not to move the ankle too much, a delicate porcelain doll rolled out of Eva's pocket onto the grass and lay face down among the plucked elderflower blooms.

The Operation

Georg swung himself behind the steering wheel of his fastest car, the cream Mercedes. He was already regretting snapping at his daughter who looked so small and pale in the arms of her mother. Margarete was left in the care of Irma the maid, who had been instructed to prepare supper for the boys. Four children, a busy practice, increasing demands on his time and the gnawing tiredness that came with managing relentless headaches, were taking their toll. Edict after edict had been arriving on his desk every few months over the last six years as the new Chancellor drove through the reforms of his regime. They all sat in his oak desk drawer, quietly ignored but festering in his mind like a black cloud.

Georg turned on the ignition, and carefully manoeuvred the long nose of the car round the drive and up onto Gartenstrasse. Every bump and jolt sent Eva into fresh waves of screeching. Hannelore tried to soothe her daughter as they drove over the cobbled road towards the main highway. It was not an easy journey, even with the Mercedes' magnificent suspension, and Eva retched several times into the enamel bucket her mother had wisely thought to bring with her. Eva was her youngest child and not the first to fall out of a tree, but her mother sensed that the shock of this fall would not be so easily soothed with soft words and cuddles.

The journey seemed interminable. Long, endlessly straight roads that scratched across the flat arable landscape of Northern Germany, punctuated only by the odd farmhouse, and wandering farm labourers heading home to their villages after a day in the potato fields. A landscape that no doubt inspired the more brooding nineteenth century novella to find popular acclaim and revealed the aching soul of Germany; acres of flat green fields yielding their harvest of solid root vegetables, but to Hannelore its very desolation was often soothing. It didn't impose itself like the majestically beautiful mountains of Bavaria, or engulf one in mystical, towering, dark Black Forest pines; it didn't entwine itself seductively around the heart like the rolling vineyards of the Mosel. Rather it allowed an altogether different emotion to take root, one forged in a less fairy-tale world of pretty castles, one that etched itself across the mind and brutally left the human spirit to find its own courage and hope. It was free from the vanity that Hannelore so despised in those who draped themselves in fine clothes and bedecked their homes in the latest fabrics. She loved the simplicity of this landscape with its country labourers. There were no city airs and graces here. Against this backdrop, all that really mattered was the intellect and the spirit. It built character. It was a stoical landscape.

But right now - how she longed for Italy!

How she longed this summer for sunlight, sparkling on a turquoise sea, for tall cedars and the ochres and terracottas of Tuscan farmhouses, dripping with vineyards and olive groves. Her mind was already preparing itself for what Eva's broken ankle would mean for the rest of the summer ahead. Georg, too was deep in thought, both parents concerned for their daughter, but for Georg who had already diagnosed the state of his daughter's ankle, and the probable operation, his mind was wandering back to the mound of paperwork that was waiting for him at home in the surgery - death certificates to sign, reports to write up on the local prison he had been visiting earlier that morning and then appointments with officials from the local Nazi headquarters that he had been summoned to attend. The constant encroachment of political ideologies on his work was beginning to bear down on him. Why were they so obsessed with the sanity of petty criminals incarcerated in the town's castle-turned-prison. What had once been simply a matter of health checks, dental checks and periodic prescribing of medication was becoming an oppressive request for minutiae. Georg was now expected routinely to interview each new prisoner on their genetic background to at least the third generation, as well as current health history. On and on the Mercedes sped, jangling the whimpering bundle past village after village, a dot to dot of red and black flags visible to Eva through the blur of tears and vomit.

At last they arrived at the Marienstift hospital, a towering, imposing red brick edifice opposite an even more imposing church after which it was named - the Marienkirche. Georg had not got through on the telephone with lines being continually jammed, but the staff here recognised him and nodded in courteous recognition as he strode through the heavy wooden doors into the reception area of accident and emergency.

'Guten Tag, Herr Doktor,' exclaimed the pretty young nurse, rising from her note taking.

'My daughter fell from a tree in the garden. She's broken her ankle, possible concussion. She will need an X-ray.'

'Of course. Please take a seat. I will 'phone through for you immediately.' The nurse looked kindly on Eva and wrinkled her brow in concern. Eva liked her, but her tear-stained face was set in a grimace.

Georg and Hannelore slumped in the waiting room chairs with their whimpering daughter. Her ankle throbbed painfully and she just wanted to be able to go to sleep. She nestled into her father's soft brown waistcoat and fingered his gold watch and chain, a gift from the town of Borkhausen to their fine philanthropic doctor. Georg had noticed the plight of mothers who needed childcare and had masterminded the building of a Kindergarten. He had pioneered and partly funded the enterprise and within the space of a few months it had been the talk of the town and the local newspaper. The Kindergarten was run by the much-loved Sister Elizabeth, and every morning this kindly nun would gather her flock of little children and sit them down to pray before the fun began, smiling at the cluster of small fat fingers clasped together and eyes tightly screwed shut,

'Dear Lord Jesus, we are your lambs whom you care for and you are our good Shepherd. We ask that you would be our friend this day and play with us and teach us your ways. Amen.'

'Amen,' chimed in the children who knew that this was a signal for them to run out into the courtyard filled with ropes, balls and bats and - the best thing of all - a swing hanging from the largest branch of the oak tree in the middle of the garden. Eva had loved her Kindergarten and her heart burst with pride at the civic ceremony when the mayor presented the gold watch to her father in front of all her friends and their families and local dignitaries.

'You can go up to X-ray, Doktor Hoffmann,' said the nurse on reception.

Georg heaved his daughter up in his arms and climbed the stone stairs, staggering occasionally against the iron railing, sweat beading on his forehead. His footsteps echoed up the stairwell. It reeked from disinfectant and Eva could see the cleaner out of one eye a few floors ahead of them. Normally she loved that smell. It reminded her of the open-air swimming pool round the corner from her house, the smell of cleaning day at home when Irma scrubbed the kitchen, hallway, surgery, and bathrooms all the way down into the cellar.

'That will keep the mice from scuttling in from the garden,' she used to tell Eva. 'They will faint from the clean smell!'

But today it made her feel quite ill and she longed to be out of this huge, cold building and back home with her doll, Johannes, who had been left lying on the lawn in the garden. The doll had been a birthday present which she had only just received the week before. His beautiful, porcelain face, delicately painted with rosebud lips, was much kissed by Eva and already she had made him a little bed out of a fruit crate she had found in the cellar.

'Johannes will be lonely and frightened in the big garden all on his own,' she sobbed.

'Shh! Eva, mein Schatz!' soothed her mother, stroking her long blond hair, 'Margarete will have put Johannes into his little bed on your table. He is waiting for you to come back.'

Eva was laid on the crisp, white linen bed and the consultant bent over her leg, muttering to her father as he did. Hermann Gerbich was an old acquaintance of Georg's and there was a mutual respect between the colleagues. They had known each other at medical school and had both served on the Eastern Front as junior doctors. Hermann had decided then that he wanted to be the finest surgeon in the land and make a name for himself in this field. He had learned a lot from the chief surgeon in the field hospitals and had absorbed voraciously every new technique and experimental operation the doctors were forced to try under almost impossible conditions. Georg had absorbed altogether different things as a result of this experience and he knew that his own future could only lie in the path of general practice. Hermann was brutally frank and not famed for his bedside manner. For Georg, he was a little too interested in the science and not enough in the patient's sense of wellbeing. That said, he was the best surgeon in Brunswick and Georg knew his daughter was in good hands.

'Yes, it is definitely broken. The X-ray will confirm this I am certain, but it will show us whether an operation is needed. Our facilities now are somewhat superior to the mobile Roentgen machines of 1915, Georg!' he said, laughing to himself.

A huge machine was wheeled into the theatre and positioned over the broken ankle, and everyone left the room, the radiographer giving strict instructions to the small waif-like patient to be very, very still. Eva was trembling with the shock of the fall but bit her lip and tried her utmost to do as she was told.

After an age of waiting, Gerbich returned to her parents and confirmed that she would need an operation immediately to re-set the bone and then to cover it in plaster. He seemed a little less cavalier in his manner.

'There is no guarantee that she will walk confidently again. There may be some permanent damage but let us hope for the best. For the daughter of Georg Hoffmann, I shall perform the operation myself.'

Looking at the strained expression on Hannelore's face he patted her arm, 'Try not to worry, Hannelore. We shall take her up to theatre straightaway. She will get the very best care from all of us.'

As Eva lay alone in the huge theatre, shivering with the strangeness and separation from her parents, her beloved sister and her doll Johannes, she drifted into a deep sleep; the Schimmelbusch mask was held by the anaesthetist above her mouth and ether dripped onto it.

'Count for me, Eva, count to ten.' The kindly anaesthetist looked into her anxious green eyes.

'Eins, zwei, drei... vier.' Her eyes drooped shut and she drifted away. Her ankle could be re-set.

Gerbich worked slowly but with confidence. Ankles were complex and he needed to manipulate the bones very carefully through the swelling. Another X-ray was taken while Eva slept, and he was reasonably satisfied that they had done the best job they could. Time would tell. Eva was young and her bones were growing rapidly which was not ideal, but they were also supple and would hopefully grow back well.

The nurses took over and applied the Plaster of Paris to the hoisted leg and let it set, before wheeling her back to the children's ward.

The surgeon strode down the stairwell to the waiting room, his expression that of a consummate professional. Hermann Gerbich liked to play court with friends as well as patients.

'All done, Georg, a classic Dupuytren fracture, nasty twist - good job we caught it before she tried walking on it. Now go home you two and get some rest. My staff will take special care over your Eva.'

'How did the operation go?' Hannelore probed Hermann's face.

The surgeon didn't meet her gaze but looked right past her at the trees beyond the window.

'Ach, it was delicate, but I think we got there. She is waking up now and a little drowsy. Time will tell and hopefully all will be well. It will be some time before she can put weight on it properly. I will arrange for her to come back in one week. The swelling around the ankle will have subsided by then and we can re-plaster it. Hopefully we shall see you both soon at our house for Marlene's forty-fifth birthday? Some bigwigs from Hanover will be there – do hope you are there. Heil Hitler!'

Georg replied with a muted 'Heil Hitler' and strode off, with Hannelore scowling at the floor.

'Hermann is loving being a member of the Party rather too much. No doubt the birthday will be crawling with officials from Brunswick,' she said.

'Shh, Hanne, wait until we are in the car. Someone will hear you.'

The subject was dropped, her thoughts consumed by the events of the afternoon, and a sudden wave of exhaustion mingled with relief at what had happened that day. The relief gave way to the realisation that her little girl, usually so full of life and energy and laughter was now imprisoned in plaster.

Six weeks. The summer holidays stretched before her. How would they cope with a seven-year-old in plaster? The steps up to the house, the steps down into the cellar and into the garden, the steps down into the lower sections of the garden, the grand stairway up from the hallway to the main landing from which the bedrooms branched, the wooden stairs up to the huge, cavernous attic where Eva would often creep and - on tiptoe - peer through the window down into the back courtyard and garden, and beyond to the river and her friend's house.

Always steps.

Hannelore's mind was grappling with how to manage this new situation. The boys would help and Irma, their maid, of course, and Georg would have to help carry her. They could read many books and she could sit and help her in the kitchen when making her favourite apple pancakes. They would spend long, hot days on a blanket in the garden, write stories and sing their favourite folk songs. Gradually the gloom of the event lifted from her heavy heart and she braced herself for whatever still lay at home to deal with before sinking into bed.

Georg took the steering wheel and gently rubbed his wife's hand. He could see the anxiety in her face as she fought to fend off recriminations about the accident. She was glad of his touch, all too rare these days. Her thoughts wandered back to the time she had met her husband at Göttingen, seat of one of the oldest universities in Germany. The young student of English literature was quite swept away by the dashing, medical student fencing champion that was Georg Hoffmann. For his part, Georg had been no less enchanted with the beautiful, cerebral Hannelore Lutz, whose gentle, intellectual dreaminess had excited his sanguine, solid North German temperament. She would tease him by reciting Shakespeare's sonnets in English as they rambled through the purple moorland of northern Germany during their courtship. She read voraciously, hungry to learn more about the rapidly changing world she was growing up in and to shake free from the confines of her gloomy, depressing family home in Hanover. She couldn't wait to escape and be married as soon as it was possible after their studies had ended. She wouldn't be confined, like her awkward, fragile, depressed, older sister, to a life behind those dreary shutters, afraid to venture out beyond the massive walls of the house in the suburbs of the city, imprisoned by her own fears and dreads.

Georg was an emancipated student and to have a beautiful as well as intelligent bride at his side was quite a trophy in 1919. He had survived the Russian Front and the Western Front, and, as survivors of this devastating World War, he and his new wife were going to shape their world in a new Germany. He had been a diligent student at school and fulfilled the dreams his father had nurtured of a son who would go to university and learn a noble profession. And here he was in the home he had built himself in 1925, with an established medical practice housed in the front of this impressive wooden framed, shuttered, Fachwerk villa on the most prestigious Gartenstrasse with its extensive garden, a maid to help his wife and two strapping sons and two beautiful daughters.

He sped on reflectively as his wife rested her head back, closed her eyes and whispered a prayer of thanks that their precious daughter was safe.

Recovering at home

Some days after the operation, Eva came home and was reunited with Johannes. Margarete had tucked him in his little crate bed and wrapped a bandage around his leg to replicate Eva's plaster. It made her little sister smile. Hannelore had made up a bed downstairs on Eva's favourite green chaise longue in the corner of the family snug; it would be dangerous for her to be clambering up and down the wide, sweeping stairway to her own room - she could easily lose her balance and fall. If she were downstairs she could access the toilet at night with relative ease, and Hannelore wouldn't have to watch her quite so carefully. It would be difficult enough getting her in and out of the garden; there were stairs to the cellar, stairs to the side and front doors. Margarete would sometimes creep down at night and lie on the snug sofa with a blanket and chatter quietly to Eva about their plans for the summer holidays, feeling lonely herself upstairs where the creaking of the timbers from the cavernous attic above her a little quite unnerving.

In the aftermath of the operation, Eva looked pale and limp and became quite petulant during these long, hot days, having to succumb to the confines of a foot in plaster. Life was not going to be easy with the summer stretching ahead but at least Hannelore didn't need to get her to school every day. Eva had longed for these summer holidays, the first since she had started school and, on the brink of completing her first whole year, she had now been robbed of the joy of all the fun her friends were going to have. She shivered through inactivity and poor circulation. Her leg was becoming stiff and ached endlessly with the weight of the

52

Plaster of Paris. Margarete would come and sit with her on the sofa and they would play with their dolls while Irma, the maid, hauled buckets of peat up from the cellar and lit the stove in the corner of the snug where they sat. The warm, earthy, heathery smells filled the room on these cool summer evenings and cheered her up a little.

The Plaster of Paris was replaced at the Marienstift hospital within the week, and life in the Hoffmann household adapted to Eva's needs. Thankfully, her brothers were home from their boarding school. She adored them both, but Johannes in particular. He was a younger version of their mother with his dark wavy hair and brown eyes; not particularly tall, but to Eva her seventeen-year-old brother was more handsome than any film star and he would spoil her with sweets and give her piggy-back rides, threatening to drop her in the river that bordered the end of their acre of garden. It had been brave Johannes who had saved the life of his younger brother Max and held onto his leg when he had fallen into the river as a five year old boy, a story Eva pestered him to tell her every time they were at the bottom of the garden.

'How did you save him, Hannes? Was the water very cold?'

'Ach, Max slipped on the muddy bank. We were trying to catch fish with home-made fishing rods - just pretending - and had crept through a gap in the fence. He then leaned too far over and lost his balance. Before I knew it, he was toppling headfirst into the river. A reflex made me grab his ankle and I just held on as long as I could while I shouted for help. I wasn't strong enough to pull him out without falling in myself.'

'Who heard you shouting?'

'I think Papa was in the kitchen at the time and came hurtling down the garden, with Mama running after him. He grabbed me with one hand and Max's leg with the other and hauled us up the bank. After that episode, Papa made very sure we would never be able to get to the river and put up this even higher fence. Shall I show you how I held Max's leg, Eva?'

And, amidst screams and giggles, Eva would be dangled by her strong brother over the now very secure fence. She knew he would never let go and her screams and giggles used to egg him on.

Johannes' future was clear to him from an early age; his ambition was to study medicine and join his father in the medical practice he had established in their home. Discussions around the table revolved around universities and old medical professors and colleagues who might also give advice and support; the future looked bright. Georg had attended Marburg University, one of Germany's oldest and finest seats of learning, and had then continued his studies at Göttingen, an equally noble university town, where he had met Hannelore. Johannes was destined to follow in their footsteps soon.

Family life centred around the oak table in the spacious dining room, always beautifully laid with a white linen tablecloth, napkins, and silverware. Lunchtime was the highlight of every day for the Hoffmann children, a moment of respite from work, a signal that the school day had ended and a chance to enjoy at least half an hour of their father all to themselves. Light shafted onto the table through large windows that overlooked the back lawn, which had been landscaped with sandy pathways for children to explore, leading to large shrubs and bushes for them to hide behind. An exotic array of indoor plants adorned the window sills along with silver-framed black and white family photographs. The walls were hung with elegant pictures that Hannelore had inherited from her grandparents' home in the finer suburbs of Hanover; landscapes of her native northern Germany, brown, flat agricultural scenes of labourers in potato fields or fine etchings of the town in the late nineteenth century, but one in particular glowed with the warmer hues of Tuscany, a much more recent purchase, acquired during the unforgettable summer of their honeymoon. Georg was less keen on these warmer climes, but his darker skinned wife with her brooding eyes longed for sun and warmth and vineyards and he had yielded to her wishes. Hannelore yearned for the scene depicted in the frame; the rolling golden hills of Tuscany sweeping around an ochre villa high on a hill, surrounded by rows of poplars and splashes of potted geraniums. She had made sure the painting hung opposite her chair in the dining room, shielded from the glare of the window light, yet providing another ray of sunshine for her to feed her dreams. Beneath it stood the upright piano and she would often look at her picture whilst playing a sonata after supper. The dining room stretched into the fine sitting room, bedecked with blue velveteen sofas and highly polished mahogany side tables and cabinets, displaying beautiful cut-glass decanters and vases as well as blue and white Meissen china teacups, passed down from her grandmother. This end of the room was often sealed off from children with shuttered wooden doors during the week. Georg and Hannelore would sometimes sit there with friends in the evening, chatting over a glass of wine and cognac after a private supper when the girls were in bed.

Some weeks after Eva's accident the family was gathered for lunch around the dining room table. Eva played with the engraving on her silver napkin ring, following the ornate initials EH with her fingers.

'What's for lunch, Mama? It smells delicious.'

The doorbell rang at the front of the house and Irma slipped out of the kitchen to answer it.

'I helped Mama make it,' Margarete piped in, 'It's onion soup and pot roast with new potatoes.'

'Onion soup! Bon!' said Max with a French flourish. 'C'est delicieux!'

Hannelore smiled and nodded with a 'Merci beaucoup, mon fils' and nodded to Georg to say grace. The family bowed their heads slightly and waited for the familiar grace.

'Come, Lord Jesus, be our guest and bless what you have provided for us. Amen.'

Just as he finished, Hermann Gerbich appeared at the threshold of the dining room from the parlour, having strutted past the maid in the hall stating that he knew where the dining room was and that he only wanted to pop in for a moment to have a word with her employer. Irma had retreated sheepishly to the kitchen.

'Aha, the perfect Aryan family at lunch. What a sight! My goodness Hannelore – what smells and what fine young soldiers you have in the making there. Hello Georg. You don't mind me dropping by to see my little blonde patient with the big green eyes? And how is that ankle of yours, little Eva?'

Eva stared a little vacantly and flushed a little. Not knowing how to reply, she began peeling the hot potatoes on her plate, watching the butter slip down the sides as they steamed, and just smiled a little weakly at Gerbich.

Georg rose from his seat and Hannelore too, who was trying hard to conceal the disappointment that a sacred family moment was being shattered, second by second.

'Hermann, why how good of you to drop by. Eva is much stronger, thanks to your fine skills. You will, of course join us for lunch?'

'Well, it does look too good to decline. And I have had a rather busy clinic. Very kind of you.'

Georg placed a spare chair next to Max, and Gerbich planted his solid form firmly on the seat, whilst Hannelore busied herself with a fresh place setting.

'We have just said grace,' she said pointedly, emphasising the word 'grace', 'but we can say it again now that you are here.'

The visitor looked a little uncomfortable as Hannelore proceeded to pray without waiting for any assent from Georg.

'Dear Heavenly Father, our only creator and Lord, we thank Thee for Thy provision and bounty and for Thy goodness to us each day. We are truly thankful to Thee alone. Amen.'

All of her children looked at her wide-eyed and quietly echoed the Amen. Gerbich had not closed his eyes and just continued talking as soon as she had finished, mildly irritated by this show of piety.

'So, Johannes, what are you planning to study? You must be almost finished with school now, yes?'

'Well, sir, I am about to go to Marburg, like my father.'

'To study medicine, ja?!'

Johannes nodded, a little overwhelmed by just how loudly their visitor was talking.

'Remember me to Professor Guntheim if you meet him; he will no doubt invite you to tea with his wife, Ulla. Do you remember Guntheim, Georg? We used to have some fun in his lectures didn't we? I'm guessing that Blumenthal has now lost his position.'

Hannelore studiously looked at her plate and avoided the gaze of the intruder.

Johannes sensed the awkwardness in the atmosphere and broke in to prevent his mother making a comment that she might regret, regarding Nationalist Socialist policies on Jews holding academic seats.

'I am looking forward to seeing my lodgings and meeting the other medical students. There will be lots of societies to join, but the first one will be the fencing society.'

'Papa! Do tell us about your scar again!' shrieked Eva from the other end of the table, suddenly animated by the idea of her father entertaining them all with his famous, oft repeated tales of the fencing society.

Georg touched the left side of his face, feeling for the familiar ridges around his lip and cheek, and smiled at his younger daughter.

'Well, Eva, these scars had to be earned. As you well know they are my duelling scars from when I was in the Marburger Philipper, my fencing fraternity at university.'

'Ha-ha! We were both in the Marburger Philipper!' bellowed Gerbich.

'That's the one I want to join. I'd forgotten the name,' interjected Johannes.

Georg continued, 'We all wore rather splendid uniforms and every week we would meet with other fraternities and stage duels. And afterwards we had wonderful parties together. The more scars we carried, the more respect we earned. I had to be very brave and let my opponent cut me with his very sharp sword. I had to stand quite still, with a guard shield over my eyes and just wait for the sword to slash downwards,' and as he spoke, Georg raised his knife and sliced the air with a great flourish. 'My opponent's name was Friedrich von Steffenberg. He came from a very aristocratic family. To be cut by the sword by someone of noble blood, not to flinch, or draw back through fear – ah, that was special. It was not simply *using* the sword that earned your reputation - anyone can slash a sword at someone. It takes great courage to absorb the fear, stare at the enemy and take the pain.'

'And greater courage to slash back quickly!' spat Gerbich, who couldn't refrain from speaking even though his mouth was full of pot roast.

Margarete winced but Eva was scrutinising his face.

Hannelore looked at her husband in slight disapproval, although she confessed to her closest friends that her eye had been caught by the fresh scars of the young Georg Hoffmann when he had arrived in Göttingen.

'But why, Papa? What was the point of being cut? Didn't it hurt terribly? I still don't understand.' Eva's brothers laughed at her naivety but they all eagerly listened to what their father's response was going to be.

'Eva, in life it is very easy to hurt other people with sticks and stones and knives and,' at this Georg's face sagged, 'and guns and bombs, but it is another thing altogether to take a blow and not strike back in anger. It developed our character and gave us self-control and discipline.'

'And discipline is what we will need in the Reich if we are to be strong again,' said Gerbich, stabbing the air with his fork.

All fell silent around the table.

'Did you use a gun in the war, Papa?' asked Margarete, looking slightly awed by her father. He didn't often look this serious or talk about guns, and he never spoke to them about the war. It was part of the past and something best left buried, along with so many of his friends.

'No, Margarete, I never shot a gun. I was a junior doctor then and helped the poorly soldiers. Now, you two lovely girls, take your dolls into the snug and play there quietly. We will call you back later for some pudding.' The girls slipped quietly from their seats, a little glad to be escaping the presence of the overbearing visitor. Eva could be overheard whispering to Margarete rather loudly,

'He doesn't have a *scar*, did you notice?'

Whilst Georg coughed awkwardly, the Hoffmann sons bristled, feeling older and more important and grew visibly more serious, knowing they were allowed to stay and be part of the adult conversation.

Hannelore tidied the plates for Irma to take away into the kitchen. She left the table and busied herself at the back of the dining room where the small, cool pantry was and returned with small glasses of cognac for her husband and Gerbich, who warmed his with large, fat hands.

'Papa,' enquired Max, 'Did you really not fight in the war?' He seemed disappointed that his father had not engaged in combat. Hannelore looked sternly across the table at him.

'Max, your father was fighting for men who were dying. He was a hero, saving the lives and limbs of so many soldiers. That war was a pointless waste of a whole generation. Be glad that he wasn't one of those who fell within minutes of the battle as so many hundreds did. You would not be here now if he had,' she added with more mirth in her voice.

'I cannot agree that it was pointless, Hannelore,' Gerbich countered with a slightly sterner expression on his face, 'it showed where our weaknesses were with an outdated monarchy, where our alliances were wrongly invested. We have learned from our mistakes and we are rising like a phoenix out of the ashes. We also learned a lot about medicine from this war, did we not, Hoffmann? My God did we see some injuries. The people are loving what Hitler is doing for this country! We have rising employment, new road systems, new factories. Germany will be great again and the nations who have been laughing at us will see it and regret their triumphalism.'

His comments were met with a nodding but silent Georg, an entranced Max and Johannes and a silent Hannelore, whose lips were tightly pursed.

'Well, I must be off now. I promised Marlene I would not dally. I gave her a lift into Borkhausen so that she could visit her aunt and have lunch with her. Couldn't face it myself so I made some excuse about getting my shoes re-soled urgently. Glad to see that Eva's not limping too badly. We need our young girls to grow up strong and healthy, eh Hannelore? I'm dropping in on the branch at Fuchsburg on the way back, Georg, they want a word with me about the Jews of Brunswick – want to have a look at my patient lists. Thankfully, something you will have little to do with here in Borkhausen. Can't imagine you have many to worry about here. Will drop by again soon. I'll see myself out. Heil Hitler!'

Georg rose in his seat and replied quietly, 'Hermann.' And with that, the surgeon downed his cognac and thundered back out of the dining room as swiftly as he had arrived. Georg visibly relaxed and cradled his glass, relieved that Hannelore had not attempted to engage the intruder in further discussion.

Max was still daydreaming about the war they had been discussing and was thankfully oblivious to Gerbich's parting words.

'I would so love to see that kind of action though!' Max exclaimed triumphantly. 'To be part of a band of fellow soldiers and to make a difference in a battle. To win a medal!'

Max was almost sixteen and his cup of life was brimming over. He would listen to the political speeches on the family radio and could feel the adrenalin surging through Hitler and Goebbels. It was quite infectious - he was almost willing a war to erupt, willing them to declare it.

Hannelore looked at him seriously, noticing her husband's hopeful idealism of the 1920s in her son. Georg had always deflected questions about the possibility of war in previous conversations with his sons, but it would be foolish not to address what seemed inevitable now. Only fools buried their heads in the sand by not reading the papers and listening to the political rhetoric on the radio. Whilst he was not prepared to revisit the past war with his sons, he definitely wanted to prepare them for what might come. He and Hannelore had discussed this conversation the night before and it was right to have it now. It would not be a long conversation, but it would enlighten their boys as to what might lie ahead.

'My sons, you are no doubt aware that war is being talked about in the papers and on the radio and in the town generally.'

'Ja, Papa,' piped up Johannes, 'Rolf told me at school last term that his father had written to say our forces are preparing for war.'

'Well, Rolf's father is right, and you may well hear more and more news about it over the coming months.'

'Is it true then? Are we about to go to war? With which nation?'

'Well the Anglo-German naval treaty Hitler was forced to submit to concerning the size of our navy was renounced at the end of April, something I personally agree with. The Treaty of Versailles after the last war has punished our nation long enough and we should be given equal rights to arm ourselves as every other nation... but I am also concerned that he may not stop at this, but become more and more aggressive for land and try and reclaim some of our lost territories.'

The collective heartbeat of the family grew quicker as eyes darted from one face to another. Max was fifteen and Johannes seventeen. They all looked at Johannes. It would only be half a year until he turned eighteen and could be conscripted, irrespective of his plans to study medicine.

'We must hope that diplomacy solves the problems, but you need to be aware that the government, that Hitler himself, is set on preparing the armed forces for another war.'

'What do you think of Hitler, Papa?' probed Max, scrutinising his father's face. 'Do you think it would be right for us to go to war?'

Hannelore smoothed the white linen tablecloth with sweeping motions of her hand, waiting for Georg to give what would be a more measured reply.

'No civilised country wants war, my son, but sometimes it might be necessary. Germany is struggling and has been beaten down by years of austerity, of hardship. Hitler has given everyone hope that our country could stand up again and play a big role in the world, but...'

And his voice trailed off as he inwardly made a decision not to speak his mind fully in front of his sons. He caught Hannelore's eyes boring into his and both of them knew that to speak their mind too freely on political matters could compromise the safety of their family. '...What is important is that we work hard and do our best to make Germany great again and pray that it doesn't have to mean war. We must try and trust our government and leaders to make the right decision.'

Later that evening the boys sat with their parents around the radio, the girls already in bed fast asleep. Max had implored his parents to let him listen to the news and they conceded; having allowed him to hear their thoughts about the possibility of war meant he had the right to be informed, especially if his school friends were hearing rumours.

Johannes fiddled with the dial on the polished walnut Zenith radio that stood proudly on a side table in the parlour. Its beautiful mahogany fretwork and gleaming dials fascinated the boys, who regularly opened it up and looked at its inner workings.

It was Hannelore's pride and joy. It had cost them the princely sum of one hundred and fifty Reichsmarks and was much admired whenever visitors came to the house. For her it represented more than a status symbol, it represented a link with the world beyond Germany. Unlike the cheap bakelite radios that were being mass produced for every household to buy, it was able to receive foreign stations, and she enjoyed tuning in to British news stations to improve her English and to hear how Herr Hitler was being reported in England. Hannelore despised the small black radios stamped with their ugly black eagle and a swastika, peddled for thirty-five Reichsmarks on the High Street. She was one of the few to discern the wonderful propaganda machine that Goebbels was creating to brainwash the German people with relentless ranting speeches the whole town was now tuning into every night.

Eva loved the radio too and once a week she was allowed to climb onto her mother's lap and listen to Grimm's fairy tales being read aloud with sound effects in the background. Although she was not allowed to play with it, the radio was a lifeline for her in those weeks of confinement to the house and garden, and her mother let her listen to it more frequently now that she was so limited in what she could do.

Georg recharged the oven from the peat basket, and they settled down to listen to the latest news bulletin. A Schubert piano sonata was playing and Hannelore picked up her mending as she hummed along to the music, the boys tapping the table with their fingers, Max pretending to play the piano and Johannes hoping the rather ponderous piece would end soon so they could hear the latest speech to recite to their friends.

'The National Socialist revolution is a typical German product.' The speaker was clearly Goebbels.

'Its scale and historical significance can only be compared with other great events in human history...' Hannelore rolled her eyes at Georg.

'The same old repeat of Nuremberg,' she sighed heavily.

'The Versailles treaty of non-peace stood in its way!'

The rant continued.

'It is a warning for the entire liberal world that Germany has replaced democracy with an authoritarian system, that liberalism broke under the blows of the national uprising, that parliamentarianism and the party system are outdated concepts for us...

Defending against the Jewish danger is only part of our plan.'

The boys raised their eyebrows and looked at each other.

'Is it surprising that the German Revolution also broke this unbearable yoke?'
the orator pounded on, reciting the plague Jewry had become in German society, taking over the legal, medical and education establishments.

'I don't fully understand,' Max said thoughtfully.

Hannelore turned the dial.

'Whatever you do, do *not* search the London channels, Hannelore!' Georg threw his wife a warning glance. 'Doktor Schiller's wife was taken for questioning for listening to foreign channels. They only released her because he is a member of the Party.'

Hannelore looked resolutely at her younger son, whose question she wanted to answer.

'The National Socialist Party doesn't like the Jews, Max, because they believe that they have defiled the purity of the German race. They want to solve the racial problem and remove Jews from all positions of power and influence.'

'But why? What exactly have they done wrong?'

'They think that they have too much influence and that the German people need to set themselves free from this, which is why many of them have lost their jobs.'

'A lot of them have left the country, haven't they Papa?' interjected Johannes, 'Several of the Jewish boys at school have left and their families have emigrated to America.'

'Yes, understandably they do not feel welcome,' Georg replied, nodding his head thoughtfully. 'It shouldn't really affect anyone in Borkhausen. There are so few Jewish people here and I hardly think old Frau Samuels and the Rothsteins pose a serious threat to the German people.'

The boys laughed at the thought of the elderly lady from the draper's shop and the diminutive music teacher opposite their home being hounded out of the town.

Max then stared at his father. 'Frau Rothstein teaches the girls piano doesn't she? Will she be allowed to do that still?'

'Of course she will,' replied Hannelore proudly.

'We are extraordinarily fortunate to have our daughters taught by Leah Rothstein. And there is no need to talk about her to any of your friends in the town or at school. Hopefully, this racial nonsense will settle down soon and everyone can get on with their lives as honest people.'

'Do you disagree with Hitler then, Mama?'

Hannelore stared at Georg. The two boys looked at their father, but Georg just nodded sagely and deftly closed down the conversation.

'Ach boys, is that the time? We shall talk more tomorrow. I'm exhausted. Your diabetic old father needs his sleep.'

The Piano Teacher

A few weeks later

The evening sun cast its long shadows across the flat cobbles of Gartenstrasse. The air was heavy with the scent of roses growing in the front gardens of the imposing villas that stretched around the corner towards the town centre with its promenade of shops. Georg was heading home after making a few necessary visits to those patients who lived just ten minutes' walk from his house. It was later than he would like but the walk would do him good and perhaps clear his head and, anyway, there were a number of patients he was very concerned about and whom he had promised to check up on before the end of the day. He was ruminating over the encounters of the last hours. The Becker's fourth child, delivered the night before, was doing well and although Erna Becker had three other children, she had managed to get some sleep between feeds with the help of her visiting sister. Georg was relieved to see lots of happy faces tucking into a hearty stew around the table. Franz Holm was back from hospital with a broken arm, a fall whilst mending farm fences at Clausmoorhof, and he had suffered a nasty concussion. Georg had been pleased to see him moving more easily and no longer struggling with headaches and dizziness. Elderly Greta Muller was recovering from food poisoning, and fragile Frau Samuels, bedridden now in the upstairs apartment of her family's draper store, was gaining strength each week. A bout of pneumonia had weakened her but she was well cared for and Georg knew she would hopefully recover to enjoy many more summers. It was this last patient that occupied his thoughts the most, though.

Esther Samuels had seemed quite agitated, worried about the growing rumours of war and what that would mean for her nephew and his family, and it was clear to Georg that her concerns were echoed throughout the town. Everywhere he went, he heard stories of the impending war. Some, usually the young, were war hungry, others who remembered only too recently the horrors of the last war were more fearful. Frau Samuels was worried also for an altogether different reason and one that Georg was himself losing sleep over.

Walking towards him he saw the diminutive figure of Leah Rothstein, a blue silk scarf wrapped tightly around her head, mere wisps of auburn hair visible in the early evening breeze and a leather bag firmly held to her body almost as if she were shielding a baby from a cold wind. Georg was surprised to see her, only because he assumed the Rothsteins were away, perhaps visiting family. He hadn't seen them in weeks. His furrowed expression softened as she approached, her eyes fixed firmly on the pavement.

'Guten Abend, Frau Rothstein.' Georg doffed his hat and stood still, anticipating an exchange of words.

Leah acknowledged the greeting, brightening a little as she realised that the silhouetted figure in front of her was her neighbour and doctor, and she raised her head to meet his gaze and offered him her delicate hand. She respected Georg. He had been good to her and her husband over the years and had always made a point of saying that if they ever needed advice 'just to come straight over the road and call.' Their house was diagonally opposite the Hoffmann home. Leah had aspired to be a concert pianist in her youth, having won a much-coveted scholarship to the prestigious Mozart Conservatoire in Vienna, and was soon touring all the major cities of Europe, often appearing as a guest pianist for the most celebrated orchestras and conductors. The love of her life was first violinist Aaron Rothstein and together they had seduced the cultured elite of Austria and Germany with a repertoire of Beethoven, Brahms, Mozart, and her beloved Chopin. Tragically struck down in his thirties with polio, Leah's husband was now confined to a wheelchair. The couple had been forced to retreat from their public lives as musicians and had bought the elegant villa in Borkhausen for their enforced retirement. Aaron needed full time care and the life of the touring concert musician was out of the question. Leah also wanted to be nearer her parents and relatives in Brunswick, home to a substantial Jewish community that had established itself around the impressive Gothic and Oriental Reform synagogue there. To supplement their savings, she gave piano lessons and had begun teaching Margarete and Eva and a few other children in the town only the year before.

Georg was a little in love with Leah. Her petite elfin-like face, framed by glossy, auburn hair seemed slightly otherworldly. Pale skin reflected a life lived largely indoors, so different to the ruddy brown complexions of many of Georg's farming patients whose rough hands worked the potato and swede harvests in the plain, flat arable fields that wrapped themselves around the town. She shunned the daylight, often at home with her husband and practising or teaching her beloved piano. Her nose was larger than her face seemed to suit, but her lips suggested a passionate spirit that embedded itself not in moving words but more in the sublime beauty of her playing. In fact, Georg had noticed them move imperceptibly as if almost in silent ecstasy when she played. Was it this as well as the romance of her previous life in the limelight and a sadness he felt at her restricted and confined life, that evoked the emotion he felt for her, a mixture of desire and pity. It was not a love he could ever freely pursue, of that he was convinced, more the sort of love that intoxicates, a Greta Garbo kind of love... one he could dream about from his surgery desk.

'Guten Abend, Frau Rothstein. I couldn't help but notice how beautifully you played the other afternoon when Eva had her accident, quite enchanting. Would I be correct in thinking it was Chopin?'

'Guten Abend, Herr Doktor.' She spoke softly,

'Ah, how kind of you, yes Chopin, a nocturne, one of my favourites.' She smiled a little at the compliment.

'You could always hear a pin drop in the concert hall with this nocturne.' Her eyes were fixed on the hedge beside them, but she was lost in another world.

'I can quite imagine. It was a most welcome distraction from my work. I feel privileged to be your audience now. You must miss touring the great concert halls of Europe?'

'Sometimes,' she answered wistfully 'but my place now is by Aaron, and as you well know there is no longer a future for me in this country. I sometimes wonder what my life would have been like had I accepted the first proposal of marriage I was offered in England back in the twenties – at least then I would not find myself trapped in this country that has no room for Jews.'

Georg smiled weakly, attempting to ignore the last comment, spoken, he detected, with an edge of bitterness in her voice. She sensed his awkwardness and changed the subject.

'And how is little Eva's ankle? I saw your wife in the town recently and she thought Eva might be able to resume her usual piano lesson?'

'Ach, thank you Frau Rothstein, that would be lovely. It was a silly accident, very foolish, and I apologise for my outburst at the time, an over-anxious father... but it is healing well enough, thank you. She will be able to return to her lessons in a few weeks. The distraction might do her some good. And how is your husband? We thought you were away, no one has seen you this past week.'

Georg caught sight suddenly of the yellow star sewn crudely onto Leah's coat. She was concealing it beneath the leather bag, but her grip had slipped, and it was now visible.

She caught the look on his face and breathed in sharply.

'It is not safe for Jews to be on the streets, Herr Doktor, I would have thought you might have appreciated that.'

Georg heard the fear and anger in her voice. Leah was a proud woman, more accomplished than anyone he had ever met in this small town of five thousand inhabitants, more accomplished even than Hannelore, which was high praise indeed, and he felt in that moment the indignation she must be experiencing at being treated in this way, branded almost as a common criminal.

'I am sure you are safe in Borkhausen,' he responded. 'No-one here would want to harm you, I am certain. Everyone knows you as the cultured, gifted concert pianist, Leah Rothstein. It is outrageous to think that you could in any way be considered a threat to German society.'

'Maybe no-one here would want to harm me, Herr Doktor, but you of all people must surely realise that no Jew is safe in Germany. We have been undetected so far because there are so few Jews in the town, and we are not as obvious as those in Brunswick and Hanover. I was only speaking to Esther Samuels last week and she is very frightened for her safety. She is so old and frail and knows that she cannot hide behind her 'Aryan' nephew.' The word Aryan was uttered with disdain.

'Have you not read that Nuremburg filth?'

Georg winced, remembering the documents he had filed in his desk drawer. He chose not to respond to her statement. It was dangerous to voice any opinions, especially on the street, with many windows ajar in the houses around them.

Instead he resorted to politeness 'Please keep playing, Leah, please don't stop; even if it is just to cheer up your old doctor.'

Leah smiled weakly, lifted a little by his kindness.

'I shall. I wish to pay my respects to Frau Samuels. I understand she has not been well.'

'Ah yes, she is confined to bed at present, but I hope she will regain her strength with plenty of rest.'

Turning to walk on, Georg sighed and doffed his hat again, the courtesy not lost on his neighbour. He looked at her frail, beautiful, gifted hands, still tightly clutching the leather bag and told her he would come by in a few days to see her husband.

Once home he strode into the surgery and almost collapsed in his brown leather chair, exhausted by the day's work but more by the gnawing realisation that his country was edging towards a precipice; one that threatened not only the peace of his life but also threatened to exile those who created the truly exquisite moments in life, moments of pure ecstasy. In truth he was feeling crushed by the way Leah Rothstein made him feel, something he had not felt in the many years of having four children and building up a successful practice. He pulled open the drawer of his desk, drew out his medication and gazed at the papers in the drawer. Here were the edicts that all general practitioners had been sent by the National Socialist regime. The new Chancellor had set himself up as a self-confessed supreme 'doctor' and Germany was his patient, an ailing patient, wounded by its treatment after the last war, starved by Versailles and the crippling demands of war reparations. He would re-energise Germany and re-build a new Empire with a healthy body, a clean body; one whose swollen appendix would be cut out in order to save the body. At the beginning Georg had admired the passion with which he had promoted public health and in particular the fight against cancer, lung cancer especially, outlawing smoking and investing vast sums of Treasury money in researching cures. He had charmed a medical world hungry for breakthroughs, fame, and immortality. What doctor didn't want his name linked to a discovery that would recognise him for posterity? What price wasn't he prepared to pay to secure that dream of the top medical post at the most prestigious universities in the land? Of course, Georg had joined the National Socialist Party as so many of his colleagues had done. Wearing the badge in his lapel was a sign of medical respectability; it was something he had not agonised over in the wave of popular national sentiment that Adolf Hitler enjoyed in the first years of his chancellorship. He had even been prepared, when occasion demanded, to wear the Nazi uniform. Georg was no Nazi though. He had grown up in an altogether different world and longed for a peaceful life with his family. His days and nights were becoming more and more disturbed by these notifications of the laws and decrees that had been coming through the letterbox every few months, and which affected his position as a physician. These were more disturbing. He had stopped showing them to Hannelore; it simply wasn't worth the arguments that would ensue. He had told her at first because he valued her opinion, her discernment about these matters, but now it was becoming imperative to conceal them, to lock them in the drawer for the safety of his family. Hannelore could be unpredictable in social circles and such was the white-hot rage that she felt towards the National Socialist ideology she could not be trusted to remain discreet. It was clear to him, even in the brief conversation with Gerbich, that she would struggle to contain her opinions. He feared that she would be denounced as a Marxist sympathiser and not even he could save her then from the authorities and the merciless treatment of such 'criminals' of the state.

Gingerly he took the documents out of the faded oak drawer along with a handbook he had been given by his younger son's Hitler Youth leader. It was a red booklet issued in 1933 brazenly explaining all the new laws to the hopeful, aspiring leaders of tomorrow. His own children were either in the Hitler Youth or longing to be in it. Margarete adored her League of Girls group. It was fun, exciting, and inspiring to be part of a dynamic group of young girls led by the tall, athletic, blonde goddess Anneliese, whom they all adored. He leafed through the booklet and the papers, casting his eyes over the paragraphs that he had underlined in black.

From the study of genetics we have learned that the individual human being is inextricably bound to his ancestors through his birth and inheritance. He is bound in the same way to his descendants. The individual human being is but one link in the long chain of generations... But the great genetic river of a people can suffer many impurities and injuries along the way... 400 of every 1,000 cases of mental illness have genetic origins. But there are also physical and spiritual inheritable diseases... The worst inherited diseases are: feeblemindedness, schizophrenia, insanity, inherited epilepsy, inherited St. Vitus' Dance, inherited blindness and deafness, and inherited physical impairments, including among others bone disorders, club foot, hare lip with cleft palate, and blood diseases...Then there are inherited diseases that are of a less serious nature, or which cause internal illnesses. Here are a few of the many that could be mentioned: extra fingers or short fingers, flat and knock feet, birthmarks and moles, short- and farsightedness, squinting, cataracts (blurring of the cornea), as well as a susceptibility to jaundice, obesity, cancer, and tuberculosis...

Georg sighed wearily, removed his spectacles, and rubbed his eyes and face before reading on.

There are inherited diseases whose external effects can be treated by the art of medicine, but do not lose their genetic nature. If, for example, someone with a bone disease or a hare lip with a cleft palate undergoes surgery, the problems will still reappear in his descendants.

Although normal diseases need not be a barrier to marriage, those with genetic diseases, even if they can be alleviated through surgery, should be strongly advised not to have children... criminality also can be traced back to genetic diseases... Serious genetic disease, particularly mental illnesses, make their victims incapable of living a normal life. They rob their victims of their reasoning powers and sense of responsibility, reducing their value to the people's community... in Germany today we have: 1,000,000 feeble-minded, 250,000 cases of genetic mental deficiency, 90,000 epileptics, 40,000 inherited cases of physical handicaps...

The costs of caring for a genetically ill person are eight times as high as those for a normal person.

From a genuine sense of humanity toward the sick and from a strong sense of responsibility to the people, the National Socialist government has therefore passed laws that will hinder the further spread of serious genetic diseases.

Georg's heart was beginning to pound. He was carrying in his own body a disease with a strong genetic component. Diagnosed with diabetes in 1929 at the age of thirty-seven, he knew he held within his own genetic make-up a death sentence to his progeny. His two sons had been conceived before he knew; his two daughters after he had been diagnosed. To which one had he bequeathed this life-shortening genetic seed? How many grandchildren would carry the weight of this life sentence... how many great-grandchildren?

His eye rested momentarily on a silver-framed photograph, sitting proudly on his desk, of his four beautiful children; the boys, tanned and in their Sunday suits – fine young boys, with the whiff of manhood in their brows, hair combed back meticulously, strong jawlines and the hint of a twinkle in their eyes as they stood still for the photograph. He remembered that the moment the photographer had finished the session they had leapt on their sisters and tickled them mercilessly. The two girls stood in front of them in the frame, a picture of white prettiness in their Sunday frocks, beribboned hair, and black boots. To which one of them had he bequeathed this disease? Despite his worry he couldn't help but smile in pride at this perfect family he and Hannelore had created. Thoughts of Leah evaporated. Hannelore was his true love, his first great romance, the mother of his children, and yet latterly she seemed colder and less full of life and energy. When he tried to touch her, she would shrink a little as if the touch were not welcome. It was as if her whole being was ill at ease, bracing itself for a battle. In truth it wasn't Georg himself that repelled her at all, more her growing anguish at the political situation, coupled with his apparent passivity towards it.

He leafed through the papers in his hand, his eye resting again on passages he had marked heavily with his black ebonite pen.

The "Law for the Prevention of Genetically Ill Offspring" encourages the voluntary or compulsory sterilization of those persons who, as the result of serious genetic illness, "are likely according to medical science to have children who will suffer severe physical and mental genetic illnesses.

This law had come into force on the first of January 1934 but Georg had quietly chosen to ignore it. How could he possibly discuss such things with his trusting patients, with young couples about to get married and start their own families? His eye fell again onto the page before him.

Georg wiped the sweat from his forehead, he needed to eat something, to have a drink and clear his mind. As he sorted through the papers, his eye caught again a passage he had circled in red:

The "Law against Dangerous Criminals" provides for the castration of serious moral criminals. It is to be seen as a way of saving the criminal by freeing him of his sick drives. It will also surely prevent serious crimes in the future.

The prison in the town was his responsibility. He had full charge of the medical needs of the inmates and was regularly called on to diagnose, prescribe and treat the prisoners for illnesses contracted during their incarceration as well as ongoing maladies. Face after face appeared before him as he found himself reflecting on the crimes each one was accused of committing and the discussions he was being forced to have with the prison governor, a committed National Socialist.

He pushed ajar the window of his surgery, glad of a fresh breeze and the sweet smell of roses growing in the flower beds below. Notes filled the evening air again, this time not piano but the steady, mournful vibrato of a beautiful violin, masterfully played by Leah's husband. Crippled by polio, sitting in his wheelchair, he still drew forth exquisite sounds. It was a sign that Leah had not returned home. Usually she would accompany him if she was in the house. Perhaps he was missing her. It was the Chopin piece, the same nocturne he had heard a couple of weeks before. The minor key seeped again into his soul. It was as if he was trying to draw his wife back home; it spoke of agony. It was the first time he had heard Aaron play in a long time.

Georg didn't want to read any more of the past year's decrees, he certainly didn't want to think too much more about Leah Rothstein's worries. He had filed that part of Nuremburg in a separate folder at the bottom of the drawer. He slammed it firmly shut, locked it, pocketed the key in his waistcoat and strode out of his surgery. He would deflect questions skilfully and had grown artful in changing the subject when officials wanted to probe how he was handling his patients. In fact, he took pains to avoid encountering those he knew to be 'committed Nazis' whether within the town or in the nearby SS headquarters at Fuchsburg, ten kilometres away.

He closed the door of his surgery and wandered across the hallway to the kitchen.

Hannelore looked up at him from the table in the middle of the room, her intense, dark brown gaze seeming to penetrate his every thought.

'Your bread and leberwurst are ready,' she said softly, holding his gaze. 'The girls are in bed. Eva is managing to climb the stairs well now. They are so pleased to be back in the same room.'

'I will go up shortly and look in on them,' he said in a tired voice.

'Georg, we need to talk.'

Belts and Braces

A week later another operation, a further scar into the armpit, to search out and remove any lymph nodes that look to be affected. More waiting in hospital rooms, sucking ice cubes to hydrate slightly, more anaesthetic, more vomiting after an operation, more sleeping while Tom looks after the boys. The wound area regularly fills up with fluid. It feels as if I have re-grown the breast, and then the fluid is drained several times at the hospital.

'It will resolve gradually,' my kind surgeon reassures me. 'This is quite common.'

I nod, mildly amused by the process of draining the fluid, as a yellow liquid pours into a bucket on the floor from an extension to the tube in my arm.

Eventually the flow stops, and the tube can be removed.

He informs me that several of the nodes were affected and five in total have been removed.

'We don't know yet if there has been spread to other parts of your body. The MRI scan will make that clearer in the next week.'

The waiting goes on, an agony of uncertainty until the next appointment with the scan, and then more waiting for the results.

I have been prepped with a cannula in my arm ready for my encounter with the final test. I've been asked to drink a jug full of juice and am then led into the scanner room and told to lie down beneath a large polo-shaped machine. My eyes rest on the printed words on the top arc of the polo: Siemens. I smile wryly. Didn't Siemens manufacture the concentration camp ovens? Bizarre recollection of a documentary I've been watching recently. Iodine is injected into my arm and the polo mint moves slowly over my body a couple of times. This state-of-the-art piece of medical machinery will detect the smallest trace of cancer in my body, it may help save my life. The irony is not lost on me. Is Siemens trying to redeem itself?

A long week later, the appointment with the oncologist. It is difficult to explain the waiting, the agony of not knowing something that others know and which could be life-changing or in my case life-ending. Every day waking up to the knowledge that it could be bad news, that the mastectomy was just the beginning of the battle, not the end. I've already been informed that the tumour was very close to the chest wall. Have cancerous cells seeped into the lungs? Is it just a matter of time until that dry cough begins and the aching in the hips and shoulders?

The morning of the results arrives, and the butterflies rob me of all appetite. It is all I can do to drink a mug of tea and hold Tom's hand throughout the car journey whenever it isn't on the gear stick. We clamber out of the car and encounter an acquaintance from the play-ground.

'Hi, Krista. You OK?'

'Yeah, fine thanks, how about you?'

'Well, had a bit of a shock recently, recalled for a dodgy mammogram result and come back for a further one but it's all clear. What a relief.'

'My goodness, yes,' I reply as I watch her stride off, filled with optimism and relief.

Jolted.

Tom takes my hand.

Grimly we head up the pathway towards reception and the long shiny corridor, filled with cafés, shops and fund-raising stalls for a new chemotherapy unit. I smile weakly at the fund-raiser and hold on to Tom. We find ourselves sitting in the oncology waiting area for what seems like an eternity. One by one, patients come out of her room and are gestured to sit down. Finally it is our turn and we take our seats on two black plastic chairs. She sits, peering through her glasses at the papers on the top of my bulging health record file and then at the screen in front of her.

'First of all,' she says in her efficiently brusque voice, 'the scan was all clear.'

I gasp, eyes welling up instantly.

'I like to get that out straight away. That's good news.' Her voice softens a little as she notices me gulp back the tears. I squeeze Tom's hand. I feel his, squeezing back even more firmly.

'What I now need to show you are the figures relating to the cancer that was found. Given its grade, if you continue with treatment - and we would recommend you have a course of chemotherapy and then radiotherapy - the survival figures for more than ten years are 83%, but the survival is often a lot longer.'

The figure is embedded in my mind – that's a pretty good statistic.

Of course I will continue with treatment. I am grateful, thankful that the scan is clear. It is an enormous weight lifted. I sign the papers and leave. The worst is over, I say to myself, the rest is just 'belts and braces' as my oncologist reassures me.

A few weeks later

A cold, grey Friday morning in late January; the day of the first chemotherapy treatment has arrived.

I wake early, nervous. Remarkably, I have slept well - still tired and recovering from the two previous operations but I know the moment I awake that this is going to be an enormous day. I feel as if I am being buckled into a white-knuckle ride, the sort that lurches forward, jolts a little and then plunges unstoppably down a near vertical drop; a ride punctuated by expletives and much heart pounding. My white knuckles are clinging on to the hope that I will not be ill, that I will be able to conceal how I feel, that I will be able to carry on being Supermum for my boys. They mustn't find out what is happening to me. So far so good. They have not guessed that their mother has had her left breast removed, just that she has needed some surgery to take out 'an infection', a word the boys understand and will be happy not to think too much about. Is it disingenuous to say that? Until they actually ask me what is wrong, I will brush it off lightly to reassure them nothing serious is happening to me. I sit up in bed and swing my legs over the side and breathe out deeply. Tom is already up, and clanking sounds from the kitchen suggest he is emptying the dishwasher and getting breakfast ready. Moments later he emerges in the doorway with a steaming mug of tea and a big grin. I hold his gaze and return the smile, fortified by his love and support.

'Today's the day,' I whisper.

'You will be fine,' he encourages. 'What time is your mum coming over?'

'Ten o'clock. They want to start it at eleven and need to do a few checks beforehand and get me wired up.'

Tom has to leave early for work, another long day in Exeter. I have insisted that his work carry on as before. I don't want any routines broken. Normality must reign. Normality is my anchor. If the cart is overturned there will be apples rolling in every direction and that is the last thing I need. I don't want people talking to the boys about what is going on; I won't be able to control what is being said to them. I can just imagine conversations along the lines of 'You are being so brave, Ben, you need to be strong for Mummy now.' – the kind of comments that would terrify most seven-year-olds. No, it simply cannot happen. Words are powerful, they stick forever in the mind. What was it a teacher said to me at Primary School, an hour after I saw my best friend catapulted through the air by a car on the road in front of the school?

'Krista, you were so brave not to cry, well done. I'm very proud of you.' All I wanted to do in that moment was cry, which is what I did as soon as I had run off to the toilets. What I needed her to say was 'Are you OK? That must have been a terrible shock.'

I get dressed in the new long blue slacks I have bought for the treatment days and wear a white scoop-necked T-shirt and swallow another of the huge pills, the ones that will hopefully pre-empt any nausea, the ones I have specifically requested because I am prone to sickness – awful morning sickness and awful seasickness. Apparently there is a correlation, so I am not taking any chances. I can't afford to be lying in bed all day looking ill, paralysed by nausea, with two young boys running around. The big pill is huge – and apparently expensive -£75 a swallow expensive. I have already taken one the day before and will take the last one tomorrow along with a cocktail of steroids and other antiemetics I will be given at the hospital.

The boys are dressed for school, blissfully unaware of what is happening today to their mother. They munch breakfast happily and we walk to school blithely chattering about the day ahead.

'What do you think would be better, Mummy? Would you rather be frozen alive or burned alive?'

Am I really bothered, I am thinking to myself, but swallow my mental sarcasm and reply 'Well, Ben, both sound pretty grim, I suspect being frozen alive might be kinder? Less agonising, but more of a slow falling asleep?'

'Hmmm! Burning would be a lot quicker wouldn't it?'

'Like being cremated,' he adds, engrossed in this conversation. 'I would rather not be eaten by worms.'

'So, Reuben, what shall we have for tea today?' I toss into the conversation.

'Pancakes!' he yells, and Ben joins in, successfully distracted.

We give each other a big squeeze in the playground before they run chattering with their friends into their classrooms. I am grateful for their teachers. I am grateful for an understanding headteacher who has hugged me and encouraged me to consider counselling for the boys.

'We have decided not to tell them exactly what is going on' I say on the day I tell her the news. 'Please be discreet about who you tell in the staffroom. Obviously their teachers, but no big announcements please, the fewer people who know the better. I don't want other parents knowing, who will probably tell their children, who will then blurt it out to the boys.'

She looks at me with kind brown eyes and speaks in reassuring tones.

'Krista, we will do exactly as you wish. Another mum is going through the same thing and her daughter is seeing a schools' counsellor, but I completely respect what you want to do.'

I am relieved that I have not had to argue the point; not everyone agrees. Children are resilient they say, they adapt, and it is better if they know the truth... I am not so sure. If children were so resilient, there might not be so many mixed up adults.

I walk back home, praying that the chemotherapy will go well. I wander through the rooms of the house, checking everything is in order – the new kitchen extension looks fabulous. The builders have been amazing - all too aware, it seems, that their client has just undergone major surgery, and they have worked at breakneck speed to finish the job before the treatment starts. Even the decorator has finished the last coat of light-bouncing white paint. The only thing left to do is the flooring. The budget has dried up and so nothing more can be done until the next few pay days, and even then, we will probably have to settle for lino for such a large area of flooring. The bedrooms are clean and tidy, fresh bedding everywhere in case I am too ill to do them in the coming weeks. The bathrooms are clean too, easy meals are ready in the fridge alongside smoothies in case my mouth gets sore.

My bag is ready and packed with bottled drinks, special medicated chewing gum from America a thoughtful sister-in-law has sent, and energy bars to nibble through the experience.

I text all my friends and family to pray for me. Jane, one of my best buddies, who lives up North, responds immediately with her usual warmth and calm.

'All power, hugs and a big kiss to you. With you all the way.'

I am touched by how often she texts me during this journey, and my special group of friends that keeps me going.

I sit down at the piano waiting for my mother, my designated chemo-buddy, to arrive, and my fingers rest on the ivory keys. I begin to play, soft notes at first that become stronger. I am in a minor key but the notes are filled with strength. I sing, lost in the moment, the blissful escape music brings... has always brought during times of frustration, anger, loneliness... and also in times of great joy. That happy place where I can lift my heart to another sphere, a place nothing else can touch; a very private place. I play mostly when no one is looking or listening, a place I have not been able to visit for a very long time with the constant childcare of the last eight years. But maybe now I can find my way back to my old form and practise more. I played almost constantly when Ben was in my womb and I wanted him to hear my music and feel the sounds and cadences of my singing voice. I have a soft but clear voice and I wanted him to recognise it and to sing with me from within.

The doorbell rings and I am shaken out of the momentary respite that forgetfulness brings, reminded that the hour has come. It is time to go. In truth I am looking forward to getting on with it now, knowing that it has the power to knock out any bad cells that might be lurking and growing in the recesses of my body. This is my mental preparation: this is not poison, but a powerful weapon that will surge through my veins and blitz everything in its path.

Mum greets me with her usual radiant smile and bear hug - it lifts my spirits immediately.

'All ready? Boys OK?' she chirps as the car moves carefully down the drive to the road.

'Yes, all packed off to school for the last time this week, and then hopefully we can all have a lie-in tomorrow and Tom can take care of them if I feel awful.'

'You're in good hands. The nurses will be amazing. Dad and I will fetch the boys later and take them out for fish and chips. Thank goodness the snow has melted. The roads are nice and clear.'

'Go on, Mum, put your foot down and let's see how fast we can get there!'

We laugh, both knowing that Mum never drives above 40 miles per hour.

I am glad that I am not alone. I know that she is concealing her own concern with her bright bravado, but it is working.

We pull up in the hospital car park and wander into the main entrance, turning right and following the signs for the chemotherapy department, a part of the hospital I have never ventured into. What will the rooms be like? Will I be on my own or in a ward with lots of others having treatment?

The waiting room is cramped – a few chairs and jugs of orange squash on the table. After a short wait, a friendly nurse appears and escorts us to another even smaller room with a couple of old-fashioned, wing back armchairs. She wheels over a trolley of equipment and sits down in front of me.

'Now, Krista,' she says in a kindly voice, 'I need to warm up your arm to get your veins enlarged, ready to insert an intravenous cannula. I'm going to give you a lovely hot water bottle to hold against your right forearm for a few minutes.'

The warmth of the bottle is soothing and comforting, a familiar domestic item in a strange world of trolleys, bags of saline and different coloured liquids. I have no idea what is about to happen. All I remember from the last oncology appointment is that I am going to have a chemical cocktail called FEC-T intravenously pumped into me but I don't know how long it is going to take or how it is going to make me feel. I imagine the worst. I envisage myself throwing up all over the room within minutes and then being wretchedly and continuously sick for weeks, as I was during my pregnancies. That is why I have cleaned the house – it is likely that I will be a useless mother, my greatest fear.

The kindly nurse introduces herself as Angie, a mature middle-aged petite lady who has spent many years working in this department, and with genuine sincerity claims she 'would not want to work anywhere else.'

'This is my mum,' I add. 'She's here to make sure everything is done properly.'

We laugh. My mother puts on a mock pompous voice, 'Yes, I'm very experienced at this sort of thing – I'll be watching you very closely.'

The laughter helps.

Fact is, Mum had been a nurse herself many years ago and worked in the local TB hospital in the 1950s. I can tell she is about to reminisce, but the nurse places my arm in a bowl of warm water and distracts her. While my arm is warming up, she sits down in front of me and explains carefully and slowly what is going to happen.

'You've been prescribed FEC-T Krista, which means, as your oncologist has probably told you, that you will have 3 cycles of FEC and 3 cycles of T. I'm going to set up a saline drip to start with to make sure that your veins are working OK and then I shall manually feed in the first of the three chemicals. Each of them will take about ten minutes and if at any point you want me to stop or just slow everything down, then say so. You might feel a bit dizzy at one point.'

'What does FEC stand for again?' I inquire. If I can master the names, I might feel more in control of what is going on.

'Fluorouracil, epirubicin and cyclophosphamide.' The words just roll off the nurse's tongue. Mum and I stare at each other and spontaneously laugh – nope, we won't be remembering those!

'So, what does each of them do?' I ask, keen to know the facts.

'The fluorouracil is full of fluorine and kills off rapidly dividing cells that make the cancer grow; it will cause you to lose your hair and may make you feel nauseous,'

'OK – a good poison to have then,' I say as heartily as I can.

'Ah,' says Angie, feeling my arm, drying it off with a towel. 'It's nice and warm.' She taps the veins on the upper side of my forearm and prepares the cannula.

'Small scratch coming,' she says and in goes a fine needle.

The cannula is taped in place and attached to a saline drip.

'Well done! Try and relax and I'll be back shortly. The tea lady will be round soon if you would like a hot drink.'

'I wonder what the other poisons do?' I say to Mum.

'You OK?' she smiles back reassuringly.

'Yep, it's a breeze so far.' Deep down I know that I won't be really calm until I have got through this day and have some measure of the side effects.

Half an hour later, Angie returns with a new trolley of bags and puts on special gloves.

'OK, Krista, this is the fluorouracil, it is transparent and I want you to tell me if you feel any burning at all around the cannula area as it goes in. You should feel it going in slowly.'

I breathe slowly and deeply and nod, indicating that I am ready.

Angie sits herself down and holds the syringe, exerting a steady pressure.

'Go for it! Go zap those nasties!' I say, filling the silence of that first moment.

'Can you feel it? Does your arm feel OK?'

'Yes, it's warm,' I reply, 'but not stinging.'

'Good, that means it's not leaking into the tissue around your vein. Just try and relax, you're doing really well.'

I want to chat with this lovely nurse.

'Don't you find it depressing, treating cancer patients all the time? Especially when you know they're terminal?' I probe, curious as to why anyone would want to do this job.

'Ah, I really wouldn't want to do anything else, the people we meet are all so different. It helps if you can laugh and look on the positive side. So many patients do get well. The other day one of our old patients came in with a cake and said, "I just wanted to celebrate my death day with you!" The doctors hadn't given him more than a few years to live and here he still was five years later, celebrating the fact. Made my day!'

Mum and I smile with her. It feels a blessing to have such special treatment and to be in good hands and to hear good news stories.

The syringe empties and the next one is loaded ready.

'This is the epirubicin,' she explains,' it's pinky-red and will make your wee go red for a while but don't panic, that's quite normal.'

'How exciting,' laughs Mum involuntarily, and I grin.

'Yes, can't wait to go to the loo now!'

'You may feel a tingling sensation as this one goes in, so just tell me if you want to slow it down.'

I brace myself and nod to start.

The pink poison seeps in steadily again and almost immediately I feel my head beginning to swim.

'Oooh - that's weird. Could you slow down a bit please.'

Angie stops depressing the syringe and waits a moment for me to get my breath.

'OK?'

'Sure, just a bit slower please.'

I close my eyes and my body swims a little as this kind nurse patiently syringes for another ten minutes, allowing me time to be very quiet.

'You are doing so well, Krista, just one left to go.'

So far it hasn't been too bad, just an increasingly woozy, tired sensation.

My nurse prepares the cyclophosphamide and I brace myself for the final syringe whilst marvelling at the strength the nurse needs to sustain these long slow injections. By the time the final syringe is empty, I have eaten a sandwich from the refreshment trolley and I am glad to be able to go to the toilet and walk out of the small, confined room, wheeling the intravenous drip with me. I smile to myself, walking back into the treatment room, 'It was red!'

Mum laughs with me. I sense her relief at seeing me still able to smile. I need to shield her from some of my fears.

The nurse has collected an assortment of antiemetics, steroids, and a medical card, and slowly goes through the instructions on what I should take and how often. My mind is struggling to focus and I ask her to write these instructions on a piece of paper. I do note that I must call the number on the card immediately if I feel at all unwell with a temperature. She reminds me that my white blood cell count will start to sink gradually over the next few weeks and I will become more and more vulnerable to infection. It is going to be important to stay well and avoid coming into close contact with bugs. For this reason, I have been careful to get my teeth examined before today. A dental procedure during chemo would not be a good idea.

'Let's get you home, love,' Mum says, picking up my bags.

'Feel a bit like an old lady,' I reply, taking hold of her arm to steady myself, as we walk slowly out of the hospital and back to the car. I never thought I would be leaning on my mother to keep me steady.

'Well, that's the first one over – well done,' she says reassuringly, starting the ignition. 'You will be fine, love, we'll take each one as it comes.'

Just focus on one day at a time. Families are strongest when times are tough.

'I just hope we can keep this secret from the boys. I don't want them looking at me and being shocked by how tired I am or by how weak I might become.'

'You're not on your own, Krista. I remember my family coming together during the war and my parents trying to shield us from the news on the radio and to keep things going for us all. We will help you do that with the boys. I'm very good at keeping secrets. They only need to know that there are fish fingers and chips for tea and ice-cream.'

We smile, but through the bleariness of the cocktail of poisons I notice her biting her bottom lip.

'Yep, only five to go... just hope those antiemetics do the trick. So far so good. This is a doddle, Mum, completely overrated hype to make us all feel sorry for chemo patients.' We both chuckle and I am very glad to be driven home.

The next morning, I wake early. I have slept well and am surprisingly alert... the steroids are beginning to kick in, I think to myself. Everyone is asleep. I pad downstairs in my dressing gown, feeling rather surreal, and take the last of the huge antiemetics. Sitting in the new bay window seat of the kitchen as the sunrise hangs low in the cold, blue sky, I gaze up at the church tower, high on the distant hill overlooking the village. A lovely bucolic scene, an iconic English church that has weathered the Atlantic storms for centuries. I sit and think a long while, grateful that I am NOT sick or nauseous. Hurrah! I almost feel like dancing. This is better, so much better that I had hoped for... This is going to be OK. No, more than OK... I will be a shining light to all my friends and family, and most importantly to my boys who will never need to know that Mummy isn't well.

Hair

January 2011

Two weeks after the first treatment.

'Ben?'

I sit on the edge of his bed, stroking his fine, wavy brown hair. It has grown trendily long – he looks like a mini surf dude. My almost-eight year old has long eyelashes which flash up from the book he is reading, and his big blue eyes look into mine.

'Yes, Mummy?'

'Have you ever heard of someone's hair falling out?'

He looks thoughtful for a few seconds.

'Mmm, yes, I think so.'

'Have you ever seen anyone whose hair has fallen out?'

''No, not in real life, but I think I've seen something on telly.'

'And why do you think it happens?'

'I don't really know.' He fiddles with the page of his book. 'It just falls out sometimes doesn't it?'

I pause, relieved that the word cancer hasn't entered the conversation.

'Yes, sometimes it does just fall out, other times it falls out because of very strong medicine. If someone is ill, they might have to take medicines that are superstrong and they unfortunately cause the hair to come out as well as helping the person get well.'

He looks a little worried.

'The hair then grows back quite quickly' I add rapidly.

'Is that why some people are bald?' he asks staring at the wall of his room.

'No, lots of people are bald, mostly men, because... well they just are. It's not because they are ill. The folk who are ill are probably wearing wigs to cover it up.'

Ben smiles thoughtfully and looks back at his book.

I kiss him and leave the room and tell Tom.

We agree. If Ben doesn't know, then Reuben certainly won't know either.

A few days later we are sitting having breakfast with the boys on a Saturday morning and I casually introduce the plan.

'Boys, Mummy has had to take some very strong medicine recently, just to make sure she gets fully better, and something a bit funny will happen because of the medicine.' Reuben's eyes grow large and stare at me.

'My hair is going to start falling out. The medicine is so strong it will cause my hair to die but then after a while it will grow back again.'

'That will look funny, Mummy,' Reuben says screwing up his face.

'Will everyone see you with no hair, Mummy?' Ben adds looking concerned.

'No Ben, no one else will know. I'll wear a wig of some sort so that I look just the same outdoors, but you might see me without the wig on in the house because it will be hot. Shall we keep it as our secret, boys? I don't really want people staring at me and asking questions.'

They look thoughtfully at my hair.

'Poor Mummy,' says Ben. 'We won't tell anyone.'

Both the boys nod.

'Well done boys,' Tom adds, confidently 'Mummy will soon be better, and her hair will grow back as it is now. Now who's for another pancake?'

'ME!' the boys shout in unison.

Later that night I lie down with Reuben in bed, my long hair flowing down onto his pillow and enclosing his small head. His little fingers hold my face and stroke my hair.

'Your hair is beautiful, Mummy.'

I sink my face into the nape of his small neck and kiss him and wipe my eyes on his pyjama top, swallowing hard and smiling close into his warm, beautiful face.

Four weeks later

Two chemotherapy sessions are complete, and my hair is still intact. My oncologist seems surprised.

'You didn't use a cold cap?'

'No' I reply, breezily, 'It will grow back anyway. I would rather the poison got to every cell and that not one got away.'

'You will notice the hair loss soon. I see you have had your hair cut.'

'Yes, it seemed sensible to reduce the impact, and it will suit the wig I am having made. It's a fairly unique wig but I think it will work.'

I had been preparing for this time and had been befriended by Julie, a mum at school, who is a mobile hairdresser. She is a sweet, young doting mum who has offered to cut my hair and to help me find a wig. We found the shop, NHS wig voucher in hand, tucked up some stairs above a small hairdressers in one of the side streets. It felt as if we were doing something clandestine, secretly placing a bet on the 9.50 at Newmarket without our husbands knowing. We sat there in front of a mirror as an elderly lady produced one wig after another, all hideous, all so artificial, all completely different from the way my hair looks. I felt wretched and sensed that I would cry soon if we didn't leave quickly.

Back in the side street, the frustration burst out 'I just want to look normal! I don't want the boys to feel I look different from other people. I don't mind them seeing my head with no hair, but I want them to feel confident in public and around their friends. If they see me wearing a big fat wig, they will all start asking questions.' Julie put a reassuring arm around my shoulders and with a twinkle in her eyes said 'I have an idea. Can I drive you to a special hairdressing retail outlet? It's just on the outskirts of town – it won't take long. '

In the car Julie explained how she was proposing to custom make a wig cap for me using real hair, colour matched to my own, that is sewn into a stronger version of a nylon stocking type of cap.

'You would have to wear a beanie or cap when outdoors or in public, but it would be cooler and more importantly look just like your hair does now. The top of your head would be covered by the netting, but the sides would look very natural.'

I loved the idea. It seemed like the perfect solution and within half an hour we had chosen the necessary hair pieces that perfectly matched my dark blonde-dyed hair colour.

'Thank you so much, Julie, how long will it take to sew together? The doctor thinks my hair will start falling out soon.'

'I'll get on with it tonight – shouldn't take more than a few days and I'll give you a ring. No-one will notice.'

Within the week I notice hair between my fingers as I stroke it away from my face. Each time I make a stroke, more comes out. It is quite fascinating, and I show Ben. Reuben is equally intrigued as I deposit handfuls of fine hair into the kitchen bin. Within a week, my hair is very thin, and I am beginning to look like an old hag – I cannot abide this look.

'I would rather shave it off, Tom. Anything is better than this witchy look.'

He looks a little shocked but doesn't reply from the bedroom. I take the hairdressing clippers out from the drawer at the bottom of our pine wardrobe and shave myself as well as I can.

It is a strange sight. Completely bald. I stroke the soft skin of my scalp. Different, but quite cool, I think to myself. If Sinead can do it, then so can I. I have lost weight during chemo and the whole look is quite svelte, almost androgynous. My eyebrows are thinning too, as are my eyelashes, as is all the hair on my body. Even my nostril hair is disappearing, and I sniffle more throughout the day. I am suddenly acutely conscious of every function that hair has on my body. My head is colder, especially at night. I wear a beanie to keep warm and long for warmer days to come. I feel great empathy and sympathy for men, especially younger ones who lose their hair and feel this cold permanently. At least this is just for a short while.

Tom comes into the bathroom and grins.

'You've got a great shaped head.' He kisses me on the lips.

'I look as if I have come out of Belsen,' I quip.

'But at least *your* hair loss is *saving* you – come on, let's show the boys.'

As with all announcements and revelations, we gather them together so that they can share the moment. They are slumped in front of the television downstairs and I pop my head around the door and start giggling at them to make them laugh. It helps. They start laughing too and are both eager to feel the bald skin on my head. I then pull out the wig and beanie and pop it on my head.

'You look just the same as before, Mummy! No one will know you are bald!' shrieks Reuben

'Shh! Our secret' I say with my finger to my lips.

I quite like the look of my head without hair. I enjoy feeling the smoothness of the soft skin, glad that it has a good shape, that it isn't a round, fat head or weirdly angular, or that there is some weird birth mark across half my head. I know this won't be forever and that I cannot keep it a secret from everyone, but if I can succeed in keeping prying eyes of children in the playground at bay, then it will be worth it. I long for one friend to shave their head or even several of them so that we can truly share this bit of the journey. No one offers. It doesn't really surprise me. It's a big deal. What woman doesn't look at herself every morning in the mirror after a shower and blow-dry their locks into perfect place, or apply thick, black mascara to heighten the sex appeal of their eyes, or shape their eyebrows, having painstakingly plucked them into the perfectly arched shape to frame their whole face. Who would willingly surrender their hair for a friend? And in so doing, their identity. My mind flashes back to the pages of photographs in the Holocaust books I studied for my degree. Hollow, gaunt, hairless faces of men and women peer out from behind barbed wire fences, stripped of their identity, just a number. A clever trick, deftly dehumanising.

But it's only hair...

The Yew Tree

Early April 2011

Three chemo's down, with my mother supporting me each time, and I am well and truly hairless. I know that it is only a matter of time now before I begin to feel much weaker. Each treatment so far has followed a pattern of ebbing tiredness for a week, gradual, growing strength and fairly normal energy until the next treatment, preceded as ever by blood tests to check the count is good for the next hit to my system, steroids tablets and antiemetics. I am getting used to wearing the wig in public, always grateful for the chance to pull it off at home or in the car on my own and to let my head breathe. The boys are behaving as small boys do - consumed by their own little worlds - and hardly seem to be aware of any change in family life. I suspect they are reassured by the fact that I regain my bounce after the first week of the cycle and then forget I have been sleepier than usual in the first week. Thankfully, I have stayed well with no spike in temperature – a blessing. Every cycle I lose weight and then re-gain some, but overall am thinner than I ever have been in my adult life. Coffee and tea have lost all appeal – taste is more metallic, and I chew gum endlessly to cover over this taste and to keep my mouth from drying up.

March has come and gone and both boys have celebrated another birthday within the space of two days. Miraculously I manage to organise two birthday parties. Friends take care of Reuben's fifth birthday by making it a joint party with three of his friends who all have birthdays within a few weeks of his. The village hall is booked, as is a magician, and all I have to do is sit and watch from the side bench as twenty-five screeching five year olds marvel at enormous bubbles they can step inside and strings of handkerchiefs shooting out from a sleeve. Thankfully, the other birthday falls just before a treatment when I am at my best. We manage to take Ben's friends to a fun park. All must go on as normal; not an ounce of their happiness should be disturbed. I place my wig on carefully for such events and try to be as bouncy as possible.

The fourth treatment presents a new challenge. What will it be like? Will the new poison bring new side effects?

I have been advised that it would be good if Tom comes with me for the first of these, as the effect 'can be a little unpredictable.' I will need to receive the treatment intravenously, lying down. Tom takes the day off and waits with me in an even smaller room than before with a simple surgical bed. Trolleys are wheeled in and I lie down, nervous at what will happen.

'How long do you think this will take?' he says, glancing at his watch. He is hoping to head back to his office when he has taken me home.

'It only takes about an hour I think,' I reply, slightly irritated by the feeling that this is something of an inconvenience. I push down the feeling, just glad that he is there when so often he has not been able to because of meetings and clinics.

A nurse walks in and tells me we will start the treatment.

An intravenous drip is set up next to me and fixed to the cannula in my forearm. This time I will be left alone with the chemicals; no nurse sitting there, syringe in hand. Tom stands beside me.

'And what are the side effects of this particular drug?' I ask the nurse. 'Is it just more of the same?'

'This is the T part of your FEC-T treatment' she explains 'We want you to lie down because you may feel a little faint and - if that does happen - tell us straightaway. The side effects of the T or docetaxel vary from person to person, but you may notice that your joints ache a bit more, rather like the feeling you get when you are fluey. Your nails may well be affected and become more brittle – sometimes the nail bed dies, and the nail comes away. You may also have a tingling feeling in your fingers.'

'And nausea?' I ask.

'It shouldn't be any more of a problem than with the FEC and if you keep taking the antiemetics, that will help. You may continue to have a funny taste in your mouth.'

'And what about my hair? Will it start growing during this treatment or not?'

'Ah' she replies guardedly 'I'm afraid it causes hair loss too, just like the FEC, but your hair should grow back fine once you have finished your radiotherapy.'

I think back to a conversation I have had that week with a friend who is a GP in the village.

'Tony, are you sure that hair grows back perfectly normally after treatment?'

'I've never known anyone's hair not to come back,' he says confidently.

I am reassured.

I lay my head back and wait for the chemicals to do their stuff. Mentally I am preparing myself for the worst and praying hard that I won't be the one in ten that has a bad reaction.

Tom holds my hand and smiles at me. I squeeze his in an attempt to reassure him that I am OK. I take my mind on a journey to relieve the tension of these moments. I remember our first encounter after a church service in the small chapel my grandmother faithfully visited every Sunday of her life. It was a balmy day in June when I spied the lean, surf T-shirt clad youth leader, surrounded by giggling teenage girls at the start of the service. The first tentative conversation with him was forced mainly because we were sitting next to one another and quite quickly the curious thought began to form in my mind that he might just be 'the One.' I think back over the next chance encounters on the rocks of the beach, me leaving the surf, as he jumped down onto the sand towards the waves, surfboard under arm – a brief conversation about surfing. The sniggers of my friend as she and I tried to work out which car belonged to him in the car park and the cheeky note I leave under the windscreen wiper of his old Seat Ibiza with a Porsche 'go faster' stripe down the side - *'Great to see you again, shame about the car Kx.'* The next encounter at church some weeks later when I return to Devon and we then arrange to meet at the beach where he will be windsurfing, the sight of him speeding along the waves in the shallows, graceful, powerful and... slowly I am falling in love. The letter he sends me that gets lost at the post office because there is no stamp on it and is only discovered weeks later when I finally discover the card under the doormat, having almost given up hope of hearing from him. The elation at finally collecting the letter and reading five long pages of Tom, full of questions and details about his life. The long walk along the headland amongst the gorse bushes, getting hopelessly lost as darkness falls and we are both reduced to tears of laughter as thoughts of staying the night on Exmoor loom large. The confessions we make to one another about our lives, the complete acceptance that neither of us has been perfect. The first hand in hand walk along the cliffs, the flask of hot coffee and Hobnobs he produces from his small rucksack as we lean into the warm flat rocks gazing out into the Atlantic, sealing in my mind that 'This is my man.' The meal at his rented house and the confession that he had to buy a picture cookery book to learn how to make the fish pie, reading kilogrammes for pounds and the resulting enormous Pyrex dish he romantically set in front of me. The reunion over Christmas when he finally visited my family and the achingly romantic proposal ten minutes before midnight on New Year's Eve, insisting that he would only give me 'until next year to reply.' These memories fortify us both, I know, during these 'in sickness and in health' days that we are journeying through. I am only glad I am not having to watch *him* receive treatment – somehow it is easier to be going through it myself.

I bathe in his love and also in the knowledge that our children are blissfully unaware of what is happening to their mother as they sit at school and do their numeracy and literacy hours. I think about the silly little conversations they are probably having with their friends about pooey toilets and birthday parties just gone and imagine them playing 'It' in the playground in the spring sunshine. Easter is coming and with it yet more distractions.

The chemical drips in.

A slight tingling sensation accompanies it, but nothing more. The first minutes go by and the nurse is reassured that all is well and that I am not going to go into anaphylactic shock as I later discover can happen. Another blessing. Tom settles down beside my bed and looks relieved too.

'You are doing brilliantly' he says, 'you are a doctor's dream.'

'Just so long as I am your dream.' I quip back

'You're the one for me - my golden girl.'

'Not so golden anymore.'

'It will come back – and anyway, I rather like the Sinead look – very sexy.'

Tom always knows how to make me feel better. He is looking tired and I am almost glad he has to be in hospital with me today so that he can pause for breath and just stop thinking about work and the hundreds of daily emails that keep him at the computer until midnight.

'I'm going to pop to the canteen. Can I get you anything at the hospital shop?'

'Perhaps a cup of tea from somewhere? That would be nice when the chemo has gone through.'

He leaves, and I close my eyes and drift off, glad of a moment to sleep.

My legs are like jelly as we walk out of the hospital with a fresh batch of steroids and antiemetics.

The air is full of spring scents and the woodland banks are bursting with pretty yellow primulas as we drive the back lanes home. I start to drift away again in the car.

The next days are a haze of drugs, disgusting tastes in my mouth and for the first time the occasional retching in the sink. If I don't eat the right food quickly, I soon sink. My stomach is irritable and for days I don't feel well. By the tenth day I am beginning to despair that I will ever pull through on this treatment and start feeling better again. It coincides with Easter visitors from afar wanting to spend an hour or two with me and encourage me. All is kindness, but it is exhausting. I am beginning to understand the words of warning from my GP,

'You will feel terribly tired, Krista, there is nothing we can give you for that – you must just go through it. Don't fight it.'

I am thinner than at the beginning and trousers hang off me. Mango helps and especially chicken in mango sauce with rice. Kind friends bring me fruit salads, but never stay long. They probably think a visit will exhaust me, or maybe they just don't know really what to say. Maybe they don't want to 'catch it'. Pasta dishes mount in the fridge and freezer and it becomes a source of great amusement around the dinner table as the boys patiently tuck in to the fourth lasagne of the week.

Easter comes and with it the arrival of my brother and his family, who have travelled all the way from France where they live, to support me and take the children out to the nearest rollercoaster ride and paint-a-pot shop. Most of my days are spent weakly in the shaded swing chair on the patio where I can lie and snooze and chat to visitors. The sun is scorching that year, apparently the hottest April on record, and the ritual Easter egg hunt becomes a race for the boys and their cousins to find them before they all melt. I smile and laugh and express delight and surprise at all the soft chocolate treasures the boys race up to me with, eyes wide with the enormous boxed eggs they have found in the depths of the shed.

Another celebration survived.

The next time I go for a treatment, I tell my oncologist how ghastly my stomach has felt.

'Ah' she says, 'I will give you something stronger to help before you go in this time; it should control the symptoms better.'

'That was a pretty brutal chemical, whatever it was' I add ruefully.

'That's because docetaxel is poison from the yew tree – that's why it is so effective.'

I smile, reflecting on the sombre sight of those dark, brooding trees in our local graveyard – a deadly, yet life-giving tree.

'The docetaxel is extracted from the needles and the bark – it is proving to be an amazingly effective treatment' she adds.

The next two treatments are slightly better but each one is accompanied by a wretched few days after the initial effect of the steroids has worn off, often on a Monday. I find myself plunging into the black shade of the yew and have to tell my parents and Tom to ignore me, to leave me alone, to not take anything personally. My whole body wants to scream. I hear it's called 'roid rage', the inevitable after-effect of taking steroids. It feels as if I will explode if someone says anything even trivial to me. It is so bad that I forbid friends and family from coming to the house on Black Mondays. It is better if I am just on my own with my wretchedness. It doesn't last more than a day or two and then the fatigue sets in. My nails are dying, discolouring. I have tried to protect them with clear nail varnish and plenty of hand cream and I try and cut them as short as possible, so they won't catch. Are the boys noticing my growing thinness and fatigue? Do they look at their bald, beanie-capped mum and wonder what on earth is going on, gazing at them from a pale, eyelash-less, eyebrow-less, rather gaunt face?

'Can I have a cuddle?' Reuben often says as he nestles in beside me in bed or on the sofa during my weaker days.

'Shall we read a story together?' I ask, trying to brighten a little.

'Yes, tell me a made-up one.'

I close my eyes as he gazes at the ceiling and I summon up all my creative powers to tell a story, sentence by agonising sentence, about a worm called Willie, who lives under the ground in a cosy hole with his family and then goes on some dangerous adventures into a big apple tree. Reuben giggles and murmurs contentedly beside me and I manage to get to the end.

'Mummy needs a little snooze now, darling, go and find Ben and make me a model with your bricks.'

Off he potters in search of his big brother and I close my eyes again and disappear for a while.

Nothing in their demeanour suggests that they are concerned, and their affection is just the same, undiminished by this strange phase we are all journeying through. Piano lessons, Cubs, tennis club, swimming lessons all go on as usual. Cub leaders smile at me sympathetically but say nothing. Play dates even happen on good days. Somehow, I manage to keep going, keep doing the school run in the mornings, thankful that it is only a few hundred yards to the school gate. The only hiccup comes one day after school when Ben is eating his biscuit and slurping a milk shake at home and says rather casually,

'Mummy, Gemma wanted to know today if you had cancer. She thought you might have cancer because of your hair?'

I freeze internally but try and reply in an equally upbeat voice 'Oh, and what did you say to her?'

'Ah, I just told her it was a family secret.'

I laugh out loud and ruffle his thick brown hair. I wait a moment to see if he is then going to ask the inevitable question… but it never comes. He never actually asks me if I do have cancer.

Yes, the family secret, that Mummy lost her hair but that she is embarrassed about this and so needs to wear a wig to cover it up until it grows back. The boys have been happy to play their part in this and are perhaps relieved that their mother isn't the talk of the playground.

The mothers who are 'not in the know' are not stupid and my thinning eyebrows and disappearing eyelashes are obviously clear to many. I foolishly thought the wig alone would make it impossible to know.

The question never comes, and I take it as a sign that Ben doesn't want to know. My young son has brilliantly fielded an awkward moment and his friend probes no more.

Holly 'phones me one morning and asks to come – just for a day. My bestie, Holly.

'Are you sure you are up to it?' she asks.

'Of course – as long as you don't mind if I flake out for an hour in between.'

'No worries – oh, and we'll bring a casserole.'

'Lovely, so glad you're not bringing a lasagne!'

That Saturday, after they arrive, we go to the beach in the campervan and the dads take the children for a long walk up to the dunes for some sand-sledging on body boards. Holly and I walk arm in arm towards the sea, sparkling in the noonday sun. There is a light breeze coming offshore and I am dazzled by the colours on the headland. Everything seems more vivid. The water laps gently onto the beach, the foam dissolving immediately into the wet sand.

'You OK?' she says in her knowing way. Sharing a house with her for a few years in our singleton days has sharpened her senses.

'I'm doing better than I thought' I reply jovially '– it's not too bad. I've not really been too sick and mercifully the boys still don't have a clue.'

'Are you sure they haven't guessed?'

'Pretty sure – I can read them like a book and they're not asking any questions.'

'Are you certain you are doing the right thing, not telling them?' Holly was not concerned about offending me. That aspect of our friendship had been hurdled a long time ago.

'I really can't bear the thought of them worrying, Holly. Everyone says to me that I should tell them and that children are incredibly resilient. The school have even offered me counselling sessions for the boys during the school day if I choose to tell them. I don't want Reuben wetting his bed, and if we tell Ben then we have to tell Reuben too... I hate the thought, though, of them hearing about it from someone else.'

'How can you stop it slipping out?' she probes.

'I'm just praying hard and trying to avoid too many situations where we are all together with a lot of people who might start talking about it with me.'

'I just hope you've made the right decision. I'm not sure I would do the same.'

Holly is always brutally frank; it is a hallmark of our relationship. Sometimes it is funny, sometimes hard to take. It is the price for over-familiarity but with it comes great love.

My friend bends down, her huge brown curls bobbing almost onto the sand, and picks up a large blue mussel that is open just a crack. She prizes it open and wipes the sand away to reveal two white, pearlescent inner shells. She presses them into my hand and beams at me with her round, smiley freckled face.

'Here you are old buddy. Remember, the greater the storm outside, the shinier the person inside.'

I smile and we hug, a solitary pair on the wide, vast shore of the Atlantic Ocean.

There is more in that one hug than a thousand words and I am glad of a friend who can help me carry the burden of this diagnosis. I remember poignantly watching *Beaches* with her on a Sunday afternoon, the Bette Midler film about best friends... how one of the friends spends her dying days on the shore of the beach house owned by the other. It is a moment not lost on the two of us. I remember too, the pain of Holly's loss of a brother, too confused to cope with life, plunging himself into the River Thames one lonely, dark night, leaving behind nothing more than a knapsack on the side of the bridge, a knapsack it takes his parents five months to open.

'I think we need to turn back. My legs are beginning to wobble.'

'Come on, you old bag, let's get you home.'

Arm in arm we walk slowly back towards the dunes, towards our five screaming children and big, strong men.

'You know, Holly, I've come to the conclusion that it is not the path we journey that is ever the key thing, it is the fact that we don't journey it alone.'

She squeezes my arm.

The Light at the End

The second of the docetaxel treatments is slightly better than the first and the stomach-calming medication is helping. Black Monday comes and goes, and I hold on to the fact that there is only one more cycle to go. I am overwhelmed by the beauty of spring, and Tom drives me at weekends to the cliff tops while my parents watch the boys for an hour or two. We go for gentle strolls, watching the stonechats perch on the yellow, coconut gorse and grasses, chirruping 'squeak chack chack!' with the joy of new life. I cannot make it to the headland but pause on a cliff-sheltered bench by a path that stumbles down to the rocks below, where deep moss-green pools fill the cracks. This is the bench where my grandmother would sit when her ninety-year-old legs could carry her no further. 'You go on, Krista,' she used to say, 'I'll rest awhile and enjoy the sun.' She would slip a small women's magazine out of her worn, black leather bag and put on her pink, translucent, rimmed glasses and read, or simply gaze at the sparkling waters and wander off in her memories to younger days.

My heart swells at my own memories of my grandmother and her resilience in the face of agonising heartbreak – the tragic death of her young husband, the loneliness of raising my father on a seamstress's pitiful salary, the faithfulness of her service to dozens and dozens of Sunday School children over the years, always visiting them when they were poorly. I remember her bony, work-worn hands and can almost feel them in my own.

My hardships seem to pale knowing this is a season that will soon be over. If I can manage the radiotherapy for 3 weeks, another great unknown, then all will be well, and I can start regaining strength and returning to full mummy mode. My parents come quietly and frequently into our lives and play endless games with the children and help with bedtimes when Tom is late home. I worry about the long journeys he often makes across Exmoor early in the morning and late at night several times a week. My peace only returns when he is home. I long for him to be home earlier and to scoop the children from me at 5 o'clock so that I can lie down again, but we are managing, and I am proud of all he is trying to achieve in his workplace.

The scars are healing well but I don't seem to be getting much feeling back. It is as if the nerves have permanently died off. I still hope, though, that sensation will return when I press my fingernails into the area.

I have tried various bras and come to the conclusion I need a cupped one with a prosthetic breast slipped inside. Summoning my courage, I walk into a lingerie shop tucked discreetly away behind the market and am immediately approached by the shopkeeper. She wants to measure me and I have to take my T-shirt off in a small changing room. She sweeps her hands around my chest proficiently with a tape measure from behind and asks me about the cup size.

'A or B cup I think' I mumble, a little embarrassed.

'Yes I think a B cup will be about right – have you got a prosthetic yet?'

'No, I've just got a soft pad for now – I need to go up to the hospital to get one soon.'

The woman is very matter of fact, unemotional, disconnected from my story. We could be talking about the differing sizes of potatoes.

I feel uncomfortable. I have never liked changing rooms, have always shied away from the large ones where everyone gets changed at the same time - a memory from my youth - and to be in a small claustrophobic space with this woman feeling my chest is horrid. I can't wait to get out of the shop, having stuffed two bras into my rucksack. The cool air outside is a welcome relief – I vow not to go there again for a long time. I dread the thought of buying a swimming costume and all that it will involve. It is only slightly less ghastly than the experience in the wig shop above the hairdressers. Exhausted by the experience I leave the shop, another hurdle over.

As the final chemotherapy arrives, a sense of euphoria begins to build. Even if this is the most ghastly experience of them all, it is the last one. And it isn't particularly pleasant, but somehow the relief of knowing it is the last and that I can start looking forward, is huge.

Mum drives me home slowly and steadily. I sense she is ageing with me and carrying this disease in her own body. But she is jubilant that we have finished this bit of the ordeal.

'You know, Krista, this reminds me of the feeling we had when the war ended. It feels as if a long battle is over, doesn't it?'

I open my sleepy eyes and look at her profile as she drives. Eyes fixed on the road, she is nevertheless somewhere else in her mind's eye.

'What do you remember of that day?'

'I just remember feeling relieved to hear that Hitler was dead and that he couldn't harm us anymore. He made us feel so frightened. He ruined a lot of my childhood when I look back and think about it now. There was a lot to rebuild after the war. The whole country was in a mess and so many people had lost loved ones.'

'Do you think any good came out of it for you?'

'It's difficult to say really. I think many good things came in spite of it and I didn't let it destroy my life although I suspect I might be a different person today if it hadn't happened.'

'Different?'

'Well, it affected us all so much that it is not easy to know for sure, but maybe that whole generation would have been less anxious and traumatised by the effects of all the bombing, the constant fear of death... but it made us more resilient in some ways and I think more passionate about fighting for what is right. It strengthened my faith, I think, without question. There were times when there was only God to lean on.'

She seems to drift off into her memories but then reawakens in the present, 'It will take you time to regain strength, darling, but you will get there.'

'Do you think we've done the right thing keeping this secret from the boys?'

'I don't think there is a right or a wrong about your decision. If it is right for you then we will support that for as long as you want us to. I am very good at keeping secrets. The boys seem very happy and the worst is over now. Let's look forward to you getting properly better.'

'Thanks for journeying with me, Mum. I couldn't have done this without you and Dad helping.'

Mum smiles and looks at me quickly before heading on through the lights and back to our house. Once again I marvel at the resurgence of energy I have seen in her in the past few months as mine has dwindled. It is as if she is fighting for both of us.

A bottle of champagne is sitting in the porch from Holly. The small card attached to it reads:

'Well done old bag! A celebration is in order! Lots of Love Holly, Chris, and girls'

It is difficult to describe adequately the euphoria that comes at the end of chemotherapy. It is unlike any euphoria I have ever experienced, and Tom and the boys seemed that afternoon even shinier and more lovely than before. It is the jubilation of every exam I have ever sat, finally over, perhaps akin to the realisation a prisoner has, that his sentence is served, and the doors of the cell are being unlocked. Quite fantastic!

The horrible taste in the mouth, the aching joints, the waves of nausea and distaste for tea and coffee gradually subside after a week and a half and I begin to surface for the last time out of the drowning world I have inhabited for five months. I have no idea what radiotherapy is going to be like but have been told that in comparison to chemo it is a 'walk in the park'.

I have been for a preliminary measurement day at the hospital in Exeter and a permanent tattoo dot marks the spot on my chest that they will need to focus machines at, while I lie very still on the bed having any bad as well as good cells in the affected area destroyed. The nurse reassures me that good cells will be able to repair themselves, but the bad cells won't.

The morning of the radiotherapy arrives, and I am collected once again by dear friends from church. The journey there and back is too far for Mum to cope with and it is nice to be able to take up offers of help from others. Thankfully, the boys have no idea that I am making these daily trips. My appointment has been purposely arranged for noon, so I can arrive and leave at leisure around the school run times. The boys won't have a clue.

An hour later we arrive in Exeter and after a short wait I am shown into a large room and told to lie down on a black bed beneath an enormous white machine. The radiographers take time to line me up with the tattoo dot as their reference mark. The process takes about quarter of an hour. Machines are rotated around me to the left and right and I am told that different beams will come in at different angles onto my body. A chirpy assistant puts some music on as the staff finally leave the room. Bizarrely the music is from James Bond and as I lie there vaguely aware of a red beam glistening in the light, I can't help thinking of scenes from *Goldfinger* when Sean Connery is lying strapped to a similar black bed. It is difficult not to quake with laughter and, in the end, I have to tell the nurse that the music isn't helping. She is mortified.

The whole treatment lasts about ten minutes and I am then asked to go and sit in the waiting room for a few minutes and have a cup of tea... and then home.

'Well that *was* a walk in the park' I think to myself, settling back into the passenger seat.

The next day I choose to drive to the treatment and the day after, and then once the next week, but I am beginning to feel tired and am glad of the support of friends who drive me.

Each day is fairly uneventful, marred only by the conversation alone in a waiting room with an elderly man who is also waiting for treatment and who wants to know exactly which breast has been removed. I report the conversation to a nurse who apologises profusely and explains that some of the patients are disinhibited by their treatment. I brush it off but am reassured I will not have to wait there again but will go straight into the main room.

After one of the last treatments, a friend takes me to a café in Exeter where we have lunch. The 'phone rings and it is Ben.

'Mummy, Mummy is that you?'

'Yes, it's me Ben – are you all right?'

'Mummy I have my test results – I passed them all – I did really well in Maths and English. My teacher says she thinks I will get a 6 when I take my SATS.'

Tears start to stream down my face as I hear the news.

'That's wonderful, Ben, I am so proud, so proud!'

I hear his voice gush with pleasure at the other end of the 'phone.

The headteacher's voice speaks.

'Hi Krista – thought you might like to hear the news from Ben straight away – he has done so well.'

'Thanks so much, Anna,' I sniff, 'that means a lot – treatment almost over!'

'We are so proud of you too,' she says, 'You are an inspiration,' and I know she has been walking with me as have so many others. A sense of elation rises. The light is definitely at the end of the tunnel. Life can start again!

A few weeks later, I return to the oncologist for a final check-up.

'Ah, how are you?' she says in her usual efficient manner.

'Well, I think I have survived the radiotherapy pretty well – so much better than the chemo. My hair is starting to grow back which is a relief and I am trying to rest as much as possible.'

'Don't overdo things' she says firmly. 'Your body has undergone an enormous assault. It can feel as if it has added ten years to your life, so don't be surprised if your energy levels are affected.'

 I look at her slightly startled by this piece of news. I feel as if I am recovering pretty well and able to do a lot more with the boys. She continues in a more clinical tone of voice.

'Now, you will need to begin a course of ongoing hormonal treatment, tamoxifen, until your menopause is over and then probably five more years of an aromatase inhibitor which we are finding very effective for post-menopausal women. There are side effects to all these drugs, but we would recommend you continue with them if possible.'

'Sure,' I nod in assent, not really wanting to know what the side effects are right now. I will read the small print later. She then fires a final volley at me, encouraged perhaps by my upbeat demeanour.

'Krista, it if comes back, I cannot promise that we will be able to get rid of it.' Her honesty is brutal. This sentence hangs in my core memory, one I will never be able to eradicate. I almost wish she hadn't said it. I walk out of the room into more of my new normal and try to bury some of the reality of what she has said. Nothing will undermine the relief, though, of having finished the treatment. It is time to open another bottle of champagne.

The Jewish Question

Georg knew when Hannelore was serious, and he drew up a chair, scraping it on the stone kitchen floor and sat down in front of the buttered slice of rye bread and smoked ham she had prepared for his supper. She poured them both a cup of rosehip tea and cradled the cup in her hand while Georg ate.

Hannelore was not one for small talk.

'We need to discuss Frau Samuels,' she continued.

Georg carried on eating, dabbing his mouth occasionally with the white linen napkin she had placed beside the plate. He was hungry and glad at last of nourishment at the end of this long day of visits.

'Yes, I saw her earlier today, she is weak, but I think will rally soon if looked after properly.'

'That's not what I mean, Georg. You know what I mean.'

'Are you referring to the fact that she is Jewish?'

'Yes, of course.'

'Aren't you worried?'

'That she will be reported to the authorities? The local police must already know who she is, but I don't think Bauer would do anything. He doesn't strike me as a hard-core Nazi any more than I am.'

'But if she were reported by anyone in the town, he would be obliged to pass that information on to Fuchsberg, and they will be less concerned about her state of health than you are.'

'What can they do to her? She is an old lady who is virtually housebound. I hardly think she is a threat to the security of our nation. No one in this town is worried about the Jews, and Fuchsberg has bigger fish to fry; they are more concerned with Brunswick. Everyone knows everyone here, and Frau Samuels is well respected. Her nephew's business is a thriving part of our town centre.'

'And what about Leah, our neighbour. She is a renowned musician and everyone in the town knows she is Jewish. I spoke to her the other day on the street and she is clearly very worried. It is a scandal that she has to wear a Star of David on her coat – everyone knows she is Jewish and it has never been a problem until now.'

'Yes, I saw her today and she did look noticeably agitated. She was clutching a leather bag in her arms, trying to conceal the star on her coat.'

'How are Leah and her people corrupting the German people? I've read the Hitler Youth handbook, Georg, I know what is written in that booklet in your desk drawer. I know what they are trying to brainwash our children with. I saw a copy of it at Erne's house. Her son had brought it home; he is being groomed apparently for "great things"' she added scornfully, waving her hand in the air grandiosely, her voice growing more agitated. 'As you well know, Leah is now no longer a German citizen, but merely a subject. Leah Rothstein who played the concert halls of Europe! And now teaches our daughters piano. Are we going to tell her she can no longer teach them?'

'Of course not, Hanne, don't excite yourself. If we all stay calm and continue as normal, this business will calm down and people will soon forget, and life will carry on as usual. The government is simply trying to ensure that the German people determine their own future.'

'So why do you wear the badge on your lapel?'

'You know very well why, Hannelore - to protect our family, our children, my job, and it would help if you kept your political views to yourself and not discuss them with our friends.' Georg's voice grew uncharacteristically stern.

Hannelore played with the cup in her hand. She lowered her voice so that he did not close down the conversation. Fears of Irma, their maid, overhearing were also a real concern, even if she had gone upstairs to her bedroom at the far end of the landing a few hours ago, well out of earshot. Irma was a good maid and had worked for the Hoffmanns for many years but even they were aware that she may be being sufficiently influenced by the propaganda to betray her own employers. They were only too aware of the propaganda posters that stared them in the face every day in the town centre – huge lettering bringing a cloak of silence over the town 'Be quiet! The enemy is listening!' 'Be careful on the telephone, the enemy is listening!' Sinister, shadowy silhouettes peered around the corner in the background of these posters. It cleverly silenced open conversations within families, reinforced by the fact that their children were constantly brainwashed in school to report anyone who spoke openly against the regime. Eva would often regale the family over lunch with tales of how Herr Schwarz, the headmaster, had punished students who had not straightened their arm properly when making the 'heil Hitler' salute. They were forced to stand outside the school building and make the salute one hundred times while he watched them. The school was riddled with Nazi officials and many good teachers had been sacked because they were not suitable educators and reformers in the eyes of the regime.

'I am not afraid of those Nazis or their ungodly ideologies, Georg. I am ashamed of this government and what it is doing to our society. I long for the days of Weimar again. I know things weren't perfect, but at least everyone was free to be who they were without fear of losing their job, their citizenship, their dignity. At least it was a democracy, a young democracy. We women won the right to the vote, we were given equality within marriage, we even had a woman MP in the Reichstag. Everything is now sliding backwards.'

'Nobody had a job, Hannelore. That is why Hitler is so popular – he is rebuilding our country, our roads, the health of the people – I am impressed with the money he is pouring into medical research and into ensuring our nation stops smoking.'

'Weimar didn't stand a chance, Georg – you know that – the Kaiser and his Prussian Junkers saw to it that the country was bankrupt. If you hadn't invested so much money in property, we too would be bankrupt now. Anyway, how can you speak so positively of someone who is taking control of our children, undermining the sanctity of life, ranting on and on about the Jewish problem, classifying people into categories? Martha is quite distraught at what is happening at the Protestant Institute for the Mentally and Physically Handicapped. Since the declaration they made four years ago there have been over a thousand sterilisations. It is inhumane. Who does he think he is?'

'We can't appear to undermine the Nazis... the children must be seen at least to be part of the Hitler Youth.'

'But I shan't be reading that filth to them, Georg, and Eva will continue to come with me to my Bible study group on Wednesday evenings. And I shall be taking her to the Institute to do my monthly visits again in August.

'Doesn't Margarete want to go too?'

'She said she would rather go to the athletics field with her friends and practise for the next tournament. Eva seemed quite keen to come along with me; she is very good with the people there – they love her long plaits. Hitler Youth hasn't got hold of Eva yet and I shall not encourage these ideas amongst our children.'

'We must be careful not to denounce it, Hannelore.' Georg said slowly, quietly but firmly.

'I listen to the radio, Georg, I read the newspapers, I read their propaganda.' She picked up the paper from the side table 'Ah here – "The Jewish dominance in culture and intellectual life over the last decades has shown all Germans the destructive and corrupting nature of this people." So, Leah Rothstein's ability to play the piano beautifully – how is that supposed to corrupt us?'

Georg sat staring at the table thoughtfully. She grew more animated.

'So, no more Jewish films, musicians, professors, bankers, teachers, farmers, no intermarriage. What will happen next, Georg, will they shut down all their shops? Tell them all to leave Germany? It is bad enough that even Aryan German women in this 'new society' are being relegated to the role of domestic maids and cows to breed the new German Volk and being deprived of any significant positions in education. Am I never to teach again? Was my degree in English all for nothing? While our

131

country is being ruled by a group of ignorant school dropouts? I can bear this with some fortitude for now, but to see our Jewish friends being treated like some sub-species of human being is quite intolerable.'

Georg chuckled to himself. Hannelore frowned.

'I'm not laughing at you, Hanne. I was chatting to Hermann Gerbich the other day about my diabetes and he looked at me very sternly, you know what an old Nazi he is, and told me that I shouldn't talk too openly about it – "you know they are calling it the Judenkrankheit don't you, Georg?" ' he said gruffly, impersonating his colleague, 'as if the Jews really could be responsible for diabetes?' He laughed out loud.

Hannelore's dark brown eyes were burning.

'It's not really funny though, is it? The very fact they have now blamed diabetes in our society on the Jews is both ridiculous and very worrying – and for a highly qualified surgeon to even mention it...'

Georg nodded in agreement.

'Many Jews are already emigrating. Hermann seemed quite pleased that the senior surgeons are leaving their posts in Brunswick – suspect he has his eye on their jobs.'

'I am surprised that Leah and Aaron haven't wanted to leave,' his wife added.

'Not so easy with a wheelchair, Hanne. All their relatives are in Brunswick; she won't want to leave her parents behind. So, how many come to your Bible studies?'

Georg was not a little concerned at the strength of feeling Hanne was showing for this unconventional group. The fact that his wife had refused to join the National Socialist Women's league in the wake of all other women's groups being dissolved made her stand out uncomfortably, especially within the social circles that Georg was being invited to join. There had even been rumours that his wife's name had been noted down on some kind of 'black list' and that it hadn't escaped the notice of those high up in the local Nazi Party that Georg Hoffman's wife did not 'toe the party line.' He knew his standing and position in the town was protecting her but it worried him.

'About fifteen men and women, some from the villages. Pastor Brockmann walks five kilometres in his boots to come and talk to us. Eva thinks it very strange that he doesn't wear socks. He has a great love for the Jewish people, as do those at the Institute. What is unfolding here is evil, Georg. Be watchful for Frau Samuels and Leah. You have influence in the town.'

'I am watching, Hanne, I am watching and trying to make good decisions for us all. Trust me.'

His wife looked up at the clock, ticking quietly on the wall. It was late and she nodded thoughtfully at his final words before tidying the glass teacups and plates away into the deep stone sink for Irma to deal with the next morning. Georg's mind was occupied with thoughts of Leah and worries about his wife's growing agitation. He needed to remain calm and to try and keep their ship steady and to navigate a way through, to see the good in what the new government had achieved and to hope that it wouldn't come to war and to even worse treatment of the Jews.

As Georg rose to leave the kitchen, he wandered into the office again to check his desk and gather his thoughts. Faintly through the closed window he could hear music. He opened the window a little. It was ten o'clock and darkness had just fallen. Yes, it was unmistakeable - the same Chopin piece being played as a duet. Leah was home with her Aaron and sublimely they let their instruments soar into the heavenlies. Georg stood there at the window in a reverie, his spirit calmed by the music yet agitated by the thoughts ploughed up afresh by Hannelore.

She looked at him from the threshold of the surgery and turned quietly to mount the stairs, deep in thought. Her heart was heavy. Four children, all of whom were either in Hitler Youth or about to go to university, played on her mind. What if her beloved country lurched uncontrollably into conflict with other nations. She knew that there had been significant activity in terms of re-arming the German army, the regime had been quite open about it for the last few years. Little did she realise just how prepared Germany had been, secretly developing tank and weapons systems alongside the Russians, miles beyond Moscow. Versailles had been trampled on openly, and secretly flouted. What would happen to her two fine boys?

'We need to be watchful,' she repeated to herself as she ascended the sweeping stairway, 'we need to be watchful.'

The Piano Dies

Light was already streaming in through the bedroom curtains when Georg was awoken the next morning by a thumping on the front door. He had not slept well. The conversation with Hannelore the previous evening, as well as his encounter with Leah, had stirred in him a maelstrom of arguments and counter arguments, and the two conversations had woven themselves into almost audible voices in his head, periodically waking him. Eva had also woken in the night and was in pain with her ankle, stiff from lack of movement. She had rung the little bell by her bedside, a signal that she needed help in getting to the toilet next to the kitchen. He had stumbled downstairs and blearily supported his limping daughter down the hallway and then escorted her back to bed.

'I can't sleep, Papa,' she had said half awake, 'I keep hearing noises outside.'

'It is probably our old friend Fritzi Mader,' Georg had said jokingly. The resident house martin would leap from the trees in the garden onto the roof and scuttle around looking for holes in the eaves, something which Eva found a little disconcerting, but these noises tonight were ones she was unfamiliar with; noises from the street outside, noises from ticking clocks in the hallway, noises from the cellar as the wind blew through the grilles of the rooms, rustling leaves around the floor of the garden room below. Eva loved her father, loved his warm thick fingers as they gently stroked her cheek, loved his soft, growly voice, his brush moustache and she loved more than anything tracing the scars on his face, scars around his lip and left cheek. She smiled up at him and whispered,

'I love you Papa! I am sorry for falling out of the tree and upsetting you and Mama.'

Georg looked into her big green eyes and buried his big head in her golden locks

'And I am sorry I was angry with you, Evachen. Sleep well, little rabbit.'

Heading back to bed he paused again at the threshold of his surgery to check that there was no cause for concern for Eva. He walked over to the window and looked out towards the Rothstein villa. The curtains had been drawn downstairs but not upstairs. Leah must have forgotten or else she had chosen to sleep downstairs in her husband's room, limited as he was by the wheelchair. Georg thought nothing more of it and returned wearily to bed, treading as softly as he could up the creaking staircase.

The knocking grew louder and louder.

'Komm schnell, Herr Doktor! Herr Doktor!! Komm schnell!'

Hannelore stirred and, aware that her husband had risen to attend to Eva in the night, arose to see who it could be. The Hoffmanns were used to these early morning calls. Only officials in the town or the very wealthy or the doctors had telephones and most people came to the surgery for an appointment or would arrive at any time of the night if it was a real emergency. She could at least field the caller until Georg had woken up properly. Hannelore was used to taking all the initial notes on a case anyway and would then type up her husband's scrawled copy of the case for letters of referral on her black Olivetti.

As she approached the front door, the hammering began again and she opened it to find one of the maids from a neighbouring villa belonging to the Bertholdts, looking as if she had seen a ghost.

'Frau Hoffmann, call the Herr Doktor to come quickly to the Rothstein's house. I was there early this morning with a delivery of their laundry. I said I would take it there for them to save Frau Rothstein carrying it herself. Something terrible has happened. Come quickly!'

Hannelore took hold firmly of the maid's hands and looked straight into her eyes,

'Helga, tell me what you have seen.'

Mouth quivering with fear, the young maid could only utter a few words 'Frau Rothstein and her husband are half collapsed on the floor of their kitchen... they look dead!'

Hannelore's grip tightened, and then she let the maid go, turned, and swept up the long staircase to Georg who was rapidly pulling on his trousers and shirt, aware that the noises below were urgent.

'Georg, there's something very wrong at the Rothstein's – come quickly. They have both collapsed in the kitchen.'

Hannelore quickly began to make herself respectable before following her husband down the stairs and out of the house. The Rothsteins had long since had to release their maid because it was illegal to have Aryan Germans employed by Jews so she told the maid to run for more help as getting into the house might be difficult.

Georg ran around to the back of the house where he knew Leah's kitchen was. He had often enough used it to call on Aaron when Leah was out. He strained to look through the window and saw Aaron slumped in his wheelchair and next to him, collapsed by the side of a chair, the delicate form of Leah Rothstein. Ramming the locked door to no avail, he finally smashed its' window with his medical bag. He was then able to unlock the door and enter past the broken shards into the kitchen, immediately spotting the wide open oven door. Poison gas filled the air, and Georg began coughing as it seeped into his lungs. Clutching a handkerchief to his mouth he turned off the oven, managed to open the windows and doors into the room and ran out gasping for fresh air.

'Ach Gott, nein!' he gasped, holding his forehead in the handkerchiefed hand. He had realised immediately that the pair had been dead for many hours. Their pale bodies were limp and there was not a trace of colour even in their lips. Hannelore rushed up to him and he held her tightly as if to say, 'Go no further.'

'Hannelore - the room is full of gas. They have gassed themselves. We need to wait for the police.' He then turned and ran into the kitchen, still clutching the handkerchief and knelt down beside Leah, grasping for her pulse... nothing. Aaron's... nothing. Their hands, white in death, were rigidly entwined in one another's like a Romeo with his Juliet. Beside him on the table was the violin he had been playing that evening, his other great love.

Georg began coughing and ran for air again, at least now absolutely certain that there was nothing more he could do for them.

He told Hannelore to go home, to be there for Eva and Margarete and the boys; none of them should hear of this or know what has happened.

She acquiesced, sensing the importance of this secret, but was also stunned by the terrible transformation that had come over her husband's face. His eyes were dead; a look of utter dread was etched around his jaw. Gone was the look of the professional GP dealing with the unfortunate death of his patients, and in its place stared out of his grey blue eyes the very heart of Georg Hoffmann, revealing a man who has just gazed into an abyss and seen his own soul lying there in torment. It was a look she had seen only once before when his own mother had taken her life two years previously. It was the look that fixes itself upon the face of those whose childhood dreams are one by one being shattered, a look accompanied by silence and confusion, and perhaps a sliver of self-rejection. She knew how much the death of his mother had affected him, the mother who had faithfully written to him throughout his time on the Eastern Front in 1915, who had sustained him literally with warm woollen gifts and bars of treasured chocolate and long, long letters of home and things to look forward to on his return. The mother he had not been able to revive from the brink of hopelessness, just months after the death of her beloved husband.

Hannelore touched her husband's arm lightly and squeezed it reassuringly, as if to bring him back, draw him out of his stupor, but he just nodded at her silently and gently steered her with his hands to return home. She was shaken by what she was seeing. She turned and headed back across the cobbled road to the house, aware that Eva was now peering from the threshold of the front door.

'What's the matter, Mama? What was all that banging on the door? Are the Rothsteins very sick?' Hannelore smiled weakly and led Eva inside.

'Papa has had to visit the Rothsteins, Eva. He will be back soon. Shall we have some breakfast together, just you and me?'

Eva was used to hearing of poorly patients in the town and thought no more of what was unfolding across the road.

'Oh ja, Mama! Can we have boiled eggs...? No... Pfannkuchen?! Hetty has laid so many big eggs. Bitte, Mama.'

Hannelore could not resist the beseeching look of her daughter and she knew that her apple pancakes would help, even if she had no stomach for food herself. She set the coffee pot on the stove and poured the beans into the wooden hand mill for Eva to grind at the table. This was a much-loved job and Eva would listen to the beans crunching and sigh deeply as the aroma of the roasted beans wafted out of the small drawer in the mill. While she ground the beans, Hannelore walked swiftly across the hallway to the surgery window and stood looking out towards the ominous house opposite. She was shivering. She found herself wringing her hands to warm herself. The conversation of last night had also made Hannelore restless in the night and she now knew that what she had begun to dread was beginning to unleash itself across her country. The Rothsteins were just the beginning.

Georg slumped against the wall of the villa, breathing slowly and deeply, hardly daring to go back into the kitchen. He knew he should wait for the gas to escape for fear of explosions, but he needed to see Leah again, to have at least one minute before the police arrived to begin the official paperwork. Death certificates would need to be signed and family members contacted.

He waited one more moment, breathed deeply and then walked again into the kitchen. The silence was broken by the gentle ticking of a clock on the wall. The kitchen was clean and tidy, and pots had been stacked and cupboard doors closed. There was no food on the table, just two glasses of half-drunk red wine and an open bottle of vintage Bordeaux. By the position of Leah's body she had clearly sat down beside Aaron in front of the oven and had slipped onto the floor as the fumes overcame her. Her hand had resolutely gripped her husband's. Her head was resting in his lap, and she was wearing a red dress that Georg had never seen her wearing before. Aaron was dressed in a black suit. It was as if they had both just performed in one of the great concert halls of their youth.

This was their swan song, Georg thought to himself. They wanted us to see their dignity, to see them as the world used to see them and not as 'dirty Jews'. Georg bent down and with a trembling hand lifted her eyelids to see once more those dark brown eyes. They stared coldly into the distance. Trembling, he closed them and let his fingertips touch her lips and chin, and then lifted the hand that was not entwined. It was lifeless, cold and heavy. His own eyes grew moist. Laying it down gently, he rose and walked into the hallway and music room where the magnificent Bechstein grand piano stood. Ornately gilded oil paintings of bucolic landscapes lined the walls alongside photographs of glittering orchestras and signed portraits of composers and famous admirers, including royalty.

Georg sat down at the piano, his hands trembling and touched the keys, just to hear once more some of the last notes she would have played. It was as if he wanted to retrace the last movements of her fingers. There was no music on the stand. Whatever she had been playing had been memorised. He was lost for a moment, deep in thought when he heard steps in the kitchen.

Police officer Bauer had arrived and as Georg re-entered the kitchen, he saw him bending over Leah and Aaron.

'They are dead, Sergeant, gas poisoning from the oven... joint suicide I would say.'

Georg tried to sound official and professional and was hoping that Sergeant Bauer had not seen the damp around his eyes.

'Your neighbours, Herr Doktor. What a waste, such talent - to think this would happen on Gartenstrasse, right in front of your house.'

The Sergeant took out his notebook and began filling in details and asking Georg official questions about the estimated time of death and how exactly it was discovered.

'And what about next of kin?' He enquired of Georg, 'Do you happen to know if they had any relatives?

"I remember Frau Rothstein saying that she had family in Brunswick. No doubt there will be papers in their bureau.'

'They were good people Herr Doktor, Jews, but good people.' He sighed, shaking his head.

'The Gestapo will be all over this no doubt,' Bauer mumbled.

'Yes' Georg sighed, ignoring the last remark. 'Good people.'

Dreams and Nightmares

1942

The number of Jews in the German Reich is generally said to be around 500,000. That is however only the number who are of the Mosaic faith. The Jew has always tried to conceal himself by changing his name or religion, so the Jewish population is in fact much higher. An official report estimates the number of full Jews who are not members of the Mosaic faith at 300,000, and further estimates that there are about 775,000 partial Jews (Mischlinge). The number of those not of German blood in the German Reich is therefore about 1,075,000. This number reveals the strong infiltration of Jewish blood into our people. The high number of partial Jews is tragic proof of the lack of racial instinct in the past. Pride in race and opposition to racial defilement were awakened again by National Socialism. Race mixing is also prohibited by law. The "Law for the Protection of German Blood and Honor" of 15 October 1935 establishes severe penalties for relations between those of German blood and those of foreign races, and determines precisely what percentage of foreign blood causes someone of mixed blood to lose his membership in the German people.

Georg gazed down at the now well worn Hitler Youth handbook for leaders and swept a hand over his receding grey hair. He had turned fifty and was in reflective mood at the end of a long morning of seeing patients in his surgery. Although of a naturally benign and sanguine nature, his thoughts had become darker in recent years. It was difficult to dislodge from his professional mind some of the more harrowing experiences since his country had engaged in another war. Whilst the newspapers raged on about this offensive and that offensive in the West and the East, waves and echoes resounded alarmingly in his otherwise peaceful town. No battles were being fought in Borkhausen itself other than the nightly drone of aircraft overhead, heading from England towards Berlin, but explosions were happening in many households... and Frau Samuels was still bed-ridden in her room above the shop. Schwann's Haberdashery had been closed, but thankfully not vandalised by the authorities on that fateful November night four years ago, although the entire stock of fabric had been seized and divided up as spoils of war amongst some of the other haberdashery retailers in the town, all thanks to a business informant within the community. The taint of Jewish blood was sufficient. Even though Herr Schwann had an Aryan German father, his mother was Jewish and, although deceased, the evidence of this marriage was visible in the form of Frau Samuels, his maiden aunt. His shop front could not bear the stamp of 'pure German business' that so many other shops proudly displayed on the doors, and no one should be encouraged to trade with those of Jewish blood, albeit a 'Mischling'. The Schwanns were in all other respects well thought of within the town and their two fine sons were famously athletic, always captains of their sports teams and popular in their peer group.

'Can't they just leave these few Jews in peace? Must everyone be hounded out of their homes and businesses?' Georg muttered under his breath. He had begun talking to himself more and more; somehow the pressure of keeping his views to himself expunged itself in quiet murmurings in the privacy of his study or on long heathland ramblings on Sundays with his wife and daughters.

Frau Samuels was still sheltered within the community, the closure of Schwann's draper's store making her thankfully invisible. Intentionally, no one spoke about her in the hearing of strangers and officials, and her kind doctor would drop by to see her whenever he was passing at the end of the day and slip in through the side entrance to the apartment above the main shop. Georg's mind was occupied more by the other visits he had had to make, the drive to the Schmidt's farm to attend to a nasty cut on Herr Schmidt's arm, leaving Max in the car to wait for him, walking into the kitchen just minutes after the postman arrived with the news for the Schmidts that all three of their sons had died in action, a nightmarish howling erupting from Frau Schmidt as her husband, bleeding, held her. Georg tried to help, to tend to the wound, to pour them all a schnapps, to give Frau Schmidt something to calm her and help her sleep, but all the time his thoughts were with his own sons Johannes and Max and what might happen to them. Max would soon be conscripted if this war went on much longer.

On returning to the car, he found his son burying his head in his hands at the unforgettable sound of Frau Schmidt, a sound that the young sixteen-year-old would never forget. A fear of sudden disaster hung over every household, including his own. Was it just a matter of time before the postman called at Gartenstrasse?

It was difficult to sleep. Johannes was now in active service on the Eastern Front, the ghastly territory where Georg himself had spent anguished months during the summer of 1915. Georg returned to his surgery and worked through notes and letters he needed to write, trying to busy himself with the distraction of patients. An hour later, Eva poked her head around the door of the surgery,

'Papa, lunch is ready.'

'Ach, hello little rabbit. My, how tall you are growing.'

She skipped over to her father and made herself look even taller, dressed in her smart Young Girls League uniform. She was so proud finally to be able to join, unaware that her mother detested the sight of the regalia, festooned as it was with swastikas.

'I take it you have an afternoon meeting?'

'Yes Papa, it will be so much fun! We are having an athletics competition. I have been practising sprinting in the garden.'

In spite of the slight limp that Eva had from the elderflower fall, she was determined not to be left behind and to be the perfect little German girl. Indeed, her shimmering blonde plaits and piercing green eyes were fine credentials and her brown eyed, brown haired sister who adored her Hitler Youth meetings was quietly envious.

Georg closed the manual in front of him and put it back into the drawer of his desk.

'Komm, Eva, we need to feed you up if you are to be the fastest little rabbit.'

Later that night Georg gazed down at a photograph of his older son as he lay in bed resting. Johannes smiled back at him in his fine uniform, peaked cap at a jaunty angle. There was a tenderness about the soft brown eyes that mirrored Hannelore's and a softness in the skin. Georg's hand began to tremble slightly as he tightened his grip on this picture that had been sent just before his most recent posting on the Eastern Front. How strange that his son, too, should find himself in that same icy wasteland of a country. He had received only a few letters from him, an indication that 'things were bad'. He had joked about the rats, the freezing temperatures and the limited diet of eggs and yet more eggs, about the other doctors in his regiments and how all the junior doctors were half terrified most of the time about making a huge mistake... Georg smiled reflectively as he remembered how he too had gone to war as a medical student. He placed the photo by his bedside and opened the drawer of the bedside cabinet, removing a thin, worn red notebook and opened it up and began reading. Hannelore walked into the room in her nightdress, removing hair clips, depositing them on a glass dish on the dressing table and picked up her silver hairbrush. She glanced at the book.

'What are you reading?' she asked, not recognising it as one of the books he had been reading of late.

'Ach' he sighed, 'My old war diary. I found it in a box of documents in the cellar and wanted to re-read it. If I remember rightly, I scribbled down a lot of medical notes in it as I couldn't take my books with me. I had only been studying medicine for a few years before the war started and I didn't want to make too many mistakes even though I wasn't fully qualified. Johannes is a similar age and almost in the same area that I was.'

At the mention of their older son's name, Hannelore's lips tightened, and her heart pounded involuntarily. She was used to this; it had almost become normal when thinking of her son fighting in this pointless, lost war. Every day was a miracle of survival for him, she knew, especially in the face of the fearsome Red Army that was advancing every day to regain territory.

A letter slipped out of the diary, one addressed to his mother and father, which must have found its way back into his diary after they had died a few years ago. Georg remembered rummaging through their things and had found this one letter and decided to keep it as a memento. He hadn't read it since. He unfolded it slowly in his hands. The paper was dirty and written in pencil, but it was still legible.

'Listen to this, Hannelore, I wrote this before we met. I don't think you have ever seen it,'

Hannelore stopped brushing her long, greying hair and sat on the edge of the bed.

'I wrote this in the August of 1915 from the Eastern Front. I must have been in my early twenties.

Lieber Papa, Liebe Mama,

Firstly, thank you for the socks and mittens you knitted — my last ones are quite worn through and I simply have no time or desire to darn and mend. The days are long and full, and it was a great joy to open your packet and smell your hands in the wool, dearest Mama.

It's 2 o'clock in the morning and the sound of the guns has finally stopped. It has been relentless the last twenty-four hours, but at last it has stopped. I would try and sleep but the excitement of the last day has robbed me of tiredness. The moon is full and bright, and it is almost impossible to drift off under the brilliance of this sky — I can see the Plough high above me and it makes me think of home and all of you during this season of crops growing in all the fields around Borkhausen. I wonder what you are all doing right now and how many ovens you have fitted in the last months, Papa. I would so love to be warming my hands now on those hot smooth tiles around the chimney breast in the parlour. Even though it is now August, the nights are cool, and we are outside almost all the time. You would be proud of your diligent son. Before leaving home, I managed to scribble whole extracts from my medical journals into the tiny notebook we were all issued with as part of our standard kit. They have been most useful and a handy reference when I have had some time to read and revise my physiology classes. I shall certainly have a very good grasp of essential, emergency surgical procedures after this experience in the field hospital and my suture skills are much improved.

Please do not fret, the news is good. After marching the whole morning yesterday our regiment made camp today and we have learned (Hurrah!) that the Russians are now in retreat. Over 40 of the regiment we have joined up with have been awarded the iron cross for bravery in the field - all are most jubilant. Hopefully, we can rest a while before marching on. We have camped in a deserted village and I have settled my small troop of faithful soldiers in an abandoned farmhouse; such was our joy when we discovered kitchen cupboards containing honey, pears, sour milk and other such things. We have feasted our stomachs on all we could find.

Ah dear Mama and Papa, it was with such sadness that I learned in a letter from Frau Weiss, how Rolf Schuster and his father fell in Galicia. I am so sorry to hear this. Poor, poor Frau Schuster. I shall so miss Rolf. He was always playing the fool at school I remember.

Dreaming helps to pass the time between rounds of artillery fire, and my dreams take me to Göttingen. Do you remember our visit there one summer three years ago when we looked at the University and visited Tante Gertha? I remember our conversation and hope I can transfer my final semesters to that medical school. Who knows? I may even meet my future wife?'

A faint smile passed Hannelore's lips. He looked up at her, smiled as well and then continued,

'That dream sustains me; that and the thoughts of being home with you all again. It feels important for me to dream some of those future hopes into reality;

149

somehow, when my legs cannot march any longer and when I have felt so weak from hunger as rations dwindle, I dream about my future home, the one I wish to build for my family. I see my wife and children around the large table and bowls of steaming soup and meat balls floating in a great tureen. I hear the laughter of my sons and daughters and see us picnicking together on the moorland, singing folksongs, and striding out on warm Sundays. I even see my grandchildren living in a better world and having wonderful lives.

Forgive my ramblings. My diary is full of names of towns and villages and battalions and regiments, but I did not want to bore you with those details. I shall tell you more when I get home. There is a chance our battalion may be sent home on leave soon. The men are weary, and frostbite has been a real problem during the winter and still affects them badly. How I look forward to seeing you all again. Kiss Henne and Rudi for me and the best kiss for both of you.

Your loving son, Georg.'

The letter was laid down on the white sheets of the bed. Ah, August 1915 – how glad he was that he had not written more; there was so much more he could have written. Georg's eyes seemed to mist over, frozen in thought. He hadn't really explained how he felt about this war, how he would lay awake at night and think of all those other friends from school days who had already fallen, how every day felt like another day he had diced with death, how in those darker moments he would wonder how much time he had left. How naive he had been when he set out on this adventure as a junior doctor 'escaping his studies for the real thing', the opportunity to work every day as a doctor in extraordinary conditions, hoping to return a hero. Little did he think in July 1914 that he would be stuck half starved, half frozen in some remote bleak village. Marburg, beautiful Marburg seemed so far away with his luxurious warm study, afternoon strolls along the banks of the Lahn as it wound its way below the great castle and the exquisite St Elizabeth's church. Neither did he explain how he felt he had aged a decade in these twelve months and that he would return a different son from the one his parents kissed goodbye for the second time last winter.

Hannelore looked into his tired eyes, glad of a brief, reflective moment and savoured the youthful hopefulness and optimism expressed in the letter by a much younger Georg. She laid her hand on his and gently squeezed it.

'How war has robbed us of our best years' she sighed, 'robbed so many we have known. I hope we hear from Johannes soon.'

She stood up and headed towards the bathroom, leaving Georg to drift off to sleep, bleaker memories of those dark days weaving themselves into his dreams.

The few weeks after he had written this letter had been some of the grimmest months for Georg. He became unwell during one of the long advancing marches through Russian territory and, on finally arriving in the market square of a derelict village at the end of the day, was barely able to stand. He collapsed in the marketplace and was examined on the spot by the senior medical officer. He had a temperature of 39 degrees and was sent immediately to the nearest field hospital. For several days he lay drenched in sweat, aching and in the grip of rheumatic fever and as weak as a baby. The next day he was transported a rumbling 60 kilometres further south to another hospital in Galicia where he received excellent care and gradually recovered, but it took a couple of weeks before they would let him re-join the Regiment. During this time of near delirium, the young Georg seemed to hallucinate, half awake, half unconscious;

images of his own grandchildren rose up before him although he didn't seem able to communicate with them, faint likenesses were visible in their young faces, boys and girls running wild across a meadow. They seemed wonderfully happy... as if blissfully unaware of war and conflict. He knew they were his grandchildren even though there was no sign of their parents. He tried to reach out for them, but they didn't seem to be aware of his presence in the meadow. But even in the desperate weakness of those days, miles from home in a bleak, foreign landscape, it cheered his spirit and when he awoke properly out of the fever the clarity of the dream did not vanish.

Georg blinked up at the ceiling of his bedroom, shaken out of his dream, and thought about those children now. He held on tightly to those images. Would his son return alive and not only alive, but well, from this war? His eyes closed involuntarily, the letter still beneath his hand. His sleep that night was not filled with the faces of beautiful grandchildren but of his own Johannes, a long way from Gartenstrasse and the bosom of his parents. The nightmare that recurred throughout this year had come back to haunt him again, its grip merciless. His head was aching dully which roused him in and out of consciousness, but the nightmare was always waiting for him again as he dozed back into a deeper sleep.

Shouts, gunfire, explosions surround the grimy, wooden hut he is standing in, as mangled body after body is brought in. The patients never stop coming. No sooner has he dressed one wound than another comes in... and another... and another... bodies are beginning to pile up and bizarrely even be laid upon one another. The bodies at the bottom are slowly, very slowly, suffocating. His eyes travel to the pile of bodies and look at the faces closely. Panic grips him as he sees the face of Johannes at the very bottom of this mountain of human misery, lips growing whiter, eyes beginning to roll. 'Papa! Papa! Hilf mir!' His son gasps as his eyes close. He frantically begins pulling down body after body, but the more he pulls, the more bodies seemed to appear, a never-ending stream of blood and half-conscious, leering faces flailing against him with their arms. Georg turns, helpless, back to the patient he is treating, and sees the face of Johannes looking back at him. 'Let's go home Papa' he whispers before closing his eyes under the anaesthetic the senior doctor has just administered. Johannes' gangrenous leg is then amputated as Georg looks on. He walks to open the door of the hut to get some fresh air but cannot move beyond the threshold – a mountain of bodies blocks the exit and seems to soar high into the sky – he pushes against it but it remains solid, immovable.

These scenes played over and over in the nightmare in an endless cycle and Georg was thankful to be woken by the 'phone ringing beside his bed, his face beaded with sweat. Blearily he answered, wiping his face with a handkerchief. Even in the middle of the night a needy patient and a long drive to a remote village was welcome relief from the haunting faces that plagued his dreams.

Christmas Eve

Fresh snowfall in the night had left a white, sparkling blanket over the Hoffmann garden. Eva bobbed in front of the curtain, still clutching a blanket around her shoulders, and scratched at the frosted bedroom window. She opened her mouth wide and breathed on the icy pane to melt a window hole and rubbed it with her nightdress sleeve, squeaking with delight as it dawned on her afresh that it was Christmas Eve. She peered out through the window at tiny trails the robins had made as they hopped around the meagre scatterings of stale bread that Hannelore had thrown out, pecking furiously and skittering away in low flight back to the evergreen hedges.

Leaping out of bed and padding over the cold linoleum floor to the sleeping Margarete, she whispered in her sister's ear,

'Wake up, Greta – it's Christmas Eve! It's snowed again in the night!'

Margarete stirred and murmured, snatching the sheets firmly around her chin, a defence against the cold air, but her heart was pounding, equally excited and blinking open her eyes she was met by the twinkling gaze of her sister, just inches from her own.

'We must finish the presents quickly, Eva, I've still got a few rows to stitch before this evening.'

'And we might get to hear from Johannes too!' squeaked Eva.

For weeks now the sisters had been making preparations for the most exciting night of the year. Eva was close to bursting as the day drew nearer. It was growing ever more difficult to conceal the details of all the secret presents she was making. Three years of war heightened the need and longing for something joyous and special, the desire to make Christmas even more wonderful. Eva was now old enough to think about what she could give to her family and she and Margarete had buried themselves in their bedroom with a boldly scribbled 'No entry' sign on the door as they plotted what they would make together. They had been dealt a hard blow when post from their beloved older brother Johannes had arrived earlier in the month. They had last seen him three months ago at the end of September, and his most recent letter had been scribbled in late November on a grimy, mud spattered piece of note paper.

'Dear Mama and Papa and Rotters!

Very little time to write before we march on to the Rzhev salient. I am busy and there is little time to stop and write Christmas cards, but I am missing you all. It now appears unlikely that I shall be home before January.

I shall make every effort to telephone on Christmas Eve.

Your loving son,

Johannes

P.S. Tickle Eva for me otherwise she may become insufferable!'

Georg had rubbed the smeared note in his hand that mid-December morning and even held it up to his nose as if to try and extract something more of his son from the grimy paper. He sighed audibly; the lack of detail in the note suggested that Johannes was putting a brave face on what Georg knew only too well would be unbearably cold nights and days and the ever- present danger of sniper fire on moving, marching battalions. The bullet did not differentiate between the doctor or the regular infantryman. The fact that he would not be home signalled too that the situation in the Caucasus was intense and troops could not be spared. He strode out of the surgery and forced himself to smile reassuringly as he relayed the contents to his family around the breakfast table. Eva was crestfallen, and no amount of cajoling could shake her out of her despondency for days. A Christmas without Johannes was unthinkable; the family had never been apart on this most special of days. Even the snow seemed suddenly to be wet and slushy in their eyes. Artfully, Hannelore had sprinkled cinnamon, icing sugar and joy into their hearts again with plans to send Johannes a small package of special treats. The girls had baked gingerbread, embroidered a handkerchief with a 'J' on it and drawn cards for him to read and had excitedly carried the parcel to the post office with their mother. The days rolled by and at last Christmas Eve arrived with that promising blanket of snow.

Eva and Margarete raced downstairs in their nightdresses and danced around the kitchen making their mother quite dizzy, until she sent them upstairs to get dressed and come back down for breakfast.

All morning, nerves were on edge in case the call came early in the day. Every time the telephone rang all activity ceased, and faces turned with bated breath to see if it was Johannes. Call after call came, one patient after another needing extra medication for colds, influenza, even toothache. Georg's list of afternoon patients was mounting and his agitation to get the day's work finished was visible.

Over lunch he tried his best to be jolly with his ten-year-old Eva in particular. 'Now, Eva, do not be tempted to sneak into the Christmas room and see what is happening. If you do, you may scare the Christkind away and there will be no presents for you.' He pretended to scowl in an exaggerated way as he always did every Christmas Eve.

At the back of the Hoffmann villa, was a circular room, partitioned from the long dining room that Hannelore had created into a beautiful parlour; a room that could be sealed off from the dining room with two lockable wooden doors. Most of the year the room displayed its treasures to the rest of the house, its folding doors standing proudly open into the long dining room, revealing a beautifully carved round chestnut dining table and chairs, an upright piano and a soft blue Bauhaus sofa with reclining arms. The children would rarely enter this hallowed space except to tiptoe across the highly polished parquet floor to practise the piano, but once a year it became a room cloaked in magic. From the 23rd to the 24th December it was sealed for Christmas preparations and the children were forbidden to peer in through the cracks in the door.

Eva knew the double doors to the room were locked anyway and there was no use trying to peek a view from the garden side as the shutters had been closed too. The night before Christmas Eve, Georg and Hannelore had secretly carried the Christmas tree up from the cellar where it had been delivered by one of Georg's farming patients and they had set it in place on its iron stand in the corner of the room by the window. Chocolate rings, handmade straw stars and small red candles pressed into their clips were arranged all over the tree. Almost immediately, pine scent filled the room and Georg and Hannelore set about preparing the room for the following evening. Small tables were set in place for each of the children's presents to be laid out, each with a beautiful tiny Christmas tablecloth. The children always received hand-knitted gloves or mittens and scarves, and always a new book as well as a colourful plate filled with spiced biscuits, marzipan, and an apple. This year Margarete was given a doll's house dining room and Eva a doll's house kitchen, replete with beautifully carved wooden dolls, clothed in scraps of old material that Hannelore had made in the late autumn evenings. These gifts were then covered over with brown paper to conceal them until the very last moment. Eva and Margarete knew that they would have to sing before they could remove the paper, a ritual they had grown used to.

'Shall we lay Johannes' table?' Hannelore whispered to Georg.

'Yes, I think so,' he smiled lovingly at her, 'the others will want to see it there and we can keep it safe until he arrives.'

'Hopefully, he got our parcel - I'm sure they will make a good day of it wherever his battalion is stationed.'

'Do you think Mama will like my present?' Margarete whispered to her sister, later that Christmas Eve morning, not knowing quite whether her mother was listening behind the door of their bedroom. She was feverishly putting the finishing stitches on a small tablecloth she was embroidering.

'It's lovely' crooned Eva, wishing the stitches on the little mat she had embroidered were as regular as her older sister's.

'Have you wrapped our present for Papa?' she added.

'Not yet, but I have found some nice tissue paper in one of the boxes my shoes came in and some old ribbon from my hair box.'

Margarete carefully burrowed in the wardrobe and pulled out their gift for Georg; a new walking stick they had saved up to buy. She held it up for Eva to see and together their young fingers stroked the highly polished black cherrywood, marvelling at the small shiny brass tip at the bottom. They had secretly measured his old one with a tape measure from their mother's sewing box and scribbled down how long it was on a scrap of paper and then run off to purchase it one Saturday when they knew their father was out of the house. They had overheard their father complain of the split in his old, much loved walking stick, and they tried to match it as closely as possible. Their mother had helped them buy it as their frugal savings were not quite enough which meant the girls had to give their mother a home-made present. They wrapped the gleaming new stick rather crudely in the tissue paper as best they could and scrunched the red ribbon around the top.

'There, that will do.' Margarete said proudly, laying it on the floor.

'When shall we give it to Papa, Greta?' Eva asked, smiling at their finished work.

'I think we should smuggle the presents down and hide them in the conservatory before we go into the Christmas room, then we can find them quickly to give out when we go in.'

It was a good plan and after lunch, when footsteps were to be heard clipping down into the cellar, they suspected that their father had set off for his afternoon rounds. They waited another few minutes before hearing the growl of the Mercedes crawling up the drive, crunching over the icy puddles and snow. The girls crept down the long curved staircase, Eva going first to check if their mother was still hovering in the dining room after lunch. Max was lounging in the family snug, but Hannelore was not to be seen.

'The coast is clear,' she whispered loudly. and Margarete swiftly glided down the staircase with all the presents under a blanket. They placed them carefully behind a cupboard in the conservatory and, giggling excitedly, the pair skipped into the kitchen to find their mother washing dishes.

'Come and help me, you two, I have given Irma today and tomorrow off to visit her parents, so I need a bit more help from my lovely daughters. We have to get the table ready for supper before we go out to the crib service.'

'Ach Mama, I am so excited,' gurgled Eva as she picked up a cloth to dry the dripping plates.

Hannelore looked into her younger daughter's eyes and smiled happily. Of course her thoughts were filled with a longing for her family to be complete on this day, but Eva's happiness was infectious.

'If only Hannes was here,' Eva said reflectively, almost sensing her mother's carefully concealed sadness.

'He will be thinking of us all, Evachen, and we must pray for him during the crib service.'

'It seems so unfair that he cannot be here, Mama' moaned Margarete, 'I hate this stupid war.'

Hannelore said nothing. Her daughter expressed everything she was feeling.

'War is an evil thing,' she added thoughtfully after a long pause of silent drying up of dishes. 'But God is more powerful than leaders of countries and He will have the last word. We must trust Him and Him alone.'

They continued drying up in silence.

'What's that noise, Mama?' Eva interjected.

A faint tap could be heard against the kitchen window as if a stone had scraped the glass. It happened again. The three turned and moved towards the window and peered through the lace curtain.

Beaming up at them from under a handsome cap, wrapped in a long greatcoat, buttoned to his chin was Johannes. They gasped in shocked delight and ran as one huddle towards the side door, normally locked, to let him in, Eva leaping down the steps into the arms of her twenty-year-old hero brother. Margarete almost knocked him over and dragged him up the stairs into the hallway where Hannelore cupped his cold, tired but grinning face in her warm hands and kissed him repeatedly. Their deep brown eyes both filled with tears as Johannes buried his head in his mother's shoulder and wept with relief.

'Johannes! Johannes! You are here! On Christmas Eve!' Eva shrieked as Max hurtled out from under his books in the snug to wrap his older brother in even more hugs.

Johannes' tear-stained face beamed up at his brother and sisters and they all chanted 'Christmas! Christmas! Christmas!' dancing on the spot.

Hannelore wiped her eyes in her apron and clasped her hands together in joy.

'How is this possible? We weren't expecting you at all!'

'We were given very late notice only a few days ago. It was impossible to contact you as we've been on the move for the last two days. Reinforcements arrived to relieve us for a week.'

Johannes peered into the surgery from the hallway.

'Where is Papa?'

Hannelore steered him into the kitchen.

'He's busy on his rounds, seeing the last patients before Christmas. He should be back around 5 o'clock, snow willing.'

Eva's eyes suddenly grew even larger with excitement.

'We should hide Johannes, Mama. We should hide him in the Christmas room. Don't tell Papa. It can be a great surprise for him!'

The Hoffmann children all chimed in as one voice 'Yes!'

'Is good, is good!' beamed Hannelore, flapping her hands at them to be quiet, 'but first a hot meal, my son?'

'Ah, that would be heaven, Mama. We have eaten nothing but eggs and boiled swede for the last two months.'

Johannes peeled off his heavy coat and his brother dragged it off with his kit bag to hide it in their bedroom so that Georg would not see any trace of his older son. Meanwhile, the girls sat rooted to the table with their beloved brother and gazed up at his sunken brown eyes as he regaled them of the journey home in freezing trucks and train wagons.

'Mama – please can I have a bath? I must smell dreadful and I am cold to the core. Ah, thank you.'

Hannelore had set a steaming bowl of hot vegetable and pork broth in front of him, along with a chunk of rye bread. He closed his eyes and smelled the broth as if in a reverie and began to gulp it down much to Eva's amusement.

'Margarete, get the bath ready. I will boil up some extra water and bring it up shortly.'

Margarete dragged the huge enamel bath that was usually stored against the kitchen wall near the larder closer to the stove, ready for Hannelore to pour boiling water into. Shortages of fuel had necessitated that baths be taken in the kitchen rather than upstairs. Once prepared, the family left Johannes to his bath and donned their warm coats and mittens and scarves and scampered down the cellar into the garden. The rest of the afternoon was spent in a state of frenzied excitement with the girls giggling involuntarily and japing around with Max in the garden building a Christmas snowman 'for Papa'. Hannelore bundled the filthy uniform into an empty sack in the cellar until she had time to wash it.

Johannes sat, scrubbed, and dressed warmly in his old clothes, which now seemed to hang a little around him, shrunken as he was by months of marching and broken nights dealing with the wounded and maimed. He was glowing now from the warm bath and the hot tea she had set before him at the kitchen table, as she buttered slices of honey bread for their traditional Christmas Eve treat.

He munched on the soft spiced bread and started talking to his mother about the long journey home through wastelands of snow, past frozen lakes, and stark pine forests. He said nothing of the time he had spent on the Eastern Front, focusing simply on the details of the last few days travelling. Hannelore could see the strain in his eyes and the involuntary yawns between mouthfuls.

'We shall talk more later, my son. Why don't you go and lie down on the blue sofa in the Christmas room and snooze a little until Papa comes home. At least he won't find you there. I shall make sure the doors are locked again - I have the only key!'

As Johannes entered the room in the waning light of this December afternoon, his throat filled again with emotion. He had little imagined that he would be back for Christmas when the leave came through, and he now felt as if he were in a dream. He breathed in deeply the smell of the Tannenbaum and spiced biscuits and looked up at the decorations on the tree, recognising crudely painted sourdough stars he had made at Kindergarten, half broken but precious remnants of his childhood. He gazed down at the four small tables heaving with gifts and tears filled his eyes again. Lying down on the blue sofa, he stared a long time at the achingly beautiful scene before him and then closed his heavy eyelids, slipping into a deep sleep for the first time in months.

It was dark outside when Georg's Mercedes could be heard rolling carefully down the icy driveway into the garage below the kitchen. Eva and Margarete were barely able to contain their excitement and had struggled to compose themselves at the candle-lit crib service. For a few moments the magic of the giant wooden crib distracted Eva, and then her thoughts would turn to the secret present hidden in the sealed room and she would giggle to herself behind her handkerchief at the thought of her father's face. She had completely forgotten about the presents she was soon to receive and even the gifts she had spent weeks preparing with her sister. The girls had been sworn to silence by Hannelore and to prevent them blurting out Johannes' arrival to their friends in the pew in front she had said a courteous 'Happy Christmas' to her friends and acquaintances and swept them away from church as soon as the service was over.

She was now busying herself in the kitchen with the girls, preparing the sausages and potato salad they would enjoy after the presents were revealed while Max was stoked the peat oven and tried pretending to be grown up and serious for when their father walked through the door, winking at Eva whenever he could behind his mother's back to make her laugh.

Georg plodded heavily up the cellar stairs with his bag and, concealing his tiredness, swept open the door to the kitchen twinkling at his family. 'Happy Christmas everyone! Has the Christkind come, I wonder? Mmm... is there any of that honey bread left for an old diabetic doctor? Just a tiny slice?'

He wrapped his arms around Eva who flung herself at him and leaned over to kiss Hannelore who smiled calmly, hoping her pounding heart would not betray itself in her expression.

'Any calls from Johannes?' he enquired.

'No, Papa... not yet.' said Margarete a little too excitedly

'Well let's make sure we don't miss his call.'

Georg strode into the surgery, deposited his bag by his desk and left the door wide open so that he would hear the 'phone, while Hannelore prepared a cup of rosehip tea for him.

'Yes, we are ready to start the celebrations, Papa.'

The family moved as one into the main dining room, leaving the kitchen door wide open as well and stood in front of the double doors to the secret room.

Hannelore, key in her hand slipped through the doors, closing them behind her while the family waited, and Johannes - who had by now woken with the commotion in the kitchen - concealed himself behind the long curtains, winking at his mother. She carefully lit the candles on the tree, surveyed the beautiful scene for a moment, drank in the fragrant smells of pine needle and spiced biscuit and whispered a prayer of thanks under her breath before grandly opened the doors to her waiting children and husband.

Georg beamed, and the children, enchanted by the candle-lit tree and tables of gifts, gasped, eyes racing around the room to see where Johannes was. But Hannelore, a twinkle in her eye prolonged the moment,

'Girls, before you may receive your gifts, we need to hear you sing.'

And down she sat gracefully at the piano in the corner of the room and leafed open the Christmas carol book at the traditional song for Eva and Margarete to perform - *Ihr Kinderlein kommet.* The girls could barely contain themselves but played along with big grins on their faces.

Georg smiled as their pure, high voices struck the first notes, his eyes twitching nervously towards the open doorways to the hallway and beyond, the surgery. He strained his ears to hear between the high notes in case he missed the bright bell of the telephone. At the end, he and Max joined in with the final verse and applause broke out, again muted by the need to hear the 'phone.

'Well done. Well done girls, but we must be a little quieter now so that we do not miss Johannes' call.'

Margarete and Eva began to giggle, which Georg simply put down to the excitement of Christmas Eve, but Hannelore broke the moment, aware that her children would not be able to contain themselves much longer.

'Papa, we have a very special gift for you, one we think you will like,' she said loudly, as if she were back in her old grammar school classroom addressing a group of students.

And out from behind the heavy curtains stepped Johannes, beaming at his father.

Georg stood for a moment, blinking in disbelief at his tall, thin son.

'Johannes! Mein Sohn!' He rushed forward and enveloped his boy in his arms, laughing in surprise at seeing the son who had cost him so many sleepless nights of worry.

The children joined in with the embrace and Eva shrieked in delight.

'We hid him, Papa! Isn't it just the best present?'

'The very best, Eva,' he said not breaking his gaze from his son, 'the very best.'

Georg held him a long time, blinking furiously, repeatedly rubbing his son's arms and laughing with his children. The war, his patients, Borkhausen, the whole wide world could be forgotten. Georg Hoffmann's family was all together again.

Christmas carols were sung around the piano, gifts shared, many sausages and biscuits munched before all collapsed, exhausted by so much laughing into their beds, the girls giggling long into the night over the events of the day. Georg and Hannelore stayed up late talking to Johannes over a precious bottle of Cognac reserved for special occasions before finally turning in, Georg rubbing his son's shoulders all the way up the staircase.

As Hannelore and Georg wandered into their bedroom, he excused himself for a moment,

'I think I left my glasses on the table in the dining room - I shan't be a moment.'

Georg slipped silently back downstairs, grabbed a coat from the hallway stand and then disappeared quietly down the cellar stairs into the back yard, out into the freezing, starlit night. He crunched his way through the snow to the back of the garden as far from the house as he could and stood for a moment below the great willow tree whose long, swaying branches stroked the freezing river.

Wrapped in a grey, woollen coat, Georg held his arms tightly as he shivered in the still, clear night. A million stars stretched out across the galaxy as he looked up at the cold, white moon. The shivering became shaking as he rocked on the spot, his shoulders heaving up and down almost uncontrollably. For the first time during this war Georg Hoffmann allowed himself to weep, to weep for the son he thought he may never see again.

'Thank you,' he whispered.

Eva couldn't sleep for excitement and got up to peer out of her frosty window at the snowman she had made with her sister and brother. In the distance she spotted a dark figure at the end of the garden. She recognised the silhouette as her father. *He looks sad*, she thought, as he wandered back along the pathway around the lawn into the cellar.

A New Life

It is autumn and a warm, low sun hangs over the horizon. The treatment is a distant dream. The sea glistens gold as the currents lap around the rocks, shelving white water at low tide. I park the car near the cliff edge and walk the familiar path through the Otter gate, past the white modernist house set confidently on the plot of the old Craggy House that the Coombe family owned and lived in a hundred years before. I gaze up at the dinosaur back of headland that stretches out into the Atlantic, arching to the right of my path. Sheep bleat, brambles tumble around the last remnants of the yellow gorse amidst the still fragrant blooms of wild honeysuckle. Bees dozily bungee around white butterflies, and birdsong seems to hang in the air; light notes from invisible beaks tucked away in the gorse. Molehills spill out on either side of the soft green pathway.

I reach the Point and stare at the craggy rock faces lined up one behind the other in the distance. I love these places, the high places, the steep places, solid rock pitted with clefts to which all living things cling at low and high tide, resolute against the storms that pound this coast, in season and out. They seem immovable in spite of the landfalls onto the long golden sands of one of my favourite beaches nearby, the inevitable erosion of this limestone coastline.

Lone female walkers trek past smiling - faster and more energetic, maps and cameras in hands, marching on to the next long stretch of sand around the corner. Cormorants swoop down the sides of the cliffs as I dare myself to walk nearer to the very end of the Point, reached by a narrow, treacherous path. I sit at the end and recline on the rock. Beside me I notice a previous visitor has left ten roses, wilting slightly but still a deep red velvet in the petal. The memorial touches me, this small poignant act of human love, the need to place something beautiful and living in memory of a lost loved one, something precious to fill the dark, empty lonely void. I am grateful that Tom isn't laying roses for me, that my children have not had to know the truth and that my life can regain some normality, that I can help others on this journey, perhaps, in the future. I am grateful to those who have helped me, sat with me as chemicals dripped in, made meals for the family during the weaker days, looked after the boys for whole days at a time, driven me to radiotherapy when I was too tired to drive myself, sent cards, flowers, texts and quietly prayed. There is much to be thankful for.

I journey home, tired but thrilled to have walked the three miles, another victory in a year when walking two minutes into the village between treatments was exhausting.

Tom's work continues to be relentless and his evenings are swamped more and more by longer meetings in Exeter and a never-ending inbox of emails that regenerate every day. I even dread us going away for short holidays, knowing that the hundreds of emails will have multiplied into a thousand. More and more frequently the lava within spits out and I vent my mounting frustration at him. 'Why so much work?' 'Why so little time with me and the boys?' 'What is the point?' 'Everything you do will be reversed anyway when you leave.' 'We are losing the best years of our lives!' 'I don't care about the money.' 'What was the point of surviving?'

He listens patiently, nods, murmurs agreement and yet is caught in a web of wanting to see the job through, to feel that something he is implementing will make a real difference. The Government slashing budgets and demanding that cuts are made is an impossible task, I tell him. He knows. He is working so hard. I feel guilty for complaining and dashing his dreams, but I cannot help myself and frequently now I stomp around the house on my own, firing expletives into the air when the 'phone call comes through at 7pm 'Just leaving Exeter.' I could scream. Another hour and a half before he walks through the door. Another hazardous journey home at the wheel.

His face is weary and apologetic when he finally arrives and I know that he is tired and hungry. We eat. I barely say a word. This isn't life, this isn't why I survived. I can't blame him, but I do. The anger seethes well below the surface a lot of the time, buried beneath layers of concern about his own health, the fact that I love him, the fact that he is a good husband and father. Most of the time I try not to acknowledge the anger, it would make me feel too guilty, too immature, too selfish.

I sit alone and contemplate what I should now be doing with my life, how I can make sense of it again and do something worthwhile. I do not want to simply live at the end of the commute, fretting about the impending accident my overworked husband has, a thought that plagues me every week.

The following spring, I bump into an old school mum at the parent café whose eyes sparkle with the news that there is a job vacancy at a local private school, a twenty-five-minute drive from home. It is the perfect job - part-time, small class sizes and no real responsibility other than simply to teach. No longer do I crave the management burden of my old teaching career, peaking as a Deputy Head in a large comprehensive school.

It would be madness not to go for it - I may as well be sitting marking books in the evening when the boys are in bed; Tom is working anyway until midnight most evenings; it will give me something to do, a chance to re-build my confidence. Tom scans the advertisement with me later that evening.

'Looks really good, Kris, are you sure you are ready to do this?'

'The job wouldn't start until September and the holidays are longer than the boys' ones. There is even a chance that if we choose to send the boys there, we can get a reduction in the fees. The job will be a doddle – only Year 7 to Year 11 with no A Level teaching required.'

Tom can see the excitement in my face.

'Well, why don't you have a go and see what happens.' He seems relieved that I might have something better to think about than his workload.

I apply, request a preliminary meeting with the head of department and head off to tour the school.

Like Hogwarts, the school towers up slightly menacingly at the top of an Exmoor climb and my little car strains into second gear before levelling out through the village that has given the school its name. I park at the front of the great Victorian façade, heave open the solid arched doors and am greeted by a friendly secretary, who asks me to take a seat while she calls the head of department.

A few moments later a jovial, tweed suited man in his late forties, strides into the reception area and declares, 'And is anyone here interested in a job in the History department?'

I smile to myself. He is going to be a character, and indeed Mr Chad doesn't draw breath for the next half hour as we wander into the quadrangle and up the steep stone steps past the geography and religious education departments to the two history classrooms. Piles of file paper lie strewn across the front table of his teaching room, next to toppling mountains of textbooks. Every inch of wall space is dedicated to famous quotations from historical characters. The effect is as stimulating to the enquiring mind as it is intimidating. We talk university jovially, sketchily look at the curriculum and eventually I prize open the conversation to ask about the other member of the department. I learn that Mr Rivers is retiring after decades of loyal service to the school as housemaster and teacher. I encounter him briefly in the corridor, a sweet, cuddly, elderly, bearded man with a gentle voice. I like him and sense he might be missed. Slightly overwhelmed by my visit to the school but impressed by the smart and courteous behaviour of every student I see, I decide that I am in teaching heaven and it would be foolish not to grasp the chance to work here.

The following week I am invited to interview, don my new grey trouser suit, and black heels and head off to be observed as I teach a lesson on Dictatorship and Democracy to a group of Year 9 students. Having sped through the rise of Hitler and Stalin, I am then grilled by one of the senior teachers and Mr Chad, and finally interviewed by the Headmaster, Mr Montagu, in his comfortably spacious study. My head is spinning.

I have been candid in my written application about my recent medical history, but nothing is mentioned, and the interview is polite and friendly, questions revolving around what contributions I can make to the wider curriculum of the school.

I leave, slightly dizzy after several hours of having to field a series of staccato questions in interview and realise that it has been a long time since I had to 'perform' at that level. I drive home with the windows wide open and hope that the right outcome will be the right outcome. Surely by September I will have the stamina to cope with twelve lessons a week.

The telephone rings the next morning.

'Mrs Templeton?' I strain to recognise the voice on the other end of the receiver.

'Yes, speaking.'

'Ah Mrs Templeton, it's James Montagu here, we would be delighted if you would accept the part-time post of History teacher. We would like to recognise your previous significant experience too and award you a salary that reflects this.'

I flush and sit down on the edge of the bed.

'Well, thank you – I would be pleased to accept.'

'Oh splendid! – we all agree that we have made a wonderful choice and are very conscious that you are quite a catch.'

'That's kind of you to say, thank you.' I am aware that my previous experience has given me an edge in the field, but I am still flattered.

'No, your competition didn't come near you. Well, I shall be writing to you shortly with a contract for you to sign and my colleagues will be in touch regarding the timetable in due course. Do pop in and familiarise yourself with everything too. We look forward to seeing you soon. Goodbye.'

I put down the receiver and punch the air.

Yes! I did it! I am a normal person. I can get a job. I will do a brilliant job. I will look smart, I will buy new suits, new make-up, even a new small car. I will tell no one in the workplace what has happened to me. A chance to reinvent myself again.

Yes!

The Black Eagle

The induction days are over and the first day of teaching has arrived.

I stand in front of my first class of students, sweating beneath the new dress, hoping they don't realise just how fast my heart is pounding. The summer holidays have been spent poring over powerpoints and a new examination course I have never taught before. The students have queued outside and file in meekly. I am aware they are weighing me up but I also know that this is a school with high standards of behaviour and it is unlikely that they will be disruptive, as so many of my previous students tried to be in the first year I began my teaching career.

I think back to those days when lessons with the older age group felt like an exercise in babysitting with barrages of, 'Miss, Miss. He stole my pen, Miss!' 'How much do you want us to write Miss? Is one sentence enough?' 'Miss, I don't understand the question.' 'Miss - he stole my pencil now.' The classroom heaving with up to thirty-four students at a time all clamouring for attention and 'trying it on' with the collective 'humming' routine or the 'name swapping' routine to see if Miss would crack or fall for it.

By the time I left eleven years later I commanded respect throughout the school, but it was bloody hard work getting to that point in the first two years. I prided myself on having the best displays outside and inside my room and sharing my wisdom with student teachers from the local training college. Those were the glory days, but I knew I could never return to that intensity of teaching again. A small part-time job in a private school would be perfect.

These students are quiet, well-behaved, and respectful, pristine in their traditional blazers and smart grey trousers, the school emblem proudly emblazoned on the top pocket. Sports badges, music badges and house colours drip down one side of the lapels and it is clear immediately who the alpha children in the room are. These students are used to hard work and expect homework once a week from every teacher. Their faces are brown with the summer holiday sun. I have spent the summer in the shade, avoiding on medical advice any more damaging rays on my body. The initial curls of hair that grew back have been cut into a smarter short style and I long for it to return more thickly. It is just a matter of time I think to myself, the students don't know my story anyway, they will just think it is normal for me to have thin hair.

The lesson goes well. The summer holiday slog of late night lesson preparation was worth it. The students respond politely and participate, and I begin to learn their names and master the technology I need to get the You Tube clips and powerpoint working. The thrill of each lesson grows and I am loving new outfits, a new sense of self esteem and the rigour of meeting deadlines and being part of a small team of History teachers. I can teach again! I hoped I might even do this before I was diagnosed, but I never thought it would come so quickly. My life is back on track and it is wonderful to be earning money again. We don't really need it, Tom is earning so well, especially with this new job, but it is great to be able to buy things with money I have earned myself. I relish each lesson and the chance to make a difference again, to teach something worthwhile and to see those wonderful penny-dropping moments when students 'get' something new and achieve good grades.

The following summer, my first cohort of Year 11 GCSE students achieves a record-breaking number of A* and A grades in History. I punch the air again on results day. Life couldn't be better.

Two-and-a-half years into the new job

I am driving, unsteadily, anxiously towards the hospice. My breathing is irregular, and I have to sit upright in the car seat so that my lungs can expand as fully as possible. I hold one side of my face as I drive with the other hand. Somehow, holding my face helps me - the feel of a hand on my cheek calms a little, as does sucking a mentholated sweet. Small strategies that help me navigate this unfamiliar phenomenon of hyperventilating.

My mind shafts back to the last few weeks which have led to this moment: the near fainting episode in church, the defiant struggle to get to work that week and teach my Year 8 class as the floor swims beneath me and my head grows foggy amidst mounting, irrational agitation with the students, walking out of the school knowing I cannot teach the next lesson, driving with laboured breathing back through Exmoor to town, having to stop to recover in the car park of a supermarket and 'phone Tom, managing to get home in tears, confused and frustrated at what is happening to me. Later discussions with Tom alone in our bedroom,

'Tom what's going on? I've never felt like this before? Is it my thyroid levels? My calcium levels? Why am I so breathless? Should I get this checked out? I can't function like this? How am I supposed to teach?'

'I'll 'phone the oncology department' he says reassuringly, 'and have you checked out. I'm sure it is nothing sinister.'

The drive to oncology a couple of days later, as tingling sensations spread around my arms and fingers and breathing quickens, my head feeling woozy, and panicking that I am not going to get to this important appointment on time. My car descends steeply into one of the villages, high Devon banks seem to close in on me. Should I stop and call an ambulance? I need to get to the hospital. I must do it. I must keep going. Not much further. I speed on, sobbing to relieve the tension. 'O God, please just get me there.'

The effusive hug of Spanish oncologist Dr Morales who examines me, reassuring all the time.

'Krista, you need time. Give yourself time. I am going to refer you for a brain and body scan so that you will have complete peace of mind.'

'I - I don't think I really need that.'

'I know' she says firmly, 'but I want to take away any other anxieties that you may be having at the moment.'

The scan appointment comes through within a couple of days.

I sit in that familiar waiting room. My veins are shot away – getting blood is always a challenge – fitting the cannula is only possible for the very skilled.

'Into the wrist might be best' says the nurse on duty. She warms the skin with a hot pack and successfully prepares me for the iodine injection that will show dense in my stomach on the scan. I lie down on the bed beneath the great polo mint of a machine that is the somaton scanner. Siemens is written large on the top.

'Impressive looking machine,' I say to the nurse to pass the time.

'Yes, we've only had it a few years - it cost a quarter of a million. OK, we're ready. I'm going to inject the iodine now and you will have a warm sensation around your chest and pelvic area – you may even feel as if you have wet yourself.'

We laugh.

'That should be interesting.'

'You will see lots of red lights whizzing around as you go in and out of the scanner. Just lie as still as you can and hold your breath when we tell you to.'

Behind the glass window the radiographers look intently at the screen in front of them. What are they seeing?

Sensations and flashing lights stop, and I am back, recovering for ten minutes in the waiting room. It is over, and I just have to wait for Dr Morales to let me know the results. Won't know until tomorrow at the earliest, I convince myself.

Within hours of the scan, though Dr Morales 'phones through,

'Great news, Krista, the scan, the head, the body – everything is absolutely clear.'

My whole body relaxes in a fresh wave of relief. All the blood tests are clear too. An ECG later that week is also clear. I knew all along that this is what she would say. There is still relief... and yet...

Confusion.

I can tell my mind that my body is fine and that there is nothing to worry about – there are no sinister shadows lurking on a hospital screen or more importantly within the vital organs of my body. My right breast is clear, good, whole – I am well. So why am I feeling so unwell, so fragile, so lost in this unknown country I don't know how to navigate? The relief is tinged with guilt.

Holly's cancer is growing.

It is growing so that she looks pregnant. Six months ago, she had spotted a swollen abdomen and eventually her worst fears were realised – ovarian cancer. Perhaps the thought of her own battle raging has added to the stress levels that have clearly been building in my own mind. I have no energy to drive to her, to support her in what she is going through. If I am to be of any help, I need to get myself sorted out first.

And so to my GP. More tears, anguished questions, and explanations from me about what has been happening and finally the question I have begun to dread.

'Krista, would you consider some external help?'

The words land as profoundly as the original diagnosis.

I look at her through brimming eyes – the tears begin the moment I walk through the door.

'I cannot see a psychiatrist, no one that Tom might know. I couldn't bear that,' I plead. 'I can't have Tom's colleagues thinking that his wife is a head-case.' It frustrates me that I cannot hold back the tears.

'Krista,' she says holding my hand, 'this is not a mental health issue, this is just life.' She looks into my eyes earnestly and I try to grasp what she is saying.

'I don't feel I am cracking up. I'm just tired and have these bizarre symptoms that don't seem to correlate with the way I am feeling. I am happy. I have a great job that I love, Tom has more time than he has had in years, now that he has stopped commuting to Exeter. The boys are doing well. I am well. I couldn't be happier right now. Why is this happening?'

'The mind does strange things, Krista, it doesn't always transmit what is happening at the time. I would like to suggest a lady at the hospice, Jennifer Wade. You should get a 'phone call on Monday.'

The hospice.

The word sinks in. Why yes, how appropriate that I should face my demons in the very place that represents everything I have tried to avoid for the past four and a half years.

Two weeks later

And so I have arrived and parked my car on the road outside the building. I breathe as slowly as I can through my nose and exhale through a taut mouth, walking gingerly towards the reception area.

I am met by the statuesque Jennifer Wade. She smiles broadly but says little. In any other context she might seem intimidatingly tall and aloof but there is something in her soft blue eyes that speaks of wisdom. She must be in her late fifties and her hair is already silver grey. As the senior counsellor here, I reassure myself that she must be confident talking about cancer and dying. I need to trust her. She ushers me into a small room with two green leather bucket chairs and a coffee table. A box of tissues and a bowl full of pebbles and shells have been placed soothingly in the centre of the glass table. I cast an eye around the room, drawn to

183

the Mondrians on the wall, gentle blocks of pastels. I place my bottle of water on the table and sink into one of the green chairs stroking my fingertips through thinning, mousy brown hair. I look up at the counsellor in front of me and look down again at long black boots wrapped around navy blue jeggings. A grey fleece is buttoned to my neck. Momentarily poised, I then give way to a wave of emotion that I am beginning to become familiar with since almost fainting two weeks ago. I am still a little incredulous that I find myself sitting opposite a counsellor. I'm a doctor's wife. I don't do counselling or psychotherapy and I definitely don't do pills.

She says nothing to me at first. The silence feels uncomfortable. I am not good with silences. I like to fill them. She explains confidentiality and how long we have and then pauses again, asking me nothing.

I look at her.

I start prattling on about how grateful I am that she has made time to see me, about my symptoms and how frustrated I am that I cannot work at the moment, how my GCSE groups need me to be there and what a burden it must be for my colleague in the department, how I need to get back in the saddle. Tears flow, and I then explain my diagnosis four and a half years ago.

'I can't really see any connection though. I am well and enjoying my job. What's going on with me?'

My eyes drift to the carpet, exhausted by these first moments with this strange, rather aloof woman I have never met before.

'Tell me about that first day, that first day when you were diagnosed,' she says softly but firmly. I look up at her, eyes brimming, biting my upper lip, fighting back another wave of tears.

No one has ever asked me that question before.

And so I talk through what happened; the questions, the ultrasound scan, the consultant, the following appointment to fix the surgery date. I say it quickly and as coolly as I can, a factual report of what happened. But tears keep flowing. It helps the breathing a little, and then when I can say no more the hour is up, and we arrange to meet the following week. More and more breathlessness follows in the weeks between appointments, until the third week when the frustration boils over.

'I just want to get back to the classroom. I love my job, I can't stand not teaching. Why am I feeling like this? I just don't seem to be able to pull myself together.' I stare imploringly at Jennifer whose implacable face simply waits for me to continue.

'I've had almost three wonderful years of teaching. OK it's been hard work and it's been quite stressful juggling the school run and the boys with marking work and exam scripts but, essentially, it's a great job. I'm not afraid of teaching. I look forward to going. I love creating imaginative lessons. Why should I be having panic attacks?'

She completely ignores the school issue and skilfully redirects the focus.

'I was struck when we met a few weeks ago by how sudden your operation was, Krista, how shockingly quick the operation was after your diagnosis.'

I feel the emotion rising again. It is never very far from the surface.

'I think you need to try and articulate how the mastectomy felt to you,' she suggests softly.

There is a pause while I think about the question. She senses there is a block.

'Some women have described it as if they were wandering across the battlefields of the First World War, looking at lacerated bodies, strewn everywhere. It helps them to visualise it. See if you can find the words to describe it.'

The hour is up and deep down I know that this is something I have got to face this week.

The mastectomy.

Even the word 'mastectomy' horrifies me. It sounds like something being chewed relentlessly by a monster and then being regurgitated for a second chewing. Before I was diagnosed, I had given thought to how this might be for a woman. An acquaintance at church had recently been diagnosed and I had been shocked and concerned at what this lady was about to face in terms of surgery. How must this friend be feeling about losing a breast? I have never googled the images on the internet, never gone there even in mild curiosity, but I have thought about it and the thought has always filled me with physical revulsion. Whenever anybody mentioned it, my whole body would shudder, my fists and elbows would clench and my eyes would screw up tightly, almost as if I were chewing on a piece of lemon; as if someone had suggested that each nail of my hands be pulled off one by one. No, these were not thoughts to dwell on, research or even entertain in a personal way. It was never going to happen to me anyway – no history of cancer.

I am glad though that Jennifer has made the suggestion, glad of something to do, something to focus on, or is it in truth a relief at last to be given permission to unlock the door in the cellar and allow myself to think about the thing I have convinced myself I should not think too much about, the secret I have kept from the boys, the shame that I bear in my body... the part of me my husband is not allowed to kiss.

Tom is so sensitive to this; our lovemaking gently avoids this area, not because he is repelled, but because he knows it is difficult for me.

'If it helps,' Tom would say to me after we have made love, often with me sobbing in his arms, 'it makes absolutely no difference to me. You are so beautiful as you are now.' Tom and I had often joked over the past four years at how grateful I am that he is essentially a 'Bottoms Man.'

'Good job I didn't have a bottomectomy!' I would shriek in more buoyant moods, both of us contorted with laughter at the thought, and I am genuinely grateful. Grateful that my husband loves me, grateful that I have only lost one breast not two, grateful to be... alive. I have spent many months in the aftermath of the operation putting on a brave and hearty face to those around me, wanting my strong faith in God to prevail, to radiate to others.

But now this demon, this event that I had firmly parked in the 'I have overcome' section of my brain, has returned to haunt my mind and emotions. Day by day I am struggling for breath, struggling to control the relentless waves of emotion that rise up from the top of my chest as I try to pace my breathing. It comes out of nowhere and debilitates me to the extent that if I am in the supermarket I head for the door as soon as I can and walk shakily towards the car, slump in the seat, slam the door and sob it out. Returning to the supermarket, I collect a trolley, wet eyed and somewhat calmer before the next wave hits me as I drive home. Stopping, starting, sobbing, starting, sobbing, getting home, sobbing.

'How can I go back to work when I am like this, Jennifer? I can't have this happen in the middle of a lesson. Will I ever work again? It's been a month and a half now. I thought it had subsided, but it just seems to be getting worse again.'

Jennifer can hear the despair in my voice.

'It seems to me as if you feel that everything is out of control. What you are describing to me is so familiar for people who are experiencing grief.'

Grief. The word stuck in my mind, tears flowing again.

What is it I am grieving for? The many loved ones who have died over the past few years? The grief at probably losing my best friend? Possibly, but it is becoming increasingly clear that I am in a state of grief for more than that. Is it really the loss of my breast? I have disconnected myself so much from the moment it happened that I don't even know. I have since had other operations; a parathyroidectomy that has left a Frankenstein scar across the base of my neck which has saddened me but is simply a necessary evil, no worse really than having an appendix removed. Surely the mastectomy was also just a necessary evil? A lifeline to a woman on death row? I'm alive, aren't I? Isn't that enough?

I drive home from the hospice and look at myself in the mirror. I take a piece of string out of the bits-and-bobs drawer in the kitchen and hold it against the scar the surgery left after the mastectomy. It is a fine 'beautiful' scar as Dr Morales assures me each time I go for the annual examination, a scar that travels like a thin line against the lower breast line and tapers away beneath my arm. I go downstairs into the kitchen and measure it against one of my son's rulers.

20cm.

I reel slightly in surprise. I press my hand against my flat, almost concave chest and can feel my ribs, my heart pounding as if it were about to erupt out of its cavity. I feel so vulnerable, my heart is barely millimetres away from my hand. Someone has ripped off my breast. Some great black claw has dug into my flesh and torn it off, a great black eagle has swooped down out of nowhere, knocked me to the ground and just snatched away my precious breast, my beautiful, precious breast. The breast that has nourished both my boys with life-giving milk, the breast that was so fondly kissed by my husband in consummation of our marriage and our love, the breast that balanced my body and enhanced my swimming costume, my bra, my dresses. And as I allow myself to think and to feel, the tears come, and a deep wailing rises from a place I can only describe as the Abyss. It is the sound that must echo round the nether regions, a place where despair and hopelessness reign and howl. It scares me at first and then I simply sag to my knees in front of the sofa in the kitchen and give into it; let it have its time. For many minutes I kneel there, head buried in the seat of the faded red sofa and sob. The pain of my lost child rises as if another talon has just snatched her away too and the moaning continues.

That night as I lie in bed with Tom, I speak of the blank space on my body. Tom has seen it of course, he knows what it looks like, but he has never touched it. Thoughts flood my mind. Should I let him kiss me there? How will it be? Will it feel horrible? Will it make the deformity seem even worse?

Summoning every ounce of courage, I slowly take hold of his hand and place it over the blank space, over the 20 cm scar and let it rest there. Quietly I cry. I am not ready for him to kiss this place but somehow as we lie there, I know that a time will come when it will be possible. Tom sighs deeply and I know his heart is filling with hope that I am letting him touch the place of pain and agony in my heart.

'You'll get a good pulse reading there,' I sniff, conscious that my heart is pounding millimetres away from his palm.

'Your heart is safe in my hands,' he whispers softly.

We lie there a long time, his hand cupped gently over my chest and murmuring soft words of comfort and gratitude. It feels good to me, it feels right.

Protected.

The Revelation

Summer 2015

'But when am I going to get over this, Jennifer? It's been weeks now and I still feel as if I am not in control of my life, my ability to work? Where am I on this journey? Have I made any progress?' I grow weary that I am ever going to feel well again. The wise hospice counsellor looks at me as implacably as ever. I sense she has seen it all many times before, but so far, she has never said as much. She picks up a pad of paper and a pen and starts to draw something so that I can see it.

'Krista, I am going to draw a diagram of where you are in this process.' She then draws what looks like a big boulder. 'This is your problem.' She then draws a stick figure to the left of the boulder that is then moving towards the boulder and going over the boulder and the arrow line continues beyond the boulder.

'This is you going over the boulder and beyond it. This is you 'getting over' the problem. This picture is complete rubbish. This is what everyone around you expects you to do - to "get over it." '

Her abruptness startles me. I didn't expect her to rubbish her diagram. I was following the line of thought completely. She then starts drawing another diagram of a boulder-like circle again and this time draws more and more circles around it so that it looks like a slice of a large tree trunk.

'This is where you really are, Krista. This is your problem and these circles are your life growing around it in layers. You are not going to 'get over' your problem. It lives within you and will always live within you. But your life will grow around it and will strengthen it and gradually it will not consume you as it is doing now. This is the place of the cross, Krista, the place of greatest suffering and weakness that will in time become the place of greatest strength.'

Her wise words are like ointment and for the first time she offers me real hope that there is a way through this maze of emotions and breathlessness, hope that it will relent and that I will live again much more fully. I am startled a little also that this professional woman has used religious imagery. In our first encounter I explained that I had a faith and that it was an important part of my journey. Yes, the wooden cross on which an innocent man hung and around which the whole of Christianity has grown like an enormous tree – an apt metaphor.

'But why has this happened now? Why didn't it happen five years ago?'

'You didn't allow yourself to feel what happened to you and your mind had probably not processed it. You didn't give yourself permission to experience it fully at the time because you were protecting your boys. If you hadn't had your crash after five years, it would have happened after ten, and would have been even more devastating.'

She pauses to let me absorb what she has told me.

'Does this happen to a lot of women, then?' I am really curious to know.

'Yes, it is a grief that needs to come out. You are not alone. This is not a sprint, Krista, it is a marathon.'

She pauses.

'Have you given any more thought to talking to your boys?'

Silence.

I feel myself welling up again and fighting back the tears. It is so clearly the big issue, the one I now need to confront.

'Give it some thought. We can help you with it if you like and provide an opportunity for them to talk to us as well if they need to.'

'How should I tell them?' I ask weakly.

'Don't feel you have to tell them too much. Let them lead the conversation. Just explain that you had cancer and that you are now well. Give them time to ask you questions.'

A few days later

The sun shines warmly on our family group perched on two gleaming, stainless steel benches opposite the great clock in the square. The boys are happily munching pizzas out of a takeaway box as pigeons swoop down in the hope of some crumbs. The mood is happy. They have loved surprising Daddy at work at the end of this Thursday in late June. Midsummer has worked its magic on the townsfolk and everyone seems nurtured by the warmth of the air. Sun-worshippers sit outside cafés sipping their cappuccinos and beer and close their eyes dreamily with thoughts of a long hot summer ahead.

The day has come. It is two months after my health breakdown.

I turn and face my husband.

'Tom, we need to tell the boys today or tomorrow. It feels right to do it very soon now. I think it'll help me if I can get rid of this pressure, this burden of secrecy. Every time I talk to my friends at the moment and explain to them what's been going on with me and how the journey has come full circle, I start crying at the bit about the boys not knowing - it's as if this might be the key to unlocking what is going on. Let's tell them both when we get home.'

This is not the first time we have had this conversation, previous discussions have centred around whether or not to include Reuben in the revelation. He is only ten, a couple of years older than Ben was when I was diagnosed. Could I bear the thought of him having to carry the burden of news that Ben never had to carry? Tom has persuaded me that it would be better if they were together so that Ben didn't need to 'keep secrets' himself. There will be strength in them both knowing together and being able to talk about it together. And anyway, everything is different now. Reuben will not have to carry the fear of a very sick mother in the same way that Ben would have, had he known at the beginning.

Tom looks straight at me and nods.

'Let's do it today. That will give them another school day to distract them and then there is the trip to look forward to.'

A huge family wedding is planned for the weekend and the boys are bubbling with the excitement of seeing cousins gathering in Devon from all over Europe. Raphs and Lorna would be flying in from Bonn, Daniel from Barcelona, and Matt from Prague. More will be travelling from Cheshire and Dorset and all will meet on Exmoor for a splendid day of feasting and football!

It is the perfect time to tell the boys. There will be a momentary sadness at the news, perhaps, but that will hopefully be replaced by the excitement of the family reunion. Resolved on this course of action we head back to our cars and I follow Tom home. Reuben is beside me playing his favourite song of the moment on my 'phone. The melodic voice of Agnetha Faeltskog, the blonde member of Abba, fills the car. Being a teenager of the 70s I have snapped up her solo album and loved the nostalgia of listening to a childhood heroine singing in her later years. The voice is a little older but unmistakeably the voice of 'the girl with the golden hair.' I love the Scandinavian melancholy - it touches me somewhere deep down and seemingly touches my handsome young son. 'You made my colours fade, too close to the sun...' We sing in harmony. Reuben has a clear, strong voice, the one of our sons, who is undaunted even in church by the fact that it isn't terribly cool for a boy to be singing loudly. He always blushes and frowns when I compliment him and would never want to be in a choir, but there is no doubt in my mind that he could probably be a cathedral chorister if he wanted to. Together, my small son and I join Agnetha in the chorus and gaze in mock romance into each other's eyes. The song is over and other thoughts overtake me as the impending conversation plays around in my mind.

What will their reaction be? Once it is out of the bottle, it can never be put back. Will Ben know already? Has he suspected all along? I am curious if still somewhat anxious. How will Reuben cope with this news especially after losing two uncles to this disease? Every night he prays for God to help all those people with cancer and, a few weeks before, I decided to probe a little.

'Why do you pray so often about cancer, Reuben?' His reply comes swiftly.

'I just want it all to go away!'

Does he know? Is he subliminally aware that my hair loss and exhaustion have had something to do with cancer?

The boys spill out of the cars and start wandering through the large open plan kitchen in search of their computers. Tom calls over to them from the threshold before they can plant themselves in front of their screens.

'Mummy and I want to have a chat with you both for a few minutes. Shall we go in the living room,'

Small family conferences are not uncommon in our household but the boys sense as always that they signal an important moment. Perhaps a revelation about the summer holidays? News about some visitors, the latest regulation about internet use...

I ease myself between my two sons and draw Reuben onto my lap. Tom has positioned himself on the edge of the sofa opposite us and waits for the boys to be quiet. Here we go, I think to myself, please just say it quickly, no big details, just the bare essentials. Don't scare them.

He is a little awkward, conscious that this is a BIG moment in the life of his family.

'Mummy and I want to tell you something that maybe you have been wondering about, to do with Mummy's health four and a half years ago. Do you remember when Mummy was a bit poorly and lost her hair?'

The boys murmur and nod affirmatively. Don't scare them, Tom, just get it out. My brain is pounding.

'Well we didn't tell you this at the time because we didn't want to scare you, but Mummy had cancer and that is why she lost her hair.'

My teeth are clenched to stop myself from sobbing, and silent tears roll down my cheeks as I knead my forehead into the back of Reuben's neck.

Ben turns to look at me and nuzzles my shoulder.

'Mummy had breast cancer and we feel that you are now both old enough to know and we don't want you to worry because she has had a big scan recently and there is absolutely no sign of any cancer in her.'

Both the boys are quiet, absorbing this news and then turn in their seats to hug me.

I swallow my tears, wipe my eyes and chime in with as much breeziness as I can muster,

'Yes, we really didn't want you to be frightened at the time. We wanted you to know when I was really well. If you have any questions at all about it, you can ask anything you like.'

Silence.

'Boys, did either of you know or suspect that Mummy had cancer?' Tom continues.

'I kinda suspected a couple of years ago,' Ben admitted a little sheepishly.

Emotionally intelligent Ben.

So, Ben suspected a while back but had said nothing, had never asked, had simply let things be. I need to watch him, to reflect on how this might have affected him.

Tom breaks the silence with a comforting truth that we have often discussed with our boys.

'You know boys, we are all going to die one day. We are not afraid of dying because we know where we are going, but we are so glad that Mummy is OK now.'

Reuben jumps up from my lap. He has clearly had enough of this tense moment.

'I'm going on the trampoline!' and darts through the open patio doors that lead into the garden.

Ben lingers behind, pausing at the door.

'What would have happened if Mummy hadn't had the medicine?' he asks, turning to Tom.

'She would have died, Ben.'

Our thirteen year old looks thoughtful, nods, and leaves the room.

A few minutes later there is no sign of Reuben on the trampoline. I wander upstairs to find my ten year old slouched on his bed, playing a game on his 'phone.

'You OK, Reuben?'

'I just want to play for a bit.'

I leave him, observing an unusual quietness in my usually bouncy boy and head downstairs into the now empty kitchen to make a cup of tea. Ten minutes later he sidles up to me and asks, 'When did you know that the cancer was out of you?'

I look straight into his big, dark brown eyes.

'It came out right at the beginning, Reuben, it was all cut out. The medicine made sure that it was really gone. It was such strong medicine that it made my hair fall out. But it was worth it because it has all gone.'

'Did the Macmillans look after you, Mummy?'

I smile and shake my head. 'No, my love, they didn't need to, I had lots of help from Daddy and Granny and Grandpa.'

He seems satisfied and I hug him again, reassuring him that I'm fine.

Neither of the boys want to know what will happen if it comes back. Whether or not they would be told. Would it be another secret? I know that if it rears its ugly head again that we will tell them, that they will probably have to know.

As I sit down with my tea on the sofa, reflecting on the past hour's revelation, it is as if a huge weight is slowly lifting off my lungs. Gradually my whole being feels lighter. My mind can relax. The power of the secret has been unlocked and is gone. It doesn't matter now if the boys hear the information from someone else at school or through friends and family. They have heard the revelation from us, at home, at a time we have chosen on a beautiful day when the school year is almost over, and they can look forward with confidence. Thank you, I whisper out loud to myself. Thank you to all who have kept the secret safe over the past years and respected my need to contain this news.

Over the next hours and indeed days, I feel lighter and lighter and while the symptoms I have been experiencing are not gone, I know I am closer to finding a way through this labyrinth.

Later that evening the 'phone rings.

'Hi, Krista, Holly here.' Her voice sounds strained.

'...there are no more treatments left.'

The Growing Sadness

Spring 2016

There is some warmth in the April sunshine although sharp, cold winds blow up the less sheltered cobbled hill as I walk towards the red-brick Victorian building where Holly is incarcerated. Holly who loves all things outdoors: wild camping, muddy walks in green wellies, bird song, unusual mushrooms, bleak hillsides, cliff top rambles and picnics; picnics preferably on a green rug on a hill with all her girls around her. It is not right that some of the last weeks of her life are being spent walled up, especially in this beautiful Browning month.

Tom and I and the boys have just spent an idyllic family week basking in the warm twenty-two degree sunshine of the Canaries, a much needed holiday and the first proper break for the whole family since my 'crash' almost a year ago. The impetus for booking this completely selfish holiday came the moment I received an unexpected legacy from Anita's solicitors. Lovely, lovely ninety-five-year-old Anita, one of our old neighbours whom toddler Reuben and I had adopted some years before as a replacement Granny. We had taken her shopping every week. Nearly blind Anita who had loved Reuben and the short hour or two we were all together at the church toddler group and then the supermarket café and who never stopped talking about how wonderful it was to be taken out.

I had been told of her death some months before but was overwhelmed by the legacy and had immediately decided that some of the money would go towards a charity that I knew Anita would have loved; a charity that enabled Jews to emigrate from various countries and return or make 'aliyah' back to Israel. Her very survival as a nineteen-year-old Jewess in Germany had depended on English Quakers taking her in from Nazi Germany and she would surely love the thought of others who were experiencing persecution in the modern era benefitting from her legacy.

The rest of the money would be spent on a family holiday in the sun. We had visited Fuerteventura before and had wonderful memories of snorkelling in the turquoise green waters and revelling in the villa pool which fronted onto the beach. Across the bay towards the harbour, large ferries and catamarans made the tourist day trips to Lanzarote.

The blue skies, warm sun and luxury villa had briefly muted the pain I was experiencing as my friend deteriorated steadily at home in Salisbury, but Holly was never very far from my thoughts or prayers and I would walk the beach early in the mornings and cast my thoughts daily towards the path that lay ahead of my friend, reciting the 23rd Psalm under my breath. Black lava rocks, remnants of volcanic activity, pitted the shoreline as I prayed.

'Please God, please help her to endure this valley.'

The sun warmed and browned my pale face and I consciously gave myself permission to feel good to be alive. *Why does guilt seem to stalk those who dodge and survive death*, I thought to myself, listening to soft breezes and the gentler side of the Atlantic Ocean kissing the shoreline by my feet. Part of me was in the hospital bed with Holly, suffering and dying with my friend. How easily this could have been my journey five years ago, and yet I survived. How much harder Holly's experience had been with so many more cycles of chemotherapy and repeatedly bad news, until the last drug had been used up and there was, as the doctor put it, 'nothing left in the cupboard.' She had continued throughout to be hopeful, determined to carry on as normal, even going camping with her girls between treatments. Her energy and indomitable spirit was almost exhausting to watch and, even recently, I had struggled to keep up with her on one of our long, muddy walks through her beloved woodlands that February half term only seven weeks ago. But now, like one of its great trees swaying in a raging autumn storm, she had been finally felled and confined to bed by the tumour that was winning the battle over her body.

I wander down the long, empty, white, polished corridors of the hospital, my heart beginning to pound a little. I glance down again at the text Holly's husband, Chris, has just sent, 'Holly is on McKenzie ward which is level C towards the end of the main corridor. Reception is also on level C. Holly is in bay D4. Doors on the right and then the far end on right by the window. Love Chris.' At least she is by a window; that would give some relief from the sense of imprisonment, I think to myself hopefully. Tom has dropped me off at the hospital after our three hour journey and is en route to see Chris and the girls. I want to see Holly on my own and to have a few moments alone after the visit to walk back to her house, a few moments to gather myself.

I am waved in through double doors by the male receptionist, a middle-aged, bespectacled man wearing a dark, comfy pullover. Walking past the main desk, no one really takes any notice of my presence, all completely immersed in the innumerable jobs of the lunchtime period. I wander up to the last bay and survey the heads of a few very elderly ladies. Disorientated eyes peer at me... I look for acknowledgement in the eyes, but they are vacant, lost somewhere in a different world beyond this busy ward.

And then I stop dead in the middle of the room, my eyes locked on the prostrate sleeping form of my friend, immediately recognisable yet utterly transformed by the last seven weeks since we spent that joyful 'girlie' week together. That week in February we had driven to the Jurassic coast and drunk deep of the cliff top views, beaten by winds and exhilarated by the joyful freedom of it all – no boys, no girls, no husbands to consider and cook for; just the two of us. We had picnicked in the shelter of the car, gazing out over a vast sea, and I had let her talk of all the things on her heart; all the things that should be fully discussed and talked about before you are going to die, but which are almost impossible to articulate until the reality has finally dawned that there is only one path left to walk. Holly explained how she had finally told the girls a month ago that she was not going to survive this disease, that for one whole hour their young adolescent faces had locked onto hers, almost without interruption and held her gaze as she explained in the simplest terms she could what was happening to her. The exact words would forever remain between the members of that intimate group, but I could well imagine how agonising that hour had been; the hour that would change everything in their world of innocent hopes. This was the moment that could never be retrieved, and it came on an unforgettable day in the year - New Year's Day. A day when traditionally resolutions are made, and bright hopes stirred in young and old hearts and when the sickening memories of difficult days should be shuffled off and forgotten about as a new year is birthed with Big Ben. Not so for these three young girls whose ages spanned twelve to fifteen. For ever a New Year would signal the end of their world.

I stare at the body in front of me, and then turn again towards the face of the old lady in the next-door bed who is staring at me. I search for a glimmer of sympathy, a weak smile perhaps, but am met with a blank, empty look. I turn back towards my friend. The greying curls have grown a little longer and thicker, but her face is shrunken, eyes sunken deep and brown into dark sockets, heavy lids shut in sleep. Holly's once chubby neck is now painfully thin and the skin on her arms has begun to look papery and old, her true age revealed only in the pale, smooth skin of her hands. A baby pink hospital gown covers her distended stomach to the knee, revealing thick, fluid-filled legs which have been encased in brown compression stockings. Short white polka dot socks keep her feet warm.

I stand motionless for what seems like an age, but which is probably only a few seconds before moving to Holly's bedside. I don't really want to disturb my friend's sleep but know that I only have an hour. I gently touch her hand and Holly's eyes blink open, exhausted, a little startled, but then full of warmth. She manages a weak but definite smile at her old friend. I feel my own face crumpling and bury my hands in Holly's curls and bend over, hugging her gently.

I weep.

We whisper into each other's ears softly.

'It's a sister thing,' Holly whispers.

'Yes,' I sniff, 'It's a sister thing.'

'I love you Holly, I shall be there for your girls and for Chris and for your parents.'

'I know you will,' she says, barely audible. 'I know you will, thank you for coming.'

We talk a little while about being in hospital, the angry redness around the drain on her abdomen and the need to be on antibiotics to get it under control, about her daughter's birthday in just two days and the hope that she might be able to go home for that. And then it is clear to me that I should leave and let her sleep. I take a selfie with Holly, grin, squeeze her hand and slip a blue mussel shell into it. I see her thumb gently rubbing the soft perlescent inner shell as she drifts away in sleep. I walk out of the bay, the ward, the hospital, swallowing tears behind my sunglasses and walk down the hill, praying that I will be able to hold myself together for Holly's girls.

The Intervention

February 1943

The arrival of Johannes that magical Christmas Eve lent new strength and hope to the Hoffmann family and Max was in buoyant mood as he put on his new Wehrmacht uniform some weeks later, in preparation for his first posting to France. His unit was due to move out from Brunswick the next day.

'Look Mama, what do you think?'

The tall, gangly youth stood in the doorway between the hallway and the kitchen, standing as straight as he could in front of his mother. Hannelore sat next to Irma at the kitchen table over a mound of carrots they were peeling. She looked up into the proud, beaming face of her second son and couldn't help smiling. He was the spitting image of his father, even down to those milky blue eyes, but his uniform sagged around his slender figure, confirming to Hannelore just how ridiculous this war was, this war that sent eighteen-year-old-boys with a few hairs on their chin as fodder to be slaughtered on the frontline.

She bit her lip and forced herself to smile.

'You look very fine, my son,' she said, 'now when is it you need to catch that train for Brunswick?'

'It leaves at 10 o'clock tomorrow. I'll walk to the station Mama, I know Papa will be busy with patients and I can pick Helmut up on the way.'

'I don't mind driving you, your kitbag will be heavy.'

'No it's *fine*, thank you, Mama.'

There was something emphatic in his response that made Hannelore realise he didn't want his mother seeing him off at the station.

'Well I have baked plenty of your favourite ginger biscuits to take with you – a little reminder of Christmas - and Tante Martha has knitted you a new scarf. You will need it if this winter is as bad as the last one.'

Max grinned and headed up the spiral staircase to his room to change out of his uniform and find his sisters for a last tease.

Hannelore held the paring knife in her hand a moment and it shook involuntarily. Irma pretended not to notice. Her hand trembled more and more these days. Johannes had been back at the Eastern Front for a month now and Max would be heading west towards France, to relieve troops that had been stationed there for the past six months. She was glad that he would escape the biting easterly winter that his older brother was enduring. At least Johannes was safe from too much actual combat – she hoped and prayed that the medical badge he wore on his arm would protect him from direct sniper fire. Max would be less fortunate but at least France was safe and occupied and hopefully he would just be patrolling the Atlantic Wall rather than being in the line of fire. The threat of invasion from England was always a possibility, in spite of the thousands of mines that the German troops had laid along the beaches of Normandy.

'I want to teach, Mama, like you. I want to be a grammar school teacher and do something good for our country after this war is over and

Germany is great again,' he had declared only a few months ago, spurred on by family discussions about the need to choose his university courses.

'You don't want to become a doctor, then, Max?' she enquired, teasingly, knowing what the answer would be.

'Ach no, Mama, you know how I hate the sight of blood.'

Life on the Front would be a challenge for Max, she mused to herself. Her son often played the fool at home in front of his siblings, full of fun and always acting the clown, but she would also see moments when he was alone in his room, lying on his bed and just staring at the ceiling. He had not enjoyed boarding school, she knew that, but having Johannes there had helped and he had put a brave face on it. Every start of term was a wrench from his family and the stomach aches would usually signal it was time to return to school and leave his beloved home. He was not as academic as his older brother but his head was always in a book, usually a ripping tale of adventure on the high seas or in a jungle. But Max was like glue in the family and everyone simply called him *Bruder*. He didn't need to be called by name – his siblings just referred to him in that way and he came to represent everything a brother should be – a tease, a laugh, a joker, an arm around the shoulder, a piggy back ride and often a ducking in the lake on long, hot summer days in the holidays. Only once in the last couple of years had Hannelore come into his room to find him with his head in his hands.

'What is wrong, my son?' she had said to him as she sat on the edge of his bed.

'Mama, I had a terrible dream about Johannes. He was lying in the mud, covered in snow. Every bit of him was frozen. It was so real that when I woke up, I was convinced he had really died. I don't want him to die, Mama.'

'Shh, Shh.' Hannelore held her son's head and stroked his brown hair, wiping the tears from his eyes as she sat beside him on the bed.

'Johannes is fine,' she said softly, 'he is working in the field hospital – he will be quite safe there. It is quite normal to be worried about him. We all miss him.'

'It's not the same without him, Mama. I don't laugh as much these days. It was good to be able to talk with him at Christmas. He told me a lot about the war.'

Hannelore could see her son sinking and tried to lighten the mood.

'Why don't you go and tickle your little sisters – they need a big brother to cheer them up – they will miss you terribly.' Max appeared not to hear his mother.

'When will this war end? It's been over three years now. Surely there must come a time when the politicians agree to stop? Why are we always at war? Papa had to go to war and now we have to go to war. Why does God allow this to happen?'

She looked into his sixteen-year-old eyes and searched in her own mind for the right answer.

'God doesn't cause these wars, Max, wars come when people stop loving God and only think of themselves.'

'But surely he has the power to stop these wars if he wants to - stop all the senseless killing?'

'He loves us too much to force us to follow his way, Max. Sometimes you do things that seem good at the time but later you realise that it was selfish.'

'Like taking the last piece of cake?' he said, smiling up at her gentle brown eyes.

'Yes,' she smiled back, 'and so it is with governments, Max. God is not a dictator.'

He nodded slowly, understanding what she was saying without her having to spell it out to him.

'Does he love the Jews, though, Mama? Didn't they kill him on the cross? Is God getting his own back on them now through our nation?'

Images of that November night in 1938 were vivid in his mind. For almost ten years now, his young mind had been saturated with antisemitic propaganda.

Hannelore's eyes flashed but she tried not to show it, but her voice signalled to him that this was the wrong answer.

'Is that what your friends are saying?'

'Everyone is saying it, Mama. Our Hitler Youth leader, Bernd, at boarding school has been talking about it in meetings for years now. The posters all over the town are full of the fact that the Jews are our enemy. And all the Jewish businesses have been destroyed. Are they really so bad? Frau Samuels' family have always seemed such good sports – I can't run as fast as Konrad Schwann. And you should see him on the rings in the gymnasium – I was watching him when I picked up Eva from her meeting on Wednesday – the boys were doing a gymnastics demonstration for the girls' groups.'

'The Jews are not our enemies, Max. You are old enough to know now that I do not believe this, and your father and I have great respect for the Samuels and for others in our town who are Jewish. It saddens us to see them treated this way and whilst we do not protest about this publicly for fear of trouble from the Gestapo, we will not openly support it either. Your father will do everything he can to protect Frau Samuels from being deported to a labour camp, and I bring food to the house when I can. I do something else, Max, something you could do too – I pray for the Jewish people. They study hard, they work hard, they always held the top positions in the universities – my own professor at Göttingen was a Jewish academic in English literature and I learned so much from him. Do not talk about these things I have told you with your friends, Max, but do not join in when you see Jewish people bullied – that is never the right way to treat people. Is God punishing the Jews? I don't think so. Our Saviour was a Jew and he chose to die. Yes, he was rejected by his people, but many Jews did follow him, and all the first disciples were Jewish. The early church was full of Jews who recognised him as their Messiah. God will not abandon his chosen people, whatever this government does to them.'

Max stared thoughtfully at the patterns on the wallpaper, listening intently to his mother. His mind was a turmoil of thoughts. Going off to fight in this war was something he had been relishing the thought of, not least because it was a chance to escape school and delay university and actually have an adventure, do something important for his country. His friends at school had all been looking forward to their eighteenth birthdays, and one by one they had left with a great roar of excitement

212

down the long drive that led away from the imposing school building. For Max, it meant he couldn't start training to be a teacher. For some time, he had sensed his parents' disapproval of the government, but had never heard it articulated quite like this. He respected his mother for being open with him and knew he would need to be quiet around his sisters and friends.

Yes, Max was a sensitive soul and Hannelore vowed to pray hourly for this son while he was away.

The jingling of the telephone in the surgery shook her out of her thoughts. Georg was still out on a few routine calls which had taken him to Brunswick hospital, and she was expecting him back any moment. Perhaps he was phoning from the hospital to say he would be late. She walked in, careful to shut the door behind her as she always did when taking calls.

'Guten Tag! Is the Herr Doktor there?'

The voice sounded urgent.

'Is that you Sergeant Bauer?'

Hannelore thought she recognised the burly voice of the town policeman.

'Ja, Frau Hoffman – is the doctor there?'

'He should be back very soon, Sergeant Bauer. Can I help in any way and pass on a message?'

'It's urgent, Frau Doktor. The SS at Fuchsburg have been telephoning me this morning. They are rounding up every Jew who hasn't already been deported to the labour camps to come to the station tomorrow morning. They've clearly been investigating all their records in great

213

detail. They have said that if Frau Samuels does not come, they will collect her themselves. I know she has been a regular patient of Doktor Hoffmann and that she is not very strong,'

'What is it exactly that you want my husband to do, Sergeant Bauer?' Hannelore was very careful in how she worded the question.

'Perhaps a direct telephone call to the headquarters would help? She is elderly and frail – what harm can she do anyone, the journey would kill her. She was always very kind to me when I was a boy, always giving me sugar crystals when I went into her shop with errands from my mother. You understand, I think, Frau Doktor.'

Hannelore smiled to herself and reassured the sergeant that she would communicate the information to her husband.

A humanitarian soul, she thought to herself, *a rarity in the police force.* So many had compromised and signed up for an easy life under the regime. There were precious few Jews in Borkhausen – a relief in many ways for Bauer. He wouldn't have to cross his conscience too many times and capitulate with the Gestapo; just keep his head down and do a good job keeping the peace. Erik Bauer loved his town. His family had lived here for generations and his parents owned the butcher's. Erik's brothers had taken on helping with the family business but he had chosen a different path, albeit one that meant he could continue serving the community of his childhood.

Time was of the essence and it was a relief to hear the sound of Georg's car driving down into the cellar garage. Hannelore went down to meet her husband and sat next to him in the car so as not to be overheard by anyone in the house. Even with Irma they had to be careful, as she might be eavesdropping from the kitchen window which was always open during the day to allow a little ventilation.

'Georg, Sergeant Bauer has been on the telephone within the last half hour. He says the SS are expecting Frau Samuels to be deported from the station tomorrow. They will collect her if she fails to appear.'

Georg's face was set, his mouth a thin grim line, his hand tightened around the steering wheel.

'I will 'phone them directly,' he said, 'I will do it now.' They left the car and briskly marched through the cellar and up into the hallway. Georg strode into his surgery, Hannelore following him, and she shut the door behind them. Sitting down in the patient's chair, her eyes bored into his, as he dialled the SS Headquarters in Fuchsburg.

'Ja, here is Doktor Hoffman from Borkhausen.'

'Ja, Ja... Ja... I understand that you have sent orders for Frau Esther Samuels of Goethestrasse to be deported by train to a labour camp tomorrow? Yes, Samuels, Esther Samuels. It is quite out of the question.'

Silence.

'I don't care about the quota of Jews that you need to submit to Berlin, this lady is extremely frail and will in all probability die in transit if she were to be moved from her bed. She is not at all well and as her doctor, I cannot sanction this action.'

Silence.

'No, and *I* am telling you that as her doctor, I cannot sanction this action – she is not well enough to travel and that is all there is to say!'

Georg's voice sounded resolute even though his brow was beaded with sweat, fist tightly clenched around the telephone receiver.

Hannelore looked up anxiously into his face.

Georg lay down the receiver.

'What did they say?'

Georg looked into her dark brown, earnest eyes with something of a freshly awakened love and said simply,

'They told me they hoped she would rot in hell, and that they would be visiting the town next month to check up on her health. They hung up on me.'

They held each other's hands and nodded their heads slowly, smiling at each other. A small but also gigantic victory in the lives of the Hoffmanns had just played out within a few minutes. The significance of this moment was not lost on Hannelore.

'Well done, my husband, my good doctor, well done.'

'It's not over. They will be back. But for now we have won a little time for our Frau Samuels. Now where is my lunch?' he said, patting her hand.

After they had eaten, Georg and Hannelore walked into town together to pay Frau Samuels a visit. They walked arm in arm, something they hadn't done for many months, a quiet peace in both their hearts.

A worried looking Sergeant Bauer was hovering near the house and Georg explained what had happened.

'Hans, we need to keep Frau Samuels as invisible as possible for as long as possible. We have put them off, but if word escapes that she is recovering well and has been seen, then they may come knocking in the middle of the night and there is nothing I can do. If they contact you again, just say that her condition has worsened slightly.'

The police officer nodded, a visible look of relief on his careworn face.

Georg turned and rang the bell at the Samuels' house.

No one answered for a long time, but a twitch of the curtain led to the door being opened a crack.

'It's Doktor Hoffmann, I've come to your aunt.'

Wilhem Schwann answered the door, a short diminutive man with a receding hairline. He let Georg and Hannelore in, clearly anxious about the news that Sergeant Bauer had filtered through to them as a warning earlier in the day.

'Please come in Herr Doktor, Frau Hoffman. We are so terribly worried. What is going to happen?'

'Be calm, Wilhelm, the SS will not be coming today or tomorrow. I have told them very clearly that your aunt is not in a fit state to travel anywhere, let alone a labour camp.' He continued in a serious tone.

'But you must be vigilant. How many visitors are coming to the shop now?'

'Sadly, hardly anyone. Most of my textiles have been seized by Schmidts and Werner who have divided up the spoils between them.'

Georg looked around and noticed how little was left on the shelves of this once rich emporium of textiles and soft furnishings that was the renown of Borkhausen. Kristallnacht was a vivid memory. The nauseating hysteria that had rampaged through the large cities of Germany had even infected the mainly good townsfolk of Borkhausen, where everyone knew everyone at least by name. Thankfully for the Jews here, there was no great synagogue to target, its meeting hall having disappeared many years ago. The remnants of that community were largely Jews who had intermarried and assimilated, with little outward sign of their ethnicity. Seventy-five-year old Frau Samuels was one of the few whose parentage was pure. She loved this town she had grown up in and although everyone knew she was Jewish, they were very fond of her and respected her family. Her nephew's sons were the top athletes in the school, and everyone wanted to be friends with Konrad and Otto. Eva was in fact a little besotted with their athletic prowess, their dark hair and swarthy complexion.

'No one can beat them, Mama. They run like the wind... and you should see them doing gymnastics - Konrad can somersault on the rings, forwards *and* backwards!'

'Thank you for bringing us such good news,' gasped her nephew. 'Please come upstairs and tell my aunt yourself, she will be so happy. I will make us some coffee. I have some stored away for a special occasion.'

Hannelore went up the steep wooden stairs behind the shop first and was greeted with a weak smile by Esther Samuels, who was lying in her bed surrounded by bottles of medicine.

'Ach, Frau Hoffman, how kind of you to visit me.'

'How are you, today, Frau Samuels?'

'My back is painful, and I feel so weak in my legs, but I keep cheerful.'

Hannelore set down her basket and withdrew a large sealed glass jar.

'I have brought some stewed apple for you - we had such a harvest of apples last autumn that my cellar is overflowing.'

'That is so kind. And how are your fine sons?'

'Johannes writes when he can, and Max is preparing to go to France.'

'This war must end soon, Frau Hoffman – it is 1943, we have been at war for over three years. How much longer can it go on? Do you hear much news from outside Germany? I have relatives in Budapest.'

'I'm afraid I know very little of news from other countries, Frau Samuels,' she lied. Not even Georg knew how often Hannelore secretly tuned into the Overseas Service to hear how the war was progressing from the perspective of London journalists. Her perfect English was a great asset.

'I must let you rest now,' she continued, 'and will return in a few days with some eggs. Our chickens are laying well at the moment.'

She left the room and descended the stairs, leaving her husband alone with his patient to ask a few medical questions before coming down with a leather bag in his hand. As they walked the five minutes back to their house, a warm glow in their hearts at saving one soul from the labour camps, Georg clutched the bag tightly.

'Is that from Frau Samuels?' Hannelore asked casually.

'Yes, she wants me to keep it safe. I think she is worried that someone might steal it or that it might be taken by the Gestapo if they come calling.'

'What is inside?'

'Oh, just some papers I think. I will lock it in the cellar in one of the strong boxes until she wants it. It should be safe there from prying eyes.'

Georg glanced at the villa opposite as they approached their house, and for the first time felt a strange peace descend upon his battered heart.

'Leah will be playing a happier melody,' he thought to himself.

Hannelore placed her empty basket on the table and started busying herself in the kitchen as Georg disappeared down the stairs into the cellar. Twenty minutes later he returned, wandered into his office and, despite the cold winter air, opened the window a little and sat in his chair and stared at the pianist's desolate house.

The Rescue

The next morning was a Saturday and Irma had the day off to visit her mother and siblings in Brunswick. Armed with a bag of fruit kindly donated by Hannelore, she flew along the landing from her room at the back of the house and tiptoed lightly down the sweeping staircase and across the hallway. She needed to hurry to catch the early train. As Georg heard the side door out of the hallway click shut, he padded out of the bedroom in his paisley, blue silk dressing gown. He strode over towards the narrow wooden stairway up to the attic and pushed open the stiff door at the top which led into a gloomy cavernous space. He gazed around in the half light of the morning. In the middle of this large loft was the spine of the house, the great chimney stack that was fed from the peat stoves in all the downstairs rooms. Old, billowy cobwebs spanned a raised window overlooking the garden down to the river. Years of spiders had woven their deadly traps in this semi-darkened cave of a room. The great beams and struts of the house were all visible here, no fine wallpapers or carpets, just dusty floorboards, and a brick wall opposite the gable end with two small doors set into them. Near to the doors were orderly piles of Margarete's and Eva's toys, ones that came down periodically when they were bored with the current ones. Dolls houses sat in lonely splendour, and dolls that had even belonged to Hannelore and had seen better days but were too precious to throw away, had been carefully laid in a white pram and covered in a knitted blanket. Sometimes Eva would creep up here when she wanted to forget the war and escape from everyone and play quietly or read. Whenever her mother asked her where she had been all morning, she would reply, 'In Heaven.' And Hannelore smiled knowingly.

Georg walked over to the two doors with their spindly metal handles and latch mechanisms and pushed them open one by one. Both rooms were exactly the same size, both tiny spaces large enough for a small single bed and not much else. Inherited pieces of furniture, boxes of old family books and toys and rejected bedroom ornaments and fading lampshades were stored up here, the things that Hannelore didn't want in a cold, damp cellar. Christmas decorations and suitcases were also piled high and in the corner of one room was a small collection of cushions and blankets that Eva had arranged as a place she could come and hide and read her beloved Heidi books. Each room borrowed the light of one window set high up in the wall with only a thin wall between the two and no separate ceilings. Georg peered in and sniffed air musty with dustsheets, piled loosely in a box for when furniture needed covering during holidays. Hannelore had strung a line between two beams in the main room so that she could dry towels and bedsheets quickly in the winter. Worn pegs hung limply, unused for several months.

He turned at the sound of a creaking floorboard on the stairway and Hannelore appeared in her long, cream dressing gown.

'Couldn't you sleep either?' she said blearily, 'I heard you climbing the stairs.'

'No,' Georg replied, smiling at her dishevelled hair, always so neatly pinned back into a bun during the day. 'I couldn't switch off at all, just lay in bed thinking about Frau Samuels, and Max heading off to France today.'

'Yes, my heart is heavy. I don't think I could bear it if anything happened to either of our boys. What are you doing poking about up here?' she asked, looking curiously at her husband.

'Well, I've been lying awake thinking and thinking and thinking and you may think this is utterly ridiculous...'

Hannelore's eyes widened.

'...but I'm wondering...' he hardly dared to utter his thoughts, when his wife interrupted.

' - if we could hide Frau Samuels here?' she continued in lowered tones.

Georg looked at his wife, speechless.

'Why, yes, that is *exactly* what I was thinking.'

'I have been tossing all night thinking the same thing in between the most unpleasant dreams. I think it is perhaps the only thing we can do. The Gestapo will be back, perhaps sooner than we think, and to find her another hiding place would only put others in great danger. The fewer that know about her the better. It is impossible to know who we can really trust anyway. No one will suspect the respectable Doktor Hoffmann.'

'What about Irma?' Georg added pacing the attic floor in circles, 'she has been with us a long time.'

'But her older brother is an avid Nazi and she talks about him in glowing terms. I'm not sure she would be able to keep it secret. We will have to manage without her and let her go, Georg. Perhaps we could tell her that we are struggling to support having a maid at this time and that we need to furlough her for a while with an extra month's salary so that she can find other work. I know Frau Deichman is looking for extra help with her newborn twins and she is well able to afford Irma. I will call her later this morning.'

'Perfect,' Georg responded, 'the fewer people in the house who know the better. It would be much safer for her to be in the attic than in the cellar, less damp and much warmer. The heat from the chimney will warm this room. Any visitors downstairs are less likely to hear her if she is coughing and calling out and the girls' friends are constantly running in and out of the cellar into the garden.'

'If we black out the windows too, then she can have an oil lamp on and no one will wonder what is going on in the attic,' said Hannelore, ' but how are we going to get her here without anyone noticing and how are we going to explain away her disappearance to the Gestapo?'

Two large green eyes peered at them both from the top of the staircase.

'Ach Eva! Was machst Du? How long have you been there?'

'I couldn't sleep and kept hearing floorboards creaking, so I came up to see if Fritzi Mader was here.'

'We've chased Fritzi away. Our little house martin only runs around at night under the eaves of the house. How long have you been here, little rabbit?' her father said coaxingly.

'Not long... who are you going to bring into the attic?'

Georg and Hannelore looked at each other and Georg walked over and knelt down beside his daughter's sleepy face, framed by its mass of blonde curls.

'We will tell you later, but first we must make a fine breakfast for your brother before he goes off to the station today. Will you help Mama?'

The distraction was enough for Eva for the time being and they all descended quickly out of the attic and closed the door on their secret.

The household began to rise swiftly as if no one had really slept that night, least of all Max whose head was full of dreams of camaraderie and medals won in extreme acts of bravery. He so wanted his parents to be proud of him, for his teachers to all pat him on the shoulder as a fine young German. His stomach had also churned most of the night in trepidation at what lay ahead. The memory of a howling mother was one that would forever haunt him. But it was not going to happen to him.

He put on his newly pressed uniform and stood tall in front of the hallway mirror, his parents watching him from the kitchen threshold.

'You look very smart, Private Maximillian Hoffmann!' Georg pronounced loudly and went to wrap an arm around his son's shoulders 'My, you are tall. When did that happen? Come on, my boy, let's feed you up before your long journey across the continent.'

Ham and eggs were sizzling in the pan in the kitchen when the doorbell rang. Everyone looked at each other, dreading another patient call out on their last precious breakfast with Max. As the only doctor working now in Borkhausen, Georg was used to relentless call outs from the doorstep. He opened the door to see Gerbich's puffy red face, beaming at him. Georg was open-mouthed for a second and all the energy seemed to drain from his face. The surgeon strode past him into the hallway, saluting 'Heil Hitler' as he walked in with a pointed air of superiority.

'Georg! - how good to see you. Hannelore, Heil Hitler. My, my! Is this your Max, all uniformed up for the Reich. Well done my boy. Heil Hitler!'

'Heil Hitler!' Max responded automatically to the booming voice of Doktor Gerbich, saluting rigidly. Hannelore's arms remained frozen by her side as her heart sank into a place of deep fury.

'Hermann, to what do we owe the pleasure of this visit?'

'Mmmm! That smells good Hannelore, am I interrupting breakfast?'

'We were just about to have a last meal with Max before he catches the train to join his infantry' Georg interjected sensing Hannelore's seething tone.

'Aha! A historic day for your family then Georg. I won't stop, just wanted to let you know that Fuchsburg are stepping up operations in this area. The Führer is particularly keen for all us on the frontline of medicine to be rigorous with our patient lists and follow all the edicts, if you understand my meaning, Georg. The garden needs a thorough weeding if we are to do our job properly. I've been assigned Borkhausen as part of my new role and will be regularly liaising with Gestapo. I'm sure we can rely on you to be watchful and not let anything slip through the net.'

Georg nodded grimly.

'I will do my job properly, Hermann, you need not worry on that score.'

Eva couldn't help noticing that Doktor Gerbich looked even fatter than the last time she had seen him after her operation. It seemed odd to her, given that most people she knew had grown thinner as the war had progressed.

The family finally had some peace and sat down to a hearty breakfast, all talk of Gerbich being banned from the table. Hannelore worked hard to stifle the churning emotions of saying farewell to her beautiful blue-eyed son, and struggled to take her eyes off him throughout the meal.

Max insisted on saying goodbye at the front door. Hannelore and Georg both held their son tightly in the porch away from public gaze and told him to write often, to listen to his superiors and not to do anything stupidly heroic. Hannelore silently pressed into his hands a small prayer book and their eyes met for a moment before he broke the gaze, turned and strode out down the steps of the villa and down Gartenstrasse in the pale morning light, looking back only once to wave energetically. His sisters skipped annoyingly behind him for a few hundred yards until he met up with one of his comrades and then they sloped back to the house. Georg shut the door while the girls wandered into the garden and held Hannelore for a moment before she swept up the stairs into the bathroom and sobbed like a child on the floor.

Sometime later he joined her in the bedroom and they sat together and discussed the attic question. It was good to focus on something else. In many ways it was a relief that Max too was out of the house as it meant even fewer people knowing about the hiding of Frau Samuels, and their idealistic son may have struggled more than the girls with the harbouring of a Jew. Georg sat down on the armchair in the corner of the room and unveiled what had come to him in that sleepless night.

'Listen carefully Hanne, we do not have very much time - we must make the most of Irma being out of the house today. With any luck, few patients will call. We need to pretend that Frau Samuels dies at home, and make sure that that her body is *visibly* removed from the house in a coffin weighted with stones. Only Herr Weiss our undertaker will know. It's a risk but I think we can trust him. He has known the Schwanns for many years and they have always provided fine silk and cotton fabric for his coffins. His men will bring out the coffin that he has prepared with me and the family, ready to take to the Jewish cemetery within twenty-four hours of death as is the Jewish custom. We can make sure that Bauer writes a report to the effect of having witnessed this and I shall of course sign the death certificate as usual.'

Hannelore listened uncharacteristically open-mouthed as Georg explained this extraordinary plan.

'So where will Frau Samuels be?'

'She will still be upstairs in the house and the coffin will be downstairs when the men collect it. We must hope she is as silent as the falling snow. When the funeral is over we return late at night and drive her to our house in the back of the Mercedes covered with a blanket. Everyone is used to seeing my car out at night doing visits so it shouldn't arouse too much suspicion and I can record in my diary that I have been visiting someone in the vicinity. We then lead her into the house via the garage and up through the house to the attic, carrying her if necessary. The attic will need to be furnished adequately with a bed, an appropriate commode she can sit on comfortably, and a table and chairs.' Georg paused to let some of this information sink in, but Hannelore's mind was already racing ahead.

'I can use some of the furniture up there already from my aunt's old house and we can perhaps dismantle the guest bed and carry it up. It will be a lot more comfortable than the old camp bed that is up there. It might be better to do that once Irma has left our service and just give the attic a good clean today and sweep and scrub the floors and wash the windows. What about the girls? We cannot keep this secret from them. They are used to going up there to play.'

They looked thoughtfully out of the bedroom window. Margarete was older and more sensible, but also besotted with her Youth leader. Could she be trusted not to let it slip? Eva was less brainwashed by the regime but also younger and might whisper something to her best friend, whose family were very keen supporters of the government. They would not be allowed to bring their friends up to their bedrooms, which would be hard for them, although perhaps as a treat they could have a dedicated playroom downstairs.

After much discussion and deliberation, Georg and Hannelore decided that they would have to tell their daughters, but not until Frau Samuels was safely in the house, to prevent them blurting out any of the plan before it had been carried out.

Hannelore visited Frau Deichman that morning, and thankfully the path was paved for Irma to go and work there in a week's time. Gerda Deichman was grateful for the extra help even if a little bemused at Hannelore letting her only maid go. Swallowing her pride at appearing to be in financial need she bravely presented a positive front.

'I have lots of help from my two girls now,' she explained at the doorstep of the Deichman villa, 'They are old enough to look after themselves when I have to go out. We are all quite enjoying cooking for ourselves. You will love Irma – she is very good with little ones.'

The task of the day now was to clean the attic while Irma was out and to give the floors a good scrub with boiling water and bicarbonate of soda.

Hannelore called the girls in to help under the pretence of sorting out the attic and throwing away things they didn't need any more so that they could make a larger den in the two little rooms. Eva and Margarete both groaned but once sweeping was underway and after Georg had dealt with the cobwebs and removed the larger spiders into the garden, they were happy to help sort out old books, polish up the old chairs and tables and move them into the main loft area, relocating the suitcases and Christmas decorations into a designated corner of the loft out of the way. Hannelore shooed them all out of the attic after the sweeping and sorting was done so that she could wash the floor 'because mice might have been running around up here.' It was hard work, work that she was not used to doing, work she would ordinarily have given to Irma. But she harnessed a new energy within her, driven on by thoughts of Frau Samuels and also the need to do something to take her mind off Max and, as she mopped, she prayed earnestly for her son and for the safety of their plan.

At the end of the day when the girls were in bed and fast asleep, Georg and Hannelore crept up to have another look at the attic. It was cleaner and a little fresher. The windows had been opened to air the whole room all day and the musty drapes had been taken down to the cellar and replaced with clean blackout curtains. The two small rooms looked clean and ready with space for a small bed and side table and oil lamp. Frau Samuels would be warmer in there than in the great draughty room and she could always potter around for a bit of movement if she felt well enough. The second small room was to be used for her commode with a washstand and basin, both of which would be brought up from Johannes' room once Irma had left their service. If the girls did chatter to their maid about their attic cleaning, she would simply be told it was a 'sorting out the clutter day' and that the small rooms were to become bigger hideaways for the girls and their friends.

'This is good, it will bring hope,' sighed Georg, 'and I can keep an eye on my patient too. I will speak to Weiss on Monday morning and then visit the Schwanns, once the plan is in place. The less Frau Samuels knows the better until the last moment and the girls mustn't know a thing until she is safely with us.'

'Let us pray the Gestapo don't come for at least two weeks.'

Hannelore headed down the stairs, yawning,

'I will miss Irma.'

The Attic

Wednesday

April blossoms appeared early in the Hoffmann garden and Georg and Hannelore were strolling in the late morning sun along its sandy perimeter pathway. Their children had spent many happy hours here, charging around on scooters and little wooden wagons, chasing each other and seeing how fast a circuit they could manage. Memories of the boys flashed in front of them and they found solace for a moment in reminiscing. It was easier to think of them tumbling around the garden scrambling for Easter eggs than the thought of them on the frontline of action in strange places, surrounded by hostile villages and towns.

Their conversation turned to the pressing matter in hand as they paused in front of the fence overlooking the river. No one would overhear their conversation here. The girls were both in school for the morning and none of the neighbours were visible in their gardens. Even so they spoke in low tones, Georg gesticulating at the old willow tree as if they were discussing horticultural matters, Hannelore nodding as if in agreement.

'Weiss came this morning and we discussed the matter again and he thinks that we need to move before the end of this week. He has a cousin in Fuchsburg who said that the Gestapo have been stepping up house raids in the villages. I shall go and visit Frau Samuels shortly. I will make sure that I am seen going in and have a quiet word with her family. When you go to market tomorrow it will be important to spread the word that you are very concerned that she has taken a turn for the worse and that she may not last the week. A recurrence of the pneumonia. Explain that I am treating her and making her as comfortable as possible at home as she is too unwell to be transferred to hospital. I shall say the same to Schwann. We shall say nothing to the girls until she is upstairs and in the attic on Saturday night. There will be no school on Sunday which will give them time to get used to the idea and we can all adjust a little.'

'Irma is also settled at the Deichmans and I hear that she is a great success with the family. I think for her it will be lovely looking after babies. We may not be able to coax her back later!'

Hannelore tried to sound cheerful, but her stomach tightened and her fists clenched as she absorbed the enormity of what they were about to do. There was no turning back now. Helmut Weiss, the town's most trusted and respected undertaker, a man who knew every family in the town, now knew. Time was running out for Frau Samuels. She dared not even begin to think too hard about what would happen if the plan was discovered, or if the girls let something slip. It would be an immediate deportation to the labour camps and separation from each other and worse still probable execution for her children under medieval Sippenhaft laws that the Nazis had resurrected in these times. Any blood connection however young would be linked to a crime against the state. It must not fail and she dare not betray her fears to anyone. A verse she had memorised as a young girl came to mind, *Though I walk through the valley of the shadow of death, I shall fear no evil...* She had often wondered what that meant – the *shadow of death* ? Did it just mean when you grieved the death of a loved one? Or was it as now, a tangible darkness that you could almost feel coming towards you? Yes, this felt as if they were plunging into the *shadow* of death, walking dangerously close to the darkness. She whispered a prayer as they walked back into the house.

233

Georg headed out down Gartenstrasse on his visits by foot, trusty leather bag swinging gently by his side, doffing his hat to acquaintances he passed on the street, trying to look as normal as possible. Hannelore watched him from the window of the surgery, checked on her stew in the kitchen, an assemblage of ham and whatever vegetables she had in the house, and then went to inspect the attic before the girls returned home. In the days since Irma's departure, she had begun furnishing the little rooms with the basic items needed to make life comfortable. She had even carried up a tiny bookcase and old mirror from the snug and selected a few of her favourite books for Frau Samuels to browse through if she felt well enough, as well as a small collection of the girls' old books for nostalgia. The commode and wash basin were also in place and an enamel pail with a lid to empty the commode into. There would be regular journeys up and down the stairs to the attic but, once the girls knew, their young legs would help. Even the bed had been dismantled and carried up late one evening and prepared with sheets and blankets. Hannelore had carefully locked the door behind her and hidden the key to stop prying eyes poking about and asking questions. There was plenty to distract the girls out in the garden and, with the weather getting better now, the attic would be less interesting.

The next morning Georg went again to visit Frau Samuels and to finalise plans with her nephew. Helmut Weiss had also brought some broken pieces of stone from the workshop where the gravestones were carved and deposited them there, carefully wrapped in old rags, to add weight to the coffin. Final pieces would be brought on the day to match the correct heaviness of a coffin for his men, who had to assume they were carrying Frau Samuels out of the house. She herself would remain completely in the dark about the plan until the day she was going to be transferred to the Hoffmann attic. There was too great a risk that the shock or fear of what might happen would cause her to be gravely ill. She was already in a weakened state of health having recovered very slowly from her winter bout of pneumonia.

Hannelore headed off to the farmer's market, walking somewhat more briskly than usual and feigning a much greater interest in all of her acquaintances lives, keen to be able to drop the seed into their minds that Frau Samuels was failing. For some it was of little interest, a reflection of their politics and their disdain of all things Jewish, others who cared more for the old lady and her family were saddened but expressed relief that 'at least she may die in peace at home with her loved ones.' Most knew that she was fortunate to be in the town at all and some expressed surprise that she was still alive as so little had been heard of her for some time.

Hannelore was satisfied that her forthcoming 'death' would be no great surprise to the ladies of the town, knowing full well that it would 'happen' that evening. She walked home, basket of fresh asparagus and new potatoes under her arm, unable to share with anyone other than Georg the full terror of what they were about to do.

Over lunch the girls chattered about the school day and the plans for the afternoon. Georg mentioned to them how poorly Frau Samuels was and that he was off to visit her again later in the day. He wanted them to tell their friends at school on Friday and for the news to trickle throughout the village in the same way that news spread like wildfire when fallen sons of Borkhausen and its surrounding villages were reported in the papers. Georg had requested that Schwann report the 'death' in the Borkhausen Zeitung for everyone to read. The obituaries were compulsive reading for so many as the death tolls of young men rose each week as well as the usual mortalities amongst the elderly.

Later that afternoon, the doorbell rang, and Hannelore rose from her typewriter and went to answer it, heart pounding. It was Wilhelm Schwann. He spoke loudly in between gasps for breath having clearly run all the way to the villa.

'Frau Hoffmann, please ask the doctor to come quickly. My aunt is failing. She is struggling to breathe.' Georg, having heard the bell had already risen from his desk and strode towards Frau Samuel's nephew, knowing full well that the plan had now begun.

'I'll get my bag and come with you straight away, Herr Schwann. Just give me a moment.' Eva was on the stairs listening and Georg made a point of turning to her and saying, 'Do pray for Frau Samuels, Eva – she is very poorly indeed.'

Georg picked up his bag from the surgery and walked hurriedly down the steps with Frau Samuel's nephew, a look of concern etched on his face. Hannelore quietly shut the door and smiled reassuringly at her daughter.

'Papa will do everything he can to help, go and play with Margarete in your room.'

Hannelore returned to the typewriter and rested her fingers on the keys but struggled to type on. She forced herself to finish the letters and reports that Georg needed to sign later, to act normally and to keep things running as smoothly as possible. What spurred her on was a new pride she felt in her husband. She could not have imagined him going this far even a few months ago. For years now his compliance with the regime had bothered her more than she could ever fully express even to him, but

236

all of that now subsided. He had defended his patient with the officials at Fuchsburg and was now prepared to lay down his life for one of them. Yes, it was better to have lived intentionally and with some fire in the belly than be lukewarm, neither one thing nor the other. Hannelore wanted their lives to count for something in this increasingly meaningless war. She knew better than many in the town from her secret listening to the British radio broadcasts that Germany was crumbling. The rhetoric of glory and victory that they were brain washed with every evening was a delusion as far as she was concerned. Her great hope was that the war would end soon, and the madness would stop.

An hour later Georg returned. They both shut the door on the surgery and moved towards the window as far away from the door as possible.

'I've signed the death certificate and Helmut has been called to the house. The two of us brought the coffin in from his wagon. It's now prepared with stones and resting on the kitchen table with the lid sealed. No one will be able to look in now.'

'And Frau Samuels?'

'She is still upstairs unaware of what is happening and Wilhelm and his wife will simply tell her to be very quiet tomorrow morning when Helmut and his men come to take the coffin away, hopefully with a few passers-by watching. No one will go upstairs anyway and if there is a noise, they can all pretend it is the cat. She will need to be silent for simply a matter of minutes. The coffin will be taken to the old Jewish cemetery and prepared by Weiss's men as there is now no rabbi to organise things locally. Wilhelm told me the rabbi in Brunswick has disappeared, possibly in hiding too. So many of their community have been sent to labour camps already.'

Hannelore nodded gravely, absorbing every detail. Georg's eyes were fixed on the Rothstein villa that now stood almost as a shrine to the memory of Leah and her husband. Officials from Fuchsburg had swept through it rigorously, removing the oil paintings, the Bechstein, the violin, the books and manuscripts, nothing had been left except the heavy curtains hanging from the windows and even those had disappeared one night probably as a result of opportunist thieves looking for furnishings for their own home. There were rumours that a bigwig from Brunswick had been gifted it by the Reich as a second home, but no one had appeared yet. At least no one was occupying it and could snoop at the comings and goings of the Hoffman house. Hannelore's eyes rested on it too and she could read some of her husband's thoughts.

'We must do this in memory of Leah,' she said softly.

Georg took her hand and squeezed it.

'Yes, we cannot lose another.'

At supper, the children were subdued as Georg and Hannelore explained that Frau Samuels had died and that her funeral would be the next day according to Jewish tradition.

'But who will do the funeral?' Eva asked, wondering what a Jewish funeral was like.

'Yes, will it be our Pastor?' Margarete piped in.

'No girls, her nephew will read a special prayer, a Kaddish, over the coffin before it is laid in the ground in the Jewish cemetery. It will be fairly short, with few relatives present, but it will be respectful' Hannelore replied.

'Are you going to go?' Eva wanted to know, 'Could I come too and have the day off school? Will Konrad and Otto be there?'

'No, my little rabbit, it would not be appropriate for any of us to be at a Jewish funeral. We shall let the family grieve alone and send our condolences in a card. The boys will appreciate you signing it, girls.'

'Anyway, she was only Jewish,' quipped Margarete.

Her mother cast her a dark look and she said no more.

That night Georg and Hannelore slept very little and tried the next day to carry on as normal with their surgery, clerical work and housekeeping jobs. Life was already feeling more exhausting for Hannelore with no maid to help with cleaning, gardening, and cooking. The girls would have to start doing more, she thought to herself as she wandered up to the attic for the third time that morning with fresh bedlinen for Frau Samuels' tiny bedroom and a final clean.

The girls chattered through lunch again about their school day and Hannelore probed a little.

'Did you tell any of them about Frau Samuels?'

'Yes' piped up Eva 'I told a few of them.'

'And what did they say?' Hannelore asked.

'Oh, some of them thought that was sad, but Heinrich Stein overheard us and shouted "Good riddance."'

The table fell silent. Heinrich Stein's father was the current Burgermeister and cast in the same mould as Gerbich. It was no surprise that his son would be vocal about all things Jewish. Hannelore chose to ignore the comment and cleared away the dishes, instructing the girls to go and wash up and then finish their homework before their friends arrived at three o'clock for a few hours. Hannelore had made sure friends were invited today before their secret guest arrived so that they could have the freedom of the house and host a little tea party in their bedrooms before new rules would have to be set in place. Tables were cleared, and the afternoon yawned on interminably until the final house calls were finished for Georg, giggling friends had left the house, and the girls were quietly reading in bed.

Georg made time to come and say goodnight to them both and sat for a while, aware that the privacy and safety of their home would change for the foreseeable future. He was tired, but his soft blue eyes still sparkled as he sat down at Eva's bedside, sweeping a stray blonde curl to one side, and stroking her soft cheeks with the back of his hand. She was growing up. The little girl that had fallen out of the tree was changing week by week.

'Papa?' Eva asked, a serious expression on her face.

'Yes, my not so little rabbit?' he said smiling at her.

'Was Frau Samuels buried today?'

'The funeral was today, yes, and I hope she can now be at peace.'

'I liked her, she always used to give me sweets from a big jar when I went into her shop with Mama.'

'Yes, she was a very kind lady Eva, and it is important that we look after older people. They are full of wisdom. One day we shall all be old.'

'I hope when I am old I have lots of children and grandchildren to look after me.'

'You will, I am sure' Georg whispered as she drifted off. 'I dreamt once that you would.'

He kissed her lightly on the forehead and crept out of the room.

In a few hours, the plan could be executed. It had been agreed that Georg would drive around to the back of the Schwann shop where the main warehouse was, driving through the gates that would be left open, and then park as near to the back door as possible. The townsfolk were used to hearing Georg's car at night and it would not arouse too much suspicion if anyone were to see him, but he didn't particularly want to be seen on this night if possible. If anyone did question it, then Georg would say he had been called out to administer a sedative for Schwann's wife. After all it had been a taxing day for them all.

The spring night air was cool. The moon was thankfully shrouded in thick cloud and the streets were dark. Relentless bombing raids had created a canopy of dark over Borkhausen with blackout shutters and heavy curtains a feature of daily life. Georg drove as quietly and slowly as he could out of the garage and onto the cobbles of Gartenstrasse, turning left at the junction towards the town centre where the Schwanns lived. The large gates were already opened as agreed. Schwann had prepared them just half an hour earlier in anticipation of Georg's arrival. The car crawled stealthily into the warehouse yard and the engine stopped. Georg opened the door of the car and left it ajar, clicking open at the same time the rear car door for Frau Samuels. A blanket lay in readiness on the seat. The only sound was that of a barn owl in the distant woods, an eerie hollow sound.

The faintly silhouetted figure of Wilhelm Schwann stood at the threshold of the door, a dim light flickering behind him as he beckoned Georg into the kitchen. They both sat down for a moment at the table where earlier in the day the coffin had rested. Even though Frau Samuels hadn't died, it was still a strange thought.

'How was the funeral?' Georg whispered, hardly daring to raise his voice even though they were inside the house.

'All good, all good. It went smoothly enough. Sergeant Bauer was present too. He wanted to pay his respects I think. That's probably good as it means news will travel fast back to Fuchsburg. We didn't bring the boys but have told them. They have been very good. They know everything and will not say a word. They are old enough now, I think. They understand what is happening. Esther is waiting for you. We told her earlier this afternoon after the funeral to give her a little time to think and to organise her bag. Heidi has packed everything else for her already. There are just two bags. I will put them on the front seat for you now.'
Heidi Schwann appeared in the parlour, fear etched on her normally smiling round face. She was visibly trembling and had clearly been crying. The thought of the Gestapo raiding the house in the middle of the night had terrified her for weeks now and the only source of comfort to her was the knowledge that Fuchsburg would have been informed of Esther's death and that her name might be struck off their list.

'She is ready,' she whispered, swallowing hard and clutching the banister rail.

'Good, good,' replied Georg, 'Hannelore is waiting for us in the cellar at home. Try not to worry. We shall not be in contact for a few days to let the dust settle a little. Do not be surprised if the Gestapo come calling to check. Be strong, both of you. Esther will be safe.'

Heidi retreated back up the stairs and reappeared a few minutes later with a shuffling Esther, coughing a little as she descended the stairs step by step, Heidi supporting her.

'Good evening Frau Samuels, shall we go? I need you to lie down very still underneath a blanket in the car. It will only take a few minutes and then you will be safe in our home.'

'That you would do such a thing for me... I cannot thank you enough...' her weak voice trailed away.

'Come, let us go.'

Georg held her arm firmly, led her to the rear of the car and helped her in, laying the blanket over her as she leaned over onto a velvet cushion that Hannelore had thoughtfully left there. She coughed a little more in the cool of the night air but at last the door was clicked shut and Georg could start the engine.

'Esther,' he whispered, 'if for any reason we are stopped, please be as quiet as you can.'

Wilhelm opened the gate and the Mercedes crept out and down the streets that skirted around Borkhausen towards Gartenstrasse. His eyes surveyed every window he passed. All seemed cloaked in sleep, not a crack of light anywhere save for the low beam of his headlights which he switched off as he turned slowly into the drive and down to the cellar garage out of view of the neighbours. He carefully reversed the car into the open garage where Hannelore stood waiting wrapped in a shawl. She swiftly shut the double doors of the garage and locked them. Georg's face was drained as he slumped for a moment in the car seat, eyes momentarily shut. Hannelore opened Esther's door and carefully pulled away the red and green fringed blanket. Esther Samuels' small dark eyes peered up at her a little anxiously.

'Frau Samuels, welcome to our home. You are safe. We are in the garage in the cellar and we need to get you upstairs into the warmth of the house and into bed.'

'Gott sei Dank!' she whispered, 'Thank you so much Frau Hoffmann. You and your husband have been so kind. I may be a little slow.'

'Take as long as you like, there is no rush at all. We may have to be a little quiet when we leave the cellar as the girls are asleep.'

Hannelore didn't want to frighten their guest by telling her the girls thought she was dead.

Very slowly Esther Samuels shuffled out of the car seat, lace handkerchief in her small, bony hand and, tightening her black crocheted shawl around her, she leaned on Hannelore and Georg as they led her through the metal door to the passageway under the house. The cellar smelled a little musty, the air here cooled by bare masonry. The ceiling was low and the twelve steps up to the main hallway seemed to take forever. How they were going to mount the main stairway and then the attic felt daunting and the old lady already seemed breathless and exhausted. They rested a while in the kitchen and Hannelore made her a cup of rosehip tea to calm her nerves and help them all sleep better. They daren't switch the light on in the kitchen even with the blackout shutters and used borrowed light from the cellar.

'Come, drink this tea and rest a moment. This has been an exhausting day for you and your family.' Hannelore set a glass teacup before Esther and quietly, between coughs, she sipped and warmed her cold hands on the cup, thankful for the rest. The clock on the wall above the stove ticked and blue and white china coffee, sugar and flour jars were visible on the shelves next to it. A lingering smell of stew hung in the air from lunchtime; everything felt very homely.

Georg headed down the cellar stairs again, fetched the bags from the car and took them straight up to the attic out of sight. The room was warm enough, he decided. They had stoked the peat fire all evening and would stoke it again before going to bed. He lit a small oil lamp on the table and dimmed it just enough for Esther to get into bed and see where she was. Hannelore had set a small vase of flowers from the garden beside the lamp and placed a Bible there too. At least she might like to read the Old Testament, she had thought to herself.

Georg padded down the narrow attic stairs, across the landing and descended the main stairway back to the hall and into the kitchen, all in the dense gloom of the darkened house. He had lived here so long now and was so used to rising in the night to visit a patient, that he could navigate his way around the house as if blind.

They would need to keep the lights off, except for the cellar light, while they journeyed up to the attic and he knew it would mean almost lifting Esther Samuels up the main stairs.

'Shall we try and get you upstairs now, Frau Samuels? I'm sure you would like to get to bed.'

The diminutive lady took a deep breath, leaned on the table, and pulled herself out of the chair, shuffling forward through the hallway, with Georg and Hannelore beside her. Standing at the foot of the stairs it felt to her as if she were about to climb a mountain.

'I'm not sure I can do this' she whispered.

Georg and Hannelore looked at each other grimly.

'We can do this *together,*' Georg replied in a soft but determined voice, 'Have courage and lean on us.'

And with hands gripped firmly around Esther's back and under her elbows, the journey began up the mountain, the pair of them almost hoisting her step by step, pausing every few steps to draw breath and rebalance themselves against a creaking banister. After many minutes, they reached the top and let their guest sit for a rest on a pine laundry chest. Georg fetched her a glass of water from the bathroom, while she muffled her coughs into her handkerchief.

'You are doing so well,' Hannelore whispered, 'we are almost there. Just round the corner of the landing is the staircase to the attic and it is then only another twelve steps.'

They knelt beside her and looked into her face as she drank. It was difficult to see in the near pitch darkness of the landing, but they could see tears welling in the face of Esther Samuels, tears of exhaustion, gratitude, fear and sadness at what she was being forced to do. She had left the home she had lived in for much of the last twenty years since her husband died and, deep down, she knew it was unlikely she would be able to return. The darkness around her seemed to envelop her now in grief and hopelessness.

They became aware of a noise behind them and Georg and Hannelore turned round to see a pale Eva, clad in a white nightdress, standing before them looking at the strange trio huddled by the pine chest.

'I thought Frau Samuels was dead.'

The Secret

Georg, still kneeling, beckoned for Eva to come closer and reached out and held both her arms, drawing her towards him. He raised a finger to his lips. She knew immediately something secretive was afoot. He looked straight into her bulging, disbelieving eyes and whispered,

'Eva, shhh. We were going to explain everything to you girls in the morning, but we didn't want you to tell anyone what was happening, so we kept it quiet.' He smiled. 'Frau Samuels isn't a ghost. We had to pretend that she had died so that she would be safe. She is our guest now and will be staying in the attic. We must be very quiet. Do you think you can keep this secret?'

Eva stared into her father's gentle eyes and nodded silently. She glanced at the elderly lady still trying to stifle coughs and smiled at her.

'Now get back to bed, little rabbit, and we shall talk more in the morning.'
Eva turned to go back to bed, but paused and said, 'Good night Frau Samuels.'

Georg and Hannelore helped Esther get up off the laundry chest and supported her across the landing for the final ascent to the summit of the house, where much-needed rest beckoned. Georg left the women alone and retreated back down the narrow stairs to bed while Hannelore helped her guest get settled for the night with the promise of a visit in the morning and some breakfast and hot tea.

'Thank you, my dear, thank you so very much. You have both been so kind. I do not want to be any trouble to you and your family.'

Hannelore smiled, her heart pounding, and in the glow of the oil lamp watched a moment as Esther's eyes closed in sheer exhaustion, overcome by sleep. *Though I walk through the valley of the shadow of death, I shall fear no evil. Though I walk through the valley of the shadow of death...* Hannelore repeated silently in her head as she looked down on the face of Esther Samuels, a woman who had lived almost all her life in Borkhausen and never harmed a soul. Her once thick black hair was now almost white and her skin had grown pale through confinement indoors. Happy wrinkles around her eyes and cheeks from smiling at her nephew's children and all the children of the town as they visited the shop had lost some of their definition, a furrowed brow had taken their place on the story of her face. Hannelore realised how little she really knew of this woman whose life they now held tenderly in their hands.

The next morning, the dawn chorus of blackbirds and thrushes wakened Eva, who had barely slept anyway. It was growing lighter earlier each day and most mornings she would momentarily forget that Germany was at war and that her brothers were both stationed on front lines in foreign countries. Blissful amnesiac sleep. But this morning it was remembrance of the night's events that came flooding back to Eva within minutes of waking and she turned to her sister,

'Greta, are you awake?'

'Shhh, I'm trying to sleep. It's Sunday. Go back to sleep, Eva.'

'Greta, Frau Samuels is in the attic.'

'Go to sleep.' Margarete was in a deep half-sleep and not ready to be woken.

Eva slipped out of bed and walked over to her sister's bedside and shook her shoulders.

'Greta, Frau Samuels is in the attic, wake up.'

'What on earth are you talking about, stop making up stories Eva, it's too early' she groaned, the last word being spoken in a long yawn.

'I'm not lying, it's true – Frau Samuels is in our attic.'

Margarete turned over in bed, feather duvet still pulled tightly around her shoulders and under her chin and opened her dark eyes.

'*What* are you talking about?' she said slowly and deliberately intending to sound annoyed with her still 'childish' younger sister.

'It's true. I'm not lying. Last night I woke up because of some coughing sounds on the landing and I heard voices so I went out to see who it was and Papa and Mama were helping Frau Samuels and giving her some water at the top of the stairs.'

Margarete's eyes widened.

'They told me it was a secret and that they were going to tell us in the morning and that Frau Samuels would be staying in the attic, that it would be safer for her there.'

Margarete sat up in bed, wide awake now, thoughts racing around her fourteen-year-old head.

Both of them crept into their parents' room. Neither Hannelore nor Georg had slept much and were sitting up in bed talking. The girls slipped under the covers next to their parents, Margarete agog with what was going on in their house.

'Is Frau Samuels in our attic, Papa? I thought she had died.'

Georg stroked his older daughter's hair and nodded.

'Girls, she 'died' so to speak, 'as far as the authorities are concerned, because we knew they wanted to take her away from her lovely, warm home and send her on a long journey. As her doctor, I knew that the journey would probably kill her and so I told them it was not advisable for her to travel as she was very poorly.'

'So why did they still want to send her on a journey?' Eva probed.

'The truth is that the authorities - the Gestapo - do not want Jewish people living in Germany. They want to send them away, including Frau Samuels. They accepted my refusal to allow her to travel but said they would be paying her a visit soon.'

'So, you have lied about her death?' asked Margarete.

Georg explained the story of the past days and how they had smuggled her up to the attic during the night. The girls wanted to know every detail but the lingering and repeated question for Eva was, why? Why would Frau Samuels have had to leave her home and why were the authorities pursuing her?

'It's because she's Jewish, isn't it?' said Margarete. 'My group leader has often said that the Jews are our worst enemy. So why are you trying to save her Papa?'

'Frau Samuels is a human being, Margarete,' Georg said seriously, looking at the girls one by one as he spoke.

'When I became a doctor, I had to make a promise, it's called the Hippocratic Oath. I promised that I would treat my patients to the best of my ability and to protect their privacy. Quite simply, Frau Samuels is my patient and I need to protect her.'

'Even when the government wants to send her somewhere else?' Margarete asked, looking confused.

'Yes, in this case, yes. The authorities do not wish her well, because she is Jewish, and I have never judged a patient because of their beliefs or because of their race.'

'But they are our enemy. Hitler says so. They were trying to take over our country. They need to leave Germany.'

Hannelore looked aghast at her daughter. She had not realised just how deeply the propaganda had seeped into the mind of her daughter. She couldn't be silent anymore. It was too late to pretend that everything was good in their society.

'Girls, the Bible tells us that God has made all human beings equal and even that the Jews are his *special* people, his chosen people. God wants us to be soft hearted towards them, not hard hearted. His word says, *'I will remove from you your heart of stone and give you a heart of flesh.'* Don't let your hearts become hard, girls, because of what others say. We need to be kind, to be loving, to be gentle and to protect the weak whoever they are. Frau Samuels will be sent to a work camp, not an old folks home. Do you really think that Frau Samuels is a threat to Germany, Margarete?'

Margarete fiddled with the corner of the duvet and did not raise her head to look at her mother.

'Well no, but that's not the point. She is Jewish.'

'But does she deserve to be sent away on a long train journey to a labour camp where she would certainly die?' Her mother pressed the point.

'That would be horrible, Mama,' Eva piped up 'She's always been so kind to all the children who come in their shop. Her sweet jar was always so colourful. Is that why their shop closed, Papa? Because she is Jewish?'

Georg sighed and nodded.

'Yes. Throughout the country all the shops owned by Jewish families have been closed down. The authorities do not want them to thrive and to grow rich. That is why Schwann's had to close, because Herr Schwann is a nephew of a Jewish woman.'

Until this time the girls had been shielded from the horrors of Kristallnacht. It had barely affected their small world of five thousand inhabitants, with only one shop in 'Jewish' hands. It had been the major cities and larger towns that had seen the brutality of that dark night and witnessed the roaring flames spewing out from the synagogues in the Jewish quarters, and the shattered shop windows plundered by a rabble of storm troopers.

Margarete was subdued, struggling to make sense of what she had been taught and the actions and words of her parents. She believed passionately in everything she had been taught in the League of German Girls. It was wonderful to be part of a huge national club of girls all thinking, feeling, believing in the same thing, the soul of Germany. The songs, the flags, the torch-lit ceremonies, all celebrating young people as the energy of the future. Was it all wrong? Were her parents about to suggest that she stopped going to her beloved group? How could she?

There *were* no other groups that were allowed. She loved putting on her white blouse and blue skirt and scarf and polishing her walking shoes. She routinely practised her marching steps around the garden, parading in her uniform. She would be bullied mercilessly if she left. And anyway, she didn't want to. No boy would look at her. She had sworn an eternal oath to Hitler, the party, and the Fatherland. Words spoken repeatedly by her beloved group leader echoed in her mind.

"Your blood is pure, it is not your blood alone, it comes from afar and everyone's blood flows through it. Keep the vessel of your immortality pure."

It was clear to her that she had to do this, clear she one day should marry a pure German and provide the Father of the nation with more children for his army. Race was the most important thing in her life, even to the extent of feeling waves of jealousy that she had not inherited Eva's extraordinary blonde hair and green eyes. Even so she felt she was part of the best nation in the world, the most competent, the most beautiful. Vivid images of the ugly Jewish faces that appeared on all the hoardings around the town and in all the magazines she read had made clear how imperfect and deformed the Jewish race was. Race, it was the most important word in the world to her. The thought that her parents were hiding an ugly old Jewish woman in her beloved attic space was abhorrent to her.

Eva interrupted her train of thought.

'What if the authorities find out that Frau Samuels is in the attic? What would happen to her then?'

Georg sat upright in bed and adopted an unusually stern voice.

'Girls, I want you both to look at me.' He paused to add gravity, saying each word very slowly.

'It is very, very important that this doesn't happen. We thought very long and hard about doing this, because it is a danger to us all if she is found.'

'Do you mean that we would be punished too?' Eva asked.

'Yes, probably,' he sighed, 'But there is no reason for anyone to know. She is very frail and perhaps may not live very long while she is with us, but we suspect the Gestapo will want to know she has definitely died which is why we made it look as if she *had* died and was buried.'

'So, the undertaker knows too?' inquired Margarete.

'Yes, and Frau Samuels' great nephews whom you know from school. But no one else. You must not tell a soul, girls. Can we trust you to help us keep this secret?'

The girls looked at their parents and each other. Eva grinned – she loved an adventure and, even more than an adventure, she loved a secret.

'Of course we can Mama and Papa – it will be fun! And I shall help you look after Frau Samuels and carry up her food.'

'Ha, ha – yes, your young legs are just what we need!' exclaimed her mother smiling and then turned to her older daughter who was still fiddling with the corner of the duvet.

'And will you help, Margarete?'

'I don't like it, I don't like it at all. I'm not sure I want to help an old Jewish woman who is going to die anyway and who is risking all our lives. I won't say anything but don't expect me to go up there and talk to her!'

She pushed aside the duvet, stood up and left the room and Georg and Hannelore looked at each other sadly.

'Don't worry about Greta,' said Eva, 'she will come round. Can I take some breakfast up to Frau Samuels this morning?'

An hour later, Eva walked gingerly up the grand staircase past the family coat of arms and paintings of her grandparents and great-grandparents, her small hands clutching a tray of boiled eggs, peppermint tea and toast. It all smelt good but she was anxious not to let it spill into the saucer. The narrow staircase would be a greater challenge and involved opening the attic door first and then retrieving the tray from where she had left it on the floor at the bottom. She was a little nervous as she entered the attic space, uncertain what was going to meet her in the tiny bedroom occupied by Frau Samuels.

'Good morning, Frau Samuels. It is only Eva. I've brought you some breakfast.'

She waited respectfully for a few seconds outside the small door and then pushed it lightly with her elbow and walked in.

The elderly lady reached for her spectacles on the side table and looked at Eva, whom she had not seen for many months.

'My, my, Eva Hoffmann!' How you have grown. And what is it you have on that lovely tray?'

'Well, these are fresh eggs, delivered this morning by Frau Braun from their farm, and the mint tea I made for you. I picked the leaves from the herb garden this morning. Mama prepared everything else.'

Eva set the tray in front of Frau Samuels, resting it carefully on the feather duvet. The old lady smiled, coughed a little and drank the steaming tea gratefully, murmuring her thanks between sips.

'I hope you enjoy it.' Eva began to move towards the doorway, feeling a little awkward and unsure of what next to say.

'Thank you, Eva, it is very kind of you to carry this all the way up those stairs. Do say thank you to your mother for me.'

'I will come and collect the tray shortly.'

Eva tripped across the attic space and descended the narrow stairway and flew down the grand staircase, her blonde plaits bobbing against her white Sunday smock, and headed back to the kitchen to join her mother. Margarete was still sulking in her bedroom and had not come down for breakfast. Georg had already been called out to attend to a farmer's wife who was in labour.

'How was Frau Samuels this morning, Eva?'

'She said thank you for the breakfast. I said I would collect the tray soon. How old is she Mama? She looks very old, much older than I remember her.'

'Ah yes, this war has aged her a lot and she has spent much time out of sight upstairs in the shop, trying to be invisible. We thought the Gestapo didn't know she was there at all, but they have many lists and research the families of every town and village like detectives. They must have heard from someone that she was still alive.'

'I think it is wonderful what you and Papa have done, Mama. It is brave and so clever. No one will think she is alive or suspect she is in Doktor Hoffmann's attic.'

'We must pray that you are right, Eva. And you are brave to help us. Now help me peel these potatoes for lunch and then we shall read the Bible together.' Mother and daughter sat together for a while chatting about how they could look after Frau Samuels and all the new arrangements in the house regarding friends visiting the girls. Hannelore looked up at the clock, aware that she needed to finish some typing in the office.

'Eva, go and fetch down the tray, please, from the attic. Our guest may not be strong enough to move it herself and see if there is anything else she needs right now. I've left some books for her.'

Eva skipped out of the kitchen and raced up the stairs when the doorbell rang.

Hannelore opened the door and Hermann Gerbich beamed at her, his fat neck creased by a crisp white collar. He was wearing a dark blue jacket with a sparkling gold Nazi membership badge adorning the lapel, a symbol of his unbroken party membership since 1933. He saluted his usual 'Heil Hitler!' and started to walk across the threshold, ignoring, as usual, anything resembling appropriate behaviour.

'Ach, I'm surprised your maid didn't answer the door, Hannelore. Ah yes,' he added pointedly,' – I remember now meeting Deichmann at the station last week and he mentioned his twins and the fact that your Irma had been kindly 'loaned' to the family? What a loss she must be to you. Is Georg at home?'

He wandered towards the surgery door and peered nosily in.

Hannelore was torn between indignation and terror at the thought of Eva descending the grand staircase with the breakfast tray and unwittingly saying something without realising that Gerbich was standing there. She raised her voice unusually loudly and feigned delight and warmth.

'How lovely to see you this spring morning, Hermann! How are Marlene and the children? Well, I hope? No, Georg is out on a visit. He will be some time. Can I pass on a message?'
She spotted Eva at the top of the stairs and tried to catch her eye, but it was too late, she had already begun her descent with the tray.

'Ach Eva,' she said loudly 'Do come and say hello to your surgeon. Doktor Gerbich is paying us a visit. Is Margarete feeling any better? Did she eat any of the breakfast?'

Eva carried on walking carefully down the stairs, Gerbich smiling at her blonde plaits, green eyes and saintly white dress and sighing with approval.

'My, my, Eva, you are quite the model German girl these days. Your parents must be very proud of you.' He looked at the tray in her outstretched hands.

'Thank you, Doktor Gerbich. I have been looking after my sister. She is not so well this morning.'

'Well enough to eat a good breakfast though?' He glanced at the empty plates, and teacup.

'Ah yes, her appetite is returning,' added Hannelore swiftly, praying fervently that Margarete would not appear bouncing down the stairs.

'Do you want me to pass on a message to Georg, Hermann?'

'Just wanted to have a chat with him about the Samuels' case,' he said, patting his nose confidentially, 'Fuchsburg wanted me to have a word before they do their own patrols in the area. I gather Georg was involved in tidying up the matter this week. Understand they were a little annoyed with the way things were going, but it sounds as if everything has been resolved satisfactorily. No doubt they will be in touch themselves.'

'I will pass on the message.'

Hannelore moved towards the front door of the villa and held it open for their unwelcome visitor.

He saluted again and marched down the steps towards his gleaming sable-coloured Opel and sped off down Gartenstrasse.

Eva exhaled. Hannelore removed the tray from her trembling hands, and she followed her mother towards the kitchen and flopped on a stool.

Margarete appeared out of nowhere at the threshold of the kitchen, looking pale.

'I heard everything Doktor Gerbich said. I was at the top of the landing. You are going to get us all into trouble. Is it really worth it?'

'It's too late now, Margarete. As your parents, we have made the decision to help our neighbour. We need you -'

'- She isn't even our neighbour,' her older daughter interrupted. 'She doesn't live next door to us.' Margarete's lips pouted.

'No, she doesn't live next door to us…' her mother began.

'But she's still our neighbour, Greta,' piped in Eva, 'she's still German.'

'She's still a human being,' Hannelore said quietly and walked out of the kitchen.

Heidi

Every morning Eva would climb the mountain of stairs to bring breakfast up to Frau Samuels as well as lunch when she got home from school. In between, Hannelore and Georg would call in on her, check how she was and sit and talk a while. Her nephew and his family could not of course come but Georg would make sure he called by and reported to them on her health and carried any messages to her from them all, warning them not to loiter around their villa or look up at the attic windows and draw suspicion to themselves. Margarete remained cold and aloof and continued regaling the family about what she had been doing in the League of Girls. She asked if she could move out of her shared room with Eva and have 'her own space' for her own things. It did not seem unreasonable and anything that placated their more tempestuous daughter might help the situation become more bearable for them all. She moved into Irma's room at the back of the house and rapidly made it into her own private space, annoyed only that she wasn't allowed to take friends upstairs anymore, so would often spend afternoons in her friends' homes when not doing her homework.

One Saturday morning, two weeks after the arrival of Frau Samuels, the doorbell rang again. A black car had parked in front of the villa on Gartenstrasse and two men had clipped quickly up the steps, wearing dark civilian suits, unbuttoned mackintosh coats and trilby hats. Both carried black briefcases. Georg was in the hallway when the bell rang and answered it himself.

'Heil Hitler! Doktor Georg Hoffmann?'

'Ja, I am Georg Hoffmann. How can I help you?'

'Gestapo. Kriminalkommissar Schwarz and Kriminalassistent Becker. May we come in?' The voice was cold and efficient and any social niceties were transparently shallow. Georg breathed slowly and deeply through his nose in an attempt to appear calm.

Georg led the men into his surgery away from any family members and shut the door firmly. Hannelore, who had been straining to listen from the kitchen when the men arrived, now hovered as near as she dared to the closed surgery door without her silhouette being spotted through its small frosted window. The words were still audible, the Kriminalkommissar making no attempt to lower the tone of his voice.

'Doktor Hoffmann, we've come to speak to you about Esther Samuels.' Their spectacles glinted in the light streaming through the window, their mouths locked rigid as they scrutinised Georg's face. These were experts in human behaviour, they had learned the art of unpicking artifice and disguise, stripping away masks of deception. Their supreme mission was solely to uncover the Jewish disease wherever it lay festering in the body of Germany, and to ensure that no stone lay unturned to uncover it.

Georg was equally a consummate professional, used to hearing shocking news, used to securing above all his patient's confidentiality and used to shielding his family from the daily grime and horror of his work during this and a previous war. He lifted the shiny black ebonite pen from his desk and played with it in his hand, stroking it slowly with his right thumb and tapping it into his left palm. The action soothed his breathing a little more and was designed to create an air of nonchalance and mild irritation on his part.

'What exactly do you want to know? I believe I submitted the death certificate on the day that Esther Samuels died, and as far as I am aware, the funeral took place the following day.'

Schwarz unclipped his black leather briefcase and drew out a file and began scanning the document inside.

'And in your professional opinion, Doktor Hoffmann, what was the medical cause of death?'

'Bronchopneumonia,' Georg replied promptly.

'And was this expected? We were informed that she had made some recovery from a previous bout of pneumonia and was in a weakened, but stable condition.' The voice of the faceless interrogator grew louder.

'It was something of a surprise to hear she had died so very suddenly,' Georg replied. 'I think, as you well know, I informed your office as to Esther Samuel's state of health and that it was precarious to say the least. It is not uncommon for a woman of her age to decline very rapidly and it was so in this case. It confirmed to me that I was correct to report her as unfit for any form of travel.' Georg tried his utmost to sound indignant and authoritative.

'I think you need to be reminded that ultimately *we* are the judge of that, Herr Doktor. In our experience some doctors have vacillated in their duty to the Reich and although we recognise you are a Party member, it has also been noted that we have had very few referrals and reports from your surgery in line with the edicts that you have been sent. We can only conclude that the good citizens of Borkhausen are peculiarly free of defect and hereditary disease.'

They both continued to stare out of their hollow eyes into Georg's face, watching intently for any betrayal of emotion or flicker of a lie in any movement of his body.

Georg had not been taken unprepared. Anticipating this visit ever since Hannelore had described Gerbich's spontaneous arrival earlier in the week, he pulled out from his desk drawer a file and handed it to the Kriminalkommissar.

'On the contrary, gentlemen, I am studiously compiling a detailed report on the state of health of the inmates in the castle prison as well as an epidemiological study on the health of the town. We are by and large a thankfully very robust society here with many working in the fields to feed our nation. The report will take time to complete but be assured I will send it to you in good time.'

'If there is anything in your research that brings things of great *concern* to light, then we should like to know sooner rather than later, especially if any more of your patients appear to have Jewish connections, however remote they might seem. Is that understood?'

'Of course, of course – at least Frau Samuels had no children as far as I am aware.'

The men rose in their seats, the main interrogator simply retorting, 'It would be better if that were the case. May she rot in her grave!'

Georg rose in his chair and led the men to the door of the surgery and out of the front door, saluting as they left. Georg saluted back promptly to seal the disguise.

Hannelore had scurried back into the kitchen and shut the door quietly before they had exited the surgery. She had no desire to be in the presence of these deathly visitors with their air of false superiority, with their game of intimidation that seemed to give them so much pleasure. *Idiots*, she thought to herself. *I doubt any of them went to university, replicas of their trumped up little leader.* Georg was relieved too that she had not tried to enter the surgery to offer tea and to embroil herself in a confrontation. The truth was that Hannelore felt not a little fearful while they were in the house and it took most of the day to regain an inner sense of calm and to quell the anger at their intimidation.

It was a wet afternoon and the family decided to stay in rather than go out on their traditional Sunday walk to the moorland or round the lake that led through the woods on the edge of Borkhausen. Margarete was reading in her room, as the League athletics meeting was cancelled, so Eva asked if she could visit Frau Samuels.

'Take a cup of peppermint tea with you, Eva,' Hannelore suggested, 'she may be glad of someone to read to her.'

A few minutes later, Eva tapped on the door of the attic and pushed it open, savoured the smell of bare wooden floorboards, adjusted her eyes to the relative gloom and walked over to Esther's bedroom, clutching a pretty china saucer cradling a wobbling cup of tea. The elderly lady had been dozing after lunch but was now sitting up with a letter in her hands, a pale pink shawl wrapped around her shoulders and a slim brown leather bag on her lap.

'I've brought you some peppermint tea,' Eva whispered, setting it down carefully on the bedside table next to the Bible. A little of the hot water spilled into the saucer. Frau Samuels smiled as she coughed into her lace handkerchief.

'Ach, Danke, Eva, you read my mind. I was feeling a little dry in the mouth and I do so love your mint tea.'

'I hope I am not disturbing you, Frau Samuels. I can come back another time.'

'No, no, child, come and stay a while. I would enjoy a little company. I miss seeing my family – and Muschi my cat. I was just reading through some letters and feeling a little sad. I could do with a cheerful face and some news of what is going on outside the attic.'

Eva perched on the edge of Frau Samuels' bed as there was no room for a chair, and straightened the creases in her pale blue dress.

'I don't know very much about the news, I'm afraid. Mama doesn't let me listen too much, but I did hear that the English Air Force bombed Stuttgart quite badly. We have heard a little news from my brothers which is good. They both sounded well and haven't been injured at all, so that's the main thing. I do miss them though.'

Esther Samuels immediately perked up with the news of Stuttgart and at the opportunity of cheering Eva up.

'Yes, you must miss them Eva, this war is not easy for you either. We must all be as brave as we can be. Muschi my cat is very funny when a strange cat tries to come into our back yard and onto her territory. She growls a low growl like this... grrrrrr and her whole body wobbles like this...' and the old lady shook her head from side to side, making Eva laugh 'and then she lunges forward as if to jump but just stands her ground until the invader disappears.' Exhausted by the effort of the story, Frau Samuels sank back against the pillows chuckling to herself.

'Do you ever get scared?' Eva looked into the small watery dark eyes of this little Jewish lady huddled under the duvet.

'Yes, I do. I suppose I have been living with fear for many years now and do wonder when it will ever end. I sometimes sing to myself if I feel afraid. My favourite song was one written by Rebbe Nachman of Bratislava. He was a famous rabbi my great-grandfather told me about, who lived many years ago.'

Esther began croakily singing some words in Hebrew. She paused to catch her breath and then explained to her rapt listener,

'It means *"all the world is a very narrow bridge, but never, never, never be afraid, no, never, never, never be afraid."* Rebbe Nachman lived in the time of tuberculosis – his wife died of it before she reached the age of forty. Three of his children died before they grew up and a fire burned through Bratislava, where he lived. When his own home was destroyed he was forced to move to a neighbouring town. A few months later he himself died there of tuberculosis. He more than many understood the narrowness of the world's bridge. So yes, Eva, I am afraid, but I have grown up knowing that the world's bridge is very narrow and I must expect hardship and suffering, that it is quite normal. Many people will fall off if they don't stay on the straight bridge.'

Eva looked thoughtful.

'Is it hard for you living in this dark old attic?'

'Not as hard as it would be to have travelled to a work camp. I am filled with gratitude to your parents for giving me shelter. I would love to hear a story though. Do you know what one of the most precious gifts we have is, Eva? The gift of imagination. I can travel anywhere in the world in my imagination. Do you ever imagine travelling far away?'

'Yes, I do. I love reading stories about other countries and one day I hope to see some of them. My favourite book is *Heidi*. She travelled a long way in her life. I'm reading it at the moment. Do you want me to fetch it for you and read you a chapter?'

'I would love that. I remember reading the first story myself many years ago when it was first published. I would often travel to the mountains with Heidi in my mind.'

Eva looked very excited at the thought of having found another Heidi friend and scurried off down the steps to fetch the book. Gasping for breath on her return, she laid it on her lap. The front cover displayed an illustration of a small girl with curling black hair stood in front of a white-haired, bearded old man who was seated in front of a mountain hut, holding a pipe in his mouth. The girl was dressed prettily in a red dirndl with blue jacket and was barefoot. She was kneeling in front of a baby goat, with a bunch of wild mountain flowers in her small hands. The paper cover of the book was snagged and a little worn from grimy fingers and Eva began flicking through to find where she had placed the bookmark.

'This is a fairly sad bit, I think, Frau Samuels, but it gets better.'

'Read on, read on,' urged the old lady, rubbing her hands in anticipation.

'It's the bit where Heidi has been taken to Frankfurt by Aunt Dete to live with Clara. She really isn't very happy as she has been living in the mountains for three years and neither she nor her grandfather really wanted her to go.'

'Ah yes,' Frau Samuels added, 'She had to look after the wheelchair bound Clara in her wealthy home. An apt chapter for you to read to me, I think, Eva!' she said chuckling.

Eva didn't fully understand why the old lady was amused but pretended to smile and started to read,

'When Heidi opened her eyes on her first morning in Frankfurt she could not think where she was. Then she rubbed them and looked about her. She was sitting up in a high white bed, on one side of a large, wide room, into which the light was falling through very, very long white curtains; near the window stood two chairs covered with large flowers, and then came a sofa with the same flowers, in front of which was a round table; in the corner was a washstand, with things upon it that Heidi had never seen in her life before. But now all at once she remembered that she was in Frankfurt; everything that had happened the day before came back to her, and finally she recalled clearly the instructions that had been given her by the lady-housekeeper, as far as she had heard them. Heidi jumped out of bed and dressed herself; then she ran first to one window and then another; she wanted to see the sky and country outside; she felt like a bird in a cage behind those great curtains. But they were too heavy for her to put aside, so she crept underneath them to get to the window. But these again were so high that she could only just get her head above the sill to peer out. Even then she could not see what she longed for. In vain she went first to one and then the other of the windows--she could see nothing but walls and windows and again walls and windows. Heidi felt quite frightened. It was still early, as Heidi was accustomed

to get up early and run out at once to see how everything was looking, if the sky was blue and if the sun was already above the mountains, or if the fir trees were waving and the flowers had opened their eyes. As a bird, when it first finds itself in its bright new cage, darts hither and thither, trying the bars in turn to see if it cannot get through them and fly again into the open, so Heidi continued to run backwards and forwards, trying to open first one and then the other of the windows, for she felt she could not bear to see nothing but walls and windows, and somewhere outside there must be the green grass, and the last unmelted snows on the mountain slopes, which Heidi so longed to see. But the windows remained immovable, try what Heidi would to open them, even endeavouring to push her little fingers under them to lift them up; but it was all no use.'

Eva paused for breath and it began to sink in that perhaps Frau Samuels too was feeling confined as Heidi was. She looked up at the old lady.

'Do you feel a bit like a bird in a cage, Frau Samuels?'

'Yes, in some ways I do, but what makes all the difference is that I am very well looked after by kind people who are protecting me. For Heidi I think it was far worse. She was used to the mountain air and missing her grandfather and Peter, and the people in the house didn't always treat her nicely.'

'I wonder if there are other Jews hiding in buildings, hidden by other people,' Eva mused.

'I hope so,' the old lady nodded, 'I hope so. Now read on, Eva, I want to hear more of the story. It helps me to leave even this lovely attic to imagine the world of Heidi.'

'Perhaps tomorrow I could read to you from the next book. You may not have read that one yet.'

Esther Samuel's eyes sparkled and she nodded, smiling and lay her head back once more against the pillow.

Eva continued with the chapter and in their imaginations the young girl and the elderly Jewess journeyed to different worlds and a different time, a wonderful escape from the clutches of Nazi Germany. Eva read until her companion dozed off and carefully replaced the bookmark before slipping out of the attic, closing the wooden door quietly behind her.

The Bullet

News from the Eastern and the Western fronts was scant. In the six months since Max had been posted to France a handful of letters had come home, but at least they had come. Each time Hannelore sensed he was putting on a brave face and shielding them from the reality of how he was actually feeling. The jokes about the lice and the food belied the fact that life was a bit grim. His posting was nearer than Hannelore had at first thought, which was good news – if necessary she could take the train from Hanover and even cross the border and visit him, although travelling was something the Hoffmanns were avoiding unless it was absolutely necessary. Frau Samuels continued to live quietly in the attic although her cough was more persistent, possibly not helped by lack of fresh air and sunshine. It would be too dangerous for her to be moved now, they could not risk her being seen from neighbours' windows and on the other side of the river at the bottom of the garden were other gardens of acquaintances they knew who were passionate about the regime.

Life had settled into a routine of caring for their elderly guest and managing their garden and an orchard they owned in another house in the town. Numerous baskets of apples were piling up in the cellar at the end of the summer and then carefully carried up to the attic and laid on great slats to store over the winter. Eleven-year-old Eva would help her mother as she arranged the apples in neat rows, smelling their fresh fragrance and occasionally stealing one and munching it as she worked.

Frau Samuels always had a bowl of apples beside her bed which Hannelore would cut up into small slices for her to eat more easily.

When not harvesting fruit and vegetables from their garden and orchard Hannelore was constantly preparing parcels to send to Johannes and Max, collecting, purchasing, and crafting provisions for her sons. One afternoon she assembled the items on the kitchen table and fetched down a large, thin, black-lined book from the kitchen shelf and slowly lifted the brass postal scales onto the table.

'We must be very careful with these, Eva, they are delicate.' Eva fingered the finely curved brass arms.

'These aren't the same as your baking scales, are they?' she enquired.

'They are called bilateral scales. Do you see the lower brass arm? That measures letters and parcels that only weigh up to 250 grams and the other arm above it measures up to 1000 grams. You must help me now and make sure that our parcels are not too heavy.'

'What would happen if they were too heavy, Mama?'

'Ach, the postman might not take them. Each soldier is only allowed to have a parcel weighing 200 grams, so we must weigh them very carefully and make sure that the address is written clearly.'

Eva and Hannelore spent the next few minutes weighing all the items that were to go into the parcels: a bar of chocolate, a small sharpened pencil, a stamped envelope with two pieces of blank paper inside, a pair of new socks and a letter she had written in her tiniest handwriting so as not to use up too much paper. The box was weighed too, and Eva totted up the sums on a piece of kitchen paper. 'I think everything will weigh 191 grams!' she said triumphantly at the end.

'Splendid' replied her mother, kissing her on the top of her forehead and stroking a stray wisp of blonde hair behind her ear, 'You are a good mathematician, Eva.'

Her mother carefully wrapped the items in a piece of light tissue paper and laid them in the box, finally placing the letter on the top before closing the lid and wrapping the whole box in a piece of brown paper with layers of tightly knotted string. She left space for the address of each unit the boys were stationed with, hoping that even if they had travelled on from their current location the parcels would find the right unit. Johannes seemed to be constantly moving around the Caucasus as his battalion edged towards the Russian oil fields the government was so desperate to secure.

'Can I put the parcels on the scales, Mama?'

'Yes, here they are – they are exactly the same, so should weigh the same – here is the one for Johannes.'

Eva carefully placed the small cardboard box on the metal plate and the arms swung apart.

'Can you read the number here on the bottom arm?'

'Yes, it is one hundred and ninety something...'

Her mother peered over her shoulders.

'One hundred and ninety-six grams – perfect! Let's just check the other parcel to make sure.' Eva placed the parcel for Max on the scales and it registered the same weight.

Hannelore began writing in the ledger with her fountain pen.

'What are you writing, Mama?'

'I am noting down what the parcel weighs, the address it has been sent to and what the contents are, to remind me. It is my way of checking that everything arrives safely. If the boys say a weekly parcel has not arrived, I can contact the postal service and let them know which one is missing to see if they can track it down.'

Eva looked into her mother's lined face and watched her as she carefully copied down the addresses. Her skin was soft, and her brown eyes narrowed to focus on the tiny print on the parcel. Eva observed her silently until she had finished. She loved her mother's face, she loved the soft curves of her jaw line that in the last few years had begun to sag a little, she loved the way her mother would purse her lips when writing and a small furrowed line would appear between her eyebrows. She loved every line and emerging wrinkle, and especially when she smiled, and her dark brown eyes would dance and sparkle. Eva made every effort to help those eyes dance, such was the longing she had for her parents to be happy. Preparing parcels for the boys was a happy event for both mother and daughter. For Hannelore it had become a weekly ritual and she took the greatest pleasure in sourcing new things to put in the parcels. Eva would sometimes draw pictures and colour them in for her brothers, to make them smile. She missed them so much, especially Johannes, and at times struggled to remember what their voices sounded like. So many months of her life had been spent apart from them, either because of school or because of the war. She kept pictures of them both by her bedside and would kiss them every night before lying down with her Johannes doll tucked beside her. Her greatest joy was when her mother received a letter and there was always a special kiss for her from them at the bottom, with a silly comment to their father to make sure he tickled her every day to keep her from being too cheeky.

Hannelore laid the parcels in her basket in the hallway next to the mahogany coat stand and turned to find her daughter in tears.

'What is it, Eva?'

'I miss them so much, Mama.'

Hannelore sat down on the kitchen chair and wrapped her arms around her daughter and squeezed her tightly.

'Shall we pray, little rabbit?'

'Yes,' Eva sobbed, her big green eyes brimming with tears.

Together they bowed their heads and Hannelore raised her greying head and whispered a reverent prayer for the safekeeping of her sons and that their packages would arrive safely. Eva nodded her head throughout and whispered 'Amen' at the end and squeezed her mother tightly. They sat there for a few moments until Margarete walked into the kitchen from the cellar having cycled over to a friend in one of the villages a few miles from Borkhausen.

Eva slipped down, wiping her tears, and turning away, a little embarrassed to have been seen with wet eyes and on her mother's lap, something she only ever did now when upset.

Margarete pretended not to notice and just flounced on through to the dining room and sat down to play the piano.

'Now Eva, I'm going to the post office and I want you to get ready for your girls' group. Your uniform is hanging on your chair. Wash your face, get changed and then come down for some tea – I have left it for you in the larder. Tell Margarete that she needs to hurry up too, please.'

'Ja, Mama.'

Hannelore disappeared down the side steps of the house and headed off to town, glad of a moment to herself and a chance to breathe deeply and collect her own thoughts. She would have gladly wept with her little daughter but knew that she had to be strong. She would have done anything to protect her from the reality of this war if she could. As she strode off into town, her basket hinged on her elbow, she whispered prayers over her daughters and over her war-swept sons.

By the time Hannelore returned, the house was empty. Eva and Margarete had gone to their youth meetings and Georg was still out visiting patients. Hannelore wandered into the surgery office and began to sift through the paperwork that the morning clinic had generated. There were notes Georg had left for her to type up and letters to write to the hospital regarding certain patients who needed surgery.

She sat down at the typewriter and began working, breaking off only to make herself a cup of camomile tea. The doorbell rang as she was walking back through the hallway.

'Frau Hoffmann?' The postman stood at the door, holding out a telegram.

Hannelore froze inwardly. Everything seemed to move in slow motion as she took the envelope from his hand and looked into his serious face.

'Thank you, Herr Gruber,' she said, closing the large white door behind her and walking back into the office. She shut the door to the surgery and sat down, her hands trembling now uncontrollably. She was suddenly aware of everything in the room, the ticking clock, the smell of disinfectant, the large round black and silver keys of the typewriter in front of her with half written notes on it.

She managed to slit open the telegram with a silver letter opener on the desk and slowly opened it.

'Dr and Mrs Hoffmann,

Your son, Private Maximilian Hoffmann sustained a bullet wound to his arm and chest on the 10th August. No mortal danger. In infirmary near to battalion at Dijon. Visits possible, accommodation not provided.'

Hannelore sank back in her chair and exhaled deeply. She didn't know whether to laugh or cry. *'No mortal danger'* A bitter-sweet relief. So many of her friends had received the worst news and she had fully expected to hear that one of her sons had fallen in this war. Hannelore rarely cried, but like her daughter earlier that day she gave way to an aching sob. All she could think of was how Max was right now, whether he was scared, what the wound was like, how he would want to be with his family. All she could utter between sobs was, 'Thank you God, Thank you God. Thank God he's alive.'

As soon as she had collected herself, she picked up the telephone receiver in the surgery and dialled the number on the telegram of his battalion's headquarters.

'Hello? Hello? This is Hannelore Hoffmann, I have just received a telegram concerning my son, Private Maximillian Hoffmann. I have been informed that I can visit him in the infirmary. Please can you tell my son that I shall be making my way there as soon as possible... thank you.'

The major at the other end of the telephone growled a response, clearly stressed by the recent engagement with the advancing enemy troops. 'Frau Hoffmann, you will have to find your own accommodation locally, it will not be appropriate or even safe for you to stay too long.'

Hannelore replaced the receiver and sighed deeply. At least her son would know she was coming.

Eva jumped up the side steps of the house, panting with having run all the way home with Rosa from her meeting. She had left Margarete to stroll home alone with a boy from her school year, Klaus, who had been at the Hitler Youth meeting.

'Mama! I'm home!'

Hannelore stepped out of the surgery office and Eva flung herself into her and squeezed her mother hard.

'I'm starving, Mama, is supper ready?'

'All in good time Eva,' her mother replied as calmly as she could, 'go and wash your hands and then come into the kitchen and tell me all about your meeting.'

Hannelore was preparing the breadbasket and cold platter of meats and cheese when Eva came and sat beside her and helped her to arrange the salami slices.

'How was your meeting? Did you learn anything interesting?'

'It was fun today, Mama, we did lots of singing.'

Eva began repeating a rendition of *Raise high the flag*, as she stomped around the kitchen, marching to the song. 'In hope, to the swastika, Rise the eyes of millions, Dawn breaks for freedom, And bread for all man...'

Hannelore's eyes were on the platter, not her daughter as she sang, and her mouth was shaped carefully into a guarded smile. Horst Wessel's song was sung at every meeting and Hannelore was beginning to be weary of the relentless pounding march as it spewed forth from the radio every day.

'Sit down Eva and tell me what else you did.'

Eva flopped onto the stool beside her mother.

'We talked a lot about what we could do for the soldiers fighting in the war, Mama, and I told our leader what you and I had been doing this morning. She was very pleased with me and gave me a sweet at the end. She actually smiled for once. Next week we shall be knitting in the group and making little squares to sew together into blankets for the soldiers in the hospitals.'

At this she grew a little thoughtful again.

'Maybe Johannes' hospital will get the blanket with my squares in. Do we have any wool I can take, Mama?'

Hannelore's thoughts sped immediately to Max lying wounded in France. She would not tell Eva today what had happened. She did not need to know the full story yet, especially after her tears this morning. She would discuss the matter first with Georg and explain the trip to France as an opportunity to visit Max in person and take him a bigger parcel of provisions.

'Yes, of course - do you want to practise your knitting with me after supper? We could do one or two together so that you are an expert next meeting. Now go and take off your uniform and help me lay the table in the dining room. I will need you to take up a tray to Frau Samuels as well. My legs are aching this evening and she will be so glad to see you – perhaps without the singing though? I'm not sure she wants to hear about the swastika.'

After supper it was still light, and Georg and Hannelore strolled into the garden with their girls to enjoy the wonderful scents of a small bed of roses that Hannelore had refused to turn into a vegetable garden. She had afforded herself the luxury of these delicate pink roses with their heady scent because they were so blessed with provisions from Georg's farming patients and their orchard. They had not known *real* want or hunger during this war that had ravaged so many and Hannelore liked to think they had passed on the gifts to those in the town who had real needs. She wandered up to the roses and touched their velvet petals and held a particularly full bloom to her nose, closed her eyes and just for a brief moment tried to forget everything that was erupting around them. She wasn't sure that she could hold any more tension from dying, bereaved or distraught patients whom she met on a daily basis on her walks into town or to their homes. The pressure of the subterfuge in the attic was also pressing in on her, but today it was the news about Max that filled her heart and mind to the exclusion of everyone else's problems and all she could think about as she stood by the rose was how her fragile nineteen-year-old son had almost been felled by a single bullet.

A familiar sound shattered the moment completely. The town sirens pierced the evening air and the girls, now all too familiar with the procedure, stopped the knitting they had brought with them, and looked up at their parents.

'Sirens!' shouted Margarete and all turned and headed towards the open garage door and into the cellar they had used for years now as a bomb shelter. They headed straight for the peat store. Its' warm, earthy smell was comforting as they sat on small wooden stools against the only wall that was not stacked high with the freshly cut fuel. The wagon had arrived early that morning and the girls had watched the 'peat man' as they called him pile the squares of thick, drying turf. A small window at the top of the wall opened onto the drive through which the peat was passed to another workman who then layered it in the largest cellar room. They loved the rich, earthy smell that then lingered in the cellar, mingling with the damp mustiness of smooth, plastered walls that had never dried out fully in the sun and air.

The girls carried on knitting their blanket squares as the sound of hundreds of enemy air force planes droned overhead.

'Another raid towards Berlin.' Georg mused despondently.

'I can hear explosions, Papa,' Eva piped up excitedly.

'Yes I think you are right, Eva,' her father replied. 'They are a long way away. They must be bombing Brunswick. We will be all right, don't worry, it will pass over soon.'

'I hope Frau Samuels is not frightened all alone there in the attic.' Eva murmured.

It was impossible to move their elderly, much-weakened guest into the cellar – the effort and time involved would endanger them all and completely exhaust her. It was a risk they had to take. If the roof was hit, she would not stand a chance.

The family sat and waited. It was completely silent. The all clear siren didn't sound but Eva grew bored and jumped up.

'Can we go upstairs now, Mama, I need the toilet.'

Hannelore nodded. Borkhausen had never been bombed. There were no factories or armament depots nearby, just endless fields of swedes and potatoes. She knew they were safe.

Eva hopped up the stairs, wincing slightly when she landed too energetically on her weaker ankle, and walked into the hallway at the top of the stone cellar steps. As she skipped towards the toilet, her whole body was thrown backwards by the force of an invisible hand. The top of the side entrance to the house opposite where she stood seemed to bend inwards and shake as if an earthquake had erupted beneath Gartenstrasse. And then more deafening sounds exploded around the house. By this time, Georg had leapt up the stairs, grabbed his daughter and half dragged, half carried her back into the peat room.

Eva stared wildly at her parents, dazed by the sounds and half deafened by the booms she had heard, her ears ringing and making her head spin. Margarete was holding her ears with her head between her knees.

The family was paralysed by the relentless sounds of explosions which carried on for many minutes but seemed like an eternity. All were shaking slightly, Eva wrapped up in her mother's arms and curled up as small as she could make herself, burying her head under Hannelore's chin. It was too deafening to speak, the very walls of the cellar seemed to tremble.

Was another bomb about to hit their beloved home, destroy their lives completely? Were they all going to die?

Eventually the noise and tremors stopped. The siren sounded and the family weakly, nervously, rose towards the kitchen. Georg went to pour himself and Hannelore a cognac he had been saving for Christmas, a bottle he had eked out over the last years of war. Through the kitchen window a great fire billowed in the distance, and smoke drifted over the town like a sinister ghost. Fire engines and the sound of shouting soon followed. Georg ran down the steps of the house to the top of the drive and walked towards the commotion. After a few streets, he bumped into Sergeant Bauer who was organising a group of Hitler Youth to help with the fire.

'Bauer, what's going on?' he shouted, 'Is it the station?'

'Yes, Herr Doktor. A munitions train had stopped there for the night and has just been bombed. All the wagons have exploded one after the other. Unbelievably bad luck! Stay at home and look after your family.'

The policeman ran off with his troop of helpers.

Eva and Georg crept up to the attic to see if Frau Samuels was all right.

They peered in through the bedroom door, tapping on it lightly and found her with her hands pressed firmly over her ears and eyes tightly shut, shaking under her favourite pink shawl, moaning.

'It's just me and Eva, Frau Samuels. The bombing has stopped, there's nothing to be frightened of now.' Georg spoke to her in soothing tones, holding her hands, and lifting them away from her ears. She looked into his blue eyes and began crying and coughing.

'Oh Doktor Hoffmann. I am so sorry. I was just so frightened. I thought the bomb was landing on this house.'

Eva slipped beside her father and put her arms around the elderly lady's neck and whispered in a lilting song,

'Never, never, never be afraid. No never, never, never be afraid.'

The old lady calmed a little, touched by Eva's soothing voice, and rested back onto her pillow. Georg and Eva stayed a while to help her settle.

Later that evening Hannelore and Georg talked long into the night about the evening bombing raid of the station, as well as Max's injury, and decided that Hannelore would leave in the morning and take the train from Hanover and stay a couple of days near Dijon in a hotel he would organise in the morning. She could take a taxi to the battalion infirmary. He and the girls would be able to cope admirably without her for a few days, he reassured her.

They both slept fitfully that night, the reality of the news and trauma of the evening robbing them of any deep sleep. The telephone broke the night for Georg who had to make a visit to a young mother in labour. The midwife was calling him out to assist with a forceps delivery. Achingly tired he collapsed into bed at 5 am and drifted finally into a deeper sleep for a couple of hours.

Eva lay awake for a long time. Her mind was stuck somewhere at the top of the cellar steps when the world around her had suddenly started moving in slow motion, and she felt locked into a dream-like state of unreality. The next morning, she woke late. She heard voices outside on the landing near the staircase to the attic and wandered out of her room.

Her father, still in his pyjamas, having overslept himself, was looking agitated and her mother still in dressing gown was pacing the linoleum.

'What's going on?' Eva said blurrily, rubbing the sleep from her eyes.

Her parents looked at her simultaneously and her father knelt down on the floor in front of her and held her hands. She grew a little anxious.

'Eva, Frau Samuels has died. We heard her coughing a lot in the early hours of the morning, probably brought on by the anxiety of the bombing. I sat with her a while and gave her some linctus, but when I checked on her just now, I found that she had died in her sleep. Her heart had given up.'

Eva began to cry, a release from all the shock her young body had stored up since she had been hurled across the hallway the evening before. She cried into her father's shoulder, sad at the thought that their guest had died alone in the attic.

'She would have felt no pain, Eva, it was a peaceful death and she knew she was loved and protected. We must be glad that she was not sent to a work camp. I will let the Schwanns know and they can see her briefly to say goodbye before Herr Weiss is called.'

'What will be done with her body, Papa? She is supposed to be dead, isn't she?'

'Ah, we will make sure between us all that she is buried secretly in her own grave in the Jewish graveyard. It is a quiet place the other side of the woods and no one will be there at night. Herr Weiss can dig up the original coffin, lay her body there and cover it up again. We have already discussed this plan some time ago, knowing this might happen.'

'Can I say goodbye to her too, Papa?' Eva asked reverently.

'Yes of course,' he replied in a gentle voice, squeezing her hand.

'We shall go together and look death in the face and not be afraid.'

Dante's Inferno

April 1945

It was a cool, overcast Saturday afternoon. On the horizon, darkening clouds were gathering and rolling menacingly east towards Borkhausen. Hannelore had wisely decided not to water the freshly planted vegetable garden the day before, sensing that a storm was coming. The house was empty and quiet, almost peaceful, and Georg wandered around his home, deep in thought. The girls were out with friends, busily plotting Eva's thirteenth birthday. All had eaten a frugal lunch of chicken soup followed by boiled new potatoes and soured herb cheese. Dessert had been a small dish of stewed apple, the last of the winter preserves. Georg strolled into the surgery and sat down at his desk to tidy up his notes after the morning clinic. He was intending to take a nap in the hope that the telephone would be quiet for just one hour, just long enough to regain the energy to face the afternoon visits which would no doubt stretch into the late evening. The young doctors who had left Borkhausen to serve on the front had not yet returned to their practices and Georg's days began at six in the morning and ended rarely before ten o'clock at night. He couldn't remember the last time he had said goodnight to his daughters although he would always look in on them at night and kiss them gently on the forehead, stroking their cheeks softly with the back of his hand.

A sharp knock at the door punched away his thoughts. He sighed heavily, laid down his ebonite pen and peered through the net curtains of the surgery window towards the raised front doorstep. The American captain stood at the door, hands rammed onto his hips, standing squarely, grim-faced, with a young woman at his side. She couldn't have been more than nineteen or twenty years old, her face pale and gaunt, dark hair short and thin, her eyes sunken, her dress drooping around her slim frame. Georg recognised the American captain. He had commandeered the Bergman's villa next door as central headquarters in the town, but he didn't recognise the girl. He plodded wearily out of the surgery and opened the door. The dark-skinned captain stared at Georg for a few seconds, eyes narrowed, jaw set, and lips pursed, and started to speak in a garbled drawl that Georg didn't quite understand. Hannelore was at the market and wouldn't be back for another hour, otherwise he would have called her to help translate.

Almost as soon as the captain started speaking, the young girl, concentrating hard on what was being said, began speaking in fluent German. She explained that she was a displaced German from Breslau who could speak a little English and that she would translate what the captain was saying.

'We require your assistance immediately to help support the newly erected hospital in the region of Bergen. We urgently need medical professionals to support the thousands of patients that are quartered there at present. There is a typhus epidemic in this region, and it must be contained. Please prepare whatever medicines you might still have in your surgery to treat prisoners of war suffering from typhus. We shall escort you there and back for the rest of this week. All non-emergencies in the town will have to be put on hold for this time and any serious emergencies directed to Brunswick. Our car will wait outside your house while you pack your supplies.'

The girl fell silent as the captain stopped talking, and stared implacably at Georg, her eyes dark, but inscrutable. She seemed to be scanning the hallway behind Georg, absorbing all the sights and smells of the Hoffmann house - the shimmering wooden balustrade that swept up to the landing, the smell of chicken stock that still hung in the air from the kitchen and she inhaled deeply.

The blood drained from Georg's face. There was no time to get a message to Hannelore; he would have to leave a note on the kitchen table explaining where he had gone. Irma, who had returned to service at the Hoffmann's having helped Frau Deichmann through her postnatal recovery, would have to look after the meals and children for the rest of the day. He had heard the rumours of typhus breaking out in various prisoner of war camps and detention centres; it was fairly predictable given the multitudes of people that were often confined in close spaces, but the rumours had not been verified until today. He was also aware that there was a large prisoner of war camp in the area. Many stories had emerged of how vast it had grown over the last year, presumably because of prisoners from labour camps who were being moved from the East as the Red Army advanced.

Typhus. The word made him shudder. He was used to dealing with lice in children's hair, something that happened fairly regularly amongst the large families of Borkhausen, many of whose children shared a bed with each other, but typhus was something he had never had to deal with on a large scale. He had read of outbreaks in Africa, extreme situations where human beings were in closely confined spaces with poor hygiene. Places where lice could spread like wildfire. He also knew that it had plagued medieval Europe - but Germany in the 20th century? It must be typhoid fever, he thought to himself, they have misdiagnosed it, the symptoms are similar. It must be poor nutrition.

'Can I wait until my wife gets home? She won't know where I am,' he stuttered.

The young woman translated, and the Captain immediately shook his head and replied,

'This is an emergency – we need all medical personnel in the vicinity to come immediately. The staff at the hospital are in urgent need of help, there are many children who are extremely sick. The British forces who have occupied the camp have just flown in medical students to help, but the task is considerable. Pack your medical supplies immediately.'

Georg had no choice. He mumbled assent and strode off towards his surgery to scribble a note for Hannelore, and then searched for what meagre supplies of medicine he could muster, as well as his mask and surgical coat and gloves. The priority was to stay well, as well as he could. Georg's head was already pounding. The headaches that were becoming a daily occurrence were almost constant and often accompanied by weakness. Georg Hoffmann was ailing. He was ailing and he knew it; the diabetes was sucking the life from his kidneys.

He should have died fifteen years before; fifteen years ago when he almost slipped from this world to the next through a diabetic coma, saved according to Hannelore by her Hezekiah prayers and perhaps the insulin injection he received at the hands of an insightful doctor in Brunswick. Ten years earlier and he would have been a dead man, but the discovery of insulin in 1921 had marked a new era in survival rates and although still in its developmental stages, there was at least hope of a longer life. It was now known that renal failure and eye disease loomed as clouds over the diabetic, but Georg did not dwell on these. He was glad to be alive and to see his daughters born after his initial diagnosis; added blessings and something to live for, even in the broken world that now surrounded his family and beloved town.

He mopped the veil of sweat from his forehead with his pocket handkerchief and breathed rapidly and deeply at the thought of journeying now with the Army Captain and this haunting-looking ghost of a girl. She sat with a quiet grace and resolute stare beside the soldier in an open top jeep. Everything within him wanted to lie down and sleep, to sleep and forget just for a moment the black days of the last six years, perhaps the last twelve years. Heaving himself into a seat in the back, he closed his eyes, hoping there would be no need to talk. The jeep rumbled down the cobbled roads in the centre of the town and sped off down the long, straight highways that etched through the ploughed fields of the north, the sky a dense mass of charcoal grey clouds hovering on the horizon.

They passed farmhouses and small dwellings with pretty girls skipping in the gardens and old men resting under trees, enjoying a quiet afternoon snooze. Spring flowers were established now, and explosions of cherry blossom erupted around every corner, defiant in the face of a war-torn landscape. Life would go on again, thought Georg to himself. The boys will return soon, and all will be well, and we can rebuild again. Georg was always hopeful. He had to be strong for his family, for Hannelore. In spite of everything, they would salvage something from the madness of the past years, years which should have been filled with school celebrations, family holidays, ice creams on the Baltic islands, family gatherings, campfires... peaceful evenings in front of the peat stove, work put aside, no telephone ringing incessantly, no icy nights of visits along treacherous roads in the blackouts, no scurrying into the cellar during air raids as RAF bombers headed for Berlin.

Georg lifted his aching head for a moment and caught the silent girl looking sideways at him from the front passenger seat. There seemed to be a look of scorn on her face unless it was just the way her face fell, hollowed cheeks, sunken jaw. Her eyes were intensely dark and belied a beauty in spite of her thinness. No doubt she was one of the many refugees from the East who were now homeless in the face of the relentless march of the Red Army towards the River Elbe. Families had been fleeing their homes in complete terror at what the Russians might inflict on innocent civilians out of revenge for the Nazi invasion. They had a reputation for brutality. The poor girl probably escaped with just the rags she was wearing from her home, he decided.

'Where have you just come from?' he asked her in an attempt to make some conversation, curious too as to why she was working for the Americans.

There was silence for a long minute.

Then turning her head and looking straight at him their eyes locked. She did not break her gaze, as if to burn the words onto his mind.

'I have just spent the last year and a half in Dante's inferno,' she replied.

The jeep rumbled on now through the juniper and heather sandy moorland, birch trees lining the rough road as they neared their destination. No one spoke anymore. Georg was too tired to try and probe the girl about her comment and it was clear that she wasn't going to illuminate it. His head sagged to one side as he tried to doze and ease the pounding ache in his temples. Sleep was always a brief respite, so often broken by a drilling telephone or a pounding knock at the door, even on Sundays. He would never forget the Saturday call at the door at 7am when Frau Bertholdt's maid, Helga, screamed from the doorstep as she hammered for him to come and help Leah, crumpled on the kitchen floor next to her husband. He would wake sometimes sweating at the memory of that morning even when the telephone was quiet, and no one was at the door. Beautiful, pale Leah, whose eyes had closed peacefully in a deep, deathly slumber, her long pale fingers entwined around her Romeo's in a tragic sleep. Those fingers that would never again enchant Georg at his surgery desk, haunting him forever with notes that spoke of longing, and love, and gentleness in a world that seemed devoid of much that was beautiful. Or was it the memory of seeing his dead mother, Marlene, lying on the kitchen floor in front of the oven in his own childhood home before the war, overwhelmed by grief, unable to face a future without her beloved husband. Why did all the beautiful people want to destroy themselves?

So many, too, had died prematurely during this demonic war. It was as if the heart of the nation was ailing and as if a silent, painless disease was spreading throughout its body, imperceptibly destroying all these young men, cell by cell, until it was too late. It had invaded so many families who had lost all their young, hopeful healthy sons on the front. Grandparents had seen their sons and then their grandsons perish in two futile wars. A pall of death seemed to hang over the countryside, even in April, the month when hopes for a better future always seem to rise in even the most hardened heart. To Georg, drenched as he had been in his life with the rhetoric of war, it felt as if his beloved country would probably never recover from this disastrous reign of terror, never be able to lift its head high again in the world... never be forgiven.

Georg's exhausted worry-ridden dreams were suffocated temporarily by a ghastly stench that filled his nostrils and caused him almost physically to retch in the back of the jeep. He was used to the smells of freshly fertilised fields in the spring and autumn, but this was beyond anything he had ever experienced, even as a medical student in the last war serving on the brutal Eastern Front and dealing with gangrenous wounds of half-dismembered young men. The captain had placed a handkerchief over his mouth, the girl seemed oblivious to what the men in the jeep were experiencing, and Georg quickly removed the handkerchief from his top pocket and stuffed it in front of his nose and mouth.

'What on earth is that smell?' he gasped.

The girl turned languidly round in her seat once again and spoke in her lyrical tone,

'That is not an earthly smell, Herr Doktor, that is the stench of hell. You are about to see a symphony of suffering.'

The girl's lyrical turn of phrase underlined that she was educated. She spoke slowly and clearly almost as though she wanted to torture Georg with her words, spitting the word 'Doktor' slowly in his face.

Georg furrowed his brow, straining to see what was ahead as a collection of wooden barracks came into view a kilometre in the distance. The stench grew stronger if that was possible and could only be likened in Georg's mind to rotting meat, a smell that defied description, the smell of death.

The jeep halted in front of the camp gates, guarded by British servicemen. Large signs outside warned of the typhus epidemic next to a speed limit sign of 10km an hour. The captain explained that the camp they were entering was like a dust bowl and that typhus could be spread by dust. Georg surveyed the scene before him. A few faded pink huts stood amongst what appeared to have been an area occupied by far more huts. Raised areas of soil stood beside the charred remains of what presumably were other buildings that had been burnt to the ground. Smoke spiralled from these charred areas, but the acrid smell was not simply that of wood smoke, but something quite revolting, quite unforgettable. The girl was observing his reactions out of the corner of her eye. In the distance was a huge black mound that must have measured 60 feet long by 10 feet wide by 12 feet high. The captain drove the jeep slowly towards it as if he wanted Georg to look more closely.

'Are these shoes?' Georg asked the girl.

At the bottom of the pile, the staggering mountain of shoes had been pressed flat by mud, rain, and sheer weight. There must have been thousands of them, black and brown boots of all sizes; tiny bootees tumbled out beside what had once been fine stilettoed shoes ground shapelessly into pairs of ugly labourers' boots like flattened liquorice.

'Yes, Herr Doktor. You are looking at the shoes and boots of thousands of human beings who died before the British arrived.'

Georg's face looked puzzled. He had not dreamed that a typhus epidemic could reach these proportions. Who were all these people? Russian prisoners of war? Criminals? He knew that many of them had been transferred to a barracks in the region, as well as other political prisoners.

'I don't quite understand. What exactly is this place –this was a detention centre wasn't it? Did all these people die of typhus?'

The girl translated to the captain and he muttered something back to her. The captain had clearly given her permission to explain everything in her own words; he himself seemed unwilling to talk very much. The girl then spoke words that Georg would never be able to purge from his mind. 'Herr Doktor. You are in Bergen Belsen. You are standing in what remains of a Nazi concentration camp run by the SS. Within an hour of your front door, thousands upon thousands of Jews have been systematically degraded and treated worse than animals. They were brought here in cattle trucks, many dying on the journey, and were crammed in huge numbers into tents and huts, two or three to a bunk, barely a blanket and a crust of bread a day and disgusting watery soup. The mountain of shoes you see belonged to just some of these people; many thousands more have already been buried. The only crime many of these people had committed was to be born a Jew. The conditions in this camp have been so poor that epidemics have swept through. Hundreds have died every day for months. If you had come here a week ago when the camp was first liberated by the British, you would not have believed your eyes. Corpses piled up with nowhere for them to be buried. You may have thought, Herr Doktor, as I did when I arrived, that this was a convalescent camp. It is certainly not an extermination camp like the one I managed to survive in Poland, but the end result has been the same. Thousands of people have simply perished here, murdered by neglect.'

'What are these areas that have been burned?' Georg managed to enquire.

The girl looked at the mounds of charred remains.

'These were huts that had to be burned because of the typhus epidemic. They were swimming in human faeces and lice.'

'Did you arrive here with the British?' Georg asked her, wanting to be polite, not able to process everything she had told him.

'Herr Doktor, I have been living, if you can use that word, in this camp for over ten months. I am Jewish. I have lost almost all of my family and I have only survived because I am a musician who your Nazi swine were happy to keep alive to entertain them. I hope you are proud of your country's noble achievements; quite astounding. Germany truly is a most efficient nation.'

The sarcasm was not lost on Georg.

His face went grey. The blood drained from his face as the truth of what many of the townsfolk had only half suspected began to sink in. It was true. Jews had been detained here in overwhelming numbers and there had been a massive death toll. The neglect beggared belief. The Germans are decent people, a civilised people, he kept reciting in his head, Beethoven, Schubert, Bach... This can't possibly be true. Yet every face that Georg looked into and studied, carefully echoed the same silent, deafening truth, that this had been the scene of a nightmare.

Georg just looked at the mountain of boots, trying to understand what the girl was saying to him. He had heard rumours about this camp, heard that many people were dying, heard that the British had entered it and that there was talk of an outbreak of typhus... But mass deaths on this scale were... medieval.

The captain then spoke with a greater sense of urgency in his voice.

'We need to drive the doctor to Camp II and show him what is needed.'

Georg climbed back inside the jeep and was driven off for a couple of kilometres to another part of the camp where there were more buildings and personnel wandering about. He couldn't help noticing how thin some of the people were, skeletal in fact. Their clothes hung from them, cheeks hollow, eyes sunken and dead. They seemed to move around in a daze, as if unable to grasp that their time of imprisonment was over. Their clothes were in wonderful condition though and some looked brand new, but sagged for the most part off the shoulders of these emaciated people. He later learned that local townsfolk had been ordered to give away their clothes and local clothes shops were stripped of their merchandise for the same purpose.

They drove up to a large building and switched off the growling engine, and the captain pulled himself wearily out, shouting, 'Follow me,' to Georg and the girl.

As they turned into a doorway, they were met with the most extraordinary sight Georg had ever seen in all his medical life as a doctor – a sea of beds that stretched as far as he could see, filling a huge hall, a vast lake of emaciated bodies lying on camp bed stretchers, a ghastly moaning the only sound.

The captain began explaining to Georg, while the young woman translated, that this building was to act as a field hospital.

'This used to be the Panzer Barracks, a tank training school. The British forces found tons of food here as well as a large bakery and also a dairy nearby producing cheese, milk and butter. It is remarkable, is it not, Herr

Doktor, that all of these provisions were just two miles from the hell you have just seen.'

Georg had nothing to say. His mind had gone numb in the face of the appalling reality of what had been going on so close to his home for months and months.

'The British regiment has also managed to requisition all available beds from the surrounding villages as well as clothing, medicine, and blankets, and German army doctors have been collected from Prisoner of War camps to assist. You will join this group and work hard to save the lives of as many of these people as possible. You will be assisted shortly, as I said before, by a group of British medical students who are travelling from London. We are dealing here with typhus, typhoid fever, dysentery and tuberculosis.'

Georg nodded but inwardly collapsed. His wife and family had no real idea what was happening and here he was at real risk of being infected himself, already exhausted by his workload and weakened by the poor availability of insulin and quality care for his own disease. But the burning thought in his own mind was, 'What was he going to tell them? How could he face his family with the truth of what he was witnessing? How could he look into the big green eyes of Eva and tell her what had happened to girls her age.'

He was ushered into the stable block of the barracks and donned his white coat and mask and joined a group of other silent doctors and nurses who were running a 'human laundry' for inmates of the camp who were to be washed and deloused before they could be safely admitted to the wards in the main building. British Army soldiers supervised the procedure to ensure the patients were handled properly and with decency. Numbly,

Georg was shown a table that the patients were to lie on, and the washing could begin. Soldiers carried the sick into the stable on stretchers or assisted those able to walk and hoisted them onto the tables.

Gaunt, hollow-eyed men and women, mostly Jewish, looked into Georg's eyes, frightened that they would be tortured and mistreated. The British soldiers did their best to reassure them that they were safe now and most of them appeared to understand the basics of English. Some even spoke back to the soldiers, thanking them in English.

Georg stared into the hollowed eyes of the patients who were processed before him. The eyes bored into his. He dared not open his mouth to speak. He didn't want them to know he was German. Silently he manipulated their frail limbs and washed and deloused them in a putrid solution of chemicals. Hour after hour, without a break for lunch or tea, the small army of doctors worked on, barely communicating with each other as if in a collective stupor. Georg recognised one or two of the doctors as coming from Brunswick.

One young man, less feeble than the others, stared at Georg as he washed him down, unable to take his eyes off the face of the man now caring for him. It was as if he was scrutinising him. Georg glanced at his eyes and then abruptly looked away to what he was doing, uncomfortable with the intensity of the gaze. A million questions filled those eyes.

Sweat was pouring from his temples and lack of hydration and glucose was weakening him as he finished the last patient of the day. As he leaned against the wet bed that had been sprayed down with disinfectant his head began to swim. Black.

Georg woke up with a pounding headache in the Marienstift hospital in Brunswick, his old colleague Gerbich leaning over him and scrutinising a chart in his hand.

'Ah. Welcome back Georg! We nearly lost you there. Good job I knew who you were when they brought you in. We've checked your bloods and given you some insulin. You were dangerously hyperglycaemic. What were you thinking of, not taking your insulin?'

'It's a long story, Hermann. Where is Hannelore? Does she know? '

'She's on her way with the girls. Your boys still at the Front?'

'Yes, both of them, God willing still safe, although we are not entirely sure where they are. They are probably on the move with their units or in the hands of enemy forces.'

'They will be back soon, old man. Things are looking bad in the hospital, stocks here are low on everything; we are running this place on a shoestring. Now look here, you are not going back to work for a while. I'm writing you a sick note for a few months.'

'I can't possibly take that time off, Hermann, what will happen to my practice?'

'There are plenty of doctors coming back from the front who can take over your patients as you have taken over theirs. It's time you had a rest and recovered properly. Have a break. Find a place away from the house to rest for a while and start back again in September. Your war is over, Georg. You are a fine doctor.'

'Hermann - Belsen.'

'I know.'

Gerbich's face looked severe and lined, the resolute face of a convinced National Socialist. There was no trace of regret, or shock or pain in that face. The eyes were dead and lifeless, a consummate surgeon used to the scalpel, used to the anaesthesia of political rhetoric. He sniffed, turned away and said less enthusiastically than before, 'The gangrenous appendix of Germany had to be removed' adding quietly as if by force of habit 'Heil Hitler!'

Georg closed his eyes and prayed for a dreamless sleep.

The Fugitive

June 1945

The central market square of Borkhausen was framed against the backdrop of the impressive and imposing St Nikolai church, its pale pink walls glowing in the sunlight of the early summer of 1945. The clean simple baroque exterior contained the jewel of this small town; a beautiful altar, painted in gold, pink and white and adorned with cherubs. This was a giant of a church, a great footprint of the Reformation on a simple, agricultural landscape. The townsfolk were proud of their church and in its shade every Wednesday the market stall-holders would gather, and farmers would drive in their wagons of fruit and vegetables, the cobbled square would swarm with women clasping their wicker baskets. No bombs had fallen on this part of Borkhausen and everything appeared strangely normal.

All the chatter that day amongst the farmers and the women was of the lost war and missing sons and husbands. A trail of American jeeps, duce trucks and tanks had rolled into the town at 8 o'clock one morning, and with them, an awful truth dawned on the inhabitants of the small, sleepy town. They were at the mercy of the allied enemy troops. What would happen now? A collective terror fell upon every household at the thought of what vengeance they might wreak on the helpless townsfolk. Stories of the Red Army raping young and old women were rife further east of the Elbe. Would the Americans do the same? Fears mounted as soldiers drove recklessly through the fences and front gardens of many of the finest homes in the town, completely disregarding the premises, turning homes upside down as they searched for possible weapons. They hammered on the front doors, barked orders in a drawl no one could understand, requisitioning homes for officers and troops. They came too to the Hoffmann villa and demanded to speak to the owner. Hannelore brusquely explained in perfect English that her husband was the only doctor working in the town and needed his surgery. Sheepishly the soldiers retreated but only after they had painted a large red cross on the front door. Neighbours who were driven out of their own homes came to stay for a few weeks at a time with the Hoffmanns until the soldiers finally moved out.

Eva liked the soldiers – she had never seen black men before and she thought their broad white grins very funny. She was particularly pleased because they threw chocolate to her and her friends as they lined the kerbside to watch the procession of jeeps in the road. Her father strictly forbade her to accept these treats, but she gleefully hid them under her pillow to share with Margarete at night. In spite of a curfew at 6 pm for all citizens of the town, she would creep out along the back gardens and visit her friends in their gardens and homes. She had just turned thirteen and felt very grown up now.

Hannelore set off at a brisk pace down Gartenstrasse early that summer's morning, basket slung over her arm, pale summer coat flapping in the June breeze. She had left her daughters to clear away the breakfast bowls and to start reading their English grammar books. Georg was still sleeping. The marketplace was buzzing with activity as she walked down the high street, her eyes gazing up at the shimmering grey tower and gold clock of the church. It was 8 o'clock and already half the town's women were bustling around the stalls and tables.

'Hanne, Guten Morgen!'

Silke Behring waved as Hannelore approached. Silke was a good friend, not one of the gossips she used to dread meeting in the square.

'The new potatoes have arrived this morning – look over there by Wachsmuth's stall.'

'Ah, Georg will be pleased, and Eva. She was asking me only this morning if they might be ready yet.'

'Any news?' Silke searched Hannelore's lined and taut face.

'No, still no news. I heard on the radio last night that the Americans are moving captured soldiers around. I can only think that Max is being transported somewhere until he can be processed and sent home. We have no idea how long that will take. '

'And Johannes?'

Hannelore bit her lip involuntarily. 'God only knows.'

Both women knew of the unspeakable horrors that might await any 'Nazi swine' that fell into the hands of the Red Army.

'There is talk of another wave of refugees fleeing from the east now that the war is over.'

'Yes, I fear for those poor souls too ill or infirm to travel. There will be no mercy,' Hannelore added.

'There are rumours too that we shall have to take those fleeing into our homes.'

'We must be prepared for all eventualities, although I don't know where I would put anyone. All our bedrooms are occupied in the holidays; the girls are already sharing a room again now that Irma is back, and Johannes and Max will be too. My mother and sister are in the sitting room downstairs.'

'Will they return to Hanover?'

'I think it is unlikely. The street is rubble, everything lost... they were fortunate to have been in the air raid shelter at the time. My mother is too frail to rebuild her life again there, and my sister...'

Hannelore's voice trailed off as she shrugged her shoulders, somehow unwilling to articulate the dark, brooding moods that hung over her sister, moods that had plagued her adult life and which the war had simply intensified. Hannelore was resigning herself to living her life around the edges of everyone else's. How she longed to just sit down for a few hours and immerse herself in her beloved books, to have all her family seated around the oak dining room table and to restart their lives. She could settle to nothing these days through either sheer worry about her sons or ailing husband, or the relentless busyness of each day's domestic demands.

The friends parted, and she headed back slowly to her house, relieved that at least her neighbours had been able to return to their homes as a troop of American soldiers had moved on. It was lunchtime before Hannelore had finished her morning's tasks at the market and paying bills at various shops along the route home. She plodded a little wearily up the side steps to the hallway, feeling the weight now of her basket of potatoes and onions. She left them on the kitchen table for Irma to attend to before heating up the vegetable soup on the stove.

Eva and her friend Rose had perched themselves at the top of the main steps to the house. Both girls had finished their studies at home for the morning, quietly glad that the school was still closed and being used as an infirmary.

'Are you sad the League of Girls has closed down?' Rose asked her.

'I miss the sports and the craft and the singing,' Eva replied, 'but I don't miss that Anneliese barking orders at us. I never liked her. Her face was always so hard and if she didn't like you, she made sure you knew it.'

'I know what you mean – I think she liked me because I could run fast,' Rose replied.

'Yes – you are definitely the best runner in our school year, Rose.'

'You would be too if you didn't struggle with your ankle.'

'I know – my brothers are both very good runners, especially Johannes.'

'My brothers are faster than me – Gerd is so fast that he was used as a runner between battalions in France, he wrote to my mother. I'm looking forward to seeing him again soon.'

'I'm looking forward to us all going for long walks on the heathland again with a picnic – I really miss our Sunday outings – it's not the same when it's just me and Margarete. Papa doesn't seem to want to go there much any more since he has been so poorly. I worry about him, but Mama says he just needs lots of rest.'

At that moment Rose's brother Conrad appeared around the bend in the road and called her home for lunch. She jumped down the steps and dashed after him, shrieking, 'See you later, Eva!' her tight brown curls bobbing as she sprinted.

The warm sun pinned Eva to the top step of the front door, and she watched the world go by for a few more minutes before lunch. Wafts of the delicious soup floated through the open surgery window from the kitchen. In the distance at the far end of the road, her eye caught sight of a ragged figure staggering towards her in the distance. She squinted in the sunlight at the unfamiliar shape of a tall, slender man. He was walking quite fast, if a little hunched at the shoulders. She remained seated, curious as to who this character might be. As he drew nearer to her, she looked up again and he motioned to her to be quiet, raising his finger to his mouth. The face was dirty and the short hair blonde but greasy. Grimy fingernails hugged an old grey blanket around his shoulders, concealing what was clearly a German soldier's uniform.

'Max!' Eva stifled a gasp and her green eyes widened in shock, surprise, and utter delight.

She ran up to him and threw her head against his chest and hugged him.

'Max! What a wonderful surprise! We didn't know where you were.'

'Shh! Eva – don't say anything more. Wait until we are inside the house.'

'You don't smell too good, Max.'

'Shh!'

They were almost at the front of the drive and Eva headed at a pace towards the steps to the side entrance, but Max motioned for her to walk down to the bottom of the drive where the garage opened onto the back garden.

Once inside the garage, Max put his arms around his little sister and held her, and then placed his hands firmly on her shoulders as if to prepare her to listen carefully. His blue eyes looked intently into hers and in a half whisper he said,

'I don't want any of father's patients to see me, Eva. Can you go up to the kitchen and tell Mama to come down to the cellar. Tell her that you want to show her something. Don't blurt anything out – do you think you can do that?'

'How exciting, Max, it's just like Christmas Eve with Johannes. Yes, I will be very serious, but Papa isn't seeing patients at the moment, he has a locum doctor standing in for him – he has been quite poorly and has been resting for some months now – didn't Mama tell you in her letters?'

'Ah yes – she did say something but not in any great detail – her letters were always full of what you and Margarete are doing. Now go, and if Mama is with a neighbour or friend, then come back and tell me.'

Eva ran off through the garage door that led into the dark corridors of the cellar, striding past the laundry kitchen, preserve store and peat room, her heart pounding. She walked up the stone steps into the kitchen to see her mother serenely stirring the soup, and Irma taking cutlery into the dining room for lunch. While Irma was laying the table in the next room, Eva sidled up to her mother, trying hard not to look flushed.

'Mama, there's something I want to show you in the cellar.'

'Ach Eva, we are about to eat – can it not wait until after lunch. Papa is due to come back any minute and Margarete is washing her hands. Could you do the same and we can eat in a few moments.'

'But it is really important that you come N-O-W.' Eva spelt the words out as if to emphasise the importance of the request and looked hard into her mother's eyes. Hannelore sighed, put down the ladle and called to Irma to watch the soup for a moment.

Eva smiled and led her mother down the steps into the cellar towards the garage where Max was slumped on a pile of old potato sacks.

He jumped to his feet as soon as his mother entered the garage and embraced her before she could fully take in what was happening. He held her for a long time, his body shaking as he sobbed out his fear and pain and relief.

'Thank you, Jesus!' was all Hannelore could whisper over and over again in her son's ear as he wept.

Eva stood beside them both wrapping her arms around her mother and brother's waist, absorbing this special reunion.

'Mama we must tell Papa and Margarete.'

'Max, why are you here? What has happened?' Hannelore eventually asked.

Max smeared his eyes with a grimy hand and began explaining the events of the last days.

'My unit was seized by the Americans a few weeks ago and we were detained until more troops arrived. We were then told we were going to be moved on to another prison camp out of France to the north of Germany. I knew there was a chance we might be driving near to Borkhausen. After days of travelling and sleeping in the wagons I began to recognise some of the signs around Brunswick and I panicked. I had no idea how much further they might take us. I overheard the American driver joking about throwing us all on the mercy of the Red Army. I ran off into the nearest woods in the middle of the night and have been walking under cover of darkness, sleeping by day in barns. I stole a horse blanket from a stable to disguise my uniform and have been terrified that the Americans are hunting me down. I could be shot as a prisoner...' At this Max broke down again in tears, sobbing uncontrollably.

Eva looked on, sadness spreading across her eyes and mouth. The thought of her brother being shot as a prisoner of war was ghastly. No one was going to touch him – they would hide him if they had to. They had managed to hide Frau Samuels and they could hide him in the attic too.

'Max, Max – it is all right. The war is over. We will sort this out. Don't worry.' Hannelore spoke soothingly but with an assertive edge. 'Papa will make sure you are safe. Now, my son, you need to be fed. I will send Irma off to town for a few hours while we decide what to do. Wait here for a few minutes. Eva, come with me.'

Hannelore and Eva headed back up the cellar steps into the kitchen and she began scribbling something on a piece of kitchen paper and making up small paper bags of tomatoes from the basket in the cold larder.

'Irma, you have eaten your lunch already haven't you?'

Yes, Frau Hoffmann.'

'I need you to go to town and fetch me some more flour from Wernecke's. And could you also take these tomatoes to the addresses on this paper – a small bag for each of the families. Don't rush back – you deserve a little time off. Enjoy the sunshine.'

'Thank you, Frau Hoffmann – I will be back before afternoon Kaffee.'

'Do use the side entrance today. Eva will lock the door after you.'

As the key turned in the lock, Eva leapt down the steps two at a time and joined her mother in the cellar. Max was weak. He had not eaten in two days and the rations he had been given by the Americans were meagre. They led him up the cellar steps into the familiar kitchen and he sat down at the table, as Johannes had done three years before, and ate several bowls of leek and potato soup.

A delighted Margarete had been fetched down by Eva and all crowded around the kitchen table to listen to Max's tale of escape. He seemed older, more serious, and even thinner than when he had left as a gangly eighteen-year-old. He was only just twenty-one but seemed much older. His eyes looked different. The boy had disappeared. At last Georg arrived back from his walk to the castle to visit an old friend working in the prison office.

As he walked into the kitchen, his face bleached, all colour drained away and he swayed slightly before grabbing his son's shoulders and squeezing him tightly.

'Max... my son. You are home. Welcome home, my son! Max!' Georg held the back of his son's head with his left hand and cupped his cheek with his right as if holding a precious object in his hands.

'You need a bath my son. And fresh clothes – if any of them still fit you, that is – we need to fatten you up a bit with some of mother's apple pancakes.'

'Yes! Yes!' the girls shrieked in unison, 'please Mama.'

Hannelore smiled and they all enveloped Max in more hugs. While he bathed in the kitchen the rest of the family sat and had their soup in the dining room. Georg and Hannelore sent their daughters off to go and find a towel and some clothes for their brother and discussed what they needed to do before Irma returned.

'We must conceal him somehow.' Georg spoke in low tones. 'The American authorities will be searching for him without a doubt, although goodness knows how much time they have to hunt down runaways in the middle of this chaos the country is in. Let's hope they are not as vigilant as the Gestapo were. I will ask our locum to admit him to the school hospital here in Borkhausen. They won't think of looking for him there, and he looks as if he could do with some complete rest anyway.'

Georg went off to see if his locum was still there. He was writing up notes from the morning's surgery. Their voices spoke in hushed tones, and then a telephone call was made to the infirmary. Max was dressed in his old clothes that hung off his gaunt frame, and after another hearty meal of pancakes with his family, was driven under a blanket through the town by his father to the small hospital nearby and checked in with instructions of complete bed rest for a few weeks, enough time hopefully for the search for his whereabouts to be abandoned. Georg left him to settle in and returned later that evening during visiting hours.

Max lay in a freshly laundered bed in the corner of the ward, surrounded by familiar townsfolk, who all nodded and smiled as his father walked in and sat beside him in a chair, taking his pulse. It was racing.

He looked into his son's eyes and smiled reassuringly, speaking quietly.

'You are safe now, my son, they will take care of you here – no one will betray your whereabouts. If anyone does ask, just tell them you were wounded at the end of the war and were sent to recuperate back home. That's what we have told the hospital administration. If any Americans come looking, tell them that you are shell-shocked and that you don't remember anything that happened to you before you came to be in this hospital.'

Max nodded and looked into his father's eyes.

'I thought I was going to die, Papa, I was buried alive and I thought I was going to die.'

Georg held his son's hand and patted and rubbed it.

Max was gritting his teeth as his mouth trembled and eyes welled up.

'We shall talk more soon, my son, we shall soon all be home together and Johannes will be back soon as well. You are safe now, thank God. Don't distress yourself right now. Just rest and sleep.'

'What was it all for, Papa? What was it all for?'

This time Max's eyes stared soullessly at the polished stone-tiled floor.

Georg patted his son's hand. He had no words.

'We will talk more soon. I shall return tomorrow, try and get some sleep.'

As he walked slowly down the ward, he turned his head to look at his son. Max's head was still locked intently on the floor and he could see the words forming again in a whisper,

'What was it all for?'

Georg strode back to the car, sweating and clutching the blanket he had draped over his son when he had brought him into the hospital, and thought again about the multitude of secrets he had been and still was holding on to; the hiding of his son from the enemy forces, the secret love he had borne Leah, Esther Samuels' existence in the attic, the ghastly scenes at Belsen he had not disclosed even to Hannelore, and perhaps the one he was currently most worried about, the extent of the weakness in his own body.

Autumn Leaves

23rd September 1945

Summer was relinquishing its vibrant hold on the Hoffmann garden. That moment had come late in September when autumn's beautiful but deadly hand was hanging in the air. For Eva, though, it was a wonderful season. The excitement of leaves transforming from rich greens to a myriad of yellows, oranges, and reds before wafting fairy-like earthwards was thrilling. The fact that this would inevitably be replaced by the gradual darkening carpet of dank, decaying sludge on the ground was far from her thoughts at this time. Every inch of her thirteen-year-old being was longing for change and her only thoughts were of what might be around the corner. Even war had not managed to crush Eva's spirit. So much in their lives had been oppressed by the madness of the past six years: the broken schooling, the bombing raids heading to Berlin, the constant news of fallen soldiers in the town, her brothers' absences, the endlessly long hours her father was 'away' from home on visits or in his surgery; hours of writing notes, receiving calls, snatching meals, until he had been forced to take six months sick leave as the war ended and take on a locum doctor to cover his practice; the ever present concern that waves of refugees, fleeing the advancing Red Army in the east would mean they had to take families in and share their home...

But Eva's heart was full of hope that all was going to change and return to normal. The war was over, her brothers were home at last! And her heart was brimming with excitement. Her family was together again around the dining room table, and her beloved Johannes had finally returned home two weeks earlier to great celebration, a little thinner but even more handsome in her eyes. Miraculously the Hoffmann boys had survived the war.

Eva wandered, limping almost imperceptibly through the garden, picking the late raspberries, watching the last lazy bees hum around the chrysanthemums, and fading roses, as she bathed her face in the warmth of summer's dying rays. It was quiet. Wonderfully quiet. No more sirens, no more air raids, the American tanks had long gone and a sense of normality was returning to the town. The new delayed school term was about to begin again after the mopping up after the war had ended, and pictures of Hitler had been unceremoniously ripped down, along with all the propaganda posters that had scarred the walls of the buildings throughout the town. Germany was quietly removing its shame and a conspiratorial silence descended across the stores and streets of Borkhausen.

Today was the first day her beloved father had started back at work and she was looking forward to greeting him at the end of the day.

It was two in the afternoon.

As she turned to head back into the house after her stroll, she saw her parents coming down towards the driveway from the cellar garage, car door keys and leather bag in hand. Her father looked exhausted. There were some afternoon visits to do and Hannelore had persuaded him to let her drive him. She had clearly sensed that he was still not fit to drive. She was ill at ease at the decision to return to work and had tried to persuade him to take more time to get well, perhaps take a cure in the Harz mountains, but Georg was adamant that he start to provide properly

319

again. If he didn't return soon, then they would be forced to sell one of their properties and in this financial climate they would get nothing close to the real worth of their estate. No, work was the only option, and anyway it would do him good to get out again and see his patients. Doing something useful would take his mind off the events of the past six years and perhaps even drown out the voices from the trenches that continued to fill even his waking hours during convalescence.

The truth was that although Georg really did not feel well, he knew that if he did not work he would begin to go slightly crazy. Images of what he had been forced to witness in April on that fateful day when the captain and the strange, mysterious girl had driven him to Belsen were beginning to inhabit his dreams. Bizarre images from both the wars merged into ghastly apocalyptic scenes. Skeletal humans wandered in and out of muddied forests in the Caucasus. Soldiers clambered over mountains of boots and shoes, collapsing onto piles of emaciated corpses. The angry stares of the British medical officers, soldiers and nurses, the haunting, accusing glare of the Jewish patients burned into his head, pounding in his mind in time to the ever present throbbing headaches that racked him most mornings on waking.

'Hallo meine schoene Eva, how you are growing.'

Georg smiled at his beautiful, blonde daughter and held out his arms to her. Her hair was almost translucent in the sun, shimmering, flowing free instead of the usual plaits. She was becoming a young woman and he had barely noticed. Her green eyes seemed larger, and her face was already recognisably finer and more mature, although something of the pouting five-year old still lingered in her mouth. Georg was not going to let her see his weariness. He would push on through this tiredness and their family life would return to some kind of normality again – just another season to get through before he could enjoy watching his daughters grow into fine young women and his sons break through on their career paths.

She sank her cheek against his chest, burying her head beneath his chin.

'Ach, Papa. Must you go out again?'

'I won't be long, Mama is coming with me, so you must help us and occupy yourself this afternoon. School will be starting again soon. I bumped into the new Headmaster on the High Street and he was looking forward to getting you all into school after the extended break. Try and read that last chapter of your story... and you can tell me about it over supper. I want to hear what you thought of the ending.'

'Ich liebe Dich Papa.'

He smiled and caressed her hair.

'Ich liebe Dich, Eva. Ich bin ganz stolz auf Dich.' He was proud of her and wanted her to hear it.

Hannelore kissed her daughter 'I've left you and the others some raspberry jelly in the fridge for tea, Schatz.'

'Danke. Liebe Dich Mama.'

Georg slumped in the passenger seat of the Mercedes, rested his head back a little and closed his eyes. Hannelore turned the ignition key and the great car growled gently up and out of the drive, turning onto the cobbled road, and then headed steadily out of Borkhausen towards the outlying villages. The relentless stream of 'phone calls all morning from surgery could not be put off until tomorrow when yet more would come. Georg's workload had trebled since the start of the war and having taken six months off meant there was a huge case load to catch up on before it settled into a more normal pattern of work. Two of his younger colleagues who had returned from their postings as army doctors had taken over their surgeries again, but it would take time for them to catch up too and for things to adjust. Just under half of all the medical practitioners had been sent to the front lines during the war and Georg and his other colleague in the town had carried the full weight of their absence. His patient list had grown to over a thousand more than at the start of the war and it was only now starting to plateau.

Eva headed upstairs to find her book and crept up with it to the upstairs sunroom at the back of the house where she clambered out of the great window overlooking the garden onto the flat roof of the veranda, gazing perilously down onto the driveway below. It was terrifyingly high, but it was a test of her bravery and she loved the fact that her parents had strictly forbidden it. She rolled over onto her back and bathed in the warmth of the autumn sun, joined by Margarete who knew where to find her daring sister.

'Do you remember when I fell out of the elderflower tree, Greta?'

'How can I ever forget that day?' her sister scowled back as if in mock rebuke at her sister's foolish behaviour.

'Do you remember how angry Papa was?'

'Ach ja, but only because he was so worried about his precious little blonde Eva! We both know that you are his favourite! You have wrapped him round your little finger.'

Eva smiled and poked her sister in mock rebuke.

Margareta closed her eyes and smiled too and thought about her father. She loved her father -perhaps more than her mother. She admired her mother's hard work, she understood that it was hard for her to manage a busy household, she realised that her mother had worried about her sons all these years, but she always seemed too serious; she was always buried in books if she had a spare moment... seemed to love books more than life itself; she couldn't remember the last time her mother had laughed at the meal table. Why did everything have to be so serious, so sad? The war had ended hadn't it? Of course, Germany had lost and the news on the radio was full of broken cities and recession, but Margarete's heart was bursting with dreams of romance and a life of excitement and yearnings for adventure. She couldn't have felt happier at this moment, and her father made her feel beautiful. He would tousle her wavy dark brown hair and pinch her cheeks and let her go cycling off with her friends without any great discussion about when she should be back... ah Papa. She sighed deeply, eyes still shut in the warm September sun.

Eva read on, gripped by the last chapter of her story, desperate now to finish so that she could tell her father what the final twist was. She had begun to read it with him some evenings, now that he had felt a little better and she treasured this time more than anything - time alone with him, his full attention. His soft, deep voice rising and falling with the different characters in the story. He seemed to enjoy these times too, enjoyed the fantasy of different worlds full of mountains, dense mysterious forests, and tumultuous lightning storms.

It was some hours later that Georg and Hannelore returned and finally parked the dusty cream Mercedes in the garage.

Georg heaved himself and his bag out of the passenger seat and steadied himself against the car.

'I'll make you some camomile tea,' Hannelore said soothingly, trying to beat down her own feelings of exhaustion. Her mind had been wandering all evening. In two days' time it would be Margarete's sixteenth birthday and she still had to finish making the dress she had been secretly sewing for her. She had made polite conversation at the homes of the patients this evening, but all the time she was thinking through the jobs at home that needed doing. The girls would be going back to school shortly after an extended summer holiday, and the boys would need to continue their studies and find university places. Johannes was determined to finish his medical degree and take over his father's practice one day and Max whose life had been shattered so suddenly now wanted to study theology. Inaudibly whispered prayers in thanksgiving for her sons had been uttered on the drive home as Georg dozed beside her. Hannelore had spent the war praying, especially for Max.

'Thank you, that would be nice, I'm really thirsty,' replied Georg, 'Thank you for driving.'

Hannelore headed out towards the garden.

'I'll be up in a moment. I just need to pick those last ripe tomatoes.'

She headed off towards the vegetable patch where most of the roses had once bloomed. Her brown hands, once always pale, had become adept at gardening and tending the precious fruits and vegetables that had helped see the family through the war; that and the many bounteous contributions from farming patients.

Georg watched his wife for a moment, grateful that she was nearby, and then wiped the sweat from his brow and blinked his eyes a few times as his body started to sway. The ground felt as if it was moving beneath him. Hannelore's voice seemed dull and distant even though she was only a few metres away. Georg staggered into the garage, through the heavy iron door into the cellar, along the corridor and then heaved himself slowly up the stone stairway, every step an effort of will as he grasped hold of the banister rail. He turned into his surgery and dropped his bag on the floor. After a few minutes Hannelore followed behind him and urged him to go and lie down on the sofa in the family room. He sighed in assent and wandered through to where his boys were. He could be heard as he chatted briefly with his sons, who were slumped in armchairs, catching up with their studies, books piled high around them on side tables. Johannes was regaling Max with tales of life on the Russian front, how the rats had chewed through their knapsacks and how they had endured freezing temperatures, though Max was strangely quiet. Georg listened, smiling, attempting to chuckle along with the conversation, and then slowly dozed off.

Hannelore busied herself in the kitchen, setting the kettle to boil and washing the tomatoes ready for supper. She made the tea and brought it through to where her menfolk were gathered. The boys had returned to their books to let their father doze. Margarete was coming down the stairs, book in hand, but there was no sign of Eva. Hannelore walked over and placed the tea tray on the table and turned to look at Georg. Something was not right. Sweat poured down his face and his mouth was slightly open.

'Georg, Georg!' she took his hand, cold and clammy, and patted it. He groaned but didn't lift his eyelids.

'Georg! Wake up. What is wrong? Johannes! What is wrong with Papa?'

Johannes by this time had leapt to his side and was holding his father's wrist.

'I can feel a pulse, Mama! But it is weak. We need to get him to the hospital quickly. I'll go and call.'

Johannes ran off to the surgery to 'phone the hospital.

'Georg, Georg. Come back, can you hear me? No, don't leave me now, not now.' Hannelore pleaded.

His head stirred, his eyes blinked open for a second and his mouth seemed to move.

Within minutes a taxi roared up the cobbled Gartenstrasse. A shortage of ambulances had left the townsfolk dependent on volunteers manning taxis to see to local emergencies. Hannelore held her husband's head in her lap on the sofa, stroking his clammy forehead and wiping away the beads of sweat. Johannes was by his side too, holding his pulse. Max's face glazed over as if in a trance. Everything to him seemed to be moving in slow motion. He knelt by the sofa urging his father to hold on, praying quietly under his breath, trying to soothe his mother.

'Hold on Papa. Please Father God take care of my father... it will be all right Mama. Please make him well... the taxi will be here soon...'

Johannes held onto his father until the taxi came and spoke with the attendants as Georg was lifted into the back seat, describing his symptoms and pulse rate. Hannelore climbed in beside her husband.

'Stay here Johannes and take care of the others. I shall telephone you when I have news.'

'Gott befohl dich, Mama. He will be all right. Don't worry.'

Johannes tried to sound more hopeful and dearly wished that he was in the back of the taxi himself but did as his mother requested. Margarete who had watched everything in trepidation from the threshold of the room turned and ran upstairs to her sister. Where was Eva? She rushed into the back bedroom, peered out of the window, and spied her sister, book open beside her and dangerously close to the edge of the roof. Without wishing to startle her, she crept quietly onto the roof, heart pounding with the shock of what she had just witnessed downstairs and held her sister firmly round the shoulders and whispered urgently into her ears.

'Eva. Eva. Wake up!'

Drunk with sleep, her eyes still screwed tightly shut, Eva murmured 'What's wrong, what time is it?'

'Come off the roof, Eva, you could have fallen off – come on, schnell, into the room.'

Eva crawled to the window, shivering slightly from having lain so long in the cool of the early evening, and only then did Margarete look her sister fully in the eyes and say,

'Eva, Papa is not at all well, he has been taken to the hospital. Mama is with him.'

Eva's heart started to pound. She could see from Margarete's eyes that this was serious. She turned and ran out of the room to find Johannes downstairs, Margarete following her at a pace. Eva's book lay open still on the roof, pages fluttering in the breeze.

It was a long evening for the four Hoffmann children. They sat up late in the family room talking, slouched on the low brown sofas around the walnut coffee table, the two brothers only too conscious of Margarete and especially Eva; wanting to reassure them, yet only too aware of how sick their father was. Of course, they had known he had diabetes since they were small, but it had become part of their routine lives that he would inject himself with insulin and take care with what he ate. They knew that he had not been well, but none of them had really seen quite how exhausted their father had become. Johannes knew more than the others just how precarious his health was, but no one realised how hard he had been working and how much he had worried about their safety on the various battlefronts. The hours ticked by. Georg had collapsed at seven o'clock and it was now ten. Still no news.

'We should pray for Papa' said Max reverently after a long silence 'That is what Mama would do.'

'Yes, that's a good idea' added Eva seriously.

Max smiled encouragingly at his little sister. They all bowed their heads and he prayed for his father, lying in a diabetic coma in the Marienstift hospital in Brunswick. Eva screwed up her eyes tightly and clenched her hands together as if to exert some force of will into the prayers. She hadn't closed her hands in prayer since she was a small child, sitting on her mother's lap at bedtimes. She so wanted to have her mother next to her now, to feel her safe and reassuring presence, the smell of her familiar cologne, the softness of her cotton dress, the knowledge that everything was going to be all right. After a few minutes, her eyes started drooping and in sheer exhaustion she headed up to bed with Margarete, her ankle feeling even heavier than usual. Margarete had moved back into their old room after the return of Irma, but now she was glad of the presence of her little sister. They undressed automatically, brushed their teeth, the ritual habits of their childhood so ingrained that they barely thought about them, and then silently lay down, unable to speak to one another; Margarete went to the window to draw the curtains. The harvest moon hung huge and low in the clear sky. A vast array of stars shafted through the heavens as far as she could see, a twinkling mass of eyes gazing down at her and for a moment she was lost in awe at the vastness of space. She turned and crept under the cool sheets of her bed, pulling the blankets around her. She peered over to Eva who was clutching her now slightly battered but much-loved doll Johannes tightly. The girls lay in the milky darkness of that pale night, only the sound of creaking beams above them in the attic, and the distant droning voices of their brothers could be heard, talking in the family snug at the foot of the grand staircase below them. Eva, wrung out by the evening's events, dropped off to sleep within minutes, but Margarete lay there wide awake. The day after tomorrow it would be her sixteenth birthday, the first birthday in years when war was not raging around their lives. She had been planning her little gathering of friends for weeks now and it had dominated the conversation around the meal table ever since her brothers had returned: what would she serve her friends at the little tea party they were allowed to have? What kind of cake must Mama bake this year? Apfelkuchen or Quark? Both were favourites – the apples had been so plentiful this year - and what little sugar Mama was able to salvage each week was carefully put by for birthday cakes. She had barely noticed the weariness around her father's eyes as he fought off the relentless pounding in his head. He rarely complained, how was she to know? And yet she suddenly felt guilty that she had not noticed, had not said much to him today, had missed seeing him as he left for his afternoon visits because she had been too busy with her friends upstairs. Tears welled up in her eyes. Silent tears that she shielded from her sister and wiped into her soft goose down pillow. Gradually sleep took hold of her and carried her to a more peaceful place for a few hours.

Early the next morning, around seven o'clock, the silence was pierced by the all too familiar ringing of the telephone. Johannes was the first to the 'phone, having spent the night lying on his parents' bed, but every one of the children heard the ringing; all of them were wide awake already and huddled around him.

The telephone was on Georg's bedside table next to a silver-framed sepia photograph of Hannelore as a young woman. In it she posed serenely for the camera, her beautiful dark brown hair parted in the middle and swept back into a bun. A fine aquiline nose joined a sculpted mouth. Around her neck hung a gold chain which slipped secretively below the white frill of her dark dress. Ornamenting her right hand, a gold band. She looked beautiful, a thinner version of her fifty-three-year-old self, one taken before she became a mother, with pale smooth skin, a gaze that was penetrating, intense, self-possessed and quietly defiant. It was as if she were questioning and even challenging the camera to tell the truth.

The children all ran into the room and sat on their father's bedside next to their eldest brother, his dark eyes staring at the floor.

'Ja, Mama, we are all here together.' His eyes fluttered towards the anxious faces of his siblings and then returned to the dark polished floorboards, his fine fingers twirling the twisted cable that hung down from the black receiver in his hand.

There was a long silence.

'Ja, Mama, I will do that. I will do that. We love you.'

Another long pause. After what seemed like an eternity, Johannes replaced the receiver with a quiet clunk onto the handset.

Silence.

Three sets of eyes bored into their elder brother's.

Johannes looked into the eyes of his brother and sisters and decided in that one moment that he simply had to say it as he had heard it from his mother.

'Papa died last night around midnight. Mama was with him. There was nothing the doctors could do for him. It was very peaceful she said. She is with him now and will stay for a bit longer at the hospital before coming home.'

Disbelief hung in the air for a moment and then punched each of them in the gut.

'Nein, nein, nein, Papa! Nein!' Margarete exclaimed as she burst into tears beside her brother, and Eva on the other side started sobbing simultaneously. Max and Johannes put their arms around their sisters and together the Hoffmann children cried, each one of them. All their hopes and dreams were in one minute shattered, everything they had fought for in France and Russia was in pieces. All those wasted days and months and years away from their beloved father, for what? How would they cope without their father? What would happen to their home and family? Rivers of tears began to flow on that bed that day in September, in that year when a war had ended. For this family it was as if it had only just been declared.

Eva crept up the wooden stairway to the attic with her notebook and pencil and stayed there a long time writing in the small bedroom that Frau Samuels had once occupied under the heavy beams of the roof. Johannes fielded 'phone calls from patients, and Max stayed with Margarete and tried his best to console her, but whilst Max tried to smile, his eyes were dead. His eyes had died in France when he had been buried alive, and again the panic was rising within him, suffocating panic that he was sinking once more into the sodden, devouring trench as yet another bomb exploded next to him. Sporadically over the next few hours until his mother returned, he had to lock himself in the toilet and try and conceal and quell the shaking of his hands and the profuse sweating all over his body. He too wept to the point of utter dehydration but never let his sister see more than the first tears they had all shed at the start of that brutal new day, the day that would change all their lives for ever.

Irma, their maid, looked tearful too and worked quietly in the kitchen, preparing breakfast for the family, expecting any moment for Frau Hoffmann to return from the hospital. What in heaven's name was she going to say to her mistress? She had great respect for the Herr Doktor and realised that her own position in the family she had worked for all these years might once again be very fragile. Her time at the Deichmans had been a welcome change, a nice diversion, but she had rejoiced to be back with Hannelore in the familiar surroundings of the Hoffmann villa.

Breakfast was eaten in virtual silence, each of the children picking at the bread and jam, sipping the now cold tea.

Eventually their mother returned. A taxi had brought her home and the children saw her from the surgery window, climbing out of the car and walking soberly up the side steps to the house. She appeared pale and exhausted and suddenly older, her hand clutching a lace handkerchief. She looked into her children's eyes as they surged towards her from the kitchen, chairs scraping simultaneously on the stone floor, Eva running towards her and bursting into tears again, glad that at last her mother was home.

No-one spoke, they just held each other in an enormous embrace, and the girls' sobbing began again, Eva burying herself in her mother's coat. The boys, wet eyed, tried to be stronger and calmer and enveloped the women of the house in their young arms as if around a great tree. Irma, who had hidden herself momentarily in the pantry at the side of the kitchen, stepped forward, respectfully held back for a moment and then broke the silence,

'Frau Hoffmann, would you like some mint tea?' Hannelore, whose head was buried in the shoulder of her eldest son, didn't look up but answered weakly,

'That would be nice, Irma, thank you.'

The maid busied herself with the hot water and cups, glad of something to do and Hannelore led her children into the family snug. They huddled together on the very sofa where Georg had collapsed, and sat quite still for a moment, remembering the shock of that moment, and holding it in their collective memory.

The children sat, waiting for her to speak, none of them knowing what to say to her.

'Your father never woke up, but he squeezed my hand when I told him how much you all loved him. He didn't want to leave you. His kidneys were just not strong enough, the diabetes defeated him in the end. Your father loved you all so very much and was enormously proud of you, every one of you.' At this, she stroked Max's face gently and looked intently into his clear blue, tragic eyes that had once danced and sparkled more than any of her children's.

The silence continued as the children listened to their mother as she explained more about the renal failure that Georg had experienced. All her children were old enough to know the full truth about the diabetes. Johannes' eyes misted over. He understood more than the others how much of an early death sentence this illness represented in the times they lived.

'We must be thankful for all the time we had with him' she continued. 'We must be thankful.'

She repeated the phrase as if to block out any bitter root that might take hold of her own spirit. There was much that Hannelore could be bitter about, but she was trying, at least in this overwhelming moment, to fight off the canker and help her children make some sense of this tragedy in the context of a ghastly war that had already robbed her of so much.

'What shall we do without Papa?' whispered Margarete for whom the world had simply ended, her dark curls soaked in tears around her normally vivacious, at times tempestuous, eyes.

'I don't know' replied her mother honestly, fighting back the black wings of despair that were hovering above her, its talons ready to strike at her heart 'but we are together, and somehow, God willing, we shall cope.'

Right now, God felt a long way off to Margarete, in some distant land where children believed in fairy tales. What use was believing in God if he snatched away your extraordinary father, the one beacon of light and hope in what had increasingly felt like a dark, destructive world. Her father had been like God to her, always warm, comforting and endlessly patient, a strong tower against all enemies, the soother of all nightmares, the protector against the nightly bombing raids of the Allies, the provider of all that they owned and needed, the architect of their wonderful, magical house and garden, the one who accorded them all such status in the town, to whom all doffed their hats in respect. This man, this giant of a father, this hero was dead and with him died all of Margarete's childlike beliefs.

She pulled away from her mother and ran upstairs to her room. Eva sat buried in her mother, already exhausted from the last hours of fitful sleep and crushing news. She clung onto Hannelore with the desperate passion of one who having lost one great love, fears being robbed of all. She began to shake and cry again.

'We prayed for Papa and you, Mama – did God not answer our prayers?'

'Eva, God heard every one of your prayers. Papa was very sick. I feared this day would come but we have had Papa longer than I thought we would. He almost died fifteen years before you were born, and I prayed then for him and he came back to me. I don't understand why God did not give him back to us again, but he has not abandoned us and we must trust in him for the future.'

Something within Eva accepted this. She absorbed her intelligent mother's strong, unquestioning faith and in that moment she made a decision that day to trust, not to feel too deeply and to try and get on and help her mother. She was old enough to see her mother's pain and she knew she must help. No more tears flowed for her father, not for a very long time.

'Children, I would like you to come with me to the hospital and say goodbye to your father. Johannes, would you mind driving?' Hannelore drank the mint tea and nibbled at a piece of rye bread and jam that Irma had prepared and talked briefly with the maid, and then they all quietly filed down the cellar stairs to the garage, each lost in thought as they drove the half-hour journey to where Georg lay in the hospital, Eva squashed between Max and Margarete. The children felt a cold shiver as they stepped out into the cool September morning, half dreading what they were going to see, half longing to touch the hand that gave them life for at least one more time. Hannelore guided them silently up the stairs to the ward where Georg had spent that night, she nodded to the nurse on duty at the desk who respectfully acknowledged her, rising in her chair with a courteous 'Frau Hoffmann,' and then nodding to the four children as they walked past her towards the private room that Georg's colleague Gerbich had ensured Georg received on arrival at the hospital. The door was unlocked and the room with its polished floor and stark white walls was empty but for a bed, an old wooden chair, and a small bedside table with a water jug on it. On the wall was a picture of the Virgin Mary who looked mournfully down on the small gathering. The Hoffmann girls held hands and the boys followed in after their mother. They all held onto each other as they stood before the bed their father lay in, Hannelore resting her hands on the shoulders of her daughters and Johannes protectively placing an arm around his mother. Eva took out from her smock pocket a small notebook that she had been scribbling in whilst sitting in the attic and tore out a small piece of scrawled paper. She carefully folded it and edged towards her motionless father, whose face and arms were still visible above the bedsheet. Hannelore had requested that they leave him uncovered until her children had been able to come and say goodbye. Eva's fingers began to tremble as she carefully pushed the piece of paper under her father's hand. She laid her hand over his for a moment, so familiar and yet so cold and heavy. Her hands were a younger version of her father's; strong, stout fingers with a short thumb, an echo of farming ancestors from a previous age. She seemed to be whispering imperceptibly under her breath and then bent down to kiss his cheek.

Max's eyes were brimming with tears. His father had been his saviour. He would never forget the day he escaped home a few months before and how his father had admitted him almost immediately to the town hospital to prevent him from being apprehended and arrested by the American forces. This younger son moved slowly towards the far side of the bed and knelt down and sobbed into his father's other hand. Hannelore closed her eyes momentarily and leaned weakly into Johannes as he squeezed her shoulders reassuringly. She wanted to awaken out of this nightmare and open her eyes to a different day, a day where her husband was alive and all of them were able to go on holiday together and walk through the woods surrounding their town once more as they used to on Sunday afternoons before the war. She knew now those days would never return and that this day would be frozen in her mind forever. Georg, the man she had loved since those enchanting student days, was dead. She was now a widow. She knew in her heart she would always be a widow and her job was somehow to complete the work they had begun together in bringing four children into this world. Did she have the energy? The will? The desire to live on in this now shattered Germany? Could her world ever be rebuilt into something beautiful, safe, and lovely ever again? She walked over to the bed behind Max and leaned over her son's head to stroke for one last time the cheek she had kissed so many times before in passion and in dutiful affection, her forefinger lingering to follow the line of his scar. Her fingers stopped for a few seconds against his lips and she pursed her own, transmitting one last kiss through her hands. 'Auf Wiedersehen mein Liebling.'

Swallowing her tears, she waited a moment longer, not wanting to break the solemnity of this imprinted moment, and then gently touched the back of Max's head and urged her sons and daughters to come away.

'The nurses need to attend to your father now' she whispered. The children of Georg Hoffmann kissed their father one last time on the forehead and followed their mother, only Eva turning to look back at her father, eyes flitting from Georg's strong but calm face and resting on that motionless hand.

Holly

Effufa put her hand on my cheek: 'Sister, you have need of a sister-friend because you need to weep and you need someone to watch you while you weep.' (Maya Angelou)

A few weeks later

The text arrives late on the Thursday evening from Chris, 'Please come if you can... I'm exhausted. Could you help sit with Holly at night?'

I know that Chris would not have texted lightly for help and my mind starts to race. I have to go - and Tom will have to look after the boys; I could not consider anything else. This is another opportunity to be with my friend and I cannot miss it.

'Tom, I need to go and see Holly, it may be the last time, Chris thinks the end is coming now. Would you be OK looking after the boys, this weekend? I can drive down early on Friday morning and come home Sunday afternoon.' Tom senses the urgency in my voice.

'Of course, don't worry – go and be with your friend.'

Tom, always giving, always understanding, always releasing. I kiss him on the cheek as I bury my head into his shoulder and think about the ordeal that is facing me. I am not feeling hugely resilient, but I know I have at least one visit left in me in terms of stamina. It isn't even the physical demand of sitting through the night with my friend that daunts me, but rather the thought of how she may have changed physically and emotionally. Once again, I will have to look death in the face and be brave.

I set off early the next morning, rising long before my family, when the Devon roads will be empty of holiday traffic, and when I can lose myself once more in the beauty of the landscape that will accompany me all the way through Exmoor, Somerset, Dorset and finally Hampshire. It is a crisp morning in late April and the trees glow with the luminous green of new leaves. My mind and heart are resolved on doing the best I can to help Chris and the girls and hopefully to have a good conversation with Holly; yes, that would be wonderful, to be able to share some last thoughts. I drive on, focused on the goal ahead, barely noticing the majesty of ancient standing stones as I sweep past Stonehenge. From the road they seem so small and insignificant in the grand scheme of human experience. Whenever I see these stones, I only ever really think of Tess of the D'Urberville's sad fate, as she lay almost sacrificially on the great slab, sun rising between the stones, a victim of the bigotry of her day. For Tess, the awe and wonder at these stones was replaced by the exhaustion of the journey, the flight from the long hand of the law, the inevitability of her execution for murdering the man who abused her. My mind wanders back over three decades to my A' level English notes and the central theme of fate dealing cruel blows. Is Holly's plight a blow of fate? A cruel twist in an otherwise happy, responsible, caring life? Instinctively I know that fate has nothing to do with her dying; I will never be able to sanction that weak interpretation of life's road. There must be a greater plan, a bigger picture, a beautiful side to the messy tapestry I know might only ever be visible this side of eternity. There has to be a meaning behind even the senseless things of life, not simply a random trust in the mythical three goddesses of fate. It is more uncomfortable to think of a

340

good God somehow allowing these tragedies to unfold, but then I reassure myself that Christianity is not a comfortable religion. It impales an innocent man to a wooden tree and calls that justice. God was scapegoated then in his incarnate form just as God is scapegoated today when things go wrong. I am more at ease with a faith that absorbs suffering, acknowledges that life is a mess sometimes, that believes that God still loves us in spite of the problems we usually cause on this planet. I reassure myself too that my understanding is limited and that I need to trust the bigger plan to His wisdom. We are not the centre of the universe and everything doesn't have to revolve around us. I remember the photograph from the amazing Hubble telescope of our tiny sun on the edge of the Milky Way, and how there are thought to be at least two hundred billion of these galaxies in the universe. It helps me to reflect on humanity's smallness, it reduces the tragedy that is unfolding - just a little.

I arrive shortly after half-past ten. The household is already up and I am met by Holly's middle daughter, Jess, who smiles and allows me to hug her. Hugging the girls is not something I take for granted; they are private, lively at times in conversation, but not particularly tactile, and I value the warmth of this moment. Chris appears behind his tall willowy daughter and throws me a toothy grin,

'Hello Krissy. Come on in.'

His face is pale and drawn, lines have etched themselves around his watery, grey-blue eyes; the life, I suspect, left them some time during the past weeks when all hope had disappeared of a more prolonged illness, of just a bit more time with his wife of twenty years. Strange how the mind builds fences of hope against the impending doom, until the last fence is ripped down and all that is left is an honest look at death staring you in the face. There would be no more conversations about next summer, next autumn, next winter and next... Christmas. It was now a question of weeks and maybe days. I am glad I have made the journey. It is time to be a godmother and a good friend.

Before going upstairs to see Holly I glance at the kitchen, the beautiful kitchen that the couple have designed together, with its spacious extension into the garden, crowned by an arched window reaching high and cascading light onto the slabbed stone floor. The black granite work surfaces shine around the range and everywhere pale blues and greys fill the room with calm around the dainty sofa and window seat. Beautiful fabrics adorn these cosy corners where Holly would usually have sat with her girls, chatting about the day. The dining table facing the blue painted dresser stacked with multi-coloured American-style glass tumblers and odd white plates that have survived over the years from different sets is brimming with perfect tulips, gifts from friends. But there is also a neglect hanging in the air. The floor is unusually dirty, unwashed crockery is stacked on the draining board, the cushions look slightly bedraggled and unloved. There are jobs to do and no one but very close family and friends is being admitted to the home at this time; the cleaning lady has been given leave to stay away for a while.

But first I need to see my friend.

'The nurses will be here shortly,' says Chris as he makes me a cup of tea. 'They take quite a long time, so I shall take the girls off to do some shopping.'

'Ok, I'll just pop up and say hello.'

'She's beginning to sound a bit confused, it's the morphine.'

Holly and Chris's bedroom is at the top of the circular 1930s stairway and the landing wraps around it, lending a perfect view down into the hallway from every angle. I spot Holly's two other daughters, Millie and Beth, hovering on the landing. They are getting dressed for the shopping outing and say a sheepish 'hello'. I beam at them and peer around the corner into the master bedroom. The whole room has been emptied out. A single hospital bed has been placed against the window and the large double pine bed has been dismantled and put in the garage. Another single bed for Chris lines the wall at right angles to the hospital bed and there, propped on a mountain of pillows is the ever-shrinking form of my once chubby friend. Once again, I am taken aback, though braced more for what I might see this time. She is recognisably Holly, but her eyes are sunken even further and her arms are noticeably thinner. The swelling in her legs and abdomen has grown worse and yet, as she flutters her eyes open as I approach her bed, there is still the warmth in the chocolate-brown eyes and a smile spreads weakly across her face.

'Hi, Krissy, thank you for coming, it's good to see you' she whispers.

I bend down and hug my friend, unable once again to stop the tears.

I struggle to find words, I just want to hold her, and remember this moment.

'Are you in any pain?' I ask her at last, wiping away the tears and trying to pull myself together.

'No, think we are on top of it at last' she whispers grimly 'but I don't sleep too well.'

'The Marie Curie lady was here last night, and she was lovely, very kind.' Each sentence summons energy, and her eyelids droop heavily.

The doorbell rings and voices below make it clear that the nurses have come to help Holly with draining off fluid, redressing her abdomen and washing and making her comfortable for the day. It is painfully exhausting to watch.

Two hours later the two large, jolly nurses leave, having checked medication stocks and sanitary supplies. The room is full of boxes of meds and toiletries. Not a lot of fluid is draining off now, the tumour is spreading to fill the abdomen but thankfully Holly can still use the toilet herself - a half-hour operation which exhausts her.

I hope once again to be able to talk to my friend, but she is too tired and just sleeps for the rest of the afternoon. I busy myself with cleaning downstairs and making the place look ship-shape. At least this is something I can do that is useful. I bake Welsh cakes with the girls, something I know Holly often did with them, and chat about school, exams and friends and then rope them into hanging out and sorting laundry. They are subdued, but happy to engage and be around me unless they are just being polite. There are even a few laughs as we forget to add sugar into the recipe and end up sprinkling the finished cakes very liberally at the end for sweetness. Holly's parents arrive and sit with her upstairs. The arrival of the Welsh cakes on a platter in her room breaks the serious atmosphere and it is good to see everyone smile for a moment or two. It is unbearably sad to stay in the room and I slip away to give them precious time alone. Throughout the illness they have been uppermost in her mind. Neither of them is in good health and Holly's plan had always been to move house to be nearer to them and care for them in their old age. That hope has dissolved and all have had to readjust to what is now an inevitable reality – that they will bury another child.

I wonder what the night shift will be like, slightly anxious about how exhausting it might be, when the 'phone call comes through that the Marie Curie nurse is able to come again. Relief washes over me at the thought that I might get some sleep and after an early night I rise for breakfast with the family, who then leave to go to church. I stay and prepare the Sunday lunch while the nurses come again. Once the chicken had been plated up, I take it up to Holly and sit with her and at last we have the space to chat.

'Krissy' she says earnestly, looking at me intently as she lays aside her plate at the end of the meal,

'I need you to help, Krissie. Chris needs to talk to the girls with me. They need to know that I am sorry I didn't do everything right, that I could have been a better mother. Chris will find that difficult. Could you talk to him and maybe help him do it with us? With us all here together?'

I hold my friend's thin hand and squeeze it gently,

'You have been a wonderful mother, Holly, none of us gets it right. I'm always apologising to the boys for the way I treat them. I will talk to Chris if you like.'

It is clear to me that Holly is agitated. Is this the morphine talking or her anguished spirit? The girls are clearly finding it difficult to know how to relate to their bedridden mother. The fluid in her legs is just too heavy to enable her to walk up and down stairs anymore and although they bob their heads in to look at her and fetch and carry, none of them stay long by her bed to talk and just be with her. It is as if they are gradually preparing themselves and distancing themselves from the inevitable reality of what is unfolding before their eyes; their mother is slipping excruciatingly slowly from them and whilst they long deep down for their mother, they cannot bear to look too closely upon her suffering. I remember how often I have been told when considering talking to the boys about my own diagnosis, that 'children are so resilient - it is amazing what they can cope with.' I struggle to buy into that notion; it has always felt like a convenient lie that adults tell themselves when seeing children cope with difficult situations, simply because children don't always appear to 'fall apart.' It seems to me more likely that children bury the suffering, not knowing quite how to process it, subconsciously parking it somewhere in the hope that it will never actually surface – a coping mechanism. How often have I seen adults displaying childish emotions because they didn't know how to handle life when they were children. Hidden injuries, not resilience, I sense. How many nervous breakdowns are rooted in early childhood damage? How many depressions?

How Holly's daughters would ultimately cope with their mother's death would remain to be seen, but I have concerns that they are to a greater or lesser degree beginning to retreat from the horror of it. In a quiet moment later that day, I relay Holly's message on to Chris and he sighs audibly, a look of anguish spreading across his face.

'We've had this conversation before. She knows the girls love her really. She is becoming more confused, the other day she was convinced that I was going to kill her. That was a dark day for me. It is hard to see this. I am losing Holly.'

Chris looked utterly drained of life and hope. It was all he could do to stop himself from breaking down. This was almost worse than the fact that his wife was dying, to see the real Holly disappear in a fog of confusion and paranoia. I touched his hand and squeezed it. There was nothing to be said.

The spectre of grief was already leering in at the door of this home. It would not be content to just leer but would gradually envelop the household and linger over every future event – every birthday, anniversary, and 'happy' occasion; every examination, job interview, results day, wedding, holiday... The holidays would be the worst. Holly had always wrapped her girls up in tent canvas and bundled them off for summer holiday adventures on some wild campsite while Chris had to work.

'The wilder, the better, Krissy' she would say. 'All we need are good books, a good stew and plenty of chocolate.'

I head up the stairs one last time to say what I know will be a final farewell to my friend. Her closed eyes flutter open and she smiles weakly. Holly knows that this is the last time – I sense she herself wants to go. Her body is weary, and she is withdrawing into herself in preparation for the final lap of this marathon. I take one last selfie of us together, and Holly tries to smile one last time for me into the 'phone.

I bend close to her and hold her hand.

'Do you still believe in the goodness of God, Holly?' I whisper.

'I know it, Kris, I know it now more than ever. He is a good, good Father and He loves me.'

'And so do I' I whisper back. 'Goodbye.' I kiss my friend and leave quickly. Holly is ready to go.

Two weeks later.

It is the warmest day of the year so far – temperatures are hitting twenty-seven degrees in London and the southwest of England seems bathed in a warm, balmy haze. Even at the coast the winds soothe and warm pale skins, and a light T-shirt and cardigan are all I need as I stride across the beach with Tom beside me, reflecting on our lives, on how Holly is and on how desperately I want to be able to go back and visit her again before she dies. Reuben's Year 6 SATS start tomorrow. It is going to be an impossible task to get away without seriously letting my own family down. Holly has stopped texting and Chris hasn't texted either. I suspect that she might be slipping in and out of consciousness.

'Why don't you try phoning her?' Tom suggests.

'I don't know that she would be able to talk on the 'phone that easily' I reply, but actually the idea doesn't seem that bad at all. I will go home and text Chris and arrange to 'phone on Monday afternoon when the girls are still at school. Maybe Holly could at least listen to my voice and be cheered by her friend.

Hand in hand Tom and I walk a mile down the beach, praying for Holly, before turning back towards the beach café for a shared ice-cream and coffee and home in the camper van.

Back home, I walk into the kitchen just as the 'phone rings. Reuben grabs it and passes it to me without even talking to the person at the other end.

'Krista? It's Chris here. Are you on your own?' There was a pause.

'Yes, yes I am on my own,' I say as I wander into the lounge, half sensing what is to follow.

'Holly died this afternoon,' he says almost inaudibly.

'Oh Chris, bless you, bless you, bless you,' I choke back .

'Thank you, it was a peaceful end, her breathing was becoming laboured, she was a bit confused and they were going to fit a catheter. They thought she may not cope with that. Half an hour later she died.'

I can feel the tears welling up.

'How are the girls?'

'They all saw her today and she knew they were there, and I told her they were all smiling at her. There have been some tears.'

I can feel Chris's own voice breaking and I try to hold it together.

We don't talk much more; I know he will have more calls to make and that there are things to do. Holly is still at home. That is good. They were so right to stay at home, rather than go to the hospice, and for everything to be as she had wanted it with her family around her to the end.

Tom has come into the room, aware of what has happened from hearing our conversation. He wraps his strong arms around me and I sob, more in relief that Holly's suffering and her family's suffering for the time being is over, but somewhere deep in the sorrow are tears selfishly for my own great loss, for my sister-friend has died and left me behind. I cry because I have dodged death's card and Holly has picked it up. I cry too for Holly's three girls, for her husband, for Holly's parents who now have no child left in the world to care for them and be there at their own deathbed.

It is May the 8th. Ironically for Holly who never had any real sense of history or of world events, she has died on the anniversary of the unconditional surrender of the German armed forces back in 1945. The battles are over for her. They are only just beginning for her husband and three daughters.

Who will buy them their charity shop clothes? Cook those amazing curries she inherited from the years as a missionary kid in India? Who will watch all those school events? Help her girls through those endless cycles of exams that are looming in a year? Who will take them camping during the long summer holidays? Who will teach them to sew on her beloved sewing machine? Who will nag them to wash their hair and lay the table and feed the guinea pig and take them to dance classes?

Chris of course, Chris.

The Package

The 'phone rang as Krista headed down for breakfast. Everyone in the house had left for school or work. The spring sunshine was streaming through the hallway window as she came down the stairs.

'Hello,' she said jovially, picking up the receiver.

'Hello? It's Mum. We've just had some sad news from Tante Margarete.' Her voice sounded strained.

Krista's heart sank.

'Uncle Max died this morning.' She could hear her mother's wet voice at the other end, swallowing sadness and trying to keep talking.

'He went to the bathroom and fell. He never regained consciousness. The doctor came but there was nothing that could be done. Annaliese and Bernd were with him.'

'Oh Mum, I'm sorry.' She paused to let her mother cry. 'I'll be over after breakfast.'

Krista replaced the receiver and sighed deeply. This was not unexpected. Uncle Max had not been well for some years and it was a miracle that he was still alive, given that he had been so frail. Krista remembered visiting him on his ninetieth birthday a couple of years before in Hanover. Even so, it was something of a shock as the end was so sudden. Strangely, inexplicably, Krista also began to cry. Her softly spoken, thoughtful, kind

351

uncle had been a gentle presence in their lives; a distant but palpable link with the grandfather she had never met. Uncle Max had filled something of the missing grandfather hole she had always felt, facially similar to her own mother, clear green-blue eyes and a kind face. It was as if a piece of her DNA had fallen away. He was a man whose passionate love of music had so inspired her in her youth on family visits to their home. Their eldest son, her cousin, a competent pianist himself, had given her Carl Bach's Solfeggietto to learn and unusually she had memorised it, often losing herself in a frenzy of presto arpeggios.

She made herself a cup of coffee and toast in a slightly numb daze, thinking about the effect this news would have on her mother. Would she struggle to cope yet again with the death of another sibling? Uncle Johannes had died some years before of diabetes when he was in his early seventies and that had taken its toll, not least because of the way her parents had visited him in the last weeks of his life, travelling to Germany to help his wife with the relentless round of nursing care that was needed as he lay on a bed set up for him in his old surgery near to the kitchen.

The letterbox spewed fresh post onto the door mat and she collected it to browse over her coffee. A bundle of letters, mostly printed and dull, were thrown into Tom's post tray on the kitchen desk, but one caught her eye, the now horribly familiar font of the hospital; her mammogram results from the week before when she had faced the annual ritual of walking into that room in the hospital again. Shaken still from the news about her uncle, she tore the envelope open, hardly daring to read the contents. She unfolded the familiar crisp, white hospital letter, her eyes skimming rapidly past the addresses and dates to the essential information.

'Dear Mrs Templeton,

Thank you for attending for your mammogram on the 8th March. We now have the report of this from the radiologists and I am pleased to be able to inform you that they have reported this as normal. A copy of the report has been forwarded to your GP for their records.

Yours sincerely'

Hands trembling, she sank to her knees in the kitchen, relief waving over her, mingled with the sadness of the telephone call. Life and death were jostling for position in her soul. Relief. Fear. Relief. Fear. Her head began to swim, and her breathing became momentarily laboured, a sign that her labyrinth, whilst over, yet threatened to unhinge her at any moment. Krista had taken beta blockers on no more than a couple of occasions to help her cope with a wedding and an appearance at her workplace to say goodbye to colleagues. Her work as a classroom teacher was over for now as her 'sympathetic nervous system' as Tom explained it to her, had been overloaded and she needed time to let it recover. Teaching required too much of an adrenalin rush to allow that healing to happen. She ate her toast and jam to give herself a boost of sugar, and finished her coffee, still elated by the news from the hospital. The mammogram was a loathed mountain she had to climb every year, loathed because so often the image was blurred and the whole ghastly process of having her breast painfully clamped between two Perspex sheets had to be repeated. And then the agonisingly long wait, sometimes three weeks before the final verdict.

Krista arrived at her parents' house a short while later and went into the small living room where her mother sat, red-eyed, peering through her glasses at some photographs that lay on her lap, milky green eyes reddened by the news of her brother.

'Hi Mum, I'm so sorry.' Krista hugged her mum.

'It's such a shock, even though I knew he wasn't well – it's still a shock.' Her mother whispered. 'I haven't seen him for such a long time.'

The tremor in her hands seemed more pronounced as she was holding a black and white photograph of a young man in his Sunday best suit, gazing handsomely back at the photographer. There was a fragility about the look in the young, pale face that stirred Krista.

'He was a fine-looking young man, Mum.' Krista said taking the photograph from trembling hands and scrutinising the face.

'Yes, he looked so like my father. This picture was taken the year my father died. Max was devastated. I remember clearly as if it were yesterday – it was as if the world had ended. I crept up to the attic to write in my notebook and to be alone for a while, and after an hour Max followed me and sat beside me. He helped me finish a poem I wanted to write about our father. I couldn't quite find the words. I have a copy of it somewhere. Max suggested I should leave the poem with our father so that he would always know what we thought about him.'

She sorted through the photos and papers next to her on the sofa.

'Ah, here it is, you may take it home with you if you like to read it later.'

Krista took the folded aged paper and skim-read the title and dedication next to it: *It is accomplished' (to our father on the day of his death (23.9.45).* She folded it and laid it carefully in her handbag.

Mother and daughter talked on a while, reminiscing about the past and about how Uncle Max's wife, Elisabeth had sounded on the telephone and how their three children would be reacting. Eventually Krista rose to leave so that her mother could 'phone her sister.

'Oh, Krista. A package arrived with some things in it for you from Tante Elsa. It arrived a couple of days ago. Dad and I were going to bring it over, but you may as well take it now. You know she is clearing out the old house ready to sell, well she sent on some things she found in the attic which she thought we might like.'

Krista recognised immediately the familiar script of her godmother aunt in Borkhausen.

'I'll take it with me Mum if that's alright. Try and get some rest later and drink lots of tea so you don't get dehydrated. By the way, what else was in the package for you?'

'Oh, some old diaries from my father, from when he was in the war as a young man, some letters I wrote my mother when I began my training as a nurse here in Devon all those years ago. We'll look at them together some time.'

Krista's mother saw her out of the door, leaning on her stick, before limping unsteadily back to the sofa. Her father waved her off as she walked to the car and started the engine. Driving home, her thoughts were filled with remembrances of her uncle and his family in Germany. She remembered the old house in Borkhausen she had lived in for a year after finishing her O Levels, longing to connect somehow with her family there and learn the language properly. How chatting to Uncle Max on the 'phone on her sixteenth birthday had inspired her to pursue that dream and how Uncle Johannes had welcomed her staying with them for a year in that special house. A year full of homesickness but also fun with her cousin making elderflower champagne in the cellar, tearing around the surrounding woodlands on bikes and sitting in the old kitchen around the table and eating fresh bread rolls they had collected from the bakery. When the house was quiet, she would creep up to the piano in the blue sitting room with its elegant sofa and armchairs and gaze up at old paintings and photographs on the wall, finger through the music books Uncle Johannes had on the shelf and play to herself. When she was sure no one was around, she would wander into the surgery and gaze at the photo of her grandfather on the wall, sit in the old leather chair and lean back enjoying the smell of antiseptic.

She pulled up onto the drive, turned off the engine and looked at the package next to her, deciding to open it in the quiet of the car. Slipping her fingers inside the envelope she drew out an old, worn music book of Chopin Nocturnes. On the front of the book, scrawled in beautiful, faded ink were words written in English,

'Music, when soft voices die, vibrates in the memory - with love from Jacob 1925.'

Krista was slightly startled – she recognised the line from one of her favourite poets, Shelley.

Underneath the beautiful writing in a faint pencil, another note by a different hand was scrawled in German. *'For the good Doctor. In the event of unfortunate circumstances, Frau Samuels will convey this to you – thank you for your many kindnesses. L.R. – 1938'*

Paper-clipped to the front of the music book was a note written by Krista's aunt, again in German.

'Krista, for you and your musical boys – I think this must have belonged to your grandfather - my children suggested you should have it. Your uncle Johannes would approve; he was very fond of your playing. Loving Greetings, Tante Elsa'

Dear Uncle Johannes, how lovely to receive something from the old family home.

Krista held the old piano music to her face and inhaled the musty attic she often crept up into with her cousin during that year in the old house, to peer out of the window onto the river in the distance far below them. Old dolls house kitchens and children's toys and dolls with painted ceramic faces, lay in a corner, carefully tidied away. A small room with old suitcases stored in it and a faded green sofa had always intrigued her too and she would sometimes creep in through the creaky wooden door and sit and read on the old couch when she was feeling a bit homesick. The thought that her mother had grown up in the villa gave her great comfort in those moments.

Later that day she set the music on the piano stand and began to play. Ben, now fifteen years old, wandered in from the kitchen to listen.

'Do you like it, Ben?'

'It's so sad, Mum, it almost makes me want to cry.'

'I'll let you have a look at it, you will be able to play the first page quite quickly.'

Krista left her curious son fingering the notes and then tentatively beginning to play the cadences of one of Chopin's most haunting nocturnes. It was a strange thought to her that her grandfather would have heard or played the same music all those years ago, perhaps her mother too who also played for many years. She couldn't help wondering what kindness he had shown to the mysterious LR on the front cover.

The Epilogue

O'er all the hilltops
Is quiet now,
In all the treetops
Hearest thou
Hardly a breath;
The birds are asleep
in the trees:
Wait, soon like these
Thou too shalt rest.
Goethe (Longfellow)

A few days later, as the Easter holidays drew to a close, Tom and Krista headed off to collect Reuben from a holiday camp with friends. It had been his first full week ever away from home and it hadn't been easy, waving him off the previous Saturday. It would have been a challenging week for him but an important opportunity to grow up a bit and stand on his own two feet. They arrived early at the grand public school where the camp was being held and, with a few hours to kill, turned into the equally majestic looking arboretum directly opposite the school.

'The trees will be in fresh leaf, Tom – it will be amazing. I really miss trees, lovely though the coast is.'

Tom and Krista wandered hand in hand between enormous Scots pines, marvelling at the height and girth of these specimens and then gasped at the blaze of colour in the azalea garden. The air was warm, and Krista was drawn to a bench that wrapped itself around an enormous oak tree to have their picnic. Leaning back against the roughly etched bark of this ancient tree, Krista mused to herself how much Holly loved woodlands, especially at this time of year when the bluebells spread out their glorious carpet. They ate their sandwiches and then Tom wandered off to the café to fetch some cold drinks, leaving her to gaze up at the huge canopies overhead, sparkling sunshine shafting through the dense layers of branches and leaves in the welcome breeze.

A year ago the funeral group had stood under the arched branch of another enormous Scots pine tree. The memory came flooding back as if it were yesterday and she allowed herself to drift back to that day in May when her best friend was laid to rest beneath a tree. She and Tom and her boys were there by the grave, standing stiffly in their black jackets. Ben, standing taller than his mother at fourteen years of age, had been asked by the minister to carry a staff alongside another teenage son of an old university friend who was given a rod to carry, both symbolic references to Psalm 23. The boys held them seriously, standing like young Davids on the hills of Judea. Krista hovered by the freshly dug grave, noticing a large rosemary bush planted on the neighbouring grave. The name 'Rosemary' was engraved on the stone.

'That's nice, Holly would like that' she thought to herself. The bush reminded her of the rosemary plants that arrived at Holly's parents' house in the wake of her brother's suicide twenty-five years ago. 'Rosemary is for remembrance,' Holly's mother had explained.

The hearse had pulled in through the gates below and wound its way up the lane at the edge of the cemetery towards them. Krista felt her eyes well up at the thought of seeing Holly's girls and Chris. She wondered how they would have dressed that morning, who would have decided what they should wear, whether Chris had been able to sort it out on his own or whether the girls had made these choices. Jess, their eldest was the first to step out of the car that had also brought her grandparents. Krista hurriedly wiped her tears and put on a serious, but reassuring smile. She felt the pain of Holly's parents intensely, almost as if she were their daughter. She had spent many, many weekends with them and Holly dealing with the aftermath of their son's death, cloaked as it had been in the uncertainty of whether he was the one to have jumped off that London bridge. His bag had been found but nothing much was in the bag to suggest suicide. A lingering wisp of hope hung in the bungalow that just maybe he would walk through the door and be there again with his big gingery smile spreading across his freckled face. But then the policeman's knock had come while Krista was visiting one weekend and a fresh wave of grief swept over them, as a body had been discovered, and dental records had confirmed their fears; it was their John. His flat would have to be cleared and a funeral arranged and always came more tears. Krista had driven them in Holly's small blue Skoda that day and she had held onto them through the ceremony as their bodies trembled in disbelief, this diminutive man and his wife who had once been faithful missionaries serving in India. And now here they were again, older, less racked with disbelief but grief stricken nevertheless.

Chris and his two younger daughters stepped out of the large hearse and posies of beautiful pink roses, bluebells and white freesias were handed to each of the girls. A wicker coffin was carried in front of them and placed carefully on wooden struts that had been suspended over the grave. Krista couldn't help smiling – of course an Occupational Therapist would choose a wicker casket for her coffin. The thought that Holly was lying in there was harder to grasp. A slightly surreal beauty surrounded this funeral as psalms and prayers were recited, as the achingly pretty vintage posies were laid on the casket by her daughters, and all those gathered tossed the bluebells they had been given into the grave. Even the church window sills had been filled with jars of bluebells, and potted young trees were arranged like a woodland at the front. It was all quite beautiful, and all planned by Holly down to the last detail. The minister had read those poignant words as the coffin was lowered.

'Though I walk through the valley of the shadow of death...'

Krista understood those words only too well; so much of her journey was lived in the shadow of death, the fear of cancer returning, the shadow that seems to hang over every survivor's life. The thought every morning on awakening, *has it returned?* Would the shadow ever leave her?

Tom returned with the sparkling elderflower bottles and they drank and sat close to one another breathing in the life of the trees. 'Speak to us, Lord,' Krista whispered.

Just as they were about to leave, they turned to see a high footbridge, suspended on huge telegraph pole supports. Circular platforms were built around the trunks of gigantic pine trees that hugged the main bridge. A sign invited visitors to wander along the bridge and explore the wooded scenery from a spectacular height. The sun blazed in the heat of the day, but there was a cooling breeze up in the crown of the arboretum and the two of them wandered along the bridge, enjoying breath-taking views in all directions, stopping occasionally to read small signs attached to the trees which gave information about different species and ages of the canopy below.

Tom paused for a few minutes at one particular sign, nailed to one of the poles, and his eyes began to twinkle.

'Krista, come over here and look at this. I think you need to read this.'

Krista peered at the plaque and, after a minute, tears began to roll down her face.

Underneath the title *Dead Strong,* these words were written: *'At the centre of most trunks lies the heartwood. Amazingly, heartwood, which may account for as much as 90% of a tree's overall woody framework, consists almost entirely of dead wood. But this doesn't mean it is redundant. As well as providing support, heartwood provides durability (decay resistance). As trees add wood each year, the older sapwood ceases to function as sapwood and turns into heartwood. This makes sense: living sapwood takes energy to maintain: heartwood, being dead, doesn't. Heartwood is usually denser and more durable than sapwood thanks to the addition of different chemicals: the darker the wood the more durable it tends to be. When a tree is injured, the cells in the surrounding area change chemically and physically to prevent the spread of decay. New cells then line the cut area to create a callus that covers and seals the injured area. Over time, this callus will blend in with the rest of the tree's bark. The sapwood outside the heartwood is the major transport area for water and nutrients and is lighter than the heartwood and is soft and moist. The heartwood is mainly for strength of the tree.'*

'That's it, that's exactly it, that's how it is,' she spluttered to Tom who stood beside her, smiling. In one single moment, Krista's mind was awakened to a truth that until now had been only half-formed in her mind. She recalled the conversation she had had with Jennifer concerning the diagram of a cross-section of a tree. Hadn't Jennifer said that the centre of a tree was a place of strength. At last she understood what that meant. What she hadn't realised was that trees at their core really are dead, and not only are they dead but incredibly strong. Standing on that platform, wrapping her arms around Tom's neck, she resolved that this cancer was not going to overwhelm her or sap her strength for ever, nor would it remain a place of weakness. This thing of death that lived within her would become her strength, it would quietly reside within her, but would not dictate who she was. It was OK to acknowledge that a part of her had died, that it would always be dead but new life would grow around her, new green leaves of hope of seeing her children grow into adulthood, of holding in her arms her children's children, of being and doing something new, something positive. Her heart felt free.

Hand in hand the couple walked through the avenue of heartwood trees, down the steps towards the car. Krista couldn't stop marvelling at what she had just read.

'I was meant to read that, Tom. That was just for me.'

They swept up the drive to the school and soon spotted Reuben in the reception area of the school. He ran over to them and they enveloped him in their arms.

'Mum! Look, my last baby tooth came out in a piece of mango!'

Their younger son's childhood was almost over.

'Thank you, God,' Krista whispered to herself as they sped off along the driveway and out of the gates of the school. Today felt good.

The family was reunited later that evening after a three hour journey in which Reuben eagerly told them of all the week's activities and adventures before falling asleep on the back seat. It was late by the time the boys had headed up to bed and Krista sat down for a few moments at the piano. The Chopin was still open, and she began to play the first lines. The notes soared high in a minor key, but the very sadness of these cadences filled her heart with a strange peace and joy. It reminded her to look at the poem her mother had written in the attic all those years ago. She fetched it out of her handbag and carefully unfolded what looked like a crumpled page. The German was difficult to read in the tiny spidery

writing of thirteen-year-old Eva Hoffmann, but she was able to make out
a few lines that she had composed as a prayer and dedicated to her father.

You loved him, for he was so good and only You know why he left,
Of comfort, only this remains for those of us who are bereft,
That he abides within Your arms.
Give us the strength and courage now, to find our purpose, work, and life,
To thank You through this raging storm, and not to yield to hopeless
strife,
But know You shielding us from harm. Eva and Max

Krista laid the poem down and thought about the girl who had written
these words in a dark, dusty attic with her brother on the day their father
had died. This was her mother's heartwood and she would learn to carry
her own.

She sighed and wandered back to the piano and studied the yellowing
pages in front of her. It felt special to her that this manuscript had been
held by her grandfather and she stroked the pages with her fingers and
smelled again the mustiness of that old attic. Her eyes followed the lines
of notes. There was an ecstasy in this nocturne, an ecstasy heightened by
the andante tempo. This was a piece to be played steadily and with great
feeling, not one to be rushed in a frenzy. It was comforting to her to know
that these notes had been played in another house and that they had been
significant to the grandfather she had never met. Krista gently stroked
the keys of her piano and began to play.

The next morning, she woke early. Easter Sunday. The sun shone
brightly, and she arose before the boys, padded down the carpeted stairs
into the hallway and walked through the kitchen towards the bay window
and out into the garden. The air was cool with the promise of warm
sunshine to follow, the silence only broken by a lone seagull, screeching

as it flew high over the village rooftops. Krista knelt down beside the pink salix and laid a fresh circle of perfectly white pebbles and shells around its' young slender bark. They had been gathered from a small beach on the shores of Brittany the year before.

Bending down, she said a prayer and stroked the delicate pink leaves tenderly between her fingers and kissed the young stem of this baby tree. She barely noticed Reuben in his pyjamas sidling up to her in the garden.

'Those stones are pretty, Mummy, they look like a necklace. Is that for Hope?'

Krista, too choked with emotion to speak, just murmured assent and gratefully sank her fingers into her son's thick brown hair and kissed his head.

Acknowledgements

My thanks go to those who gave up many hours of time to read and check the manuscript at various stages of the process, who proof read and helped edit and shape the final version and even shed tears with me over the story: Jane Perry, Julia Moore OBE, Sian Campbell-Colquhoun, Angela Moore, Clare Fisher, Alison Bancroft, Jacqui Ratcliffe, Jane Moore, Shelley Kerslake, Liz Hall, Gill Gillett, Laura Summers, Debbie Beard, Katie Major and Antoinette Ferraro.

Tim for invaluable help with all matters technical.

Maria Martinez, without whom this book would not have been written at all, Alison, the most selfless nurse I know, and Dr R G and Dr KS who reflect daily what is so great about our National Health Service.

Thank you to my mother, Eva and my aunts, Annerose, Edith and Annegret in Germany, my cousins Jutta, Andreas and Carolin, all of whom shared from the collective archive of their memory and made this family story come alive. The historical documents and diaries they allowed me to use were invaluable. My hope is that this book will be translated into German so that they can read it too.

Matthew Mayer for his beautiful front cover design.

Sharon, Dirk, Robin, Angela and Lindsey for advice and encouragement.

Additional debts are owed to Leonard Berney's *Liberating Belsen*, Michael John Hargrave's *Bergen-Belsen 1945, A Medical Student's Journal*, and Anita Lasker-Wallfisch's *Inherit the Truth*.

My greatest thanks go to my husband and sons who bore with me and encouraged me to complete the story. To Josh for brilliant advice, Tim for all his kindness and Stefan for being proud of me. It is, I hope, a legacy for them and one which may help them better understand the journey we have been on as a family. I am grateful to God for every day I have with them.

This is a work of fiction in that names and places have been altered and some details changed a little, but it is based on the true story of my life and that of my mother. In changing autobiographical details, it became a novel rather than a memoir which gave me the freedom to create. The old villa in Germany was sold recently after many years of being in the family. It felt sad to say goodbye to it and all the secrets it held.

If you have enjoyed HEARTWOOD, then please follow more background to the story on Facebook by searching the **Heartwood by Kerstin Moore** page. There are a collection of more photographs of those that inspired this story.

The sequel to this story is being prepared entitled DRIFTWOOD.

Printed in Great Britain
by Amazon

70203779R00222